Also by Chris Ryan

Non-fiction
The One That Got Away
Chris Ryan's SAS Fitness Book
Chris Ryan's Ultimate Survival Guide
Fight to Win
Safe

Fiction
Stand By, Stand By
Zero Option
The Kremlin Device
Tenth Man Down
Hit List
The Watchman
Land of Fire
Greed
The Increment
Blackout
Ultimate Weapon
Strike Back
Firefight
Who Dares Wins
The Kill Zone
Killing for the Company
Osama

In the Danny Black Series
Masters of War
Hunter Killer
Hellfire
Bad Soldier
Warlord
Head Hunters
Black Ops

In the Strikeback Series
Deathlist
Shadow Kill
Global Strike
Red Strike

Chris Ryan Extreme
Hard Target
Night Strike
Most Wanted
Silent Kill

CIRCLE OF DEATH

CHRIS RYAN

CIRCLE OF DEATH

CORONET

First published in Great Britain in 2020 by Coronet
An Imprint of Hodder & Stoughton
An Hachette UK company

3

A CIP catalogue record for this title is available from the British Library

Hardback ISBN 9781529324853
Trade Paperback ISBN 9781529324891
eBook ISBN 9781529324860

Typeset in Bembo by Hewer Text UK Ltd, Edinburgh
Printed and bound in Great Britain by Clays Ltd, Elcograf S.p.A.

Hodder & Stoughton policy is to use papers that are natural, renewable
and recyclable products and made from wood grown in sustainable forests.
The logging and manufacturing processes are expected to conform
to the environmental regulations of the country of origin.

Hodder & Stoughton Ltd
Carmelite House
50 Victoria Embankment
London EC4Y 0DZ

www.hodder.co.uk

ONE

Julian Cantwell sat in his lavishly furnished office and felt the fear twisting like a knife in his stomach.

He knew he shouldn't be worried, of course. Cantwell had faced down dozens of major crises in the past. In twenty-plus years as the country's most expensive political consultant, he'd helped to ward off countless threats to his clients. Enemies had been blackmailed or paid off. He'd buried scandals. Masterminded the downfall of political rivals. Overseen campaign strategies. Those tactics hadn't made Cantwell many friends, but by god, they had worked. He'd helped his clients win elections in countries around the world, from Senegal to Lithuania – and in the process, he'd grown extremely rich.

When it came to looking out for his clients, there was no one better than Cantwell; no problem that he couldn't fix.

Logically, he knew he shouldn't be anxious about this new threat.

It was nothing at all.

But the feeling in his guts told him otherwise.

He shifted his mouse, checked the time on his screen: 13.57.

Three minutes until the meeting.

Three minutes until his world potentially shattered.

Cantwell's office was on the third floor of an art deco property situated on a quiet side street in Fitzrovia. The heart of London, but you wouldn't guess it from looking out of the window. The view from his office overlooked a betting shop, a yoga studio and a block of crumbling redbrick flats. Except for a handful of pedestrians, the street was empty. You didn't get many tourists in this neighbourhood. Most stayed within the orbit of Oxford Street several hundred metres to the south, or Marylebone to the west, or Regent's Park to the north.

The offices for Cantwell's company were not well advertised. There was no large sign outside the building, no corporate branding. Just a small metal sign fitted next to the buzzer outside the ground-floor entrance, bearing the name of Cantwell Consulting Group.

Few people knew that his business existed. Fewer still understood the power that he wielded.

He had worked his way up from a modest background, with none of the privileges of his Eton-educated colleagues. He had grown up in Coventry, in a modest three-bedroom house on the outskirts of the city. His parents were strictly middle class. Both were teachers; both regularly attended church. They were proud people, but their horizons were limited. Cantwell himself had been determined to make more of his life.

He had shown promise from an early age, eventually going on to study PPE at Merton College, Oxford. After graduating, he'd taken a job as a junior journalist at Sky News, then spent six years working as an adviser in Westminster. Nine years ago, he'd left the firm to start his own political consulting company.

The walls of his office were lined with his achievements over the past couple of decades. Almost every spare inch of real estate had a frame hanging from it, displaying campaign posters of the many elections he'd worked on around the world: Namibia, Georgia, Aruba, Guatemala, Montenegro. Several photographs on his mahogany desk showed Cantwell with some of his clients. In one snap, he was shaking hands with the Sierra Leonean president; in another, he was celebrating with the Polish prime minister. In a third, he was lurking in the background, smiling as the future leader of Burkina Faso addressed a crowd of supporters.

There were a handful of photographs of Cantwell with various figures from British politics, but he had never truly been accepted by the establishment at home. He was considered too eccentric, too unconventional. Many of his former colleagues failed to understand why he had traded the bear pit of Westminster for the chance to work on less glamorous overseas campaigns, but they missed the point. He preferred operating in the shadows. He was a maverick, breaking new ground. Pushing the envelope and the limits of what was possible. You couldn't always do that in London. Too much oversight. There was less scrutiny abroad. It was easier to stay invisible in foreign countries.

Until six days ago.

When the email had landed.

Cantwell had been working late at the time. Nine o'clock on a Friday evening in late March. He had been in his office, about to make an important call to a major client, when the message popped up in his inbox. The subject heading had read: *We need to talk.*

Which sounded like some kind of spam. A dating scam, Cantwell had assumed. The sort of message sent out by low-rent criminals in some impoverished Romanian backwater, targeting the wallets of desperate middle-aged men. He had gone to delete the email.

Then he'd caught sight of the sender's address.

From: Nick Gregory <nickfgregory73@hotmail.com>

Cantwell had frozen. He had recognised the name immediately.

Nick Gregory.

Nick fucking Gregory.

The journalist who had very nearly destroyed his career.

Two years ago, Gregory had been working as a freelance journalist, writing articles on Cantwell's supposed shady dealings. One article, published for an online news outlet, claimed that he had links to the Kremlin. *Powerful British fixer linked to alleged Russian spy*, the headline had screamed. Gregory had accused Cantwell in print of conspiring with Moscow to dig up dirt on Ukrainian politicians opposed to the Russian President. It was all nonsense, of course, but Gregory was quickly making a name for himself as an investigative journalist, at Cantwell's expense – and so he had decided to take action.

After all, a fixer was only effective as long as they were invisible, and Gregory was threatening to bring Cantwell out of the shadows. Into the light. He couldn't operate in those conditions. Worse, the newspaper reports were beginning to have an impact on his bottom line. Clients began to abandon him. Colleagues stopped returning his calls. Everything he had worked for was coming under threat. Gregory's one-man war against Cantwell Consulting Group had to be stopped, no matter what.

So Cantwell had launched a counter-attack. He'd tasked one of his employees with hacking into Nick Gregory's private accounts. The hacker had struck gold. Along with a few minor embarrassing details, they had discovered that Gregory had been fabricating details in a number of the articles he'd written over the years – inventing quotes and embellishing details in order to jazz them up and sell them for a higher price to his editors.

Gregory had made his name off the back of several high-profile cover-ups involving key figures in the establishment; the revelation that the journalist responsible for those stories had been making stuff up had been enough to wreck his career. All of a sudden, Gregory became toxic. No self-respecting editor wanted anything to do with him. He had committed the cardinal journalistic sin: writing fiction as fact. His career was in the gutter.

It had been brutal attack, Cantwell reflected, but necessary. If he had failed to act, Gregory would no doubt have continued to tarnish his good name in the media. Cantwell had managed to salvage his career. Eventually, most of his former clients had returned. He'd managed to add some new ones. Had even moved to a larger office. His business turned a decent profit. He'd weathered the storm.

But now Gregory was coming at him again.

In his email, Gregory had explained that he was writing an article. A freelance piece that he intended to sell to one of the daily newspapers. He had spoken with several people, done some deep digging and unearthed some troubling claims. Gregory had briefly summarised them, without going into any specifics.

Then he'd asked if Cantwell wanted to comment.

He had given Cantwell a week to respond. Otherwise, Gregory had said, he was going to his old editors with what he had.

Ordinarily, Cantwell would have dismissed the threat out of hand. That was rule number one for dealing with journalists. But the claims Gregory had alluded to in his email, true or not, were extremely damaging. If published, they would completely destroy Cantwell's reputation. And that wouldn't even be the worst of it. The consequences would be far, far worse. There was no way he could risk the allegations being exposed in the media. It would be the end of him.

He couldn't simply ignore the threat.

Gregory had almost killed his career. Cantwell couldn't afford to risk letting the guy attack him again. Something had to be done, clearly. He could try to discredit Gregory once more, but there were no guarantees that his hackers would be able to find something incriminating.

There was only one thing for it, Cantwell knew.

Which is why he had agreed to meet the journalist. He would make his case to the guy, face to face. Persuade him to drop the story. Which wouldn't be easy, especially given the history between the two men. It was going to take all of Cantwell's legendary powers of persuasion. But even then, it might not be enough. Gregory was a stubborn bastard, after all. One of those hypocritical self-righteous types who were hell-bent on exposing every tiny shred of corruption, no matter the truth of it.

If he failed – if Gregory went ahead and published – the fallout would be catastrophic. His career and business would go down the tubes. He might have to sell the holiday home in Nice. But that, he reflected morbidly, would be the very least of his troubles. Even thinking about what might happen brought him out in a cold sweat. He had hardly slept over the past few days.

Which is why Cantwell had arranged for a failsafe.

A backup option, in case the charm offensive failed.

Either way, he wasn't going to let Nick Gregory fuck him today.

No way.

At exactly two o'clock, Cantwell's assistant stepped through the door to his office. Elsie was one of his longest-serving employees, joining a week after he'd founded the company. She was nearing thirty, maybe two inches over five feet tall, with plump cheeks and hair the colour of a tangerine peel. A curvy figure, but strangely unattractive. She was also pathetically loyal, a quality Cantwell looked for in everyone who worked for him.

If someone messed up, he could forgive them. Most things were fixable. But if anyone dared to betray him, God help them.

'Mr Gregory is here,' Elsie said in her husky Durham accent.

Cantwell sat upright in his chair, nodded briskly. 'Very well. Tell him I'll be right along.'

His assistant turned on her heels and trotted back down the corridor. Cantwell took a final drag on his e-cigarette – he would have much preferred a hit from the real thing, but at the age of forty-two one had to make certain compromises. He rose to his feet and headed for the office door.

He was impeccably attired, as always. Cantwell considered himself a man of immense good taste and dressed formally around the office. Today he wore a herringbone jacket, beige trousers, a blue shirt so crisp you could almost snap it in half and a pair of tan leather oxfords. With his short red hair and silk pocket square, he looked like an Edwardian gentleman heading for a day at the races.

He knew many of his colleagues and rivals gently mocked him for his extravagant wardrobe. The clothes gave the impression that he was a cultural dinosaur, a man out of step with the times. Cantwell ignored their limp jokes. The clothes were in fact part of an image he had worked hard to cultivate over the years, along with the cut-glass accent and the taste for fine wine. Leaders in developing countries, he had discovered, did not generally appreciate being lectured by Brits with thick regional accents and dressed in off-the-rack suits. They preferred the classical look. It made them feel as if they were being addressed by an equal. Someone of great importance.

At the far end of the corner he hooked a left and approached the conference room. He stopped in front of the frosted glass door, took in a deep draw of breath and stepped inside.

The conference room was more blandly decorated than Cantwell's office. The floor was covered in some sort of hard-wearing industrial grey carpet. The walls were white-washed and bare except for a couple of generic landscapes. Sunlight seeped through the tall windows and spilled onto a rectangular oak conference table laid out like a coffin in the middle of the room. There was a projector screen at one end of the room, and a security camera mounted to the ceiling. Half a dozen leather chairs were arranged around the table at regular intervals.

Sitting at the far end of the room was Nick Gregory.

For a moment Cantwell didn't recognise the guy. The man in front of him had aged ten years in two. He'd lost maybe thirty pounds, and most of his hair. A few spidery threads draped either side of his bald pate. Prominent crow's feet protruded like wings from the corners of his eyes. His face was gaunt and pale and had more cracks in it than a pair of old leather shoes. His jacket was threadbare, with patches on the elbows. He wore no tie and faded jeans, and his shirt had a greasy stain down the middle.

Life had recently been a struggle for Nick Gregory. That much was obvious.

At the sound of Cantwell's footsteps the journalist looked up from his phone – a dated Samsung Galaxy model with a cracked screen, Cantwell noted – and rose to his feet.

Cantwell put on his most charming smile and strode confi-dently over to the man who had almost wrecked his career.

'Nick,' he began in a chummy tone of voice, thrusting out a hand. 'Bloody good to see you. Thanks for taking the time to come in. How have you been?'

Gregory looked down at the outstretched hand as if he might get Ebola from it. He kept his arms by his sides and lifted his piercing gaze to the consultant.

'Better, actually,' he said in his heavy Bristol accent. 'No thanks to you.'

He stared coldly at Cantwell. The latter smiled apologeti-cally. 'As I said before, I am terribly sorry about all that. That business about you fabricating stories, it really had nothing to do with me. A rogue employee, I'm afraid. It should have never happened.'

Gregory stared at him for a long cold beat. Cantwell could see the anger simmering behind the man's eyes. He smiled warmly and said, 'Anyway, I'm glad to see you looking so well.'

Which was a lie, Cantwell knew. Cantwell himself had lost a little of his old sheen. His hair was thinner these days, and at five-six and weighing seventeen stone, he had grown fat in his middle age. Too many boozy lunches at the Dorchester, too many late-night drinks in the City with old colleagues. But compared to the guy standing in front of him, Cantwell looked like he belonged on the cover of GQ magazine.

'You're doing well, I see,' Gregory said, glancing around the conference room.

Cantwell offered a humble shrug. 'You know how it is. The work never stops.'

'I bet.'

Gregory grunted. He finished casting a judgemental gaze over the furnishings and then swung his gaze back to Cantwell.

'This was a surprise, I'll admit,' he said. 'You agreeing to meet with me.'

'Oh, nonsense, old chap.' Cantwell waved a hand dismissively, as if swatting away a fly. 'Water under the bridge and all that. You were just doing your job.'

'That wasn't what you said at the time, as I recall. What was it you called me again? An inbred West Country fuckwit, wasn't it?'

Cantwell wrung his hands. 'Some things were said in the heat of the moment. I regret saying them. Honestly, Nick, I bear no malice towards you.'

He gestured to the chairs. 'Please. Sit down.'

Gregory planted himself back down in his chair. There was an A4 legal pad in front of him with lines of scribbled notes, a couple of biro pens and his phone. Cantwell took up a seat opposite the journalist, reached for a bottle of sparkling water and poured himself a glass. On the other side of the table, Gregory swiped to unlock his phone and tapped open some sort of voice-recording app.

Cantwell cleared his throat. 'Actually, Nick I'd prefer it if this conversation was off the record.'

Gregory opened his mouth as if to protest, then took a snap decision and shrugged. 'Fine. As you wish.'

He closed the app, put his phone to sleep and adjusted his thick round glasses.

'I'll get straight to it,' he said. 'As I've already explained, I've been researching some disturbing claims made by a former senior employee of yours. Stuart Goodwin.'

Cantwell smiled thinly. 'I'd hardly call him senior, Nick. As a matter of fact, I barely knew the chap. Stuart worked here for a couple of months, as I recall, before we had to let him go.'

'Mr Goodwin claimed that he was forced out of the company unfairly.'

'That's not how I remember it.'

Gregory tilted his head and frowned. 'Oh?'

'The reality is – and this isn't a very comfortable topic, as you might imagine – Stuart was a troubled individual. He struggled badly with addiction. Drugs, alcohol. It got to the point where it affected his work and the environment we're trying to create here. He was given several warnings about his conduct, but nothing changed.'

'So you sacked him?'

'We had no choice. Stuart needed professional help, but he wouldn't listen. We had to let him go. He didn't take it very well, of course.'

Gregory paused to glance down at his scribbled notes. 'This was in November of last year. Two months before Mr Goodwin was found dead at his family's home in New Zealand from a suspected overdose.'

Cantwell nodded solemnly. 'I was greatly saddened to learn of Stuart's death. Such a terrible waste of talent. But what has any of this got to do with me?'

'I was just getting to that.' Gregory laced his hands in front of him and leaned forward, propping his elbows on the table. 'A week before he died, Mr Goodwin contacted me.'

Cantwell felt the knife plunge deeper into his guts. 'You met with Stuart?'

'We spoke on the phone several times. Secure encrypted communications only. Mr Goodwin was very concerned that he was being watched and felt quite sure that people were monitoring his email and messages.'

Cantwell shifted. 'I wasn't aware that you two knew each other.'

'We didn't. Mr Goodwin reached out to me after reading some of my work. He said he had information he wanted to share, and he felt that I was someone he could trust.'

'I see.' Cantwell coughed. 'What did Stuart tell you, exactly?'

'I won't go into specifics right now. You've already seen the broad outline of Mr Goodwin's claims.'

A thin smile played out on Cantwell's face. 'That list of vague allegations you mentioned in your email? That hardly constitutes a cast-iron case.'

'Mr Goodwin gave me a lot more than that. A hell of a lot more.'

Cantwell sighed. 'Look, Stuart was deeply paranoid. The chap was prone to delusional episodes as a result of long-term substance abuse. He's hardly a reliable witness. I suggest that anything he has told you should be taken with a great big pinch of salt.'

'Actually, I found him to be highly convincing.'

'Christ, Nick. Don't tell me you're taking anything he said seriously?'

Gregory straightened up. 'Some of Mr Goodwin's claims initially struck me as outlandish. But he supplied me with dates, locations, names. Details that I was subsequently able to corroborate.'

'Really? Perhaps you'd be so kind as to share them with me.'

Gregory shook his head. 'I don't think so. You can read about it all when the story goes live. All you need to know is that I have enough evidence to take this to my old contacts.'

'Impossible.'

'Would I have bothered reaching out to you unless I had something concrete?'

He flashed a gap-toothed smile at Cantwell. The latter felt the knife twist inside his guts again, like a bayonet. 'And I suppose you want me to comment on the ludicrous allegations you alluded to in your email? Is that it?'

Gregory shrugged. 'This is an opportunity for you to give your side of the story.'

'But you can't possibly think there's even a grain of truth in what Stuart told you. It's all fantasies. The product of a demented imagination. Surely you can see that?'

'I know that Mr Goodwin was scared for his life when I last spoke to him. I know that he worked closely with you on a number of campaigns. He also told me that you had been recruiting a number of individuals to work on this particular project with you. Everything was on a need-to-know basis, according to Mr Goodwin.'

'Ridiculous. Absurd.'

'Well? Do you deny Mr Goodwin's claims?'

'Of course I bloody do.' Cantwell threw up his arms in exasperation. 'Special projects, secret conspiracies ... really, Nick, I'm very disappointed. I thought you were better than that. Frankly I'm surprised that you're even spending time on this piffle.'

'So that's a "no", then? You're denying everything?'

Cantwell closed his eyes, took in a deep breath and composed himself. He tried a different approach. 'Look,' he said calmly. 'This isn't about me. I'm trying to do you a favour here.'

Gregory raised an eyebrow in suspicion. 'Really?'

'Think about it. What will happen if you approach your old boss with some nonsense about a secret conspiracy, based on the spurious claims of a known drug addict? How do you think that will look? You'll be laughed out of the building, for god's sake.'

'I don't think so. Not with what I've got.'

'If you drop this claptrap story of yours, it might be to your benefit. I could give you a big news story. Something really juicy. Something that isn't based on lies.'

'Bigger than what I've got from Mr Goodwin?' Gregory chuckled. 'I very much doubt it.'

'Perhaps we can come to some sort of financial arrangement, then.'

Gregory stared at the consultant with widened eyes. A look of horror fused with outrage swept across his face. 'Are you actually trying to bribe me, Julian?'

'I wouldn't call it that,' Cantwell replied smoothly. He spread his fat hands. 'I'm merely suggesting that I compensate you – very generously, I might add – for the time you've spent investigating this nonsense. In return, you agree to drop the article and pursue some more meaningful stories. We both get to move on with our lives.'

'I'm not interested in your money.'

'How about a job? I could have a word with my friend over at the *Standard*. I'm sure he could get you a gig over there.'

Gregory shook his head firmly. 'You don't get it, do you? I'm not after a bribe.'

'What do you want, then?'

'Simple.' Gregory stared hard at Cantwell, his eyes glowering with barely suppressed anger. 'I want people to know the truth. I want the public to know what kind of a man you really are. That's what I want.'

'You're making a big mistake, Nick.'

Gregory raised an eyebrow. 'Is that a threat?'

'Of course not,' Cantwell replied. 'I'm simply pointing out that it's in your best interest to walk away from this story of yours. That's all. Now, perhaps if we discussed numbers, we might come to an agreement—'

Gregory raised a hand, cutting him off. 'Save your breath. You can't buy your way out of this one, Julian. Not this time. This story is going to get published, whether you like it or not. The world is going to find out what you've been up to. And nothing you can offer me – *nothing* – can change that. So take your offer and shove it.'

The journalist sat back, bristling with rage. Silence passed between the two men for a beat. Cantwell exhaled and smiled sadly. 'Well,' he said at last. 'That's a great shame. I had really hoped we could come to an understanding today.'

'Oh, I think we have. Just not the one you were looking for.'

'Pity.' Cantwell stood up, signifying an end to the meeting. 'Thank you for coming in, Nick. I'm sorry this wasn't more productive.'

His friendly, courteous manner evidently took Gregory by surprise. For a moment the guy just sat there, dumbfounded, looking at Cantwell with a bemused expression, a deep groove forming above his brow. Cantwell tapped his watch.

'I'm afraid I have to make a phone call. So, unless there's anything else I can help you with . . .?'

Gregory snapped out of his shock, then shook his head. 'Thanks, but no. I've got everything I need.'

He eased out of his chair, stuffed his belongings into the tattered leather man bag he'd brought along with him and pocketed his phone. Cantwell ushered him out of the conference room and paused briefly just outside the doorway, patting Gregory on the back. As if he was bidding goodbye to a dear old friend.

'Elsie will show you out. Thanks again for coming, old chap. It's always a pleasure to see you.'

'Er, right. Yes.' Gregory was still staring at him in puzzlement. Like a patient in a clinic, trying to make sense of a Rorschach card. Cantwell smiled.

'Best of luck, Nick. Really. I mean it.'

He turned and beckoned over Elsie from her desk. She strode over, smiled at Gregory and escorted him back down the grey-walled corridor, towards the main reception area.

Gregory hurried along after her, pausing to glance back quiz-zically at Cantwell. He wore a look on his face like a participant on stage at a magic show, trying to work out how he'd been tricked. Cantwell gave him a cheerful wave.

A few moments later, Elise led the journalist out through the main doors, towards the bank of lifts in the hallway. Cantwell watched him disappear from view, then dug out his phone from his inside jacket pocket.

He swiped to unlock, swiped twice to the left and tapped open an app called HideMyTracks. Cantwell used it whenever he wanted to communicate in secret. The app essentially converted his smartphone into a burner mobile, creating a string of temporary phone numbers he could delete as soon as he was finished with them. He wasn't sure how it worked – Cantwell was hopeless when it came to technology – but the principle was broadly the same as using a pre-paid phone to call someone. It was a way of sending encrypted messages without leaving any trace of the text or its contents.

Which was important in this situation.

Absolutely vital, in fact.

He punched in a six-digit pin code to unlock the app, opened a Hidden Contacts list, selected the only number on the screen and typed out a short message.

He's leaving. On his way down now.

Cantwell hit send. Then he waited.

The message, he knew, would automatically self-destruct within ten seconds of being viewed, wiping it from both users' phones. The number he had messaged wouldn't show up on his phone bill, and no one would ever be able to tell that he had sent a text to it.

There was a pause of maybe eight or nine seconds. Then his phone buzzed with a new message from the other person. A one-word response.

And?

Cantwell wrote a hasty reply, fat fingers dancing over the screen.

Don't worry. He doesn't suspect a thing.

There was another short wait. A few seconds later, Cantwell's phone trilled again. A second message popped up on the screen.

Good work. Stay there. Will let you know when it's done.

Thirty seconds later, Nick Gregory emerged from Kimberly House into the washed-out greyness of a Monday afternoon in London in late March.

He felt a sort of nervous excitement. And relief. As far as he could tell, the meeting had gone quite well. He had guessed that Cantwell would try to deny everything, of course. Nothing unusual about that. But the clumsy attempt to bribe Gregory into killing the story had been an unexpected development. But also welcome.

Because it told him that Cantwell was desperate.

Desperate to bury the story.

Which meant that the guy had something to hide.

Gregory smiled to himself. At first, he hadn't been too sure about the allegations. The conspiracy Stuart Goodwin had outlined had seemed too staggeringly vast in scope to be true. Even as he uncovered more evidence, that tiny voice of doubt had remained, niggling away at him.

Is this really true?

But now he knew for certain. Julian Cantwell was lying.

Nick Gregory was going to break the story of the century.

Better than that, he would redeem his own reputation in the process. The plot he had uncovered was shocking in its breadth and ambition. Gregory would be forever known as the intrepid journalist who had exposed the greatest conspiracy of recent times.

He paused outside the entrance and glanced round, looking for somewhere to set up his laptop and make notes from his meeting while it was still fresh in his mind. Cantwell's office was located midway down a tree-lined side street, on a one-way system running south to north. Directly opposite Kimberly House stood a parade of shops and a row of redbrick flats, with a faded Edwardian charm. A hundred metres to the north, at Gregory's three o'clock, there was a budget hotel and a concrete block of flats. To his left, a hundred metres away to the south, a Greek cafe and a pub with a green-tiled exterior, with a long line of cars parked along the side of the road.

At half past two in the afternoon, the street was practically deserted. Which wasn't a surprise. Fitzrovia wasn't Green Park, or London Bridge, or Tower Hill. There weren't many tourist attractions in this corner of the city. It was a patchwork neighbourhood of student housing, small-sized companies, old-man boozers and fancy restaurants. The few people who worked around here were probably hunched over their desks, slowly losing the will to live.

There was an overweight guy outside the betting shop on the other side of the road, sucking on a cigarette. Ten metres to the north, at Gregory's one o'clock, he spotted a middle-aged guy fiddling with the chain lock on his bicycle. He wore an orange waterproof jacket and black jeans. A pair of wireless buds jutted out of his ears. Further along, twenty metres away, a jogger was going through a warm-up routine. A short, barrel-chested guy dressed in a loose-fitting T-shirt, gym shorts and a baseball cap. His hands were planted against a lamp post, with one of his legs stretched behind him. He looked like he was trying to push a boulder up a hill.

From a distance, the guy didn't look much like a runner, thought Gregory. He had the physique of a professional wrestler. His muscles bulged through his T-shirt like basketballs in a sack.

Gregory turned left and set off down the side street, heading south. Away from the jogger and the cyclist. Towards the cafe and the pub on the corner of the street. He would find a table at the Greek cafe. Set up his laptop there. Make his notes.

Then he'd call one of his old editors and arrange a meeting. He would have to move fast, though. Cantwell would almost certainly try to block publication. The sooner Gregory could sell the story, the less time Cantwell had to prepare his defence.

Life had been a struggle for the past two years, but once this story broke, everything was going to change. The editors of all the major dailies would be fighting to sign him up. There would be lucrative offers to write books. The Americans would be interested as well, no doubt. Maybe he'd get a spot as an analyst on one of the cable news channels over there. Earning the big bucks.

Nick Gregory smiled to himself again.

Life had been shitty. But it was about to get a whole lot better.

A hundred metres to the south, the driver sat behind the wheel of the grey rental van and watched the target emerge from the building.

There were two of them on the team, the driver and the guy in the jogging gear. The driver was the bigger of the two. In his younger years his body had been pure muscle, but now everything was covered in a layer of fat. His belly protruded, straining against his Gore-Tex leather jacket. His legs were squeezed tightly into his waterproof trousers. The extra-large black leather gloves he wore barely fitted around his thick hands.

He had been given many nicknames over the years, but the one that had stuck was Tyson. He had once been an accomplished amateur boxer, demolishing rivals with ruthless efficiency. He had been in some hard fights, too; had the busted nose and the puffy ears to prove it.

Then he had failed a drugs' test. His hopes of turning pro had been wrecked.

In another life, Ty would have been sparring with the likes of Floyd Mayweather and Manny Pacquiao, raking in millions, headlining fight nights at the MGM Grand. Living the big life.

Instead, his life had taken a very different turn. For ten years he had served in the military, where his brute strength, stamina and aggression had helped him to reach the summit of his profession. Then he had done a stint on the private circuit, working for mediocre pay in shithole countries in Africa and the Middle East. Places most people had never heard of. Now, after fifteen years of fighting other people's wars, he was about to take part in his own.

Ty had moved into position first. He'd arrived two hours ago, parking the van in an empty space at the side of the road, next to a dingy-looking pub. Some sort of local hang-out, with net curtains drawn like cobwebs across the windows and a chalk-board sign fixed to the wall outside promising *Cold beer and warm food*. Which was setting the bar pretty low, in Ty's opinion. Surely that was the very least any respectable drinking establishment should aspire to?

The Ford Transit was facing north down the one-way road. A hundred and fifty metres away, he saw the other guy, the jogger, warming up near the other end of the street. He had been browsing the goods in a nearby sports store until he got the call to move forward. Which they both felt was a necessary precaution. The van wouldn't arouse suspicion. Whereas a jogger hanging around the same street for too long would draw unwanted attention.

Once they were in position, they had settled down to wait.

They were both patient men. They had been shadowing the journalist for the past three days, establishing his routine. Close observation of the target had confirmed that he lived alone, had few friends, didn't own a car, rarely used taxis and either walked or used public transport on the few occasions he left his flat. Such a guy would be unlikely to take a minicab from Crouch End to a meeting in central London, they had concluded. They had planned their operation accordingly, studying the roads around the offices of Cantwell Consulting Group. Checking for security cameras. Looking for the best spot for their attack.

Their boss had insisted that it be made to look like an accident. He had been very keen to emphasise that point. *Make sure they can't link this to us.*

If they fucked up, they had been warned, there would be consequences. They both knew their boss's reputation. The things he was capable of. He wasn't someone they wanted to piss off.

Thirty seconds ago, the message had come through.

At which point the jogger had hurried forward to his starting point close to Cantwell's building and Ty had cranked the ignition on the Transit. Then he had sat and waited, engine rumbling, observing the entrance to Kimberly House a hundred metres away.

Thirty seconds later, the target stepped outside the building. He paused briefly while he scanned the street.

Then he turned left and took off, heading south.

Towards the Transit.

Ty felt a nervous tic in his throat. This was it.

He released the parking brake, shifted into first gear, pumped the accelerator and gently steered out of the parking space. Pointing the wagon north down the one-way street.

Heading directly for the target.

A hundred and fifty metres to the north, the jogger in the purple baseball cap broke into a gentle trot.

He was ready.

He was one of the newer recruits to the team, and he looked it. He was five-seven and about as wide, with the squat, muscular frame of an Olympic powerlifter. He had short dark hair, a swarthy complexion and a trimmed black goatee. His name was Vecchio, but the veterans on the team called him Caesar, on account of his

Italian ancestry. It was a way of belittling Vecchio, of putting him in his place. Letting him know that they were the ones calling the shots.

Which was partly why the vets had chosen him for the operation, Vecchio knew. It was a way of testing him. Seeing if he had what it took to be a part of the team. So when they had told him he was going to London, Vecchio knew what was at stake.

He just had to hope that Tyson didn't fuck it up.

Vecchio had been with the gang long enough to know that Tyson was a loose cannon, totally unpredictable. There was no telling what the guy might do.

He crossed the road, passing the bald-headed guy unlocking his bicycle, and came up behind the target. The journalist was twenty-five metres downstream from Vecchio and moving briskly down the street. He had the quick, impatient walk of city dwellers the world over.

A hundred metres further to the south, the Transit slithered out of the parking bay and began slow-crawling down the road. Tyson was keeping the speed very low, moving along at maybe ten or fifteen miles per hour.

They were closing in on the target from opposite ends of the street.

Vecchio was approaching from the north with Tyson, in the Transit van, further to the south. The journalist was thirty metres down the street from Cantwell's office. He didn't look back at Vecchio at his six o'clock. Didn't seem to be worried about being followed. He just continued heading on a southerly bearing towards the cafe at the end of the street.

Vecchio was fifteen metres behind the target now. He kept moving at a steady canter, not wanting to draw too close and risk startling the guy. Up ahead, the van was sixty metres from the journalist and closing fast.

In the periphery of his vision Vecchio caught sight of an old man walking his dog. At the end of the street a woman in a pencil skirt and dark jacket sat outside the Greek cafe, tapping away on her laptop. A few metres further along, a balding guy in a pinstripe suit was marching down the street, phone glued to his ear.

No one was paying any attention to what was happening on the street.

Good.

Vecchio looked ahead. He was ten metres behind the target, with the wagon forty metres further ahead. Engine growling, tyres hissing as they rolled over the rain-slicked blacktop. The journalist was still looking down at his phone, totally unaware of what was about to happen.

Vecchio quickened his stride. Arms and legs chopping as he surged forward, like an athlete sprinting down the home straight. An athlete who had lifted too many weights in the gym.

Eight metres to the target. Six metres.

Four.

In the next beat he drew up alongside the journalist and thrust out with both hands, shoving the guy aside. The impact caught the target by surprise and knocked him off his feet. He stumbled and then fell away with a pained cry, landing in a heap in the road, a metre or so from the kerb.

'Hey!' the journalist cried.

Fifteen metres ahead, the van suddenly accelerated.

There was no time for the man to scramble clear of the wagon.

Vecchio ran on. Head down, the baseball cap concealing his face from any CCTV cameras on the street. Behind him, the target screamed in terror.

Which was the last sound that ever left his mouth. Because the next thing that Vecchio heard was a sickening crunch as the Transit smashed bumper-first into the journalist's sprawled body, three thousand kilograms of metal hitting him at around twenty miles an hour. He heard the thump and shudder of the body going under the tyres.

When he was twenty metres away, Vecchio risked a glance over his shoulder. He saw the Transit jolting as it raced on for several metres with the journalist trapped beneath it, his limbs scraping against the blacktop. Then the driver gunned the engine and the Transit shot forward, and there was a final judder as the target's ragged body tumbled out from beneath the back of the van and rolled over a couple of times before flopping to a rest. The van picked up speed as it arrowed north, leaving the bloodied body in its wake, hurtling towards the far end of the street.

Which is when Vecchio saw the cyclist.

He was shaven-headed, wearing a distinctive orange jacket and riding in the middle of the road. The same guy he had seen unlocking his bike a few moments ago, Vecchio realised. At some point between the target leaving the building and the attack, the guy had set off down the street. He was trundling along, unaware of the collision behind him, his earbuds cutting out the background noise.

The Transit was twelve metres away from the cyclist and hurtling forward.

No time for the guy to dive out of the way.

Vecchio looked on in surprise and horror as the van ploughed into the back of the cyclist. There was a dull thump as the impact knocked the man from his saddle and in the next instant he went under the wagon, the wheels crushing the frame of his bicycle and mangling the rider's body, grinding organs and snapping bones.

Further to the south, outside the Greek café, someone screamed.

The Transit didn't stop. The rear wheels bounced up and then the van sped away, leaving a tangle of limbs and twisted bike parts in its wake. Vecchio saw it race north for another eighty metres before it hit the corner at the other end of the street. Then the wagon swerved to the right, tyres screeching as it took the turn at speed. A moment later, it disappeared from view.

Vecchio paused for a cold beat.

Then he turned away and started running south.

He crossed the junction, hit the other side of the road and sprinted past a barber's shop and a curry house with rubbish bags piled up outside. After another twenty metres he stopped and glanced over his shoulder. He saw the woman in the pencil skirt rushing over from the cafe, dropping to a knee beside the journalist.

At the same time the balding guy in the pinstripe suit was pacing up and down, jabbering on his phone. Calling for an ambulance, presumably. Two more customers bolted out of the cafe and raced over to the cyclist, a portly guy in a Liverpool shirt and a younger man in red cords and a tweed jacket.

Both victims looked to be in a bad way. The journalist lay slumped on the blacktop, leg twitching. The cyclist wasn't moving at all. He was just lying there, next to the mangled frame of his bicycle. Hard to tell from a distance, and Vecchio wasn't a doctor, but he didn't give either of them much of a chance.

No one paid any attention to the jogger seventy metres to the south. Everyone was completely focused on the two victims sprawled in the road.

Vecchio turned and ran on again.

He shuttled on for another fifty metres down the side street, passing whitewashed terraced houses and art studios and boutique fashion shops. As he neared the corner he looked back again at the scene to the north. More people were crowding in the street now, rubbernecking the scene or filming it on their phones.

No one was chasing after Vecchio.

He looked ahead, hit the corner in a few more strides and hooked a left, running east down a busier main road for a couple of hundred metres. He dropped his speed to a light jog, not moving too fast or too slow, doing nothing to draw attention to himself. Just a regular guy, out for an afternoon run in the streets. After two hundred metres he hooked another left and chopped his way north down a narrow side street. Row of decrepit townhouses on his left, a construction site on his right flank. At his one o'clock, the BT Tower loomed over the surrounding buildings like some giant radio antenna.

He carried on for another hundred metres, passing a dirty-looking launderette and a dim-windowed Turkish restaurant. He made a left and then a quick right, heading down the east-facing side of a seventies-style office block. There was an underground car park built below the offices, with a ramp leading down from street level to the lower floors. The place was poorly maintained, overpriced and somewhat hidden away. Which made it perfect for Vecchio and Tyson.

He walked past the ramp until he hit the pedestrian entrance thirty metres further along the street. Exactly four minutes after the attack, he yanked open the rusted metal door and ducked into the concrete stairwell.

A stench of urine so thick you could practically hack through it with a machete. The steps were sprinkled with a confetti of cigarette butts and foil wrappers. He hurried down one flight of stairs, burst through the door to the lower-level parking area and looked around.

The place was half-empty. A handful of motors were scattered around the white-marked spaces. Nobody on foot, as far as he could tell.

He spotted the Transit parked up in a far corner and hustled over. Tyson was clambering out of the wagon, dressed in his bike leathers. The guy would have taken a circuitous route to the car park, Vecchio knew, screaming down a maze of side streets in case anyone tried to pursue him. They had gone through the route late last night, studying the maps in detail, looking at possible chokepoints or dead ends where they might get blocked in or cut off.

Tyson cocked his head at the younger man. 'Anyone see you come in here?'

Vecchio shook his head. 'I wasn't followed.'

'You better hope that's fucking true.'

Vecchio paused a beat to catch his breath. He was sweating freely, in spite of the chill in the air. 'What was that all about?'

'Fuck was what?'

Vecchio swallowed. Tyson staring at you was an uncomfortable experience. The guy was seven inches taller than him and maybe forty pounds heavier. His balled fists were as big as wrecking balls.

'The guy on the bike,' Vecchio said. 'Jesus, Ty. I think you killed him. What the hell?'

Tyson shrugged. 'He was in the way.'

'That wasn't part of the plan.'

'You would have preferred it if I stopped, got out, politely asked the guy to get out of my way?' Tyson rubbed his jaw. 'Cyclist would have seen my face, anyway. Through the window. He might have been able to make an ID. Hell, he might have even chased after us. Concerned citizen. Tailed us all the way here. It had to be done.'

'He was innocent.'

Tyler frowned. 'So fucking what? Collateral damage. Happens. Or maybe you haven't got the guts to do this stuff? Is that what you're trying to tell me?'

'I've got what it takes.'

Tyson snorted. 'Some fucking mope on a bicycle gets in my way, that's on him. No reason for you to get all cut up about it. Or maybe you want to go back to robbing liquor stores, or whatever the fuck you were doing in New Jersey.'

Vecchio said nothing.

Tyson snarled. 'That's what I thought.'

He stepped closer to Vecchio, prodding him in the chest. 'You're not in charge round here. You ought to remember that. Far as me and the boys are concerned, you're just some Italian sack of shit who's been on the team for five fucking minutes.'

Vecchio stared at Ty for a beat, then decided to drop it. The clock was ticking. They couldn't afford to stay in the general vicinity for a moment longer than necessary. By now the ambulances would be on their way to the scene of the accident. The police would probably also have been alerted. They would soon be scouring the area for a grey Transit van.

Besides, he didn't want to jeopardise his place on the team. He had been promised crazy money for his part in carrying out the mission. The opportunity of a lifetime. No way was he going to mess that up.

'It's cool,' he said. 'We're good.'

Tyson nodded. 'Let's get the fuck out of here.'

He swung round to the rear of the wagon and popped the doors. Inside the cargo space stood a BMW R1200 GS Adventure motorcycle, all sleek angles and scarlet-red bodywork. A beast of a bike.

The van was hot, they knew. If Tyson and Vecchio tried to escape in the Transit, they would quickly get snarled up in London traffic. They wouldn't stand a chance of losing the cops. A motorbike was better. They could mount pavements, weave through traffic jams and go the wrong way down one-way streets.

The perfect getaway ride.

A pair of ratchet straps were wrapped around the BMW's chrome fork legs, with the other ends fastened taut to anchor points on the floor. The front wheel was set into a solid steel chock, securing the bike in place. A waterproof helmet bag was tethered to the rear of the bike, with a cable lock threaded through the wheel.

Tyson stepped back from the doors, padded around to the front of the wagon and snatched up a shopping bag from the front passenger seat footwell. He circled back around to the rear of the van, chucked the bag at Vecchio.

'Here,' he said. 'Get changed. Hurry.'

Vecchio fished out a black Gore-Tex jacket and a pair of waterproof trousers from the shopping bag. While he slipped them on over his sweat-drenched clothes, Tyson reached into the back of the Transit and untied a folded aluminium loading ramp. He extended the ramp, lowering it at an angle to the ground. Then he hopped into the van, untied the straps from either side of the BMW and pulled the bike backwards, releasing the front wheel from the chock. Carefully rolled the bike down the loading ramp.

As soon as Tyson had eased the machine down to the ground he kicked out the side stand, rested the BMW upright and padded round to the front passenger side of the wagon. Hurried back a few moments later gripping a black full-face helmet with a clear visor.

He thrust the helmet at Vecchio, quickly folded the aluminium ramp back up inside the Transit and slammed the doors shut. Then he retrieved a second motorcycle helmet from the waterproof bag tied to the back of the BMW and slipped it over his head.

Tyson paced back round to the front of the Transit. He reached inside the passenger seat. Grabbed a plastic bag filled with human hair.

The evening prior to the attack, they had stolen a bag of hair clippings dumped in the street outside a less-than-reputable barber's shop a few miles away. Vecchio and Tyson had taken the cuttings and stashed the hair in a sealed sterile bag. Now Tyson unzipped the bag and emptied the contents inside the van. The hair would corrupt any DNA samples taken later on by police scene-of-crime teams. With all that extra DNA swimming about inside the van, there was no way the police would be able to identify the person driving it at the time of the hit-and-run. Not for a while, at least.

He tossed the empty bag on the floor, slammed the side door shut and locked the Transit. Hooked back around to Vecchio and the BMW, gripped the handlebars and threw his left leg over the seat. Then he braced both feet on the ground, retracted the side stand and fired up the ignition. A bunch of lights flashed up on the display, and then Tyson shifted into neutral, squeezed the clutch and brake and thumbed down the start button. The engine buzzed into life. Vecchio planted himself awkwardly on the passenger seat, gripping the hand-hold tightly. He tapped Tyson once on the back, indicating that he was good to go.

A few moments later, the BMW was motoring forward. Tyson upshifted through the gears, following the directions towards the exit ramp. They emerged from the gloom of the car park into the pale grey of the afternoon and rode east for fifty metres before cutting north towards Great Portland Street. Three minutes later they were tooling down Marylebone Road and heading towards Edgware Road.

Thirty-nine minutes after the killing, they were clear of London and motoring west on the A40.

They were safe.

For the time being, anyway.

They had done everything possible to cover their tracks, Tyson reassured himself. The previous day, they had carried out a detailed recce of the car park, noted the positions of the various CCTV cameras and blocked them out with green spray paint. Even if somebody saw the van enter the parking lot, there was no way anybody would be able to identify them now. No one had seen them leave the building riding on the BMW. They had also swapped round the licence plates on the Transit, stealing a set from an almost-identical van they had spotted outside an industrial estate in Tottenham.

There was nothing to tie either of them to the crime.

Or their boss.

As for the cops, they would most likely conclude that the journalist had been the unfortunate victim of a hit-and-run, along with the cyclist Ty had flattened. They might have their suspicions about Cantwell, but he would claim to have spent the afternoon in his office, going through a mountain of paperwork, unaware of the accident in the street. He would later voluntarily attend a police station near his home in Barnes, explaining that he had only heard the terrible news about Gregory after checking his phone that evening. Detectives would almost certainly focus on the animosity between Cantwell and Gregory as a possible motive. But Cantwell would argue that he bore no grudge against the man. The footage from the conference room camera would back up his statement, showing the fixer smiling and patting the journalist on the back at the end of their meeting.

Of course, CCTV in the area would have picked up Vecchio pushing the target into the street. They had done a mobile recce of the area in the days before the killing, noting the position of the cameras. They had quickly concluded that if you were planning to kill someone in central London, there was no way to avoid being caught on camera. Instead, they had decided to take a different approach, constructing a narrative that a lazy detective might pick up on. They would see Vecchio pushing the target into the street and reason that an arrogant jogger had shoved a pedestrian aside, with fatal consequences. The driver of the Transit van, in a moment of total panic, had decided to flee the scene rather than face arrest. That's what the footage would show. And there would be nothing to conclusively link the jogger with the driver.

Plausible. Just about.

Tyson smiled.

Job done.

They rode the BMW as far as Beaconsfield. There was a rented Volkswagen Passat waiting for them in a lay-by in a wooded area, several miles outside the town. They hit the lay-by at a little past four o'clock and switched motors, dumping the motorbike deep in the woods and dousing it in bleach. Then they changed into fresh sets of clothes and disposed of their motorcycle gear in a bin a couple of miles away.

They had go-bags stowed in the trunk of the Passat. Everything they would need for their onward journey: passports, flight tickets, cash, pre-paid credit cards, burner mobiles.

At 16.30 hours, they set off for Birmingham Airport. They would catch the 19.55 direct flight to Paris, spend the night at a mid-range hotel at Charles de Gaulle Airport and fly out the next morning to Atlanta. From there, they could take another flight to their final destination. Straight on to their next mission.

Tyson smiled to himself again. Everything had gone according to plan. Well, almost everything.

There was a small chance that the journalist would survive the accident, of course. The Internet was full of videos of people making miraculous recoveries from horrific car crashes. But at the very least, the guy would be seriously injured. He'd be in hospital for months, possibly comatose. Maybe even brain dead.

And if the worst happened and he did wake up, by the time he was able to talk it would be too late. The operation would already be completed. The first part of it, anyway.

If the plan worked – and there was really no reason it shouldn't – Tyson and his brothers-in-arms were going to change the world. They would be richly rewarded for their work, but there was more to it than that, Ty knew. What they were about to do, nobody had done before. They were breaking new ground. Writing history.

It was going to be fucking beautiful.

TWO

Forty-eight hours later, John Bald stared out of the window and wondered how much lower he could sink.

He was sitting at the table in the wood-panelled kitchen, on the ground floor of the bed and breakfast he had recently taken over. The rain-spattered windows looked out over a patio at the front of the property and, beyond it, a bleak and windswept landscape. A band of thick clouds hung low in the sky, stirring the grey waters of Loch Indaal a few hundred metres to the south. In the distance a series of low hills were faintly visible through a dirty veil of mist and rain.

Late March on the Isle of Islay, off the west coast of Scotland.

Shitty weather.

A business that was haemorrhaging cash.

Ten years after leaving 22 SAS, John Bald had finally hit rock bottom.

He gritted his teeth and looked down at the papers spread out in front of him on the kitchen table. Accounts for the business.

The numbers were bad, Bald knew.

Really bad.

Two years ago, he had been living the good life. Had an apartment overlooking the Caribbean Sea. Spent his evenings on a white-sanded beach, sipping ice-cold Coronas and eyeing up the local talent. Things had been pretty fucking good.

Now . . . this.

There were times when the scenery on the Isle of Islay could be strikingly beautiful. Days when the sun shone crisply in the clear-blue sky and glinted off the waters of the loch, when you could see the fallow deer galloping through the fields, and for a fleeting moment, Bald could pretend that all was right with the world.

Today was not one of those days.

He reached for his whisky glass, raised it to his lips and took a long hit of the cheap stuff. The liquid burned as it went down his throat and spread a warm feeling through his veins, numbing the rage in his guts.

Bald had bought the B&B after he'd been screwed over by a couple of ex-Regiment guys. Ramsey and Peake. Old-timers he had fought alongside in Afghanistan, leading assaults into the Tora Bora caves to flush out the last defiant pockets of Taliban resistance. People he had shared beers with. People he thought he could trust.

He had been wrong.

A year ago, they had approached Bald with a business proposition. He had been working in corporate security at the time, as a health and safety director with one of the big oil firms. He was getting good money, but the work was spirit-crushingly dull. He did a lot of travelling, attended courses, gave regular talks to a bunch of flabby-gutted executives in tailored suits. No action. No risk. Not his scene.

Then Ramsey and Peake had showed up. Told him they had a plan to set up their own private security company. They had pitched the idea to Bald. It was going to be an elite operation, recruiting exclusively from the UK and US Special Forces families, providing security for large businesses and media outlets.

Ramsey and Peake would provide the manpower and contacts in Whitehall. They were going to make millions. But they needed funding. Start-up cash. Did Bald want in?

He didn't need much persuading. He had been looking for a way out of the corporate gig and now he had it.

Big mistake.

At first, everything had looked good. Ramsey and Peake had received some encouraging noises from their contacts. But soon the costs began to spiral. There was rent to pay on the office, staff to hire, equipment to purchase. They needed more money, Ramsey had said to him. The big contracts from Whitehall were going to come through any day now. It was just a temporary cash-flow problem.

Bald had emptied his savings. Put every last penny he had into the business.

Still the contracts didn't come through. Bald started chasing his partners. Asking questions. They told him to be patient. It was just a matter of time, they said.

A few weeks later, Ramsey and Peake stopped returning his calls.

It turned out that their high-level contacts inside the MoD didn't exist. They hadn't paid any of the employees or bought any hardware. The whole thing had been a scam. They had been siphoning money out of the business and using it to fund their lifestyle. As soon as Bald got suspicious, they had upped sticks and fled the country.

He was out of pocket by two hundred and fifty thousand. Everything he had saved up over the years. Meanwhile, his old partners were now running a new company out in the Middle East. They were doing well, apparently. Last Bald had heard, they were both multi-millionaires.

He had been played. The sort of con trick he might have pulled on someone else, in his younger years.

His fault. He had got slack. Ignored the warning signs, the people telling him not to trust Ramsey and Peake.

You should have seen it coming.

After being cleaned out by people he'd once considered his muckers, Bald had decided to get as far away from Hereford as possible. Too many snakes. Too many bad memories.

He'd heard about an ex-Parachute Regiment lad who had been running a guest house on the Isle of Lewis. Tourism in the Hebrides was a growth industry, apparently. Australians and Americans were flocking to the islands, attracted by the famous distilleries and Instagram-worthy landscape. Bald had done some research and learned about an opportunity on the Isle of Islay. The owners of a B&B were looking to sell up in order to be closer to their grandchildren on the mainland. Bald had haggled over the price, sold his house in Hereford and moved to Islay.

Thirty years after he'd left to join the army, he had finally returned to his native Scotland.

The property he had acquired was situated on a barren stretch of coast, on a slight rise overlooking Loch Indaal. To the north, a belt of woodland covered a gently rising slope. A hundred metres to the south, the main road that ran from Bridgend in the east to the westernmost tip of the island at Portnahaven. Three hundred metres beyond the road, a narrow strip of shingle extended across the fringes of the loch.

There were two properties on Bald's land: a two-storey house and a smaller guest cottage. The structures were bisected by a gravel path that ran from the main road to a parking area at the rear. There were five rooms in total. Two large double bedrooms on the first floor of the main building, and three rooms in the cottage. The plot was enclosed by a waist-high stone wall with a timber gate at the entrance.

It was an isolated spot. Which was part of the appeal, Bald had figured. The nearest village was two miles to the west. The administrative capital, Bowmore, was five miles away, on the southern side of the loch. It was the perfect location for rich city folk looking to get away from it all.

But the place had needed a lot of work. More than he'd anticipated. The roof in the main house was leaking. There were damp patches on the walls, the carpets were threadbare, and the chintzy furniture needed replacing. Bald had sunk the last of his cash into an extensive renovation. He'd gutted the cottage, installed new bathrooms, paid for a modern kitchen and a landscaped patio facing out across the loch. When he ran out of funds, he had taken out a large loan to cover the work. He had paid a firm in Edinburgh to design a slick-looking website and an online reservation system. He'd even run ads on social media. Everything he needed to get his new business up and running.

Then he had waited for the bookings to roll in.

There had been a slow trickle of guests at first. A few American and Canadian couples staying for a night or two while they visited the distilleries, the occasional English couple. But that was it.

Bald kept hoping that the business would pick up. He had run promotions, paid for premium listings on booking websites, slashed the room rates. Nothing seemed to work.

The previous winter had been especially brutal. Now he was on the brink, financially. In a few months they would be approaching the start of peak season, he knew. If things didn't improve then, he was finished.

He took another gulp of cheap whisky. Tried to ignore the voice in his head. The one telling him that he should have seen this coming.

You haven't hit rock bottom yet, John Boy, the voice said. *Twelve weeks from now, you could be out on your arse. No home, no money. Your next address could be Cardboard City.*

From SAS legend to penniless bum. Big fucking comedown, that.

The kitchen door swung open, snapping Bald out of his thoughts. He looked over and saw a short figure with cropped black hair standing in the doorway. She wore a pair of skinny jeans that wrapped like cling film around her ample thighs and a plain white boyfriend shirt with the top two buttons popped.

Magda Lewandowski, Bald's receptionist-cum-housekeeper, chewed gum loudly as she folded her arms across her chest.

'We have problem,' she said in her thick Polish accent.

Bald found himself casually sizing her up. He had toyed with the idea of working the old charm on Magda on more than one occasion. Christ knows, he could use a shag. On an island of three thousand people, there weren't many good prospects, and Magda – wide-hipped, large-breasted, strawberry-lipped Magda – was more attractive than most. Her good looks were one of the reasons Bald had hired her, reasoning that he needed a friendly face to front the business. The fact that she could cook and clean and do the various admin tasks was a bonus.

'You listen, boss? I said we have problem.'

Bald shoved aside the pleasing mental image of shagging Magda and frowned. 'What is it?'

'The guests. They make complaint.' Magda rolled her eyes. 'Again.'

Bald clenched his jaws in frustration. The last thing he needed.

Two days ago, a trio of Australian backpackers had arrived at the guest house. From the moment they'd arrived they had been nothing but trouble, moaning about the breakfast and the heating and everything in between.

He gestured to the sheaf of papers on the table. 'I'm busy. Can't you handle it?'

'Is problem with bathroom. They say sink is blocked. They say they want fixed, or money back.' She shrugged expressively. 'Is man problem. You need to fix.'

'Fine.' Bald sighed irritably. 'I'll deal with it.'

He took a deep breath, slid out of his chair and ducked into the utility room to the side of the kitchen. Grabbed a bucket and plunger from a cupboard below the sink. Then he marched back across the kitchen into the main reception area. Magda had resumed her usual station behind the reception desk, flicking through a Polish-language gossip magazine. Bald breezed past her and made for the door.

'We need to have chat,' she called after him. 'This job is shit money. You want me to deal with idiot guests, I need pay rise.'

'Later,' Bald growled.

He didn't know it, but his day was about to get a hell of a lot worse.

A harsh wind whipped across his face as he stepped outside, stinging his ears and blasting through his silvery hair. He hung a right outside the main house and beat a path towards the guest cottage fifty metres away, the rain-soaked ground squelching under his waterproof boots. The cottage was a quaint one-storey stone-built structure with narrow windows and a steep shingle roof. A tall hedge enclosed a small private garden set to the side of the cottage. As Bald drew nearer he could hear a boisterous din of laughter and voices coming from within.

He marched up to the front door and rapped his knuckles twice.

The noise instantly cut out. Bald heard the muffled padding of footsteps approaching, the clack of the latchbolt retracting. A moment later the door swung open.

A huge shaven-headed guy in a Wallaby rugby jersey filled the doorway. He stood in front of it like a boulder blocking the entrance to a cave. The guy was maybe four inches shorter than Bald and about thirty pounds heavier, most of it evidently muscle. His legs were like a pair of columns supporting a Roman arch. His biceps were so big they could have doubled up as basketballs. He had a barrel-shaped chest and small dark eyes that were too wide apart.

'Help you, mate?' Biceps asked.

'Magda tells me you fellas are having some problems with the sink,' said Bald.

'Yeah.' Biceps scratched his balls and sniffed. 'Too bloody right we are. Thing's been blocked all morning. Fucking unacceptable, that. Along with everything else in this place.'

Bald bit back on his anger. 'Let me take a look inside, eh? See if I can sort it out.'

'Yeah, whatever.'

Biceps grunted as he turned and strutted back into the main living area. Bald followed him inside, closing the door behind him.

A spark of anger flared up inside his chest as he glanced around the room. The Aussies had evidently trashed the place. The bin in the kitchen area was overflowing with empty beer bottles. There was a stack of dirty plates in the sink, coffee cups filled with crushed cigarette butts. On the other side of the room, Bald noticed a reddish stain on the rug in front of the fireplace. Muddy footprints were stamped across the wooden floorboards.

One of the other guests was slumped on the sofa next to the fireplace, his boots, socks and coat tossed casually across the floor. Sipping a beer while he warmed his feet in front of the wood-burning stove. The guy could have been Biceps' paler, hairier twin. He had skin the colour of milk, an unkempt ginger beard and wild eyes. He was dressed in a pair of light denim jeans and a plaid shirt with the sleeves rolled up. Bald noted that the guy had a crude rose tattoo on his forearm.

The third guy was standing to one side of the sofas, cigarette dangling from the corner of his mouth as he ironed a denim cowboy shirt. He was a greasy-looking fucker, with lank black hair and a chinstrap beard. He wore a Green Day T-shirt and he had a braided leather necklace draped across his chest. In the background, Bald could hear music coming from one of the bedrooms. Some sort of grunge band.

At the sight of Bald entering the room, Chinstrap and Rose Tat both looked up at him.

'Here to unblock the sink,' Biceps explained.

'About fucking time,' Chinstrap said, fixing his gaze on Bald. He rested the iron on the dock, took a long drag on his cigarette.

'Shouldn't take long, fellas,' Bald said, trying to keep his anger in check. 'I'll be out of your hair in two minutes.'

'Not good enough, is it, lads?' Chinstrap looked questioningly at his two muckers.

'Ain't just the sink, either,' Rose Tat said. 'That ain't even half of it.'

Bald set down the bucket and plunger. 'You lads have got other complaints?'

'Yeah, mate,' said Chinstrap. 'We fucking do. Place is riddled with problems. Even this shitty iron doesn't work properly. No bloody steam coming out of it.'

Bald trudged across the room, snatched up the iron and inspected it. One of the fancy new cordless models that Magda had insisted on getting for the rooms. He twisted the plastic knob clockwise, placed it down on the shirt and depressed one of the buttons. A shot of hot steam hissed out of the iron. Bald set the iron back in the metal dock and nodded.

'There's your problem. Wrong setting.'

'What about all the other problems we've been having?' Rose Tat demanded.

Bald turned to face the guy, grinding his teeth in anger. 'If you've got other issues, I'm sure we can sort them out. Just tell us what's wrong.'

'How much time have you got?' Chinstrap counted them off on his fingers. 'For a start, the TV is ancient. Thing belongs in a museum. The Wi-Fi is slow and cuts out all the time. There aren't enough towels, and the ones you've given us are too hard. There's a draught coming through the window in my bedroom. I could go on all day.'

Bald raised his hands. 'We'll fix everything, lads. If you'll just give us a chance—'

'You've had plenty of chances already. This place is a dump. Ain't that right, fellas?'

Biceps and Rose Tat, the steroid twins, looked at one another

36

and nodded in agreement. Chinstrap flicked cigarette ash on the floor, dropped his stub into an empty beer can.

'What kind of a joint do you think you're running here, anyway?' he went on. 'Call yourself a B&B? Place is more like a fucking refugee camp. You should be ashamed.'

Bald felt a powerful urge to tell the guests to piss off.

'I'm sorry you feel that way,' he said.

'Sorry won't cut it.' Chinstrap folded his arms across his chest. 'In fact, I reckon you should waive our bill. Let us stay here for free. That should just about compensate us, for all the crap we've put up with.'

'Brad's right,' Biceps put in. 'You shouldn't be charging us to stay in this dump.'

Bald felt the rage simmering in his guts. 'I can't do that. But I can see you're unhappy, so I could maybe offer you fellas a small discount. Say, five per cent of the total?'

Chinstrap pulled a face. 'You must be fucking joking. You ain't fobbing us off that easily. Either you wipe the bill, or we'll give this place a load of one-star reviews.'

The guy pointed at Biceps. 'Bailey here is a bit of an influencer. He's got eighty thousand followers on Insta. One word from him and you're finished.'

'Come on, lads. Be reasonable. I've got a business to run here.'

'I don't give a toss. Either let us stay for free, or we'll ruin your rep.'

Bald shook his head. 'You don't want to do that.'

Chinstrap chuckled. 'Is that a threat, old man?'

'Just telling you how it is.'

The smile on Chinstrap's face disappeared. 'Be careful, Grandad. You don't know who you're fucking with.'

'I disagree,' said Bald. Anger pounded between his temples. He took a step closer to Chinstrap. 'I know exactly who I'm dealing with. A couple of morons who look like the missing link, and a greasy twat who's too thick to know how an iron works. That's who I'm fucking with. And if you think you can pressure me into dropping your bill, think again.'

In the corner of his eye, Bald saw Rose Tat rising to his feet, standing close to the fireplace. Wrought-iron tools dangling from a stand next to the wood-burning stove. At the same time, Biceps moved to block the entrance.

Closing in on him.

'We ain't asking,' Chinstrap said. 'We're telling you, plain and simple. Let us off the hook with the bill, or me and the lads will shit all over your business. Got it?'

Bald took in a breath.

'Okay,' he said calmly.

Then he grabbed the iron and lamped Chinstrap in the face.

At the age of fifty-six, Bald was nowhere near as well honed or as muscular as he had been in his youth. Back then, he'd possessed the body of a Greek god. Now, the decades of wear and tear were beginning to take their toll. His skin was leathery and creased. His cognitive functions had been damaged by a bullet he'd taken to the head at point-blank range several years ago, passing through his frontal lobes and leaving him with savage migraines. His shoulder joint was stiff from an old rotator cuff injury. The cartilage in his knees had been worn down to the nub.

But he still knew how to win a fight.

He moved in a rapid blur. He was half a metre away from Chinstrap, with the ironing board at his three o'clock. The iron was within easy reaching distance. So was Chinstrap's face. There was no time for Bald's opponent to block the attack or launch a pre-emptive strike. He let out a grunt as the still-hot soleplate smashed into the middle of his face and sent him staggering backwards, head tipped back, like somebody had just told him there was a fifty-pound note stuck to the ceiling. Bald struck him again, hitting him so hard the iron flew out of his hand. There was a dull thud as Chinstrap crashed back against the wall, driving the air from his lungs.

In the next instant, Bald saw a flicker of movement in his peripheral vision.

He spun round. Saw Rose Tat rushing towards him from the fireplace at his eleven o'clock, a slab of slow-twitch muscle and pent-up rage. Biceps was a few steps further away, standing in the entryway, still processing the scene in front of him. Chinstrap was at his six o'clock, momentarily stunned.

Rose Tat had reacted fractionally quicker than his mucker. He had dropped his shoulder low and was lunging at Bald, his right hand balled into a fist the size of a kettle bell, ready to unleash a punch.

Six feet away, Biceps also moved towards him.

Bald sprang towards Rose Tat and thrust out his right arm, striking the guy cleanly across the face.

There was a satisfying crack as his fist smashed into the side of Rose Tat's jaw, shattering bones and teeth. Rose Tat grunted and fell away, arms flopping at his sides, his eyes rolling into the back of his head like symbols on a fruit machine. He dropped like an anvil next to the wood-burning stove, knocking over the stand holding the wrought-iron poker, shovel, tongs and brush.

Two down, one to go.

In the same breath, Bald whipped round just in time to see Biceps launching at him from a metre away.

Fist driving towards his face.

Bald was too slow to react. The effects of the three large whiskies in his bloodstream. The punch struck him on the jawbone. Pain exploded inside his skull as a billion different nerve endings flared up. He saw white briefly, then blinked and saw Biceps swinging at him again, aiming for the throat. Bald raggedly parried the blow and shovelled a left hook into Biceps' midriff, momentarily winding the guy. Biceps scowled, his face twisted with rage as he came at Bald again.

In a flash, Bald snatched up the iron poker and spun back round to his onrushing opponent. Biceps was shaping to throw a big uppercut. Going in for the knockout blow. He didn't want to get dragged down into the trenches, clearly. He wanted the fight over.

Bald grasped the rod with both hands as he twisted sharply at the hips, swinging the poker towards Biceps. Like a baseball hitter knocking out a home run.

Biceps had no time to adjust his stance. Momentum carried him forward, straight into batting range. Bald cracked him across the skull, metal slamming against bone. His legs buckled and then his lights went out and he crashed to the floor, landing heavily alongside Rose Tat.

The latter was spitting out bits of broken tooth and reaching for the shovel on the floor next to the fireplace. Bald circled round his floored opponent, lifted the poker above his head and brought it crashing down on the Aussie's outstretched hand. Like a guy chopping wood. Rose Tat let out a howl of agony as the rod slammed against his wrist, shattering bone.

Bald heard a scraping sound at his six o'clock. He snapped round, saw Chinstrap picking himself up. Ready for round two, seemingly. Bald struck out before the guy could stretch to his full height, belting him across the knees. Chinstrap hit the deck again. Bald followed up with a merciless flurry of blows to the legs, smashing his ankles. Chinstrap curled up into a foetal position, trembling hands covering his face in a pathetic attempt to shield himself.

Bald raised the poker again.

'Still want that fucking discount?'

Tears streamed down Chinstrap's face. He shook his head frantically, his body convulsing with pain and terror.

'No,' he whimpered. 'Don't. Christ, please.'

'Aye,' said Bald. 'That's what I fucking thought.'

He held the poker above his head for a beat, tempted to unleash another torrent of blows on the guy. Then he saw the fear in Chinstrap's eyes and turned away.

Fuck him.

Prick isn't worth it.

He looked back round at the other two. Biceps was out cold. Rose Tat was sprawled on the rug beside his mucker, blood running down his chin, pawing at his shattered jaw with his one good hand. He wouldn't be pulling any pints in Walkabout for a couple of weeks.

Bald stepped over Biceps' limp body and made for the front door, the anger quickly subsiding. He glanced back. Chinstrap held his phone to his ear, speaking in a panicked tone to someone on the other end of the line.

'Police. Get me the fucking police. We're being attacked.'

Bald swept through the doorway, crossed the gravel path and marched back towards the main guest house.

No point trying to make a run for it. There were only three

ways off the island, Bald knew. There was a ferry service from Port Ellen and Port Askaig, and regular flights to the mainland from the small local airport. Easy enough for the authorities to monitor the embarkation points. Better to simply wait for the local plod to arrive.

The police station was down at Bowmore, several miles to the south. Bald figured he had maybe ten or twelve minutes until they responded to the call.

He was in the shit, he knew. The injuries he'd inflicted on the three Aussies were severe. Nobody was going to let him off with a caution or a slap on the wrist. His business was surely fucked now. Chinstrap was probably already tweeting images of his messed-up face.

But Christ, it had felt good.

Bald wasn't at the peak of his physical powers anymore, but he still had a few moves in his locker. The backpackers had figured he was a soft target. Somebody they could push around.

They had figured wrong.

But the voice in the back of his head told him something else. He had come close to losing the fight. On another day, Biceps might have knocked him out cold. The whisky, partly. But something else too. His age.

You're too old for this, John Boy.

He headed back inside the guest house, breezed past Magda. Ignored her questions about the blood speckling his face and the torn flesh on his knuckles. Ducked back into the kitchen and poured himself another measure of whisky.

Eleven minutes later, the police came to arrest him.

THREE

They arrived in a liveried police car, lights popping and cracking in the gloom. A pair of uniformed officers debussed, which Bald figured had to constitute almost half the force on the island. There was a red-haired sergeant who looked like a retired accountant, and a short round-faced woman with sympathetic eyes called PC Hourihane. They both looked terrified of Bald. He imagined they didn't deal with a lot of violent crime on Islay. Drunk drivers, probably. And vandalism and petty theft. Brutal attacks by ex-SAS soldiers, not so much.

Hourihane took statements from Chinstrap, Rose Tat and Magda, in that order. A short time later, an ambulance arrived to take the backpackers to the hospital to treat their injuries. Biceps had woken up by that point, but he was groggy and confused and they didn't want to take any chances.

The guy who looked like a retired accountant introduced himself as Sergeant James Tierney. He was tall, gentle mannered and soft voiced. He had a wary look in his eyes as he explained to Bald that he was being arrested on suspicion of aggravated assault. Tierney told him he had a right not to say anything other than his name, address, date and place of birth and nationality. He had the right to see a lawyer, if he wanted one. Bald said he didn't. Then they slapped him in a pair of silver bracelets and took him away.

They drove him six miles to the station in Bowmore. Which turned out to be a modest-looking grey bungalow with a neatly trimmed front lawn and a wooden fence. It could have passed for a pensioner's home, except for the blue 'POLICE' sign fixed to a lamp post outside.

Tierney steered the motor down a side entrance towards a car park at the rear. The two officers debussed and frog-marched Bald towards an entrance at the back of the station building. Led him down a plainly decorated corridor towards the duty desk, where a thin-lipped constable called Draper checked his keys, watch, wallet, phone and belt on arrival, sealing them in plastic bags.

They took fingerprints and mugshots and searched him. Then Hourihane and Tierney escorted him to the cell-block facilities at the other end of the corridor. Which amounted to a pair of small custody cells, one for men and another for female detainees. Both were empty. The male suite had illegible graffiti scrawled on the walls, a porcelain toilet in one corner and a lumpy mattress mounted atop a plinth. Tierney was very proud of the cells. They had been recently refurbished, he explained. A complete facelift. A big moment in the history of Bowmore police station, evidently. There was a Bible if he wanted one, and a Koran and a prayer mat.

Tierney added that food would be brought to him in due course. He stressed, again, that if he wished to speak with a solicitor he had the right to do so at any time. He seemed genuinely puzzled when Bald refused and asked for a cup of coffee instead. Hourihane obliged. She headed off to the staffroom and came back a few minutes later with a steaming hot black coffee in a Styrofoam cup. It was surprisingly strong. Not great, but not the worst he'd ever had.

Then he sat on the mattress and waited.

They came back for him three hours later. Tierney and Hourihane took him out of the cell and ushered him into a bland, brightly lit interview room located halfway down the corridor. It looked like every other interview room Bald had ever seen. There was a grey table in the middle of the room, with two plastic chairs either side of it, and a bulky piece of recording equipment against the wall, and cameras mounted to the ceiling.

Tierney led the interview. He said that they had finished gathering statements from the various parties involved. Then he asked Bald about the assault.

So Bald told his side of the story. Or at least, a censored version of it. He painted Tierney a picture of a stressed-out B&B owner dealing with the guests from hell. He hinted that they had been aggressive towards Magda. He admitted to striking Chinstrap first but claimed that he had acted out of self-defence, feeling physically threatened. It had been three against one. He feared for his life.

Tierney frowned at his notes. Hourihane stayed quiet.

'Here's the thing, John,' Tierney said as he looked up from his notes. 'We've got witness statements from Mr Metcalfe, Mr Irvine and Mr Dragovic, all claiming that you initiated the assault. We also have a statement from your housekeeper, Ms Lewandowski, claiming that you were drinking heavily shortly before you arrived at the guest cottage.'

'I had a little whisky, that's all. I wasn't pissed.'

'Please allow me to go on, John. We've also got a report from the hospital on the injuries suffered by your guests.'

Tierney consulted another sheet of paper.

'Mr Metcalfe was admitted with a broken wrist and broken jawbone. He's also lost several teeth. Mr Irvine has a broken ankle, a fractured knee and significant bruising to the ribs and both arms. Mr Dragovic is suffering from concussion and remains under observation.' Tierney looked up. 'These are severe injuries, you agree?'

'I've seen people dish out worse.'

'But you don't deny assaulting the guests?'

'As I said, it was self-defence. They were threatening my business.'

Tierney coughed. Hourihane shifted uncomfortably. 'Our colleagues on the mainland have done some routine background checks. You're ex-army, correct?'

Bald nodded. 'I spent eighteen years down at Hereford, aye.'

'That must make you something of an expert in fighting.'

'You learn how to handle yourself in a scrap.'

'Then can you explain to me why a veteran soldier would feel intimidated by three young graduate students from good family backgrounds, with no criminal convictions or police records?'

'You've seen the size of them. They're big lads. I was defending myself.'

They asked him some more questions. Then Tierney explained in his gentle voice that, based on the witness statements and evidence gathered from the scene, Bald was being formally

44

charged. An officer would escort him at the earliest opportunity to the Sherriff's Court in Campbeltown, on the mainland. However, the last ferry from Port Askaig had already departed and he could not be transferred until the following morning.

Which meant he would be spending the night behind bars.

Draper escorted him out of the interrogation room and took him back to his cell. Ninety minutes later, Hourihane brought him food in a takeaway container, ordered from a local hotel. Chicken in a garlic and herb sauce, potatoes and vegetables. She handed him plastic cutlery, a can of Diet Coke and a slice of chocolate cake. Bald thanked her. Hourihane smiled at him and noticed the bruising on the side of his face. She promised that she'd fetch the local doctor tomorrow, once the practice opened.

Then she returned to her desk.

The night passed slowly. Bald had time to think. He had slipped a long way since leaving the Regiment. That much was obvious. Back then Bald had been an outstanding operator, one of the finest Blades ever to serve in 22 SAS. Now he was a nobody, a washed-up warrior on the downward slope of his life.

In many ways, that was what the Regiment did to you. You turned up at Hereford, passed Selection, earned the right to wear the famous beige beret, and for a brief while you were a rock star. Everyone wanted a piece of you. Then you handed in your notice, and you went back to being a nobody all over again.

Bald had spent the past ten years fighting that reality.

Now he was looking at a stretch in prison.

Face it, John Boy, the voice in his head told him. You can't wriggle your way out of this one. All the dark shit you've pulled over the years. The money you've stolen. People you've maimed and killed. And in the end, you're going down for lamping a trio of Aussie gobshites.

It's almost fucking funny.

The first shafts of daylight spilled through the window grille at seven o'clock the following morning. Two hours later, there was a grating rasp as the cell door opened and a young chubby-faced constable he didn't recognise guided him down the corridor.

Bald assumed he was being taken out to a waiting police

vehicle. A short ride to the port at Askaig on the eastern coast of the island, and then a ferry to Kennacraig on the Kintyre peninsula.

This is it, John Boy.

End of the fucking road.

His mind worked feverishly, trying to look for a way out of his predicament. Maybe he could escape when they disembarked from the ferry, Bald thought. He could make a run for it and lose the cops on the mainland. Risky, but it was better than ending up in a shite Scottish prison, watching his back in case he got shanked.

He was still running through the plan in his head when the constable stopped outside the interview room.

'Here you go, pal,' he said. 'They're waiting inside.'

Bald pulled a face. 'Who?'

The constable stared at him. 'Your friends from London. Got here a few minutes ago.'

He opened the door and gestured for Bald to step inside. Bald glanced questioningly at the officer for a moment. He wondered if somebody, perhaps an old friend, had learned of his plight and called a solicitor up to deal with his case. Unlikely, but who else could it be?

He took a breath and swept into the room.

FOUR

There were two figures seated at the table in the interrogation room, a man and a woman. They weren't wearing police uniforms. They didn't look much like solicitors, either. No paperwork on the table, no briefcases or work bags resting beside their chair legs. Which was a dead giveaway. Lawyers, in Bald's experience, never went anywhere without a briefcase.

The guy looked like he was modelling for the cover of *World's Blandest Man* magazine. He wore a two-piece navy suit with a plain white shirt and perfectly knotted grey tie. Standard corporate uniform. He was forty or thereabouts, with receding hair and a neatly shaven face. Slim, but not athletic. He looked like he should be working in the accounts department for a large insurance company. The guy was so middle-of-the-road you could have used him to paint lines on a stretch of asphalt.

The woman was younger. Bald guessed she was in her late twenties, maybe early thirties. She gave off a whole different vibe. She had rose-dusted cheeks, a button nose and big blue eyes, like something out of a Japanese cartoon. She wore a dark grey jacket, matching trousers and a sky-blue shirt. Professional but relaxed. She looked sparky and confident, thought Bald. Someone who knew what she wanted from life and what she had to do in order to get it. A hint of a smile teased out of the corner of her mouth as she looked up at him.

'Hello, John,' she said.

Bald stood rigid in the doorway.

A question ricocheted like a bullet through his skull.

Who the fuck are these people?

The smile teased a little wider out of the rose-cheeked woman's mouth. She gestured to the vacant chair.

'Take a seat,' she said. 'Please.'

Mr Bland just stared at him.

Bald eased himself into the chair, resting his cuffed hands on the table. The woman waited until the constable had left, closing the door behind him. Then she said, 'You probably have a lot of questions.'

'Aye,' Bald said. 'You could say that, lass. With fucking bells on.'

The woman shifted.

'We'll get straight to it. My name is Stevie Cope. You can call me Stevie. This is my colleague, Gus Wheeler.' She indicated Mr Bland. 'As you've probably guessed, we're with the Branch.'

Bald sat up ramrod straight. His gaze shifted from Cope to Wheeler and back again. Several things suddenly clicked into place.

The General Support Branch, known simply to those who worked in it as 'The Branch', was the secret unit within MI6 that worked closely with serving and former members of 22 SAS, carrying out deniable black ops around the world. Missions that were known only to a handful of people, often carried out in places the British government wasn't officially involved in, for reasons that frequently eluded the guys on the ground. The Regiment provided the muscle for such ops. They were the guys who kicked down doors.

Bald had carried out several ops with the Branch in the past. You worked with them at your peril, he knew. If things went south, Six would hang you out to dry without hesitation.

'I'm sorry you had to spend the night here,' Cope went on. 'But we got here as quickly as we could. I'm afraid we couldn't handle this thing over the phone. Too delicate.'

Bald frowned. 'You heard about me getting arrested?'

'Of course.'

'How?'

'Our friends at GCHQ have a system in place. They constantly screen national and local police computer systems. Any information logged relating to current or former members of the security services and special forces is automatically red-flagged and pinged over to Vauxhall. Your name was flagged yesterday afternoon, in relation to an alleged assault on private property not far from here.'

'It was self-defence.'

Cope shrugged. 'Call it what you want. As soon as Madeleine was alerted to the ... *incident*, she decided to send up a team to liaise with you. So here we are.'

Bald tilted his head. 'You know Maddy Strickland?'

'Of course.' Cope's smile widened. 'She's our boss. She's the director of the Branch these days, you know.'

'Good for her.'

'I understand you two worked together on an operation once.'

'We did. A couple of years back.'

'She's full of stories about you. Said you were a bit of a legend in the SAS.'

'That was a long time ago.'

'My dad was Para Reg. Must have served around the same time as you. He was always in awe of the SAS. He'd be thrilled if he knew I was sitting here with you now.'

There was a gleam of admiration in Stevie Cope's eyes as she spoke. He detected a certain respect for the Regiment, for the things he had done for Six. There was none of the usual MI6 arrogance. She reminded him of Madeleine Strickland, in that respect. Bald found himself warming to her, against his better instincts.

He leaned back in his chair and said, 'I'm assuming Maddy didn't send you two up for a friendly chat.'

'She's concerned. She read the sergeant's report. You're in trouble, John.'

'I'm a big boy. I can look out for myself.'

'Not this time. It's three against one. Your word, versus the three Australians you floored. If the judge rules against you, with your record, you're looking at a custodial sentence.'

'I'll take my chances.'

'Listen, you thick bastard,' Wheeler snapped. 'We're doing you a favour here, so start showing some appreciation.'

Bald looked at the guy with flat eyes. 'It talks.'

Cope shot a look at Wheeler. Then she coughed and said, 'What my colleague is trying to say is that we're here to help you. We can make this problem of yours go away.'

'Forget it. No offence, love, but I'd rather stick pins in my eyes than get help from Six. Too many strings attached.'

Cope shook her head. 'There's no strings this time.'

'Bullshit.'

'I mean it. All we're asking you to do is come down to London with us for a briefing. Hear Madeleine out.'

A frown creased Bald's face. 'What's the mission?'

'We're not authorised to discuss operational details. If you want to know more, you need to speak with Madeleine.'

'And if I refuse?'

'Then Madeleine will be very disappointed,' said Cope. 'She'll still do what she can to help you avoid a prison sentence, but obviously there are no guarantees.'

'Then tell Maddy thanks for the offer, but no.'

'Meeting with her is in your best interest, John.'

'I disagree. It's nothing personal against her, but Vauxhall has got previous for stabbing me in the back. Working with you lot should come with a health warning.'

'Things have changed. It's not like it used to be.'

'It's funny. The more you people tell me that, the more things seem to stay the same.'

'The old guard have retired. New people have moved in. The mood music is different now.'

Bald shook his head. 'You can't change the nature of the beast. Back-stabbing is practically engrained into the DNA over at that fucking place. In fact, I wouldn't be surprised if you set this whole thing up just so you two could get in a room with me. Those Aussies might be working for you, for all I know.'

That drew a derisive snort from Wheeler. 'Don't kid yourself. You're not that important.'

Cope gave him another sharp look. Bald formed the impression that Cope, although much younger than her colleague, was the more senior intelligence officer.

Bald had seen Wheeler's type before. The smug grin, the posh accent and condescending attitude. Six was full of guys like that. They tended to look down on the lads in the Regiment as thick cavemen, only good for killing people.

Cope said, 'You need to consider your situation. We're throwing you a lifeline here. A chance to get back on your feet.'

'I'm doing just fine,' said Bald.

'Really?' Wheeler looked at him with raised eyebrows. 'It doesn't look that way, chum. We've seen the accounts for your business, you know. You're on the verge of closure. Best-case scenario, you scrape through the summer season and fold over the winter. Assuming you don't go to jail.'

Bald looked from Wheeler to Cope. 'What's really going on here? Six hasn't given a flying toss about me for two years. Then you two suddenly show up and start making me offers. The last time I saw Maddy, I told her I was done with all that.'

'The situation has changed.'

'Find someone else to do your dirty work. There's plenty of ex-Regiment lads hanging about in Hereford.'

'That's not an option for us. We need someone immediately. Someone known to Six. Someone we can trust to get the job done.'

'Forget it. Not interested.'

'Madeleine is prepared to make you a very good offer for your services.'

Which got Bald's attention.

'What kind of offer?' he asked.

'Madeleine will discuss the particulars with you at the briefing. But let's just say that we're prepared to offer you a generous package.'

'What about the charges against me?'

'The victims have been informed that they have outstayed their welcome.'

'Meaning?'

Cope said, 'We've done some digging. Turns out that two of the victims have been working here for several months without the appropriate visas. They've been informed that unless they retract their statements, they could be going to jail.'

'They agreed?'

'They're professional scammers. They've pulled the same trick at several other hotels, threatening management with negative reviews unless they let them stay for free. They're looking for free meal tickets, not justice.'

'Word to the wise,' Wheeler said. 'Perhaps vet your guests more carefully in future.'

Bald pointed at Wheeler. 'Fuck me, this one's full of good ideas.'

Cope ignored the comment. 'What do you say?'

'What about my staff? I can't just leave them high and dry. I've got wages to pay. Bookings to fulfil.'

'Leave that to us,' said Wheeler. 'We'll find someone to manage the sale of the business. Make sure your people get what's owed to them.'

'This is a good deal that we're offering,' Cope put in. 'Money and a get-out-of-jail-free card. You won't find a better offer.' She paused. 'Well? Do you accept?'

Bald hesitated. On the one hand, he really didn't want to get into bed with Six. No matter how shitty his life had become, it was a lot less stressful with Vauxhall in the rear-view mirror. He was sorely tempted to tell Wheeler to piss off.

But then the voice piped up in his head.

There's nothing left for you here, it said. *Nothing except a failed business and a stack of unpaid bills. At least if you go back to working for Six, you'll be doing something you're good at.*

Bald was aware that his confidence had been dented recently. He wasn't the ruthless warrior he had once been. He had tried his hand at playing it straight, running an honest business and keeping his nose clean. All that had got him was a bank account in the red and a night in a prison cell.

You can't fight who you are, John Boy.

It was time to go back, he realised. Back to being John Bald. The hardest, meanest bastard who had ever passed Selection. The guy every other Blade lived in fear of.

'Fuck it,' he said. 'When do we leave?'

FIVE

Cope didn't give him a straight answer. She told him to sit tight, then stood up and left the room to make some calls. Several minutes later, she returned with the portly constable in tow. The constable escorted Bald back to the duty desk while another officer retrieved the sealed bags with his valuables. Then a tired-looking Sergeant Tierney appeared from his office and asked Bald to sign some paperwork. Tierney expressed surprise that the Australians had retracted their original statements, glancing at Cope and Wheeler as he spoke. Bald doubted they would have told the sergeant who they really worked for. That wasn't the way Six did things. Tierney probably knew that they were with the Ministry of Defence, but nothing more than that.

They emerged from the station to a filthy grey morning, damp, blustery and cold. Droplets of rain clung to Bald's silver hair and face as he followed Cope and Wheeler over to a blue Skoda Fabia hatchback parked at the side of the road. Cope gestured to the rear passenger door. Bald folded himself into the back seat while Wheeler rode shotgun. Cope took the wheel.

They drove east and then north out of Bowmore and made a brief stop at the B&B. Bald grabbed the go-bag he always kept stowed under the bed in his living quarters. He found Magda cleaning up the guest cottage and told her that he was leaving on an urgent family matter. Someone else would be coming in to manage the lodge in his absence, he said. Magda didn't seem too bothered by the news. She asked again about a pay rise. Bald told her to take it up with the new management. Then he hurried back to Cope and Wheeler in the Skoda.

They drove south towards Port Ellen, passing peat bogs and broken hills; a grey churning sea to the west, the horizon wreathed in shreds of mist. Not a landscape Bald was going to miss, on reflection. He figured he would move somewhere warm after this. Somewhere with cold beer on tap, white sand and scantily clad women. That was more to his taste.

They reached Port Ellen twenty minutes later and drove through the small marina, passing the handful of fishing boats and yachts moored along the wooden jetty on their way to the terminal for the ferry to the mainland.

A large crowd of distillery day-trippers, island-hoppers and locals were already boarding the vessel ahead of its departure. Cope showed their tickets to a terminal worker in a hi-vis jacket and joined the line of vehicles snaking up the boarding ramp. She parked the Skoda on the car deck, and the three of them rode the lift up to the main passenger deck.

They located a bar on the upper deck, found a spare table overlooking the stern and settled in for the journey. Cope ordered drinks. Bald went for a Diet Coke. Wheeler asked for a bottle of sparkling water and Cope had a frothy latte. Bald sipped from his glass, watching the ferry pull away, leaving a foamy trail in its wake. Cope tapped out messages on her phone.

Bald said, 'What's the plan, once we hit the mainland?'

'We'll head to the airport at Campbeltown and take a privately chartered flight down to RAF Northolt. A driver will meet us there. He'll take you straight to the meeting.'

'Where's the briefing?'

'Off-site. A secure location in central London. You'll find out more once we land.'

Bald puckered his brow. 'Why is Maddy reaching out to me? She's the head of the Branch. She can tap up the Regiment for some extra muscle whenever she wants. Why me?'

Cope looked up from her phone screen. 'Madeleine would prefer to use someone from outside the system for this mission. She feels there's less risk of leakage.'

'Bollocks,' Bald growled. 'Whatever op you're running, this thing is off the books. That's why Maddy sent for me in the first place, isn't it? I've got no links to Six or the Regiment these days. I'm not on anybody's payroll. I'm a deniable asset.'

'As I said, I'm not authorised to discuss the details of the operation.'

'At least give us a clue. I've got a right to know what I'm letting myself in for here.'

'You know I can't. This operation is strictly need-to-know. That goes for everyone inside the Branch as well.' She flashed a reassuring smile. 'Everything will be clear in a few hours, I promise.'

Bald considered arguing the point. He could pressure Cope, threaten not to get on the plane unless she spilled the beans. But she seemed genuinely in the dark about the op. He decided he was getting nowhere and changed the subject. Might as well try to butter this woman up instead. Form a bond with her. Someone as young as her, she was obviously going places. She might prove a useful ally in the future.

Might even get a shag out of it.

'You said your old man was Para Reg.'

Cope nodded. 'Twelve years. He joined Three Para a year before the war in the Falklands. He was there at Mount Longdon, fixing bayonets and charging at the enemy. My brother and I would get him to tell us the story before bed. Not the usual children's bedtime stories, I guess.'

'You were never tempted to join the army?'

'I had my heart set on it. I was going to join the Medical Corps as soon as I finished school. I wanted to be a combat medic. The next best thing to serving on the frontline.'

'What changed?' asked Bald, feigning interest.

'My dad. He sat me down one night, told me he'd spoken with my teachers. They were encouraging me to apply for uni, but I wouldn't hear any of it. Dad told me that I shouldn't be trying to follow in his footsteps. He said that would be a mistake. He said he'd regretted never getting a proper education and told me I should try and make something more of my life. He kept pestering me until I eventually caved in and agreed to give uni a try. In my mind, I was only doing it to shut him up.' She smiled. 'I ended up going to Durham on a scholarship, then joined Six straight after I graduated.'

'Good for you,' Bald said, still pretending to give a toss.

She cocked her head at him. 'What about you? Why the SAS?'

'I'm a bastard. And I'm good at killing. With them skills, I was either going to be a gangster or a Blade.'

'There must have been more to it than that.'

'Not really. Not for me, anyhow. Some of the other lads went in for all that queen and country bollocks, but not me.'

'You don't believe in serving your country?'

'Not a fucking chance. The good guys are as bent as everyone else. They're just better at hiding it.'

'That's a cynical way of looking at the world.'

'Aye, maybe. But it's true.'

'Some of us believe what we're fighting for.'

'Good for you. But I'm not one of them. Never will be.'

'Why did you agree to come down with us, then?'

'Money,' said Bald. 'That's my allegiance.'

'That's sad.'

'Is it? What about young lads being sent to their deaths in Iraq and Afghanistan, because a bunch of crooked politicians lied through their teeth? You want to talk about sad, you should start there.'

'You sound bitter.'

'I'm a realist. I've fought in my fair share of wars. I know how the world works.'

Cope gave him a considered look. 'Do you miss it? The Regiment?'

'Yes and no.'

'Meaning?'

'Soldiering is a young man's game, lass,' said Bald. 'And I'm a long fucking way from young.'

'That's not what Madeleine seems to think.'

'Her opinion might be biased.'

'Don't kid yourself. Madeleine isn't known for being senti-mental. Just because you two worked together once, doesn't count for a thing.'

'If you say so.'

Cope stared levelly at Bald. 'Trust me. I know Madeleine, better than most people. If she's asked for you, it's because she needs whatever skills you've got to get this mission done.'

'Which is what, exactly?'

Cope smiled at him. 'You'll find out soon enough.'

They docked at Kennacraig two hours later. They went through the whole boarding procedure in reverse. Took the lift back down to the car deck, climbed into the Skoda and drove down the ramp leading to the ferry terminal. Cope followed the directions on the built-in satnav and took the main road running south along the coastline towards Campbeltown. The same route Bald would have taken to the Sherriff's Court.

Next time, you won't be so lucky.

Forty minutes later, they reached Campbeltown Airport.

A Cessna light jet was waiting for them on the tarmac stand. Wheeler explained that the aircraft belonged to a private security company that worked closely with the security services on various ops. Some guys called GreyWatch International. A new firm, apparently. Bald had never heard of them. He wondered why a security business was laying on a Cessna for Bald and his minders.

There was no check-in procedure. Nobody asked to see their passports. Bald, Cope and Wheeler bypassed security and were led straight through the terminal building and across the stand to the Cessna. They settled into their seats and took off at a little past four o'clock in the afternoon. Soon they were climbing through the dense clouds, leaving Scotland behind.

There was no alcohol on the plane, so Bald helped himself to coffee from the on-board pod machine and skimmed through a copy of *The Times*. A bunch of people had glued themselves to buildings in London, protesting about the climate. Economists were predicting another recession. There was a full-page article on a campaign to release a British academic being held in Venezuela. A young woman. Caroline Fuller.

The campaign was gathering momentum, according to the report. There was a photograph of Fuller before her arrest, next to a shot of a group of protestors outside the Venezuelan embassy in London, demanding her release. The article carried a report from the woman's father, criticising the prime minister for not doing more to secure his daughter's freedom.

Bald was leafing through the sports pages, searching for news on his beloved Dundee United, when Cope moved down the aisle and sat opposite him.

'We'll be landing in twenty minutes,' she said. 'Our driver is waiting inside the terminal. He'll take you directly to the meeting. Madeleine will be waiting for you both there.'

'Both?' Bald repeated.

Cope nodded. 'This isn't a solo mission, John. You'll be working as part of a five-man team.'

Bald scratched his jaw. An off-the-books op for Six, involving a team of five guys. He started to wonder what he'd let himself in for. *Maybe I should have taken my chances in court.*

'Who else is on the team?' he asked.

'They're being activated as we speak. Three outsiders, but I don't know their names. Americans. Special Forces. Plus another ex-SAS operator.'

'Another Hereford lad?' Bald asked. 'Who?'

'I believe you know him,' said Cope. 'John Porter.'

SIX

At that moment, John Porter, lifelong alcoholic and ex-Regiment hero, was standing inside a pub in east London and trying to ignore the voice inside his head.

Three years had passed since Porter had last touched a drop of booze. There had been moments when he'd almost slipped, but each time he'd managed to catch himself before it was too late. It had been hard work – the hardest fight of his life – but Porter had won. He had gone sober. Cleaned up his act.

Fifteen years ago, he'd been sleeping rough on the streets of Vauxhall, drinking cheap voddie and scrounging for pennies, blackballed by his muckers in the SAS.

Now he had a modest house on Dinedor Hill on the outskirts of Hereford. He had a steady job, working for the security services on a part-time basis, providing the muscle for field officers on ops overseas and acting as a bodyguard to persons of interest to MI6. When he wasn't doing their bidding, Porter supplemented his income by house-sitting for celebrities and wealthy foreigners, safeguarding their multi-million-pound London properties. The job was stress-free and undemanding, providing him with a safe cover story for his work with Six. Whenever they needed him, he could be taken off the job at extremely short notice and replaced with another ex-Hereford man.

His current job involved watching the Belgravia residence of the Sultan of Brunei. There could be no easier task for a former Blade. Porter worked in twelve-hour shifts with another ex-SAS bloke, patrolling the grounds and making sure that everything was in order in case the owner showed up. It was an achingly dull routine but it paid well. And it was better than begging for scraps on the streets.

Despite everything he had suffered, Porter had made something of his life.

But he could never truly silence the voice.

It was always there, nicking away at the base of his skull. Tempting him to go back to his old ways.

Telling him to have a drink.

Some days the voice was so faint he barely noticed it. At other times, it was almost impossible to ignore.

Right now, the voice was really fucking loud.

Given his history of legendary alcohol abuse, hanging out in a bustling pub in the East End was probably not the best idea. But Porter wasn't there to get pissed. At least, not today.

He was there for his daughter.

Sandy.

Six months had passed since Porter had last seen or heard from her. At the time she had been living with him, along with her three-year-old son Charlie, Porter's grandson, at his place in Hereford.

For a while, things had been good between them. It hadn't been easy for her, but she had forgiven Porter for the years he'd been absent from her life, first in the Regiment and then on the piss. He had done his best to make it up to her, taking Sandy in after she had split up with her long-term fiancé and supporting her while she raised Charlie.

And then, suddenly, everything had gone pear-shaped.

It had started last summer, when Sandy had begun seeing a new bloke. Jared. Some guy she had met on a dating app that Porter had never heard of. Sandy had a unique talent for choosing dead-beat boyfriends, but even by her own standards Jared was a special waste of space. He claimed to be a grime producer and an influencer, but as far as Porter could tell, the guy was a heavily tattooed dope fiend who sponged off Sandy and spent most of his time on his PlayStation. For a while Porter had kept the peace, hoping that Sandy would eventually see through the guy's act. Then one night over dinner she had announced that they were moving in together.

Porter had flipped.

'Dad, I'm just asking you to give him a chance,' Sandy had said. 'He's great with Charlie. He's a good person, you'll see.'

'He's a waster, love,' Porter had said back. 'I'm telling you, he's bad news.'

'He loves me. He takes care of Charlie. Why can't you see that?'

'It's all an act. Trust me, Sandy. This bloke is playing you like a fiddle.'

'You barely know him, Dad.'

'I know the type. He's fucking arsenic.'

'Why don't you want me to be happy?'

'I'm just trying to protect you,' Porter had said. 'I don't want you getting hurt.'

'It doesn't feel that way, Dad.'

Porter had tried his best, but Sandy had made up her mind.

A month later, there had been an argument at her place. Porter had noticed a bruise on Sandy's arm. She claimed to have injured herself fixing up a shelf but Porter was convinced that Jared had struck her. He had gone over to confront the guy. The two of them had come to blows, and Porter ended up striking him on the face, busting his nose. Sandy had managed to persuade Jared to drop the charges, but she had decided to leave Hereford soon after. Porter had begged her to stay.

'I can't,' Sandy had told him. 'Please don't ask me to do that.'

Porter had shaken his head. 'Why are you doing this?'

'You know why. Jared thinks you're a bad influence on Charlie. He says some space would be a good idea.'

'He's pulling the wool over your eyes, love. He's manipulating you. Just stay here. We'll work it out.'

'I don't think that's a good idea,' Sandy had said. 'I'm sorry, Dad. But you hit the man I love, in front of my son. It's going to take a long time to forgive you for that.'

Since then, Sandy had cut off all communication with Porter. She had blocked him on social media and ignored his repeated phone messages and voicemails. Eventually, he had managed to track her down through one of her friends. A former uni roommate had told him that she had seen Sandy pulling pints at the Green Eagle, an old-school watering hole on Hackney Road. After finishing his shift for the day at the sultan's Belgravia mansion, Porter had decided to head over to the pub and check it out for himself.

He sipped his sugary orange juice and scanned the crowd for the hundredth time since he'd set foot in the bar a few minutes earlier.

The Green Eagle looked like something out of a Guy Ritchie film. The walls were covered in wood panelling, the windows were decorated with engraved glass and a thick odour of spilled beer, polished wood and cheap detergent lingered in the air. At a little past five thirty, the place was half full. On the TV above the bar, there was a brief report on Channel 4 News on the campaign to release a British academic who had been detained in Venezuela. A throng of angry protestors, waving colourful placards and shouting for the government to take action.

Behind the bar, a heavily tanned guy in a silk shirt with gold rings on his fingers – presumably the landlord – chatted with a couple of weathered-looking blokes in hi-vis jackets.

Still no sign of his daughter.

He wondered how it had come to this. He thought about the degree Sandy had earned in English Literature. How proud he'd been when she'd graduated. Some of the other lads at Hereford, their kids had trained as lawyers and doctors and civil servants. A few of them had even followed in their dads' footsteps and signed up for the army. They were going places in their lives, doing things.

And my Sandy is working shifts in a rundown London boozer.

Porter took another sip of his drink and checked his smart-phone. A quarter to six. He wondered how much longer he could hang out in the pub without giving in to his demons.

A few moments later, the kitchen doors swung open and a slender figure swept into the bar.

Sandy.

She was dressed in a pair of skinny black jeans, scuffed white Converse trainers and a loose-fitting white T-shirt with a graphic print of a cityscape on the front. She carried a couple of plates piled high with greasy-looking burgers and chips and at first she didn't appear to see Porter as she threaded her way through the crowd to a table in the opposite corner. He watched her for a few beats as she placed the heart-attack-inducing meals down in front of two older blokes. One of them leered at Sandy as she turned on her heels and made a beeline for the kitchen.

Porter sprang to his feet and moved to intercept her, picking his way through the crowd of drinkers watching the football.

'Sandy,' he said, catching up with her before she reached the bar. 'Sweetheart.'

Sandy stopped in her tracks. Then she slowly turned towards Porter.

'Dad?' She frowned. 'What are you doing here?'

'I'm worried about you, love. You haven't been returning my calls. I've not heard anything from you.'

'I've been busy, Dad.'

'Working here?'

'I've got bills to pay,' she replied defensively. A thought occurred to her. 'How did you find me?'

'I'm working across town. One of your friends told me they saw you behind the bar here.'

'You're still house-sitting for that sheikh?'

'Sultan,' Porter said. 'Yeah, still doing that. Ticking over. Keeps me busy.'

Sandy nodded.

'Where's Charlie?'

'At home. With a friend.'

'What about Jared?'

Sandy made a pained face and looked away. 'He left.'

Porter nodded gravely. You never wanted to see your kids hurt, even when you knew it was for the best. 'I'm sorry, love.'

'Are you?' Sandy swung her gaze back to Porter, her frown deepening. 'You didn't look too upset when you were putting him in hospital with a broken nose.'

'I fucked up. I'm sorry.'

'You shouldn't have come here, Dad.'

'I know. But I had to see you.'

'What do you want?'

'Come back with us,' said Porter.

Sandy looked at him in disbelief. 'To Hereford?'

'Why not? The spare room's still free. You and Charlie can stay there for as long as you like. It'll be just like the old times. I can even take some time off from work, give you a hand.'

'I can't. Not after what happened.'

'For Christ's sake, love. I know we've had our ups and downs, but it's got to be better than this.'

From behind the bar, the guy in the satin shirt called out to Sandy. 'Back to work, darling. Ain't paying you to stand around chatting to punters all fucking night.'

'One minute, Phil.' She turned back to Porter and sighed. 'Look, I have to go.'

'Come with us,' Porter insisted.

'You know I can't.'

'I'm only trying to help, love.'

'I know, Dad.' She smiled weakly. 'It's just that every time you try to fix something, you end up making things worse.'

The words speared through Porter's chest. He took a step towards Sandy, looked at her with a pleading expression. 'It'll be different this time. I promise.'

'Sorry. But I have to figure this one out on my own. I'll text you later. Promise. I really have to get back to work now.'

She turned to head back to the kitchen. Porter reached out and grabbed her by the arm. 'Sandy, please.'

Sandy tried to shrug him off. Porter tightened his grip around her bicep. *I've lost her once before,* he thought. *I'm not going to lose her again. Not after everything we've been through.*

'Don't do this,' he said.

'Let go of me!'

In the corner of his eye, Porter was conscious of the other patrons snapping their gazes towards him. He heard an angry shout from across the bar and looked across to see the mahogany-tanned landlord – Phil – storming over.

'Hey. Get your hands off her.'

Porter glared at the landlord. 'Stay out of this. She's my daughter.'

'I don't give a crap. She's my employee. We don't tolerate that kind of behaviour here. This is a respectable establishment.'

Porter drew in a deep breath and released his grip. Sandy drew back from him, rubbing her arm. The landlord nodded at her. 'Off you go, darling. One of the barrels needs changing.'

Sandy paused to glance at Porter, a look of intense sadness and disappointment in her eyes. Then she turned and ducked through a door at the back of the bar. Phil the landlord watched her go before sliding his tiny bloodshot eyes back to Porter.

'You. Get the fuck out.'

'I'm not looking to cause any trouble,' Porter said, raising his hands. 'I just need to talk to my daughter, all right?'

'You've got something to discuss with her, do it later. Not here. I got paying customers.'

Porter stood his ground. 'I'm not leaving without her.'

'You deaf, sunshine?' The landlord jerked his head at the door. 'Leave right now, or I'm calling the fucking police.'

Porter caught a sudden movement. A few metres further along the bar, the two old boys in hi-vis jackets stood up from their stools and turned to face him. Sizing him up.

'Go on,' the landlord said. 'Piss off.'

For an instant Porter was tempted to crack the landlord in the face. Knock out his gold teeth. Then the anger fizzled out and he unclenched his fists, shot the guy a final glare before he turned and headed for the door.

A cold chill blasted Porter in the face as he stepped outside. The evening was grey and damp. It had rained earlier that day, slicking the pavement and flecking the windows of the shops lining the sides of the road. At a few minutes before six o'clock, dusk was already gathering. Apricot lights glowed in the windows of the flats above the shops. Pockets of warmth in an otherwise gloomy landscape.

The voice in Porter's head was deafening.

Have a drink. That'll sort you out. God knows, you could do with one right now. What's the point of staying sober if your own daughter doesn't want anything to do with you?

Maybe Sandy was right, thought Porter. You can stay off the drink, follow all the rules, try to stay on the straight and narrow. But at the end of the day, you can't change who you are.

Face it. You're just a fuck-up. A sad old fool who can't even have a relationship with his own daughter.

Porter gritted his teeth and trudged west, heading in the direction of Shoreditch. He didn't know where he was going and didn't much care. After fifty metres he passed a homeless guy sheltered in the doorway of a shuttered joinery business. He was gaunt and dishevelled and could have been anywhere from thirty to sixty. A sleeping bag was pulled up to his chest and bits of damp cardboard and newspaper were arranged beneath him as a make-shift mattress.

Fifteen years ago that was me, thought Porter. He fished out his wallet from the inside pocket of his leather jacket, took out a ten-pound note and put it in the paper coffee cup next to the guy's sleeping bag.

'God bless you, mate,' he called after Porter.

Might as well do one good deed for the day.

Before I go and get steaming drunk.

Porter carried on walking.

A hundred metres further along, he found himself stopping in front of an off-licence. A pokey little shop with a glowing sign above the entrance and rows of dusty bottles on display in the window. His eyes rested hungrily on a bottle of Polish vodka.

The voice whispered in his ear.

Well? What are you waiting for?

Porter sketched out a plan in his head. He'd grab a bottle of the voddie, maybe a pack of ciggies, head to a nearby park. Find a bench and sit there and get pissed. Have himself a little party. He wasn't expected back on duty again until midnight anyway.

Plenty of time to drink myself into oblivion.

'Mr Porter,' a voice said behind him.

Porter about-turned. Found himself staring at a burly-looking guy in a dark suit. He was standing a metre away from Porter, arms the size of pneumatic drills resting at his sides. The guy stood at six-four, a couple of inches taller than Porter. He had a face like a breeze block, with a square jaw and a forehead so big you could draw a map on it. With his drab suit, white shirt and polished black shoes, he looked like a retired boxer who had decided to take up accountancy.

A couple of metres further down the street, Porter noticed a silver Volvo SUV parked at the side of the road. The rear doors were open, the engine running. Another tough guy in an identical suit stood beside the passenger doors. He was shorter than the guy with the slab-like forehead. Had a long, thin neck, swept-back hair and black eyes like a pair of holes on a dartboard.

'Sir.'

Porter slid his eyes back to Breeze-Block.

For an instant he wondered who this bloke was.

But then he knew the answer.

They know my name. They dress like they've got a group discount at Marks & Spencer. And they act like they're the kings of the fucking universe.

'Mother sends her compliments,' Breeze-Block said.

Porter stiffened. *Mother*, he knew, was the codename for his handler at MI6: Madeleine Strickland.

Breeze-Block gestured to the Volvo. 'Step inside the car, please, Mr Porter.'

'What's going on?' asked Porter.

'Mother will explain. You need to come with us, please.'

'Now?'

'If you don't mind, sir.'

Which wasn't true. Porter had worked for the security services long enough to know the drill. Six didn't send their muscle to ask you nicely. This was an order, dressed up in polite language.

'I'm on a job,' he said. 'I'm expected back at work.'

'Alternative arrangements have been made. Your employer has been notified.'

'I didn't get a call.'

'Things are moving fast, Mr Porter. There's been no time. You need to come with us.'

Porter hesitated.

Right now, he just wanted to get pissed. Numb the anger in his guts and try to forget about the mistakes he'd made with Sandy. Instead, he was being ordered to go into the unknown.

But he knew he couldn't refuse.

When Six came calling, there was only one answer.

'Sir,' Breeze-Block said.

Porter took a deep breath.

Then he climbed into the wagon.

SEVEN

They drove west towards Old Street. Porter sat in the back with Breeze-Block for company. The guy with the long neck and pinprick eyes rode shotgun. A third guy took the wheel. He had skin the colour of chalk and a grey suit that matched the colour of his hair. Porter didn't ask Breeze-Block or the other guys where they were going or why Strickland wanted to see him. They were probably foot soldiers. Hired muscle, usually ex-Special Forces or from the MoD police, tasked with driving staff around and bringing guys like Porter in whenever they were needed. They wouldn't know a thing about the op. Even if they did, they weren't about to share any details with him. Instead, Porter settled back for the ride.

At six o'clock in the evening, the streets were choc full of pedestrians. Waves of commuters flocked towards the Tube station, some dressed in suits and carrying backpacks, massive wireless headphones clamped over their ears. Others were jogging or motoring along the pavement on electric scooters. In the distance, steel-and-glass buildings dominated the skyline.

The area had changed beyond his imagination. Porter was old enough to remember a time when Old Street had been a warren of rubbish-strewn streets, grimy pubs and abandoned warehouses. Now the tech crowd had muscled in. The greasy spoon cafes and kebab shops had disappeared, replaced by vegan foodie haunts and sleek office blocks. What they called progress. He wasn't sure how he felt about that. All he knew was that it made him feel really old.

They hit the main roundabout and looped counter-clockwise, then shuttled north on City Road. Several minutes later they hit Euston Road and got snared in the rush-hour traffic. They slow-crawled past King's Cross and Great Portland Street and Regent's Park, edging west towards Marylebone. After another mile or so they hit Baker Street and the driver made a left past the station, taking them south into Mayfair. Porter wondered where he was being taken. Vauxhall, perhaps. Or one of the safe houses they owned in the City.

They scudded south for half a mile. By now the light had faded and the lamp posts were burning, bathing the streets in a sickly orange glow. After a few minutes they hit a small square encircled by a neatly clipped hedgerow. Five-star hotels and elegant red-brick townhouses lined the square, most of them with blue plaques fixed to the walls. Almost every car they passed was a Bentley or a Maserati or a Tesla.

The driver steered the Volvo around the square and continued west down a long street flanked by limestone buildings and embassies. After a hundred metres he pulled over and killed the engine.

Breeze-Block debussed. So did the guy with the long neck. The driver stayed behind the wheel while his long-necked friend opened the rear passenger door and cocked his head at Porter.

'This way, please.'

Porter climbed out of the wagon. He followed Breeze-Block and Long Neck towards an imposing four-storey building with an ornate portico and black iron railings to the sides. From the outside the place looked like an upside-down pint of Guinness, with a white stucco facade on the ground floor and exposed dark brickwork above it. Window boxes adorned the front of the building. Stone steps led up to a red-painted door with a brass knocker on the front and an intercom panel mounted to the side. There was no indication of who lived there, or what kind of business went on inside.

Porter shot Breeze-Block an enquiring look. 'One of ours?'

He nodded. 'The Branch runs it.'

Porter could guess at the set-up. Six had similar arrangements across the globe. First, they purchased a property through a shell company linked to one of their various legitimate business fronts. Then a team of specialists was brought in to soundproof the rooms and install signal-jamming equipment to make sure no one could listen in. The Branch used such places to safeguard assets, interrogate suspects and hold confidential briefings. They allowed the Branch to operate at arm's length from the rest of the security services.

This isn't an official op, he realised.

He followed Breeze-Block up the steps to the red door and waited while the guy jabbed a button on the intercom. There was a short pause, and then the door buzzed open and they swept into a marble-floored foyer with a chandelier hanging from a ceiling rose. A bored-looking flunky in a tight-fitting black jacket and shirt sat at a desk to one side of the room, observing a computer monitor. Another flunky with a crew cut and a mean-looking expression stood beside a walk-through metal detector just inside the foyer.

The crew-cutted flunky signalled for Porter and his minders to pass through the detector. He patted them down, then led them across the foyer to a solid-looking door at the other end of the room. The flunky paused in front of the door and looked up into a security camera mounted to the wall above. There was another brief pause before the door unlocked with a dull mechanical click. He guided Porter, Breeze-Block and Long Neck through the door and down a flight of stairs. At the bottom they hit a brightly lit corridor with grey-painted walls and hard-wearing vinyl flooring, with a series of doors on either side. Porter counted eight in total. All of them were closed.

The flunky carried on down the corridor before stopping in front of a plain metal door on the right. There was a biometric scanner fitted to the plate above the chrome door handle, Porter noticed.

The flunky pressed his thumb to the plate. Held it there for a couple of beats. A light flashed green, the door made a beeping sound. The flunky wrenched the handle and motioned for Porter to enter.

He stepped inside a sparsely furnished interrogation cell. There was a metal table in the middle of the room with a couple of chairs, a flat-screen TV fitted to the wall and not much else. The walls were painted the same industrial grey as the corridor. A pair of fluorescent lights cast weak pools on the concrete floor.

Someone had left a jug of water and a plate of biscuits on the desk.

Hospitality, MI6-style.

'Wait here,' Breeze Block said. 'Help yourself to drinks and snacks.'

Porter frowned. 'What's going on? Where's Strickland?'

Breeze-Block ignored the question. He ducked out of the room and marched back down the corridor with Long Neck. The flunky closed the cell door behind him.

Porter planted himself down on the chair, poured himself a glass of water and grazed on a stale biscuit. He checked his phone. No reception. He put his handset away, flicked on the TV and watched BBC News for a few minutes.

There was the usual shit. The US president was firing off tweets threatening his enemies at home and abroad. Another high-street brand was going into administration.

In local news, there was a story about a hit-and-run in Fitzrovia. A security feed from a nearby betting shop showed a van bolting down a side street at speed, slamming into a guy in the road and ploughing into a cyclist before speeding off into the distance. One of the victims was a disgraced former journalist, apparently. The story cut to a detective standing in front of Scotland Yard, appealing for witnesses to come forward.

Translation: *We don't have a clue who did it.*

Porter channel-hopped for a while.

Sixteen minutes later, the door clicked and beeped and opened again.

He looked up.

Two figures stood in the doorway. One of them was the flunky with the crew cut Porter had seen a few minutes earlier. A second person stood next to him. Not Strickland. But someone else he instantly recognised.

His old mucker.

Jock Bald.

The flunky closed the door again, sealing Bald and Porter inside the cell. Bald glanced casually round the room and frowned at the water and biscuits on the table.

'No booze. Fucking shame, that. I could murder a slug of whisky right now.'

Porter stared at him for a long, cold beat.

'What the fuck are you doing here, Jock?' he said at last.

'Six reached out to us.' Bald dropped into the other chair and poured himself a glass of water. 'Made us an offer.'

'I thought you were out of the game.'

'I was.' Bald took a sip of water. 'Then Mulder and Scully showed up on my doorstep, giving it the hard sell. Telling me Strickland required my services. Some sort of top-secret op she was running. So here I am.'

Porter made an enquiring face. 'What happened to making it big on Civvy Street?'

'The plan's on ice.'

'I heard a rumour in Hereford. One of the lads reckoned you got into trouble with a couple of old Blades. Ramsey and Peake.'

'We had a disagreement.'

'That's not the story I was told. I heard they set you up. Fleeced you for every penny you had.'

'Fake news.'

'So what happened, then?'

'It's in the rear-view,' said Bald. 'Ancient fucking history. I'm up north these days. Got myself a business there.'

'Doing what?'

'Bed-and-breakfast on the Isle of Islay. Nice and steady, like. Tidy income. Quiet as fuck.'

Porter grinned. 'Maybe I'll visit.'

'I wouldn't. Not with your history. The place is a drinker's paradise. You can't swing a cat without hitting a distillery. Your drunken arse should steer well clear of it.'

'I'm sober these days, Jock. Have been for three years now.'

'Could have fooled me.' Bald regarded his mucker. 'You look like a bag of shit someone's reheated in the microwave. I'm surprised Six have still got your crusty arse on retainer. They must really be scraping the barrel these days.'

'Piss off.'

'Just telling it how it is.'

Porter shook his head. 'I'm not the only one getting on. You're not exactly a spring chicken yourself.'

'Yeah, but I keep myself in good nick. Got the body of a warrior. There are personal trainers who would kill to be in this condition. You, on the other hand . . .' Bald wrinkled up his face in professional disgust. 'Frankly, I've seen corpses in better shape.'

Porter gave his mucker a dark look but kept his lips pressed shut. Bald had a vicious tongue on him, but there was a grain of truth to what he said. The many years of hard boozing – getting blackout drunk, sleeping on park benches and under railway arches, his cigarette habit – had taken a heavy toll on his body.

His hair, already thinning, was now completely grey. His face was heavily cracked. The skin on his neck was beginning to sag. Physically Porter was in better shape than the average bloke his age, but he was a long way from his peak. Sitting around the Sultan of Brunei's house all day long hadn't exactly helped.

He said, 'Any idea what this is about?'

'Your guess is as good as mine, mate. You know what them suits are like. Never tell you a thing you don't need to know.'

'They didn't say anything?'

Bald scratched his stubbly jaw and shrugged. 'Just that Maddy wanted to brief us on an op. They told us it was a five-man job.'

'Five?' Porter repeated.

Bald nodded. 'Me, you, and three foreigners. Ex-SF blokes. Americans, they said. I'm guessing either Navy SEALs or some of the lads from Delta.'

Porter creased his brow. 'Why would Six recruit a few Yanks for an op?'

'Maybe they don't want anything official.'

'You think this is off the books?'

'We're meeting off-site, away from anyone who might identify us. They've recruited three foreign blokes with no formal links to Vauxhall. And Madeleine specifically asked for us.'

'Meaning?'

'We're politically convenient. A pair of retired Blades with nothing to tie us to the establishment. Something goes wrong and we get captured, Whitehall can put their hands up and claim they had nothing to do with it.'

'I don't think Strickland is that cynical.'

'I agree,' said Bald. 'Maddy is sound. But if the Yanks are involved, there's a chance they're the ones running the show. And I trust them even less than those tossers at Six.'

Porter cocked an eyebrow. 'You're calling her Maddy, these days?'

'What's your point?'

'It's not like you to say anything nice about anyone.'

'She's a good Scottish lass. Not like the rest of those English toff bastards running the place.'

'You sure that isn't your manhood talking?'

'She's not my type. Too old,' said Bald. 'Ten years ago, I might have given it a shot. Like you once did.'

Porter nodded, fondly recalling the night he'd spent bottled up in a besieged hotel in Sierra Leone, sharing a bed with an agent from Six. 'That was a long time ago, mate.'

'Probably the last time you had a shag, too.'

Bald grabbed a biscuit and chewed noisily on it. Porter checked his phone again. Still no signal.

He wondered if he should message Sandy after the briefing. Think of some way of making it up to her. Then again, maybe not. Maybe she was right, and she just needed some time alone to figure things out. He looked up from his phone. Nodded at Bald.

'Why did you agree to come down?' he asked. 'I thought you couldn't wait to get away from Six.'

'Too fucking right.'

'So why take up their offer? You're not connected to Vauxhall anymore. You could have told them to do one.'

'Cash-flow problems,' Bald replied tersely. 'Temporary issue. I'm only down here for the sake of the business. I'll do this one job and get myself back on an even keel. Then I'm done with this mob.'

'That's what you said last time.'

'Yeah, well.' Bald grabbed another biscuit and popped it into his mouth. 'This time I fucking mean it.'

Thirty seconds later, the door unlocked and swung open again.

The crew-cutted flunky stood in the doorway, nodded stiffly at Bald and Porter.

'This way, gentlemen,' he said. 'They're ready for you now.'

EIGHT

Bald and Porter followed the flunky back down the corridor until they stopped outside a door on the left. The guy went through the same routine, placing his thumb against the scanner until the LED light on the plate turned luminous green.

'Inside,' he ordered.

They swept into a low-ceilinged briefing room, long and narrow, like a Tube carriage. The floor was some sort of dark-tiled carpet. A large conference table occupied the middle of the room, with a dozen executive leather chairs arranged around it. Half a dozen figures were seated around the far end of the table. Four men and a couple of women.

The woman at the head of the table looked to be forty or thereabouts, with short dark hair and a heart-shaped face. Her eyes were the colour of emeralds and her lips were crimson-red against her pale cheeks. She was dressed in a belted wool coat and a cream-coloured shirt. A shiny ID card dangled from a lanyard around her neck, resting on her sizeable bosom.

Bald recognised her instantly.

Madeleine Strickland. His old handler at MI6. The rising star of the service. Fast-tracked through the ranks. A straight-talking Glaswegian whose friendly demeanour masked an icy ruthless streak. Now running the General Support Branch. Bald had little doubt that she was one day destined for the very top. Deputy Director, perhaps, or even Chief.

'Gentlemen, thank you for waiting,' she said in her broad Scottish accent. Her eyes lingered on Bald for a beat and she smiled admiringly. 'It's good to see you, John.'

'Hello, Madeleine,' said Bald.

'How's life up on Islay?'

'Same as ever. Too many fucking English. You know how it is.'

Strickland smiled at that. 'It's been a wee while since I had chance to visit the islands. More of a city lass, myself.'

'You should visit next time you're up that way. Get out of Glasgow for a change. See the real Scotland.'

'I'll try to remember that.' Strickland waved at the empty chairs. 'Please.'

The flunky left the room, closing the door behind him. Bald and Porter took up the nearest chairs and made themselves comfortable. Strickland cleared her throat and said, 'Before we begin, allow me to introduce my colleagues.'

She pointed to the man immediately to her right. A plump guy in his late fifties, dressed in a crumpled shirt and jacket. His wrinkled face had more lines in it than a Shakespeare play. A pair of rimless glasses sat on the bridge of his nose. His grey hair was perched like a bird's nest atop his shiny pate.

Strickland said, 'This is Hugo Merrick. He's my number two at the Branch. An old hand at Six.'

'Looking forward to working with you both,' Merrick said in a cut-glass accent.

Bald smiled to himself. Strickland was a smart one. She had evidently appointed one of Vauxhall's old guard as her 2iC. A shrewd political move, and a good way of keeping an eye on someone who could threaten her position. Bald guessed that a guy like Hugo Merrick, at his age, would have expected to take the top job at the Branch. Instead he found himself answering directly to Strickland. If he was bitter about the outcome, he wasn't showing it.

Strickland indicated the man sitting beside Merrick. A serious-looking guy in an expensive-looking suit, with a pointed chin and prominent mole on his left cheek. He was sipping from a coffee cup with the logo of Aston Villa football club down the side.

'Simon Carter,' she said. 'From the Foreign and Commonwealth Office.'

Carter nodded a greeting. Strickland then pointed out a third man sitting at the end of the table. He looked older than the others. Early sixties or thereabouts, Bald reckoned, but the guy

77

wore his age well. He had feathery white hair, thin slanted eyebrows and a strong jawline. There wasn't an ounce of fat on the guy. His body was taut and lean and he flashed a smooth smile at Bald and Porter as they turned to him.

Strickland said, 'I assume you both know Roderick Iverson, former Director Special Forces.'

'I've heard of him,' said Bald.

'Roderick is a friend of the service. Some of your old colleagues from Hereford work for his private company, GreyWatch International.'

'Always good to meet a couple of guys from the other ranks,' Iverson said.

Bald simmered. For a former SAS man, 'other ranks' was one of the most hated terms in the military lexicon. It was used by Ruperts to describe the men below them in the pecking order: the troopers and NCOs. A way for the officers to assert their authority over the guys who went out and did the business.

'I'm ex-Hereford myself, you know,' Iverson added.

'You spent time in the Regiment?' asked Porter.

'Oh, yes. Did two years with G Squadron as Troop Commander. This was back in the early eighties.'

'Before our time,' Bald murmured. Strickland waved a hand at the two figures seated directly to her left. A man and a woman. Bald turned to look at them. The guy was morbidly obese, with a salt-and-pepper beard and narrowed eyes. He wore a velvet waist-coat under a charcoal suit the size of a circus tent.

Next to him sat a stern-looking woman in a grey trouser suit, with skin like worn leather. She had shoulder-length wavy hair and wore a necklace with pearls as big as ping-pong balls. Her smile was so thin it looked like it had been carved onto her face with a knife.

'Allow me to introduce our American cousins,' Strickland said. 'Bill and Mary. They're from Langley.'

'Pleasure,' Bill said gruffly.

Mary said nothing and looked blank.

Bald exchanged a quizzical glance with Porter before turning back to Strickland. 'Nobody said anything to us about the CIA being involved in any operation?'

'I'll explain everything in due course,' Strickland answered patiently. 'No doubt you're both full of questions. Why you're here, what you're going to do for us.'

'I'm here to listen, that's all,' Bald corrected. 'I haven't agreed to anything yet.'

'Of course.'

Strickland smiled politely, then nodded at Merrick. 'Hugo, if you wouldn't mind.'

'Yes, ma'am.'

Merrick reached over to a laptop on the table, adjusted his spectacles and tapped a couple of keys. A moment later an image popped up on one of the flat-screen TVs behind the table. Bald and Porter found themselves looking at a photograph of a smartly dressed woman. She was forty or thereabouts, with auburn hair and a long slender neck. A delicate smile teased out of the edges of her mouth as she posed in front of a bookcase filled with leather-bound books. She was quite attractive, thought Bald, in an unconventional way.

Strickland said, 'I presume you both know who this is.'

Bald nodded. 'She's been all over the news. She's the swot. The one the Venezuelans arrested. Christina something.'

'Caroline Fuller,' Strickland said. 'How much do you know about her?'

'Not much,' said Porter. 'Just what's been in the press, like.'

'Allow me to fill in the gaps.' Strickland consulted a file in front of her. 'Caroline Fuller. Born in Tring, 1977. Father was a professor who taught at UCL. Mother was a child psychologist from Cambridge. Captain of the girls' hockey team at Haileybury. Earned a first-class degree in History and Politics at Oxford and completed an MA in Political Economy at King's College, London. Spent two years in Buenos Aires while studying for her PhD. Returned to the UK in 2007 to take up a post as a university lecturer. Now works as a research fellow.'

Strickland paused and looked up from the file.

'Eleven days ago, the Venezuelan security forces arrested Fuller during a trip to Caracas. They've been holding her prisoner ever since, despite several pleas from Downing Street and a concerted media campaign calling for her release. You've probably seen the coverage in the press.'

Bald said, 'Why would the Venezuelans bother to lift some minor academic?'

'They believe she's working for us.'

'Is she?'

'Fuller isn't a spy. She's never worked at Vauxhall and has never been employed by the security services in any capacity. Frankly, we're shocked that the Venezuelans would think otherwise.'

'So why did they arrest her?' asked Porter.

'We think it's to do with her research. Fuller's particular field of interest is Latin American economics. Our understanding is that she was in Venezuela to speak with fellow academics opposed to the regime.'

'I'm sure you've heard about the situation there,' Merrick said. 'It's particularly grim. The country is an economic basket case. The shops are empty, there's rampant corruption and crime. Food and medicine are in desperately short supply. Former university professors have been reduced to boiling seawater for soup and eating rats to survive.'

'Sounds like Dundee, Jock,' Porter joked.

Bald stared at him for a moment.

Merrick said, 'We think someone high up heard who Fuller was talking to, assumed she must be a spy and ordered her arrest. It's complete nonsense, of course. She's guilty of gross naivety, but nothing more.'

'There's an additional problem,' Strickland said.

'What's that?' asked Bald.

'Fuller was working on a paper at the time. Specifically, the nexus between organised crime and the economy in Venezuela. We have reason to believe that she knows sensitive information about high-level Six operations to infiltrate the cartels.'

Bald looked at her intently. 'I didn't know you were running covert ops in Venezuela. Thought that was the Yanks' turf.'

'Ordinarily, it is,' said Bill in a Deep Southern drawl. 'But it's tricky for us to operate down there at the minute. Too much heat from the authorities. Brits tend to attract less attention.'

Strickland said, 'We've known for years that President Vasquez and his inner circle are closely involved with the cocaine trade. Our people have been cultivating agents inside the cartels, using them to build cases against the key players. Including the president's own brother.'

Porter said, 'How much does Fuller know?'

'Enough to compromise our operations. If she tells her captors what she knows, we'll be forced to pull out of the country overnight.'

'Not to mention the damage to our global prestige,' Carter added in his blunt Brummie accent. 'I don't need to remind everyone around this table that our involvement in Venezuela is a closely guarded secret, for obvious reasons. If word were to get out that our boys and girls in Six have been meddling in Latin America, the press will have a fucking field day.'

'The Regiment was in Colombia for years, training up the local commandos,' Bald reminded him. 'Everyone knows about that. No one seems too bothered.'

'Different circumstances. The Colombians were happy to have us on board. The Venezuelans don't know we're operating there. It's fucking illegal. That easy enough for you thickos to understand?'

Bald shot a vicious look at the guy. An uneasy silence hung in the air before Porter spoke up.

'What do you want us to do?'

'We need you to head to Venezuela,' Strickland said. 'You're going to find Fuller and rescue her. Then you're going to bring her home.'

NINE

Strickland sat back in her chair, drumming her long fingers on the table. Carter sipped from his Villa-branded coffee cup, tore a chunk off a croissant and popped it into his mouth. Merrick wiped his glasses on his shirt. Iverson checked his watch repeatedly, as if he had somewhere more important to be. Across the table, Bill toyed with a pen in his chubby hands. Mary continued to stare impassively at the two ex-Blades.

Porter broke the silence. 'Why can't you lot press the Venezuelans to let her go? Tell them she's just some naive researcher and it's a case of mistaken identity?'

'We've tried that already. More than once. The Venezuelans aren't interested. They're convinced she must be a British spy. My people will keep plugging away, but any diplomatic efforts might take months to bear fruit. Christ knows what might have happened to her by then.'

'Simon's right,' Strickland said. 'Fuller is being held by the Bolivarian National Intelligence Service. You might have heard of them. The president's internal security unit.'

'Nasty fuckers, I bet,' said Bald.

Strickland nodded. 'They've got form when it comes to torturing suspects, as you might imagine. Fuller is a civilian with no resistance-to-interrogation training. It's safe to assume that she won't hold out for very long. Time is a luxury we simply don't have in this case.'

'There's also the issue of the protests,' Carter added. 'Her parents are kicking up a lot of fuss, demanding that the PM does whatever it takes to secure her release. We've got people on the streets and the press is on our backs day and bloody night. Downing Street wants this resolved swiftly.'

'And I want a threesome with the Olsen twins,' said Bald. 'But we can't get everything we want in life.'

Carter stared fiercely at him. Strickland laced her hands and said, 'There's more than national pride at stake, John. If Fuller spills the beans to the Venezuelans, it'll blow our existing operations against the cartels and put the lives of our agents on the ground at risk. Getting her out now is an urgent security issue.'

Bald held up his hands. 'I get it. You want this bird out. Fine. But it's going to be easier said than done. Last time I checked, Venezuela isn't exactly Butlin's these days. I'm guessing the Venezuelans wouldn't welcome us with open arms.'

'We have ways of dealing with any issues on the ground.'

'I should fucking hope so. But there's a bigger problem than that.'

'Which is?'

'Locating the researcher. She could be anywhere.'

'Jock's right,' Porter said. 'How are we supposed to find her?'

Strickland looked towards Bill and Mary, and slightly inclined her head. As if giving them the floor.

Mary said, 'We have a source.'

'Who?'

'A senior figure in the Venezuelan Air Force. Colonel Jefferson Gallardo. He fled the country several months ago after President Vasquez accused him of being part of a failed plot to topple him. He turned himself into our embassy in Bogotá. Been working for us ever since, out of an office in Colombia.'

Bill said, 'Until he decided to stab the president in the back, Gallardo was a trusted member of Vasquez's inner circle. We're talking about a very well-connected individual, with high-level access to a lot of important people. And a respected military man. He still commands a lot of loyalty among his former subordinates.'

'Even though he tried to get rid of the president?'

'Vasquez isn't as wildly popular as he likes to think. A number of senior military figures despise him. They respect Gallardo for his bravery.'

Mary said, 'Although he isn't in the country anymore, the colonel is in close contact with his comrades. They report back to him, and he passes on information to us.'

'So?'

'One of his contacts reached out to him last week. A lieutenant, now working for the Venezuelan intelligence service. He claims to know where Fuller is being held.'

'Where?' asked Bald.

'Right now, she's at the headquarters of the Bolivarian intelligence service, in downtown Caracas. Which is obviously very well defended.'

'How the fuck are we supposed to get her out of there?'

'You aren't,' said Bill. 'Gallardo's contact says that President Vasquez has ordered Fuller to be moved to a new, more discreet, location. Specifically, his private retreat outside the capital.'

'Why would he do that?' Porter wondered.

'Our source says Vasquez wants to question her personally. He can't do that in Caracas. Vasquez hasn't dared set foot in the capital for weeks. Not since the assassination attempt. He's been holed up in his various mansions for the past month. According to our source, Vasquez is planning to put his top interrogators to work on Fuller when she arrives.'

'When is she being moved?'

'We don't know. Gallardo's contact believes the security services won't risk a prisoner transfer until the unrest in Caracas has been brought under control. Which might take a while.'

'How long?'

'A few days, at the very least. Right now, half the city is on the streets, fighting the police and protesting against the regime. Could be a week before the transfer. Could be less. Our source will let us know for sure, as soon as he hears.'

Bald rubbed his jaw. 'Can we trust him?'

Bill and Mary swapped a look. Mary took the answer. 'We've no reason to doubt the veracity of his claims.'

'He might be bullshitting. Maybe the Venezuelans have sent him your way, to feed you false int. Might be a trap.'

Mary half-smiled. 'We've considered that, of course. But everything Gallardo has told us so far has checked out. Besides, it's in his interest to tell us the truth. He'll only get his reward once the hostage has been safely returned to London. Same for the lieutenant.'

Porter shook his head. 'Even if that's the case, how are we supposed to get her out of some remote mansion? That place is bound to be crawling with guards. We'll get bumped long before we can spring her free.'

'You won't be going in alone,' Strickland said. 'You'll have support.'

She waved a hand in the direction of Bill and Mary. 'Our friends at the Company have offered to supply three former Special Forces operators to accompany you on your mission.'

'Delta Force?'

'Ex-Navy SEALs, actually,' Bill replied. 'Our finest people. They did some work for us back in the day, with the Special Operations Group. I can personally vouch for them. These boys are the best of the best.'

'I'd rather have some of the lads from the Regiment,' said Bald.

'Out of the question,' Carter responded. 'We can't use active military personnel for this operation. The PM won't allow it. Too much risk of blowback if it goes wrong.'

'What about some of the blokes on the Circuit?'

Strickland said, 'There's no time to recruit and vet them. It's the SEALs, or nobody.'

'Where are they now?' Porter wondered.

'Bogotá,' said Bill. 'On a training mission down there with the Colombian security forces. You'll rendezvous with them at a FARC training camp in the jungle, north-east of Bogotá.'

'FARC?' Bald gave the American the eyebrows treatment.

'You've heard of them, I assume. Marxist guerrillas hiding out in the jungle. Dedicated to overthrowing the government. Glorified terrorists and drug-traffickers.'

'I thought they disbanded a few years ago.'

'Most of them did. But a few dissidents remained in their jungle camps. They're still operational, fighting against various cartels and paramilitary groups.'

'But your mob fought against FARC. Why would they suddenly agree to work with us?'

'A realignment of interests,' Mary explained. 'There's a new wave of drug trafficking organisations. Much deadlier than the old cartels. More militarised, more disciplined. They could be a big problem for us. Right now, the priority for the White House is to tackle these emergent organisations. The FARC dissidents are our ally in that particular fight.'

Bald nodded. He got it. It was a case of the least-worst enemy. After the bloodbath in Mexico and the billions spent tackling the cartels, the last thing anyone wanted was Colombia returning to the bad old days. If that meant breaking bread with a bunch of FARC thugs, so be it.

'What's the plan, once we get to the camp?'

'You'll train for the assault with the ex-SEALs,' said Mary. 'One of our colleagues will brief you in detail on the plan to rescue Fuller. Once you're ready, the guerrillas will guide you across the border into Venezuela.'

'Why can't we just hop on a plane?' Porter asked.

'Won't work. Five British and American citizens would look suspicious. You'd be arrested more or less immediately.'

'We could travel separately.'

'Same problem. There's too much risk of arbitrary arrest. And that's without the difficulties of sourcing weaponry and kit locally. The smuggling routes are a better bet.'

'We'll need a cover story,' Bald pointed out. 'In case anyone gets suspicious. Starts asking questions.'

Strickland grinned. 'That's where Roddy will come in.' She nodded at Iverson. 'Perhaps you'd care to explain.'

'Delighted.' Iverson sat upright and addressed Porter and Bald as if they were soldiers under his command. 'Right, chaps. This is how it's going to work. You'll fly out as private security contractors attached to my company. GreyWatch. I'm sure you've heard of us. We're a big deal these days, plenty of people know the name.'

Something clicked inside Bald's head. 'That jet that flew us down from Campbeltown. That's yours.'

'One of ours, yes. We do a lot of work with our friends in Six.'

'Sounds lucrative.'

Iverson smiled.

Porter said, 'We'll need documents.'

'Already taken care of. My team will provide you with all the necessary paperwork and accreditation. You'll be added to the company payroll as well. All very straightforward.'

Porter said, 'What's the story?'

'You're flying out to provide security to the Mendieta oil installation, in the Llanos basin to the east of Bogotá.'

'Will that work?'

'It's a big old place. There's always a few other lads like your-selves working there.'

'Like us?'

'Retired guys from the ranks, looking to make a few quid.'

'What if the Colombians don't buy it?'

'They bloody well ought to. I've sent plenty of guys out there before on similar contracts. If they start asking questions, you should be able to bluff your way through.'

'Easy for you to say,' Bald growled. 'You're not the one flying out to a country that's gone to shit. You get to sit in your nice office, making a tidy packet while we take all the risk.'

Iverson shot Bald a cold look. Bald swivelled his gaze back to Strickland.

'What about hardware? We're gonna need weaponry, explosives, night-vision kit. You can't expect to send us in to the country half-cocked. Not if you want this woman out alive.'

'The Americans will provide you with everything you need, once you're at the training camp.'

'What about intelligence?'

'The Company will provide you with up-to-the-minute intel,' Mary chipped in. 'We have a number of assets we're willing to put at your disposal. Surveillance drones, nodal analysis, signal inter-cepts. We're offering complete support on this one. Whatever you need.'

'And that is very much appreciated,' Merrick said.

A troubling thought needled Bald. 'I don't get it. I can see why Vauxhall wants to rescue this woman, but what's in it for you lot?'

Bill leaned back and rested his hands on his enormous gut, the chair creaking under his weight. 'You guys are in a fix. We're in a position to help. Nothing more to it than that, friend.'

'Well?' Strickland glanced round the room before resting her gaze on Bald and Porter. 'Questions?'

Bald thought for a beat.

'It's a ballsy plan. But that's about all it's got going for it.'

Strickland raised an eyebrow. 'You have doubts?'

'You want us to RV with some ex-SEALs we've never met, trust a bunch of Marxist guerrillas to lead us safely across the border into Venezuela, and somehow rescue this lass from the president's private gaff. Then we've got to smuggle her out of there again, without getting contacted by the local security forces.'

'You're saying you won't do it?'

Bald shrugged. 'I've taken part in hairier ops. Part and parcel of life in the Regiment. If you think this is dodgy, you should see what the geniuses in the head shed used to come up with.'

'Then what's the issue?'

'If you want us to go out there and risk our necks, you're going to have to make it worth my while.'

'I already have. You're out of a jail cell.'

'It's going to take more than that. A lot fucking more.'

'What do you propose?'

'Eighty grand. That should do it.'

Merrick did a double take. 'Who the hell do you think we are? The Bank of England?'

Bald pointed a finger at Iverson but addressed Merrick. 'I'm sure he's getting nicely compensated. Why shouldn't I?'

'You should be grateful we got you off those charges, you arrogant prick.'

'Gratitude doesn't pay the bills. If you want my services, it'll cost you.'

'What ever happened to serving your country, for Chrissakes?'

'Tried that once. A mug's game.'

Merrick stared at him, face bristling with indignation.

'I'm afraid we can't give you anything like that sum,' Strickland interrupted. 'You'll get a daily rate paid to you as contractors working for Roddy, of course.'

'How much?'

'Five hundred a day, plus expenses.'

'You're going to have to do a lot better than that, lass.'

'That's all we're offering,' Merrick said. 'Take it or leave it.'

'Bullshit. I know you lot have got a slush fund for black ops. I'm sure you can scrape together a few pennies to pay us.'

'I'm sorry, John. We simply can't agree to that.'

'Then we've got nothing more to discuss.'

'But we can give you something else.'

Bald narrowed his eyes. 'What?'

'Revenge. And a future career.'

Bald waited for Strickland to go on.

'I understand that you ran into some trouble a while ago with a couple of fellow SAS men. Ken Ramsey and Matthew Peake.'

Porter flashed a questioning look at his mucker. Bald ignored him and fixed his gaze on Strickland. 'How do you lot know about that?'

'Word gets around.'

'They really took you to the cleaners, old chap,' Merrick added smugly. 'Terrible, when you think about it. All that money they stole from you. How much was it again?'

'Fuck off.'

Strickland said, 'No doubt you'll have heard that Ramsey and Peake are running their own outfit in Dubai these days.'

'Aye. I heard.'

'We can wreck their business.'

'How?'

'We've got rather a lot of clout in the private sector, as you might imagine. A few words in the ears of the right people, and their contracts will dry up. They'll be filing for bankruptcy before the end of the year.'

'Tempting,' said Bald. 'But that ain't gonna pay the bills.'

Strickland grinned. 'Those contracts will have to go somewhere else, John. We could send them your way. Set you up with your own private company. Help you get back on your feet.'

'I'd prefer hard cash.'

'This is our final offer. You won't get a better one. Not in your circumstances.'

Bald stroked his chin and chewed on a thought. Strickland was right. He had nothing else going on in his life. If he walked away now, he'd be going back to a dull, quiet existence managing a failing business. More than that, he'd be turning his back on the chance to make some proper cash. With Six putting in a good word for him and sending clients his way, he could make a killing in the private security sector.

Play your cards right, the voice told him, *and this could be the chance you've been waiting for all these years. The chance to earn your fortune.*

'Fuck it,' he said. 'I'm in.'

'Good.' Strickland smiled. 'One of our drivers will escort you to your accommodation for the evening, immediately after we've finished up here. You'll stay at an apartment belonging to Roddy's firm, over in Paddington.'

'When do we fly out?' asked Porter.

'Tomorrow afternoon. Hugo will take care of the arrangements. Now, unless you have any other questions ...?'

Bald and Porter looked at one another and shook their heads.

'Then it's settled.'

Strickland glanced round at the other faces in the room. 'Thank you, everyone. I think we're done for the evening. Sebastien will show you out.'

The door buzzed open. The flunky with the crew cut stood in the doorway while Iverson, Carter and the two Americans gathered up their files and briefcases and nodded their goodbyes. Then they filed out of the room, the dull patter of their footsteps softening as they marched back down the corridor. Strickland watched them depart before slanting her gaze back to Bald and Porter.

'You'll need clean passports, work visas and company credit cards. Plus some walk-around money. Everything will be issued to you tomorrow morning, before you depart.'

'I'll need fresh clothes,' Porter pointed out. 'Toiletries as well. Didn't have a chance to collect my go-bag before coming here.'

'Make a list and give it to Hugo. He'll take care of it.'

'Roger that.'

'One more thing.' Strickland levelled her gaze at Bald and Porter before she went on. 'This operation is strictly deniable. Aside from the people in this room, and a handful of others close to the PM, no one else is aware of it.'

'Same old story,' Bald muttered. 'We take all the risks, while you lot get the glory.'

Strickland eyeballed him. 'I'm telling you this so you're under no illusions. We'll provide as much support as we can – and so will our friends at the Company, within reason – but once you're on the ground in Venezuela, you're on your own.'

'It could get noisy. We might have to drop bodies.'

'As long as you don't take casualties yourself. This needs to be more one-sided than that drubbing Rangers dished out to Dundee the other week. Five–nil, wasn't it? Hendrie hat-trick.'

'Totally unfair. Red card before half-time changed everything. Ref should never have sent him off.'

'You can't tackle from behind these days. Everyone knows that.'

Christ, thought Bald. This lass even knows her football. She went up in his estimation even further.

Strickland pressed her hands together.

'Now, before you two leave, there's someone else I want you to meet . . .'

TEN

Strickland gave an order to Hugo Merrick to go and fetch their guest. He promptly stood up and left the briefing room, the door slamming shut behind him. Thirty seconds later, he stepped back into the room, followed by a second man. He was short and fat and dressed like a British dandy, with a three-piece tweed suit and yellow-and-blue striped tie. A silk handkerchief poked like a spear-tip out of his breast pocket. His tan leather brogues looked like they cost more than Porter's monthly pay packet. The guy looked to be in his early forties, with thinning red hair brushed into a neat side parting. A large paunch threatened to burst out of his buttoned-up waistcoat.

He scanned the room and noticed Bald and Porter sitting to one side of the table. His gaze hovered briefly over them before Strickland rose from her chair to greet him.

'Sorry to keep you waiting, Julian.'

The guy dismissed her apology with a brisk wave. 'Not at all, Madeleine. Happy to be of service.'

He looked and sounded like a chubby pastiche of an Edwardian gent, but there was a calculating look in his eyes and a steely edge to his voice, thought Bald. As if his whole look was an act, designed to trick people into dismissing him as a joke.

'Please,' Strickland said. 'Take a seat.'

The guy made himself comfortable while Strickland made the introductions.

'Julian, these are the two gentlemen I was telling you about. They're going to be spearheading the operation.'

'I see.' He studied the two old Blades for a few moments, regarding them the way a farmer might assess cattle at a market. 'Madeleine tells me you're ex-SAS?'

'Long time ago,' Bald said. 'And you are . . .?'

'Julian Cantwell. Founder of Cantwell Consulting Group.'

'Julian runs a political consultancy across town,' Strickland explained. 'He's been briefed on the operation to rescue Caroline. Broad brushstrokes.'

'What's his involvement?' Porter asked.

'Julian went to university with Fuller. He's kindly offered to help shed some light on how she might react, when you find her.'

'This bloke's a civvy. Should he even be here?'

'This isn't the first time I've worked with Vauxhall,' Cantwell responded haughtily. 'My firm has cooperated with Madeleine in the past, sharing information and so on. I know the drill.'

'Julian can be trusted to be discreet,' Strickland said. 'I'd vouch for him personally on that front.'

Bald spread his hands. 'What can you tell us?'

Cantwell folded his legs and thought carefully before making his reply.

'The first thing to bear in mind is that Caroline is a sensitive, thoughtful soul. We met back at Oxford. I was studying PPE at Merton. She was reading History and Politics at Jesus College. We were both members of the Union.' He smiled at a memory. 'That's how we first met one another, actually.'

'You two were an item?'

'Oh God, no. Nothing like that. It was strictly platonic. Caroline was a fiery socialist, very much inspired by her father's political upbringing. I was always more of a dyed-in-the-wool Conservative, I suppose. She would never have dated some young fogey like me, but that didn't stop us from having some thrilling debates. No-holds-barred stuff.'

'Fascinating,' Bald said drily.

Porter shot his mucker a look, then turned back to Cantwell. 'Go on.'

'Look, Caroline is incredibly bright. Far smarter than me, I have to say. She'd invariably outwit me in our discussions, peppering her arguments with arcane quotes from obscure intellectuals. But she's quite an anxious individual.'

'How do you mean?'

Cantwell ran a hand through his red hair. 'We took a holiday once. After graduation. Myself, Caroline and a few others. A trip to Eastern Europe. This was in the mid-nineties. The Berlin Wall was down, the Soviet Union had collapsed; everything was edgy, raw and exciting. Just the sort of place a few politically engaged graduates would want to explore.'

He paused to take a sip of water.

'Go on,' Porter said.

'We spent the last few days in Estonia. Beautiful part of the world, by the way. Highly recommend it.'

'Get to the point,' Bald said.

'We got drinking in a bar one night and heard from a local about some frozen waterfall in a remote part of the country. The next day, we decided to check it out, rather on a whim. Well, anyway, we'd failed to check the forecast, and on the way back we got caught in a fierce snowstorm. Truly dreadful. Our car broke down, it was bitterly cold, we had no food or water and we had no way of calling for help. This was in the days before mobile phones, of course. After a few hours the car battery had died, we were all freezing, and it looked a bit worrying. We started to wonder whether one of us should leave on foot to look for help. Eventually, several hours later, we spotted a passing truck and flagged him down. He sent for help. It was rather a dramatic little adventure, but Caroline saw it rather differently.'

'How so?'

'She had a full-blown panic attack while we were stranded. Took her a while to get over the ordeal.'

'Sounds like a soft touch,' Bald growled.

'Caroline is a wonderful person, don't get me wrong. She has many, many qualities, but you must understand that she comes from a privileged background. Well-off parents, large house in the suburbs, private education. She never really had to struggle. Never had to deal with adversity. I come from a much humbler background. Had to fight tooth and nail to get to where I am today. She didn't have to suffer like I did.'

'Class system,' Bald said. 'You get it everywhere. Even in the Regiment.'

'I'm not so sure about that,' Strickland cut in. 'That's changing, even at Vauxhall. I'm proof of that. It's not about where you went to school. It's more about your ability these days.'

'Yes, that must be it,' Cantwell replied sarcastically. 'Nothing at all to do with all that diversity rubbish being shoved down our throats.'

Porter changed the subject. 'How long do you think Fuller will hold out against the Venezuelans?'

'If I'm perfectly honest, I'd be very surprised if she hasn't caved in already.'

'What happens when we locate her? How do you think she'll react?'

Cantwell set his face into a grimace. 'Badly, I'm afraid. She'll already be at her wits' end. She'll panic. You're going to have to calm her down before you do anything else.'

Bald said, 'That's going to be a problem for us. The president will have his goons out searching for us. We can't hang around.'

'It won't take long. Just a few words of reassurance. Put her mind at ease. That should do the trick.'

There was a pause, and then Strickland rose to her feet and smiled at Cantwell. 'Thank you, Julian. That's all very helpful.'

Cantwell remained in his chair. 'Is there any truth in those rumours in the press? About Caroline working for the security services?'

'I wouldn't believe everything you read in the news. You of all people should know that, Julian.'

'They're saying she was looking into Vasquez. Digging around his inner circle. That she may have found out something big.'

'She was out there doing research, speaking to academics,' Strickland said. 'Nothing more.'

Cantwell nodded then swung his gaze back towards Bald and Porter. A look of anxiety was etched across his face.

'Do you think you'll find her?'

'We can't make any promises,' said Porter. 'But we'll do our best.'

That seemed to satisfy Cantwell. He let out a breath and tipped his head at them both.

'Just bring her back safely. Whatever it takes. Bring her home, before those bastards break her.'

*   *   *

95

The briefing ended a short time later. Strickland thanked Cantwell for his help and reminded him not to talk to anyone about the operation. Then Merrick escorted him out of the room. Bald and Porter stayed behind to run through a few more procedural details with Strickland. She told them they were booked onto a United Airlines flight departing from Heathrow the following afternoon. They would fly to Houston, then change for a connecting flight to Bogotá. A local contact would meet them at the airport and escort them across the country to the jungle camp. They would RV with the three ex-SEALs and make their final preparations before crossing into Venezuela.

She wished them the best of luck.

Then she said goodbye.

They followed Merrick out of the briefing room. Retraced their steps back down the tunnel-like corridor and up the flight of stairs leading to the ground floor. Passed back through the security door with the camera mounted above it. Marched across the foyer and through the double doors to the street outside.

A charcoal-grey Vauxhall Insignia was parked in front of the building, waiting to ferry them to their accommodation for the evening. Bald and Porter climbed into the back while Merrick took the front passenger seat and gave an address in Paddington to a driver with a widow's peak. He pulled away and accelerated west, then turned north on to Park Lane before hitting traffic.

The roads were clogged with vehicles. The city was practically at a standstill. A huge crowd of people clustered in the square outside Marble Arch Tube station, staring at their phones or throwing up their arms in frustration and shouting at the blue-jacketed Tube officials. Others sat on the lawn opposite, drinking bottled beers. More people stood in long straggling lines at the bus stops, jostling for space on the crammed double-deckers. None of the traffic lights appeared to be working. Cars honked at one another. In the distance, Bald could hear dozens of alarms going off, machine-like wails piercing the night air.

He leaned forward and said, 'What's going on?'

'Blackout,' the driver replied in a hoarse south-of-the-river accent. 'All over the news, mate.'

'When?' Porter asked.

'Forty, fifty minutes ago. They reckon half of north London was down. Bloody chaos.'

'Is the grid still down?'

'Radio is saying that power has been restored. But half the Tube's still closed, along with King's Cross and Euston. Traffic lights are fucked and all. People are stranded and have got no way of getting home. Going to take a while to get you lads across town.'

'They say what caused it?'

'Some expert on the radio reckons it might be a software bug. A glitch. Like the one that happened in Paris a few weeks ago.'

Bald sat back and nodded.

Porter said, 'That's weird.'

'What is?'

'The blackout. Happening so soon after the one in France.'

'Coincidence.'

'You don't think it's strange?'

'I can think of stranger things. Such as how a lame soldier like yourself managed to pass Selection. That's a big mystery, that. Right up there with the pyramids.'

'Fuck off,' said Porter.

'Anyway, how could two power cuts in two separate countries be linked? Doesn't make any sense.'

'Someone might have hacked into the grids. Messed about with the software.'

'Like who?'

'The Russians, maybe.'

'What for?'

'Disruption? To send us a message? Or maybe they just want to mess with us for the sake of it.'

'I don't buy it,' said Bald. 'The Russians are old school. All them years their president did in the KGB. They want to send a message, they poison some poor bastard in a hotel in London.'

'They've carried out cyber-attacks before. Here, in America, and a lot of other places too. The Russians are doing this stuff all the time, hacking into government systems and planting viruses in major networks. They can close down a foreign banking system from a back office in Moscow.'

Bald looked at Porter and made a face. 'How do you know all that stuff? You're not exactly Steve Jobs when it comes to the tech, mate.'

'I've seen it on the news. Had a whole big feature on it.'

Bald looked back out of the window at the restless crowds. 'It's a coincidence,' he repeated. 'You've been watching too many conspiracy films.'

They crawled north past Marble Arch and joined the traffic on Edgware Road, inching past the shisha bars and Lebanese restaurants. It took them twenty minutes to travel a mile. Then they hooked left onto a side street and shuttled west through Paddington. The roads grew less congested as the driver made a series of quick turns until they stopped outside a gleaming new apartment block built on the edge of a canal.

'This is us, chums,' Merrick said.

He hopped out of the Insignia. Bald and Porter unfolded themselves from the back seats and followed him towards the glass-fronted entrance. Merrick took a key card from his wallet and swiped it against a panel next to the door. He led them through a spacious lobby towards a pair of lifts at the far end. They rode up to the third floor and made their way down a beige-carpeted corridor until they stopped in front of the door to apartment 317. Merrick tapped the key card against the lock. Ushered Bald and Porter inside.

The apartment looked like it had been ripped from the pages of *Rich Bachelor Monthly*. It was stylish and cold and untouched. The floors were made of engineered wood. There was a chic kitchen built into the corner of the main living space, with a breakfast bar and a Nespresso machine and retro pendant lights. Sliding patio doors led out to a small balcony looking out towards Hyde Park. There was a flat-screen TV so big the US president probably wanted to do a trade deal with it.

'Keys are on the breakfast bar,' Merrick said. 'There's a gym in the basement. Fridge is full, and there are toiletries in the bathroom. Two sets of everything. Should cover the essentials.'

He pointed to the two large double bedrooms.

'There are chargers for your phones in your bedrooms. Gym shorts, tops and trainers are in the wardrobes, in both your sizes. Jock, your go-bag is on your bed.'

Porter said, 'What about my clobber? I need a change of clothes. Shoes. All of that.'

'We're sending a driver over to the Sultan of Brunei's place to pick up your things. He'll drop it off later tonight. The concierge will call up when he arrives. Questions?'

'Anywhere to grab a decent pint nearby?'

The agent shot a cold look at Bald. 'I'll assume that's a joke. If you need anything urgent, there's a parade of shops across the canal. But try not to leave the building unless you absolutely have to. Understood?'

'Crystal,' Bald said.

Porter said, 'What about our documents?'

'I'll bring them tomorrow. Nine o'clock sharp. There's some reading material on the coffee table. Travel guides on Colombia and Venezuela. Worth a read if you've got five minutes free.' He peered at Bald through his glasses. 'You do know what books *are*, don't you?'

'Very funny. Hilarious. Side-splitting. You're a born comic.'

Merrick glared at him. Then he turned and left the apartment, closing the door behind him.

They made themselves at home. Bald tugged open the fridge door, scanned the shelves and helped himself to an ice-cold Diet Coke. Porter poured himself a glass of tap water and looked round the living area.

'Nice place. Iverson must be doing well for himself.'

'He's a Rupert,' Bald muttered. 'You know what them lot are like. Always looking out for one another.'

'You think he's only helping out Six for the money?'

'Why else?'

'Loyalty, perhaps.'

Bald considered, then shook his head. 'Nah. Not him. Bet he can't believe his luck. He gets to take part in a secretive op for Six and trouser a truckload of cash in the process. He's laughing.'

Porter set his glass down on the breakfast bar and fished out his phone. No new messages. He looked away and gritted his teeth. He hadn't really expected a message from Sandy – not after the way they had left things earlier – but the silence still hurt.

He typed out a brief message. *Love, I'm sorry. Please call me back. I just want to talk.* Tapped send and put his phone to sleep. Took another sip of tap water, and wished it was something stronger.

'What the fuck is wrong with you?' Bald snapped.

'Nothing,' Porter murmured.

'Load of crap. You look even fucking sadder than usual. Any minute now and you'll start rooting around for the voddie.'

'I'm off the drink.'

'For now. But I know you. First sign of stress in your life and you're liable to hit the bottle.'

'Not these days. That's all behind me now.'

'We're about to head out to Venezuela,' Bald said. 'Murder capital of the fucking world. There's no room for passengers. You need to be on top of your game.'

'I am.'

Bald snorted. 'You don't bloody look like it. Got a face on you like a monkey just shat on it.'

Porter clenched his jaws and looked away.

Bald said, 'If there's something on your mind, I've got a right to know.'

'You wouldn't understand.'

'Try us.'

Porter sighed. Then he reluctantly told his mucker about the situation with Sandy. He gave him the shortened version. Told him about the argument over her boyfriend. How she'd left the house in Hereford and moved to London. His efforts to track her down. The confrontation in the Green Eagle.

When he had finished, Bald grinned at him and said, 'Could be worse.'

'How's that?'

'She could have taken after her old man. At least she's not sleeping in a cardboard box.'

'Piss off, Jock.'

'You want my advice?'

'Not really.'

'She's a grown woman. Stop treating her like a child.'

Porter felt the anger constricting his throat. 'She's throwing her life away.'

'Doesn't sound like that. Sounds like she just wants to step out of her old man's shadow.'

'You haven't got kids. You wouldn't understand.'

'No, but I know what it's like to want to get away from your old man. Me, I couldn't wait. Why I joined the army.'

'You never told me that before.'

Bald shrugged. 'Nothing much to tell. Old man was a wanker. Prick used to come home drunk from work and give me what he liked to call the Friday Night Special. Beat me senseless with his fists and then give me a belt to the arse. Did that until I was thirteen and old enough to punch him back.'

'He still around?'

'Died years ago. Lung cancer. Best fucking day of my life.'

Porter stared him for a beat. He was seeing a side of Bald he had only ever glimpsed before. He didn't know much about the guy's background, other than some vague references to a tough upbringing in Dundee. There was clearly more to him than his ability to soldier, his dirty jokes and his hatred of the officer class.

He briefly wondered what else he didn't know about Bald.

He refilled his glass and said, 'What do you reckon about the ex-SEALs? Think they're gonna be up to the job?'

'If they're as shit hot as them Yanks say they are.' Bald knocked back the rest of his Coke and belched loudly. 'But it's not the SEALs I'm worried about.'

'What's that supposed to mean?'

'You're past it, mate. Bloke like you should be sitting behind a desk somewhere, filling out a form. Not going halfway round the world on a rescue op.'

Porter gripped his glass tightly. 'That's not what Strickland thinks,' he replied through gritted teeth.

'She's got a blind spot. Thinks you still know how to soldier, just because you wore the winged dagger a long time ago. You might be fooling her, mate, but not me.'

'I'm not much older than you,' Porter argued.

'Eight years,' Bald said. 'I don't turn fifty for another eighteen months. You're only a few years from turning sixty. That makes you fucking ancient, in Regiment terms.'

'I'm not over the hill,' Porter insisted. 'I won't fuck this one up.'

'You'd better not. Because if this op goes pear-shaped, Six won't be sending in the cavalry. You heard what Madeleine said.'

Porter nodded.

Once you're on the ground, you're on your own.

Another thought occurred to him. 'You think Cantwell was right? About that researcher having panic attacks?'

'Fuck knows. But I know one thing. If it goes noisy, it won't matter if she's having a breakdown. We'll have half the Venezuelan army on our backs. It'll be a miracle if we make it out of there alive.'

Two miles away, Julian Cantwell took a fortifying sip of Lagavulin and picked up the phone.

The office was dark. Outside, the street was quiet except for the hum of the occasional passing car. Strange to think that two days ago, Nick Gregory had died just a few hundred metres away from this very building. The death of the cyclist had been unfortunate, but Cantwell had understood the argument that it made the journalist's death look more like an accident. He had played his part, staying in his office and waiting until the incident hit the news before contacting the police to make a statement. There had been a brief interview with a pair of detectives, but they had swiftly cleared him of any involvement.

Now it was time to focus on the other thing.

Cantwell had returned to the office directly after his briefing with Strickland and the two soldiers. He had hacked through some of his emails, responded to questions from a few prospective clients, but in truth he was just dithering. Delaying the inevitable. At ten o'clock he had finally summoned up the courage to make the call.

He opened up the same HideMyTracks app he'd used to contact the Americans. Tapped in the overseas mobile number he had committed to memory and hit Dial.

Then he waited.

After four rings, the other guy picked up.

'One moment,' the voice said.

There was a muffled sound of someone hack-coughing. Cantwell sat and waited. A few beats later the gruff voice came back on the line.

'How did it go?'

'Well, I think,' Cantwell said.

'You *think*?'

Cantwell inwardly cursed himself. His boss disliked vague answers.

'It's hard to be definitive,' he said. 'Strickland was playing her cards very close to her chest. Habit of a lifetime, I suppose.'

'Did she suspect anything?'

'I didn't get that impression.' He hastily added, 'They don't know a thing. As far as they were aware, I was just a concerned citizen wanting to help an old friend.'

'Who you haven't spoken to in fifteen years.'

'She doesn't know that.'

'What *do* they know?'

'About the plan? Nothing, apparently. They're completely in the dark.'

The voice was silent for a few seconds.

'What about the other thing?'

'It's still early,' Cantwell replied. 'But so far, no issues to report.'

'So we're ready?'

'As much as we can be.'

The voice went quiet again.

'It's important this works, Julian.'

'I know.'

'Because if it doesn't—'

'It will,' Cantwell cut in. 'Trust me. I've got my best people on it. They know what they're doing.'

'Good.'

Another pause.

Cantwell said, 'Are your men in place?'

'That doesn't concern you. Just focus on your side of the arrangement, and we'll take care of ours. Division of labour. Makes everybody's life much easier.'

'What now, then?'

'You wait,' the voice said. 'When it needs to happen, we'll be in touch.'

ELEVEN

Bald rose at exactly five o'clock the following morning. He dressed in the workout gear Six had left for him in the wardrobe and headed down to the basement gym in the pre-dawn light. Beasted himself with his usual routine. Twelve sets of crunches, push-ups and pull-ups. An eight-kilometre run on the treadmill, followed by twenty kilometres on the bike. He pushed himself until he was lathered in sweat. Until the demons in his head were drowned out and he was ready to go to war with the world again rather than with himself. Then he padded back upstairs, showered, shaved and changed into a fresh shirt, 5.11 tactical trousers and Gore-Tex boots.

He found Porter in the kitchen, dressed in a long-sleeved olive-green shirt and stone-coloured khakis, grazing on a slice of thickly buttered toast while he flicked through one of the guide books to Venezuela. Bald guzzled down a long black coffee, fixed himself a bowl of porridge and perched on the sofa, watching the news on the TV.

The headlines were dominated by the power outage in north London. Experts were claiming that some sort of technical fault had caused the blackout. National Grid officials were saying that it was too early to comment. Reporters were out roaming the streets of Edgware, interviewing locals. There was no mention of possible Russian interference.

Twelve minutes later, Hugo Merrick arrived.

He entered unannounced, using his own key card to unlock the door. The guy looked just as tired and shabby as he'd appeared at the briefing the previous day. His grey hair was ruffled, his shirt heavily creased. Dandruff on the lapels of his jacket.

Bald and Porter gathered round the kitchen table as Merrick

laid a leather briefcase flat on the surface and popped the latches. He pulled out two wadded envelopes from the briefcase, along with a pair of plastic document folders and a couple of brand-new smartphones.

'I'll make this quick,' Merrick said. 'There's rather a lot to go through before you catch your flight.'

Porter said, 'Where's Strickland?'

'Madeleine is busy. She's asked me to handle the operational side of things.'

'Must be hard,' Bald said. 'Being Maddy's errand boy.'

Merrick stared at him. 'I'd drop the attitude if I were you, chum. Especially since we're going to be working together closely in the future.'

'What do you mean?' asked Porter.

'Director of the Branch is a stepping stone to bigger and better things. Madeleine will be moving upstairs before long.'

'How soon?'

'Sooner than you think. A year. Could be more, could be less. Word is, she's being groomed for Deputy Director. Which means someone else will have to take over at the Branch.'

'Meaning you.'

Merrick stretched his thin lips into a grin. 'Who else? I'm the second-in-command at the Branch, I've got two decades of experience at Vauxhall. I'm the natural choice.'

Bald looked at the guy, suddenly grasping why Merrick didn't seem bitter about being subordinate to someone much younger. Merrick was simply biding his time, he realised. Playing the role of the helpful 2iC, knowing that one day he would be sitting in the hot seat.

'So ... word to the wise,' Merrick went on, 'you'd do well to stay in my good books. You don't want me as an enemy when I'm the one calling the shots. That goes for both of you.'

Bald said, 'Doesn't matter to me. One last op and I'm done with you wankers anyway.'

Merrick continued smiling at him but the look in his eyes was cold.

Porter pointed to the plastic folders and broke the silence. 'What's all this stuff?'

'Identification,' Merrick replied. 'Clean passports, driving licences, plus work visas and corporate ID, proof that you are contracted employees of GreyWatch International.'

Bald picked up one of the holders, took out the passport and leafed through the pages. It looked fairly new, but some switched-on individual at Six had made sure to crease the front of the passport and include a few backdated visa stamps. He tossed it aside and looked up as Merrick indicated the two envelopes.

'Walk-around money. You'll take two thousand dollars in US currency each. Technically illegal in Venezuela but most places will accept them, now that the bolivar is essentially worthless. You'll also carry a million Colombian pesos apiece, plus credit cards linked to GreyWatch's corporate account. A credit limit of ten thousand dollars on each. They won't be much use in Venezuela, I'm afraid – the card readers are notoriously unreliable. But they should take care of any unforeseen expenses when it comes to getting out of the country.'

Porter gestured to the smartphones. 'What's the deal with these?'

'Your Six-issued phones. Standard features, really. End-to-end encryption for both voice and text, GPS tracking and an emergency locator beacon in the event you're compromised.'

'How do we reach you?'

'There's a number stored on the phones. Under your Contacts list. Call it, and you'll be put through directly to Vauxhall. Someone will monitor the line around the clock. Use it only in case of emergencies.'

Bald said, 'What's the procedure if we need to bug out of the country early?'

'We can't offer you any support on this one,' Merrick replied impatiently. 'Madeleine has already explained all that.'

'You're just going to hang us out to dry?'

'The Americans will have your backs. They'll be watching you every step of the way. If it goes wrong, I'm sure they'll do what they can to get you to safety.'

He remembered something else and pointed to another icon.

'Boarding passes for your flights are in this folder. You're already checked in. The fourteen thirty-five from Heathrow to Bogotá.

There's a short stopover at Houston before your connecting flight departs. Should arrive at six o'clock tomorrow morning.'

Porter said, 'What happens once we land?'

'One of our local contacts will meet you at the airport. Alberto Mendoza. He's connected to the guerrillas. He'll escort you to their jungle camp.'

'What about the ex-SEALs?'

'They're already en route. You'll meet them at the camp. Once you're all in place you'll receive a detailed briefing on the rescue mission from one of our chums at Langley. You shouldn't be at the camp for more than a couple of days.'

'Why aren't we moving out straight away?'

Merrick adjusted his glasses. 'The Americans are still building up the intelligence picture. There's also a great deal for us to arrange at our end. We need to prepare a cover story for Fuller's rescue. Her family will need to be briefed. And that's without the problem of gathering information without any assets on the ground.'

'Don't the Yanks have anyone?'

'A handful of people. But it's not easy, in the current climate. They're pulling together as much information as they can, but it's taking time. They want as much clarity as possible before they give the green light.'

'Not like them,' Bald observed. 'Usually they can't wait to go in guns blazing.'

'The Company's keen to keep this mission discreet. They've got as much to lose as we have if it goes wrong.'

'How so?'

'They have a shared interest in our anti-cartel operations in Venezuela. The White House is keen to bring down the main suspects. Especially the president's brother. That would be a big win for them, politically. If Fuller gives up what she knows, the brother will inevitably go underground. The case against him will collapse.'

'Let's assume the op goes smoothly. Assume we manage to lift this researcher without getting bumped by the Venezuelans. What then?'

'Once you have the package, your orders are to head for a designated extraction point. The Americans will handle the details.'

Bald grunted. 'We're relying a lot on the Yanks here.'

'We don't have a choice. Venezuela is their backyard, geopolitically speaking.'

'I don't like it.'

'You don't have to, chum. You just have to do what you're damn well told. Now, unless there's anything else, I suggest you get packing. Your driver will pick you up in an hour.'

Bald and Porter checked out of the apartment fifty-nine minutes later. They travelled light, carrying only their passports, phones and money, with the bare essentials for their journey packed inside their black nylon go-bags. They carried a change of shirts, socks and underwear, a spare pair of Gore-Tex boots, a few basic toiletries, their guidebooks and a pair of heavy-duty portable power banks for charging up their phones on the move. They left behind their personal phones, along with their bank cards and ID. Anything that might incriminate them. Their items would be returned to them once the mission was over, Merrick had said.

They were picked up by the same Vauxhall Insignia driven by the same widow-peaked guy and ferried west towards Heathrow. Fifty minutes later, the Insignia disgorged them in front of Terminal 2. Bald and Porter hefted their backpacks out of the boot and joined the stream of passengers trotting into the main building. They located the check-in area for their flight, handed over their passports and answered a bunch of questions.

The check-in guy tapped a few keys, smiled and wished them a nice trip.

They breezed through security and hit the departures lounge. Which looked more like an out-of-town shopping mall than an airport terminal. They strolled past the designer fashion outlets and the luxury jewellers and found a spare table at the back of a garishly lit coffee shop. Ordered cappuccinos and propped their backpacks against the legs of their chairs and watched the screen for their gate number.

Bald said, 'What do you reckon their game is?'

Porter said, 'Who?'

'Bill and Mary. The CIA. What are they helping us for?'

Porter poured a sachet of fake sugar into his coffee and

considered. 'Could be just like they said. Maybe they want to do us a good turn.'

'Bollocks. When did you ever hear of the Company lifting a finger for us?'

'They helped the Regiment in Iraq. Supplied us with intel.'

'When their own backs were against the wall. They were fucking desperate to bring down al-Qaeda and needed our help to do it. But this is different. There's nothing in it for them.'

'There's something they're not telling us?'

'Either that, or we're letting the American president build a shiny new hotel on the Thames.'

Porter stirred his sugar into his coffee and went quiet for a beat. 'There's something else that doesn't make sense.'

'What?'

'Why is Vauxhall going to all this trouble to rescue Fuller in the first place? Usually they'd just go through the diplomatic channels. Now, all of a sudden, they want to send in a bunch of ex-SF blokes to break her free. What for?'

'She's got int. From her research. The cartels. Maddy explained all that.'

'Do you believe her?'

'Maddy wouldn't lie to me.'

Porter cocked an eyebrow. 'You've really taken a shine to her, haven't you? Fuck me, mate. You'll be buying her a box of Milk Tray next.'

'Fuck off.'

'I'm pulling your leg. It's just strange to hear you praising someone other than yourself.'

'She's different to the rest of those back-stabbing twats at Vauxhall. She's a tough lass. A fighter. I respect her for that. But my point is, she's got no reason to lie to us.'

'Just seems like we're going to a lot of effort for some academic.'

'We've rescued civvies before,' Bald countered. 'Pacifists, charity workers, journalists. All sorts.'

'When it's clear they're about to be executed. But we're not talking about the Taliban here, Jock. The Venezuelans aren't in the head-chopping game. They're corrupt as fuck, but they'd hand Fuller over sooner or later, for the right price.'

'Maybe they don't want to bargain with Vasquez.'

'It's got to be less risky than sending us in to rescue her. What if it goes noisy? She might get slotted in the firefight.'

Bald shrugged. 'Six must have their reasons. I couldn't care less. We've got enough problems on our plate without worrying about that.'

'You mean the Yanks?'

'I mean Venezuela. We're going into a Grade-A shithole. Place was bad enough the last time I was there.'

Porter looked at his friend curiously. 'You've been there before?'

'Aye.'

'When?'

'A few years ago.'

'What for?'

'A job,' said Bald. 'With Six. Before Strickland's time.'

'Just you?'

'And another Hereford lad. Joe Gardner.'

Porter made a face. 'I knew Joe. What ever happened to him? He seemed to disappear off the grid.'

Bald cast his mind back six years. He remembered the scene vividly. A farmhouse in the French Alps. Joe Gardner's bloated corpse hanging from a rope tied to a ceiling beam. His guts hanging out of the wide gash in his stomach, the glistening pool of blood and entrails on the floor.

'Haven't a clue,' he muttered. 'We lost touch. Guess he moved on to better things.'

Porter said, 'Do you think we'll get her out of there?'

'Depends,' Bald replied. 'If those ex-SEALs are up to scratch, and the plan is sound, then we've got a fighting chance.'

'And if it isn't?'

'Then I'll walk away. Simple.'

'You can't do that. You gave Strickland your word.'

'I'm not risking my balls for some swot who got herself into trouble, mate. If the odds look good, then fine. But if it smells like a suicide mission, you can count me out.'

'We're Blades, for fuck's sake. This is what we do.'

'Not any more, we're not. I don't know about you, but I'm not planning on getting myself captured and thrown in a Venezuelan prison. That's not how the Jock Bald story ends.'

'What about Strickland's offer? The company?'

'She can keep it. I'll find some other way to make my millions.'

'You can't pull out. Not now. The ball's rolling. Jesus, you'd shaft the op.'

'Not my problem,' Bald said. 'Mark my words. If this thing looks dodgy, I'm gone. No ifs or fucking buts.'

They passed the rest of the time in semi-silence, checking their phones and the information boards. At exactly 13.40 hours, their gate was announced. A short while later, Bald and Porter boarded the Airbus A330, stashed their backpacks in the crammed overhead storage compartment and settled into their seats. Economy class. *Typical*, thought Bald as he settled into his seat. *MI6 officers get to fly first class, while blokes like us have to slum it at the back.*

They sat through a long safety presentation on the seat-back displays in front of them and listened to a bunch of announcements from the cabin crew. The crew finished their checks and buckled up, and then the plane began taxiing across the tarmac stand towards the runway. Bald stared out of the window at the gloomy west London sky and wondered what the fuck he was letting himself in for.

TWELVE

They landed at Houston Intercontinental Airport eleven hours later. A little before seven thirty in the evening, local time. Bald had spent most of the flight reading the travel guides Merrick had given them and keeping a close eye on Porter. He'd half-expected the guy to sneak off at the earliest opportunity and find the drinks trolley, maybe sink a few miniature bottles of whisky while Bald wasn't looking. But Porter had stayed in his seat, arms folded, watching the live map on the seat-back display as the plane edged across the Atlantic. Bald was quietly impressed. Either Porter was putting on a world-class performance, or he really had cleaned up his act.

They grabbed their backpacks from the overhead compartment and got off the plane, following the stampede of passengers. It took them forty minutes to clear through customs and another thirty to check in for their connecting flight and make their way to the departures lounge. By which time they still had a whole three hours to burn. They found a fifties-style diner and sat in a booth with bright-red upholstery and a Formica table and a laminated menu with about twenty different types of pancakes. A bright-eyed waitress sauntered over, cheerfully introduced herself as Kimber and took their orders. Porter chose a Reuben sandwich and a root beer. Bald went for a bacon double cheeseburger with sweet potato fries, plus a bottomless coffee. He followed it up with a generous slice of key lime pie. Polished it off and asked for another slice. He didn't know what the score was with the cooking facilities in the jungle, but he guessed the guys in the FARC unit wouldn't be serving up gourmet dinners.

He was working his way through his third cup of coffee when he saw the news.

A couple of large TVs were mounted above the long counter at the side of the diner. One of the screens was showing a basketball game. The second TV was tuned in to CNN. A report on some sort of corruption scandal in Canada. There was a brief cut back to the newsreaders, and then the camera switched to a packed press conference in London.

Two figures sat behind a long table, a man and a woman. Both looked to be in their early sixties. The man had an olive-skinned complexion and wild white hair. The woman was small and frail with hollowed cheeks and dark bags under her eyes. A caption at the bottom of the screen introduced them as *Parents of Caroline Fuller*. The father spoke into a bank of microphones on the table in front of him as his wife sat silently at his side, wringing her hands.

'It is our belief that the British government has utterly failed Caroline,' the father said. His voice trembled audibly as he went on.

'Two weeks have passed since our daughter was arrested, and the prime minister has done nothing to secure her release, preferring to shift the blame to others instead of dealing with her case in the proper way. He has refused to meet with us, or even to consider President Vasquez's demands. In that time, we have heard reports that Caroline's condition has badly deteriorated. While our beautiful daughter suffers at the hands of her captors, Peter Ashworth dithers. We call on him tonight to end Caroline's plight.'

The father paused and looked up from his prepared statement, hands shaking as he directly addressed the camera. At his side, tears welled in his wife's bloodshot eyes.

'Mr Ashworth, we've had enough of your empty promises. If you have an ounce of decency, do the right thing and secure Caroline's release. For the sake of our daughter, end this nightmare.'

The report cut to the shadow foreign secretary, a tall, lean man with round glasses, standing on the steps of the UN headquarters in New York. Addressed a horde of journalists in a grave tone of voice.

'I'm afraid that Peter Ashworth has singularly failed in his duty to Miss Fuller,' he said. 'Instead of making a concerted effort to secure her freedom, he has refused to enter into negotiations with President Vasquez. By failing to do so, he has effectively abandoned a British citizen – an esteemed academic, no less – to her fate. Now we learn that Miss Fuller's health is reportedly failing. Mr Ashworth is actively prolonging the suffering of this poor young woman.'

'Do you think the prime minister should resign?' a journalist off-screen asked.

'That's for Peter Ashworth to decide,' the politician replied smoothly. 'But I will say this. His attitude towards Miss Fuller has been scandalous. I think it's perfectly reasonable to question whether such behaviour is in keeping with the office of prime minister.'

The report cut again, this time with a recap of the deteriorating security situation inside Venezuela. There were shots of vast crowds in Caracas, waving colourful flags and banners. Masked protestors hurled bricks and Molotov cocktails at government buildings. Cars were ablaze. Smoke rose from burning storefronts. Riot police fired tear-gas canisters at people fleeing through the streets.

A country descending into hell.

'Looks like them lot in Westminster are feeling the pressure,' Bald said.

'Same old story,' Porter grumbled. 'Some tossers in Whitehall need us to save their arses. And they need us to do it on a shoestring budget, while they take all the credit.'

'If that's how you feel, why did you agree to the op? You can't be doing it for the money. Not as if you've got loads of expenses, either. Meals for one and a shite haircut once a month.'

'You don't know my life.'

'Maybe not, but I know a washed-up soldier when I see one. You're ready for the scrapheap, mate. You should be seeing out your twilight years bodyguarding celebs and house-sitting for wealthy Russians. Why this?'

'This is all I'm good at,' he said. 'It's all I've got left.'

'Not all,' Bald corrected. 'You've got a daughter.'

'Who won't speak to us.'

'She's going through some shit. It'll pass.'

'I'm not so sure,' Porter replied quietly.

'You're her father. You might be a lame old tosser as far as I'm concerned, but she'll forgive you. Daughters always do.'

'I've fucked up too many times, mate. Should've been there for her, when she needed me.'

'Forget it. Looking backwards is for losers. You did some shit in the past, tough. Get over it. Regret gets you nowhere.'

'Says the bloke without a pot to piss in.'

Bald shot him an icy glare. 'That's temporary. Once we come back from this op, I'll get my own security company off the ground. Give it a year and I'll be minted.'

'We've got to get through this op first,' Porter reminded him. 'Won't be easy, breaking Fuller out of the president's gaff.'

'Let's hope the Yanks have got a good plan up their sleeve, then.'

They finished their last morsels of food, helped themselves to more coffee and root beer and watched the TV. An hour later, Bald and Porter paid their bill, left a healthy tip for Kimber and headed for their gate. At ten minutes past midnight, they boarded their flight.

Five hours later they were touching down in Bogotá.

THIRTEEN

The Boeing landed with a jolt and a shudder. They crawled along the runway for a couple of minutes, steered on to a wide tarmac apron and lurched to a halt beside a scattering of commercial aircraft parked up in front of the terminal building. Engine reduced to a faint whine. Seat-belt sign turned off with a diplomatic ping; the passengers rose up en masse as they scrambled for coats and laptops and carry-on luggage.

Bald and Porter grabbed their backpacks and disembarked at the front of the Boeing. They made their way through customs. Got a stamp in their passports and an indifferent welcome from the security guard, who cursorily examined their work visas. They bypassed the luggage carousels and headed straight for the arrivals hall. A sea of faces crowded the hall, hugging friends and loved ones as they spilled out of the exits. Chauffeurs stood clutching signs with their clients' names scrawled on the front. Sniffer dog teams and guards in olive-green uniforms and caps patrolled the floor, searching for anything suspicious.

Bald moved to the side of the hall with Porter, dug out his Six-issued phone and unlocked it. He had two new messages, both delivered within a few minutes of each other, shortly after their plane had landed. The first was a generic text from the phone company, detailing a bunch of international data usage and messaging rates. The second text was from the UK number stored on their phones, linked to Vauxhall.

Contact is sending his two sons to meet you. Hector and Luis Mendoza. They have your descriptions. Wait outside the Barrios Coffee Shop. They'll find you there.

Bald showed the message to Porter, hit Delete and stashed the handset away. He scanned the hall, spotted the coffee shop and pointed it out to Porter. A generic-looking establishment, with wood flooring and soft lighting, next to a duty-free perfume store. They started across the hall, threading their way through the dense crowd and stopped beside the coffee shop entrance. Then they set their bags down and waited.

Thirty seconds later, two youthful-looking figures approached.

The younger kid was eighteen or nineteen, Bald guessed. He was scrawny and short, with a bumfluff moustache and a Mohawk haircut. A Barcelona football shirt hung from his skinny frame.

The taller kid was the older of the two. He looked to be in his early twenties. Had the rugged look of someone who had spent most of their life outdoors, working the land. His skin was the colour of teak. His eyes were dark and narrow, as if he had been squinting at the sun. He wore a baggy green polo shirt, tattered jeans and a pair of mud-spattered trainers, along with a bright-red baseball cap.

The older kid looked at him and said, 'Mr Bald?'

'Call me Jock,' said Bald. He waved at his colleague. 'This is John Porter.'

The guy thrust out an arm. 'Hector Mendoza.'

They shook hands. Hector grinned and gestured to the kid in the Barcelona shirt at his side. 'My little brother, Luis. Welcome to Colombia.'

He spoke good English, but with a strong accent, mangling words as he fired them off in a rapid stream. Bald could just about understand what the kid was saying.

'There a problem, mister?' Hector asked.

'I thought we were supposed to be meeting your old man,' Porter said. 'Alberto.'

Hector made a pained face. 'His English, not so good. Me and Luis, we speak better. He sends us instead.'

'Where is he now?'

'At the farm. To the east.'

'How far?'

'Many hours' drive. We'll take you there now, mister.'

Bald said, 'You're supposed to take us to the training camp. That was the deal. We're expected.'

'Tomorrow. Today, is not possible. Too far away. We sleep at the farm tonight.'

'Is it secure?'

'The farm?' Hector grinned, revealing a row of rotted black teeth. '*Si*, mister. Very safe. Trust me. Now, you come with us, okay?'

Before Bald could answer, Porter gripped him by the arm. 'We're not gonna rely on these two to get us to the camp, are we? Fuck me, they're barely old enough to shave.'

Hector's grin widened. 'Don't underestimate us. Where we come from, you learn how to shoot before you can walk.'

'Doesn't matter,' Porter growled. 'We're travelling across bandit country, with no way of defending ourselves. We need better protection than this, for Chrissakes.'

Hector gave a casual shrug and folded his arms. 'Up to you. Makes no difference to us. But if you want to join your friends, you need to come with us.'

'We could rent a car,' Porter suggested to Bald. 'Make our own way there. Get the coordinates from the Yanks.'

Which drew an amused look from Hector. 'The roads are very dangerous. Full of bandits. Narcos. Gangs. You try to go alone, you'll get captured. Or worse. Me and Luis, we know all the back routes. Been living there our whole lives. We can keep you safe.'

'I don't like it,' Porter muttered.

'Me neither,' said Bald. 'But the kid's right. We don't have a choice.'

He sighed bitterly and nodded at Hector. 'Fuck it. Let's go, kid.'

Hector promptly turned and started towards the exit, his younger brother hurrying alongside him. Bald and Porter snatched up their backpacks and followed the kids outside.

Dawn in Bogotá. A fine grey drizzle was slanting across the city, a brisk chill in the air. Bald remembered reading somewhere about the city being one of the coldest places in the country. Something to do with being 2,600 metres above sea level. But still much warmer than Dundee in the depths of a Scottish winter.

The Mendoza brothers led Bald and Porter past the taxi rank and

119

across the road towards an open-air tarmacked parking lot the approximate size of a rugby pitch, enclosed by a two-metre-high chain-link fence. They swept into the lot and beat a path down a long line of parked motors before they stopped in front of a sandy-brown five-door Jeep Cherokee. An American classic. From the angular frame, Bald guessed that it was about twenty years old. The sides were streaked with dirt and the bodywork was marked with several scrapes and dents, and at some point the radio antenna had snapped off. But otherwise it looked in decent nick.

Hector tugged open the front passenger door and indicated the rear. 'You guys ride in the back.'

Bald and Porter circled round to the rear of the Cherokee and dumped their backpacks in the boot. They clambered into the rear passenger seats while Hector sat up front. Luis hopped in on the driver's side and sat behind the wheel. Bald watched the kid buckle up and made eye contact with Hector in the rear-view mirror.

'Is he old enough to drive this thing?'

Hector laughed. 'My brother looks young, no?'

'Too fucking young.'

'Don't worry, Mister Jock. Luis, he's a good driver. Best in our village. He'll get us there safely.'

'He'd better,' Bald replied sharply. 'Otherwise I'll give him a fucking slap.'

Luis grinned at him inanely. At his side, Hector gathered up a pile of brochures and maps scattered across the dash and passed them back to Bald and Porter.

'Here. In case we get stopped.'

Bald snatched one of the brochures and took a cursory look through it. A tourist guide, written in English. There were soft-focused shots of people riding on horseback and lush savannahs and exotic animals.

'Your cover story,' Hector went on. 'If the police stop and ask questions, you tell them we're tour guides. You pay us to take you here. *Llanos Orientales*. Eastern Plains.'

Porter said, 'Will the cops buy it?'

Hector nodded enthusiastically. 'Many people go to the Plains now. Big sightseeing tours. They pay lots of money to see the birds, ride horses, take selfies.'

'Place has changed. I thought that whole fucking area was a drug-trafficking corridor.'

'Still is, in many places. Lots of narcos.'

'Are they likely to stop us?'

Hector chuckled. 'Killing tourists is bad for business. Don't worry about the narcos. They won't bother us.'

'How long?' asked Bald. 'Until we get to the farm?'

Hector fished out a pack of Lucky Strikes from his jeans pocket, plucked out a cigarette and wedged it between his lips. 'Luis can get us there in eleven hours. No problem.'

Bald caught sight of the time on the dashboard clock: 06.43 hours. Which meant they would arrive at the farmhouse at a little before six o'clock that evening.

A long drive.

'Better get a fucking move on, then,' he said.

Hector grabbed a lighter from the coffee cup holder, sparked up his cigarette and said something to his younger brother in machine-gun Colombian Spanish. Luis grinned manically at Bald and gave him the big thumbs-up. Then he twisted round in his seat and cranked the ignition and the Cherokee sputtered into life.

A minute later, they were steering out of the airport car park.

Luis pushed the Cherokee hard. The wagon bounced and juddered over the potholed road as they motored south, following the steady stream of gold-coloured taxis and minibuses shuttling towards the downtown area. After a couple of miles Luis turned off the road and merged with the traffic on a busy main thoroughfare, taking them through the western part of the city. A blue-collar neighbourhood, by the looks of it. The road was lined with eyesore apartment blocks and discount fashion shops and garages. Not a slum. But not an area that attracted much tourism, either. They carried along the thoroughfare for another four miles, then took the next slip road and drove north on something called the Autopista. Which Bald vaguely recalled was the Spanish word for *motorway*. A three-lane stretch of worn blacktop, flanked by Japanese car dealerships and American fast-food chains and brand-new high-rises.

A few miles later, the high-rises and the out-of-town malls abruptly disappeared, and suddenly they were driving through rolling green countryside. Hector lit another tab, blew smoke out of the window and tuned the radio to a station playing Colombian rap music. He glanced back at Bald and Porter.

'First time in Colombia?'

'We've been here before,' Bald answered for both of them.

'When?'

'Long time ago. Twenty-six years.'

'What were you doing here?'

'Business trip,' Bald lied.

He didn't want to tell the kids the real reason they had been in the country. They had been serving with the Regiment at the time, training up a specialist unit tasked with taking on Pablo Escobar and the drug cartels. The unit's secondary task had been to hunt down the FARC units operating deep in the jungle. He remembered what Merrick had told them back in London. About Hector's father, Alberto. *He's connected to the guerrillas.* Bald didn't want to provoke the kid by admitting he'd once helped train soldiers to kill them.

'Colombia is very different now,' Hector said. 'Lots of tourists. Lots of Americans, Chinese, English. And Venezuelans.'

'Venezuelans?' Porter repeated.

Hector sucked the dregs of his cigarette, flicked the butt out of the window and nodded. 'They come across the border every day. Thousands of them.'

'Must be shite over there.'

'Like you wouldn't believe. They come here to find food, medicine, work. Some beg on the streets. Some join the gangs. A few join the guerrillas.'

Bald said, 'What's the deal with you two and your old man? You're with the old FARC mob as well?'

'Our father used to fight. Then the army bombed their camp. Many dead and wounded. My father was badly injured. Now he works on the farm.'

'And you two?'

'We help our father around the place. Do what we can to support the guerrillas. Food, information, supplies. Whatever our friends need, you know.'

122

'How do you know our people at MI6?'

'We don't. One of the old commanders, he works in Bogotá these days. In politics. Has a contact at the American Embassy. Whenever they need something done, they speak with the commander. He tells our father, we send the message to the camp. Sometimes, we take people to meetings with the guerrillas too. Like your friends. The Americans.'

'What did they tell you about us?'

Hector made an expressive shrug. 'Just that you're friends of the Americans. They told us to take you into the jungle, to meet our brothers and sisters. Then they're going to take you across the border to Venezuela.' Hector glanced back. 'Is that true?'

'More or less.'

'That place is fucked up. The police, they're shooting people in the streets. Had to call in the army. Nobody's seen the president in weeks. They think he's hiding.' Hector shook his head. 'You ask me, anyone crossing the border is crazy.'

'I'm beginning to agree,' muttered Bald.

They rolled on through the Colombian countryside. They passed undulating green fields and low hills studded with trees, and single-storey farmhouses with corrugated tin roofs and battered old pick-up trucks dumped on dirt-track driveways. They passed fields of grazing cattle and timber-built ranches and a handful of dilapidated rest stops. Bald and Porter scanned the landscape, searching for signs of a threat.

Traffic was light. They passed delivery trucks and long-haul lorries and the occasional motorcyclist buzzing along at the side of the road, and not much else. Luis kept the Cherokee ticking along at seventy miles per hour, fingers drumming on the steering wheel to the beat of the rap music spilling out of the radio. His older brother stared out of the window at the dense grey clouds and smoked.

They stopped twice. Once at a petrol station with a small roadside diner next door, serving up tamales and fried plantains. Then for a second time a couple of hours later, in a small town roughly two hundred miles from Bogotá. A speck-on-a-map type of place with a few businesses hugging the side of the road. A motorbike repair shop, an Internet cafe that doubled up as a bar and a restaurant with a bunch of beer-bellied guys in straw hats sitting outside at plastic tables, smoking cigarettes and chatting over bottled beers. None of them paid much attention to the two foreigners travelling with the Mendoza brothers.

Half an hour later, they hit a military checkpoint.

There was a sandbagged guard hut to one side of the road and a bunch of soldiers standing around, gripping their automatic weapons. A uniformed guard marched over to the Cherokee, tapped on Luis's window and barked at him in the local lingo. Bald and Porter handed their passports over to the guard. He took a long hard look at them and there was a brief exchange with Hector, with lots of exaggerated hand gestures and gesturing to the maps of the eastern plains area.

The guard turned on his heels and marched over to the other soldiers, still clutching the passports.

'What the fuck is he doing?' said Bald.

'He says he has to make a call,' Hector said.

Bald felt his muscles tighten. 'Shit. If he suspects something, we're in fucking trouble,' he muttered.'

'It'll be fine.'

Bald watched the guard closely as he made a call on his satellite phone. He sensed that the mission was hanging in the balance. *If this goes wrong, we'll be wearing handcuffs in a couple of minutes. The operation will be over before we've even reached the camp.*

Sixty seconds passed. The guard seemed to be having a deep conversation with the person on the other end. Then he killed the call and marched back over to the Cherokee. Bald's stomach clenched tighter. *Is he going to arrest us?*

The guard handed over the documents, stepped back from the vehicle, waved them through. Bald eased out a sigh of relief as they drove away from the checkpoint.

They rolled on for another ten or twelve miles. As the last streaks of daylight tinged the horizon they crossed a rusting truss bridge and Luis took the next left turn, arrowing the Cherokee down a rutted dirt track flanked by dense tangles of forest. Like driving down a tunnel. After two hundred metres the track curved gently to the right before it widened to a driveway at the front of a modest-looking farmhouse.

Luis skidded to a halt on the driveway and killed the engine.

'We're here,' said Hector.

Bald and Porter debussed from the back of the wagon and stretched their legs as they glanced round.

The farmhouse looked rustic and run down. It had been built in the middle of a clearing, with a terracotta-tiled roof and exterior walls painted the colour of orange peel. A low brick wall surrounded the property, with cultivated parcels of land to the north and south. There was another field at the rear of the farmhouse with a pair of old bangers and a few outlying buildings. A narrow dirt track led from the back of the farmhouse towards a thick wall of jungle two hundred metres away. The area around the farmhouse looked neglected. Bald saw rusted farming equipment, old car tyres. A couple of scrawny-looking dogs chained to a painter barked at the foreigners. In a paddock to the north, half a dozen mules were grazing on the long grass. Bald had the impression of a family scraping by, living from hand to mouth, just about making ends meet.

'Welcome to our home,' said Hector.

'Nice place,' Bald replied. 'Very chic.'

The screen door rasped open, grating on its rusted hinges. An old guy in a loose-fitting shirt, waterproof trousers and farming boots emerged from the gloomy interior and limped across the patio to greet his sons. They hugged him in turn, and then Hector introduced him to Bald and Porter.

'This is our father, Alberto.'

Bald pumped the farmer's hand. He could have been forty-five or ninety or anywhere in-between. It was impossible to tell. The guy had one good eye and about three teeth. His face was all shrivelled up, as if it had been left out in the sun for too long. His hand was heavily calloused, and his hair was the texture of coarse wool. He flashed a gap-toothed grin at Bald and said something to Hector.

'He says, you must be very tired after such a long journey,' Hector translated. 'He says he's made up the beds in the spare room for you. There's food, too, if you're hungry.'

'Starving,' Bald said. 'I'll have a beer and all, if there's one going.'

Alberto Mendoza made a pained face. He said something else to Hector. Who then said, 'We have no beer. But my father says he has some rum in the kitchen.'

'Good enough.'

'And for you?' Hector asked Porter.

'Coke will do. Or juice. Or water. Just as long as there's no booze in it.'

Hector looked confused. 'I thought all Englishmen drank?'

'This one's a lightweight southerner,' Bald cut in. 'Give him a couple of beers and he's a wreck.'

Porter scowled at him. Then he swung back round to face Hector and said, 'How far is it to the training camp?'

'From here? Seven hours or so.'

'Bloody great,' Bald muttered. 'Another seven hours in a fucking wagon.'

Hector said something to Luis and chuckled heartily. Luis gave Bald another big thumbs-up and grinned at him, as if he had just said something really dumb.

'What's so funny?' he demanded.

'You cannot get to the camp by road,' Hector explained, composing himself. 'Impossible. Too dangerous.'

'How are we supposed to get there, then?'

'We won't be driving. We have another way.'

FOURTEEN

They ate dinner with the Mendoza clan – plates of bland rice and corn and boiled chicken, washed down with a sugary soft drink Bald had never heard of – and an hour later they crashed on a couple of lumpy mattresses in a cluttered spare bedroom with exposed brickwork and a small window and ceiling fan that didn't work. They woke at five o'clock the next morning with the dawn chorus. The birds in the treetops began their usual shrieking racket an hour before first light, squawking and chirruping and signalling the start of the new day. After their morning ablutions, Bald and Porter grabbed their backpacks and shook hands with the shrivelled-faced old man. Then they headed out through the screen door.

The first streaks of daylight fringed the horizon as they emerged from the farmhouse. They found Hector and Luis at the side of the paddock, fastening baggage to four mules tethered to a timber hitching post. Supplies for the FARC fighters, Bald guessed. Food, medical equipment and fresh clothing, plus drinking water and snacks for the trip. One of the mules, he noticed, had a pair of forty-five-gallon drums hooked to its sides. The lids on both drums were sealed shut.

'Can't believe we're having to ride these things through the jungle,' Porter grumbled.

'Only way to the camp, mister.'

'Screw it,' Bald said. 'Beats walking.'

'You two know how to ride, yes?' asked Hector.

'A little,' Porter said.

Bald said, 'We'll manage. What's the plan?'

'We'll meet two of the guerrillas in the jungle,' Hector explained. 'They'll be waiting for us at a meeting point. They'll lead us the rest of the way to the camp. Make sure we're not followed.'

'Not taking any chances?'

'They're wanted men, mister. They're taking a big risk helping you.'

'What do they want, a fucking hug? I'm sure they're getting nicely compensated.'

'We need to get moving,' Porter said. 'We're expected at the camp.'

Bald nodded, checked his watch. Six o'clock. If we leave now, he thought, we'll arrive at the camp at around one in the afternoon. They needed to get there as soon as possible, so they could be in position when the hostage was moved.

Every second we spend here means less time at the camp. Less time to prepare for the mission. 'Let's go,' he said.

The two Brits hefted up their backpacks and attached them to the pack-saddles on their respective mounts. Porter rode a whinnying beast called Escobar. Bald was given a stubborn mule called Scarface. Hector told them he had named them himself, in honour of his heroes. The kids helped them climb into their saddles, checked that their packs were secure and untied the ropes from the hitching post. Porter clumsily gripped his reins in his left hand, his right hand clamping the saddle horn to steady himself as his animal lurched from side to side.

Luis and Hector mounted their own mules with the practised ease of kids who had been riding since before they could read or write. They set off down a narrow track leading towards the jungle to the rear of the farmhouse, two hundred metres away.

It was sweltering hot beneath the canopy, humid and gloomy. Within minutes, Bald was sweating heavily. Drops ran down his face and trickled down his back, starching his shirt. The ground was sodden and a vile stench of rotting vegetation and dead leaves assaulted his nostrils as they pushed deeper into the jungle. The terrain was closer to bush than dense forests. There were rolling hills and valleys and small trees, criss-crossed with bushes and animal tracks. Movement was difficult, and slow.

But the route was safe, Hector assured them. There were few roads in this part of the forest, making it impossible for the army to patrol. The guerrillas had complete control of the area, he said.

'Who are they fighting?' asked Porter. 'I thought the war with the government was over.'

'Most of them laid down their arms. But some chose to stay in the jungle. Carry on the struggle against the state.'

'Why?'

'They don't trust the government. Too many broken promises. They prefer to stay in the camps and fight.'

'Bet the locals are thrilled about that,' said Bald.

'They don't have a choice. In these parts, you're either with them, and support them, or you're against them. Anyone who betrays them, bad things happen. Many bad things.'

'Sound like a friendly bunch, your mates.'

'They keep the peace. Kill criminals. Protect the farms. Without them, we would be at the mercy of the cartels and the gangs.'

As the sun climbed higher into the sky they made steady progress, following the route that Hector took. The mules were occasionally difficult but surefooted and handled the terrain effortlessly. By eight o'clock the counter in Bald's head told him that they had covered around five miles. A speed of around two-and-a-half miles per hour. Hector had said that the guerrilla camp was a six-hour ride. Which meant that the camp was roughly fifteen miles into the jungle.

After another fifty minutes or so they stopped beside a small stream for a water break and drank from the canteens the Mendoza brothers had loaded onto the saddle packs.

'How much further?'

Hector rinsed out his mouth with water and squinted at the track ahead. 'Six miles. No more. We'll get to the meeting point by noon.'

Luis nudged him and winked. 'Good job it's not much further, no? Your friend, he don't look so good.'

Which was putting it mildly, thought Bald as he glanced over his shoulder. Porter was resting on a fallen log, his body leeched in sweat, grimacing and breathing heavily between greedy gulps of water from his canteen. Bald marched over to him, wearing a contemptuous look on his face.

'Fuck me, mate. Talk about letting the side down. We're only halfway there and you're already hanging out of your arse.'

'I'm fine,' Porter snapped.

'Bollocks. When was the last time you did any proper training?'

'I've been on the job,' Porter hit back. 'That's kept me in shape.'

Bald almost choked on his water. 'Call that physically demanding? Sitting around some rich tosser's house, having brews and going for a stroll in the grounds?'

'There's more to it than that,' Porter growled.

'Bullshit.' Bald took another hit from his canteen, screwed the cap back on. 'You'd better sharpen up once we get to the training camp. Can't have your ragged arse slowing us down when we cross the border.'

'I can handle it.'

'Once upon a time, yeah. But not now. All them years of going on the piss are catching up with you.'

'It's just the heat, for fuck's sake,' Porter snapped. 'Besides, I'm not the only one with a drinking problem.'

Bald stepped towards his mucker, his expression hardening like cement. 'What are you saying?'

'Come on, mate. You've put away a lot of beers over the years too. You're almost as bad as me, when it comes to the drink. Your body's not exactly a Rolls-Royce anymore, either.'

'Maybe not,' Bald said. 'But I've still got what it takes to do this op. Unlike some.'

Porter was about to reply when Hector called over to them, tapping his watch and signalling that it was time to move on again. Porter clamped his jaws shut, biting back on his rage as he stowed his canteen and climbed back onto his mule. A few minutes later they set off again through the forest.

Two hours later they came to a shallow stream junction. Hector tugged his reins and called for his mule to stop beside the edge of the water, next to a pile of stones.

The others dismounted and waited, and three minutes later Bald heard movement coming from beyond a bamboo thicket on the opposite side of the stream. The squelching of mud, the faint rustling of branches.

As Bald looked on, two figures decked out in camouflage kit emerged from behind the thicket, crossed the river and approached, their M16s slung over their shoulders. A man and a woman. The guy was tall and skinny, with bandoliers of ammo draped diagonally across his front. Long shaggy hair and a red sweatband.

The woman was a few years younger than the guy. Early twenties. She looked tough and capable, with a strong muscular physique and a stern expression. But she was undeniably beautiful, too, with high cheekbones and alluring green eyes. She wore a multi-coloured charm bracelet and a heart-shaped locket hung around her neck. Bald found himself imagining her in a pleasingly tight-fitting dress.

The sentries and the Mendoza brothers exchanged a warm greeting, and then Hector thrust an arm in the direction of Bald and Porter, introducing them to his friends. They eyed up the ex-SAS men suspiciously.

'Guys, this is Carlos Zapata,' Hector said, pointing to the skinny bloke with the sweatband. 'And this is Daniela Reyes. They're from the local unit. Reyes's father was a teacher. She speaks some English.'

'Fuck me,' Bald said, 'they didn't tell us that FARC was recruiting Playboy models these days.'

Reyes stared at him. 'Did anyone follow you?'

'Not a chance.'

'You're sure?'

'We're ex-military, love. If someone was tailing us, we'd know about it.'

'How far is your camp from here?' asked Porter.

'Not far.' She pointed to a ridgeline a few hundred metres away from the stream junction. 'On the other side of that hill. You will come with us now, okay?'

Reyes and Zapata turned on their heels, crossed the stream again and set off up the side of the densely forested hill. Bald, Porter and the Mendoza brothers followed them on foot, leading their mules up the gentle slope. Bald gave Reyes a long lingering look and glanced over at Porter, a crafty look in his eyes.

'Tell you what. I wouldn't mind having a crack at that.'

Porter stared at him with barely concealed disgust. 'Do you ever think about anything other than shagging?'

'Come on. You're saying you wouldn't?'

'We've got a fucking mission to do.'

'Doesn't mean we can't have a bit of fun along the way.'

'You're a dirty bastard, Jock.'

'I like a nice pair of tits and a cracking arse. Nothing wrong with that. At least I know how to appreciate a good woman.'

'It's not about that.'

'Yeah, it is. You're just jealous, mate. Been so long since you've got laid, I'm surprised your manhood hasn't fallen off.'

Porter clenched his jaws and looked ahead as they carried on up the hill. A short while later they hit the ridgeline and followed a track snaking down the far side of the hill, leading towards the valley below. The ground was thickly layered with foliage and Porter could see no further than fifteen or twenty metres in front of him as they plodded along the valley floor, picking their way through the dense undergrowth. After two hundred metres they hit a patch of bamboo and navigated around it, and suddenly the landscape opened up in front of them and they found themselves at the edge of a vast camp. Like a theatre curtain being pulled back to reveal a grand stage.

'This is the place?' asked Bald.

Hector grinned. 'See, mister. Told you we'd get you here safely.'

Bald ran his eyes over the guerrillas' camp as they drew closer. To the left there was a training ground where a dozen new recruits were being put through their paces while a stout guy in an olive-green hat shouted at them. There was an accommodation area to the right, with a scattering of hammocks and shacks with tarpaulin roofs. Groups of guerrillas were chopping wood and cleaning weapons. Others washed their clothes in a stream running alongside the camp. There had to be at least forty guerrillas, Bald guessed. Some of them appeared to be veterans, grizzled old sweats who had been through the wars, but there were plenty of younger faces as well. And several women, he noticed. At the far end of the clearing he noticed a larger timber-framed structure with the Colombian flag draped outside, next to a banner with Che Guevara's mug on it.

Reyes and Zapata led Bald and the others through the entrance and down the main track until they stopped beside the training ground. Zapata told them to wait while Reyes hastened over to fetch the stout guy in the hat shouting at the recruits. She said something to him. He swung round and marched over to greet the new arrivals.

He nodded curtly at the Mendoza brothers, turned his attention to Bald and Porter. Up close, Bald saw that he had a dark pencil moustache and scars on his cheek, as if someone had been chalking off days on his face with the tip of a knife. Like the other guerrillas, he wore rubber boots and a jungle camouflage uniform, with an armband on his left sleeve bearing the FARC coat of arms: a pair of rifles crossed in an 'X' shape, over a map of Colombia, with the colours of the national flag in the background.

He said, 'You're the Englishmen?'

'He is.' Bald nodded at Porter. 'I'm from Scotland.'

His face broke out into the world's biggest grin. Half of his teeth were gold. The other half were missing. 'Land of Braveheart! Whisky! Kenny Dalglish! My favourite country. One day, I visit.'

'Good fucking idea.'

The guerrilla offered his hand. He spoke surprisingly good English, with little trace of an accent. 'Andres Uribe. Company Commander.'

Bald shook his hand. 'Jock.' He pointed to Porter. 'This is John.'

'The one who cannot ride a mule properly. My men found this very funny.'

Porter knitted his brow. 'You were watching us?'

'But of course. My men have all the approaches covered.' He indicated a high point twenty metres due west of the camp.

Bald narrowed his eyes and searched the clump of bush and trees. At first he could see nothing. Then his eyes adjusted, and he spied a cammed-up sentry manning a heavy machine gun in a position between the trees.

'There are others, too,' Uribe went on. 'We cover the approaches day and night, changing watch every two hours. Some have machine guns, others have RPGs. In case of attack.'

The soldier in Bald was impressed. The guerrillas clearly weren't slackers when it came to organising a defensive perimeter.

'We might be peasants, but we know how to fight. And how to survive.'

Porter scanned the camp, frowning. 'Where are the Americans? We're supposed to RV with them here.'

Uribe waved in the direction of the large timber building with the Colombian flag and Che portrait. 'In the meeting house. I'll take you there. One minute.'

Uribe barked an order at Zapata and Reyes. They hurried over to the Mendoza brothers, set down their rifles and helped the kids unload the drums fastened to one of the mules. Reyes prised open the lids on both drums with the tip of his bayonet. Then Zapata reached inside the first drum and hauled out several clear plastic bags filled with lumps of what looked like white chocolate.

Porter snapped his gaze back to Uribe. 'Is that stuff what I think it is?'

Uribe flashed his gold-toothed smile and winked. 'You've seen coca paste before, eh?'

'Once or twice in my life. The fuck are you lot doing with it?'

'We need money to continue the struggle. This is how we make it.'

'By trafficking coke?'

Uribe shrugged indifferently.

'What about the poor fuckers shoving this junk up their noses. Crackheads stealing to get their next fix. Their families. What about them?'

'That's rich,' said Bald. 'Coming from a broken-down alkie like yourself.'

Uribe smiled. 'You expect these poor farmers to care about some junkies in New York? In London? Around here, this is the only way they can survive.'

Bald understood. The dissidents were glorified drug smugglers now. They had spent decades trying to overthrow the government, had lost the war and now the handful of them left in the jungle were making a profit from buying up the coca paste. They would have cocaine processing labs somewhere else in the jungle, he figured. From there it would be sold on to the traffickers and smuggled overseas.

Big money. Hard to turn it down.

Uribe ignored Porter's piercing gaze, strode over to the sentries and stooped down, picking up one of the white lumps to inspect it. Bald watched the commander and rubbed his stubbled jaw.

'He's got a point. You can't make a living in these parts growing plantain.'

Porter shook his head angrily. 'We're working with criminals.'

'We've worked with worse. Compared to some of the psychopaths we did business with in the Regiment, this mob are practically saints.'

Porter said something else, but Bald wasn't listening. He was too busy counting the number of coca bags the sentries had emptied from the drums. 'There's got to be twenty kilos of base in those bags. That'll be worth millions on the streets.'

Porter rounded on him. 'Don't even think about it.'

'Think about what?'

'Lifting their coke stash.'

'I'm not thinking shit. Just making an observation.'

'Bollocks. I know what you're like. You can't resist lining your pockets if you've got half a chance.'

'Fuck off, mate. Don't tell me you're not thinking the same thing.'

'We can't,' Porter hissed. 'Jesus, we need these people to get us across the border. We can't piss them off.'

'Who says they'll notice if a few lumps go missing?'

Something snapped in Porter. He stepped closer to Bald, anger pulsing in his veins. 'If you lift their supply, they'll find out about it. You'll wreck the op.'

'There's only one prick who's in danger of doing that,' Bald said. 'And it's not me.'

Porter shot him a fierce look and felt an urge to punch him in the face. He remembered why he had always tried to keep a certain distance from Bald in the past. The world had made Jock hard-edged and ruthless. His rough upbringing had helped turn him into a brilliant soldier, one of the most skilled operators Porter had ever fought alongside. But he was also merciless and cynical and shamelessly corrupt. In Bald's world, everyone was either a target to kill or a victim to plunder. And he had a way of getting inside Porter's head. Of teasing his demons, tempting them out from the dark recesses of his mind.

The anger passed. He heard Uribe calling out to them. Looked round and saw the commander straightening up, watching with satisfaction as Reyes and Zapata carried the bags of coca paste over to one of the shacks. Hector and Luis were following close behind, while another pair of guerrillas tethered Bald and Porter's mules to a wooden post.

'Come,' Uribe said as he started down the track. 'This way. The Americans are waiting to meet you.'

FIFTEEN

Uribe led them towards the meeting house at the opposite end of the camp, passing the tented shelters and the stream on their right and the training ground at their nine o'clock. A network of old slit trenches ran through the camp, Bald noticed. Presumably built in case the guerrillas came under attack. The trenches looked badly maintained and were filled with several inches of water.

'My comrades will set you up with ponchos and hammocks,' Uribe explained. 'For your shelters. You'll share meals with us, but otherwise my people have been told to keep their distance. No questions. Nobody is to bother you. My orders.'

'Works for us,' said Porter.

Bald glanced round. 'How safe is this place?'

Uribe smiled wryly. 'You're worried about an ambush?'

'We've got an op to plan for. If there's a chance of it going tits-up because your security is slack, we need to know.'

'The camp is safe,' the Colombian said proudly. 'This place is very hard to spot from the air. Lots of tall canopy, lots of camouflage nets.' He gave Bald a reassuring pat on the shoulder. 'Don't worry. You'll be fine here.'

They trudged past an animal pen and what looked like a storeroom loaded with bags of rice, pasta and fresh vegetables. Nearby, a cluster of women in guerrilla kit tended to a vegetable patch. Hens roamed freely around the camp, pecking at the dirt. Laundry hung from lengths of paracord tied between the trees. The camp was ordered, but untidy, Bald thought. And stifling hot. Like wearing a tracksuit in a sauna.

He looked ahead as they neared the meeting house. Which technically wasn't a house at all. There was a rectangular dirt-floored space beneath a tarpaulin roof, with a timber frame on three sides and an open-sided entrance instead of a door. There was a TV fixed to the back wall, next to a noticeboard with the regimental timetable listed on it. A trestle table occupied the middle of the room, with several timber benches arranged around it.

Three guys sat around the table. They were facing away from Bald and Porter, hunched over maps while a fourth man in a white linen shirt, a pair of Bermuda shorts and a bush hat stood at the end of the table, addressing the others in a low voice. He was sweating profusely, mopping his brow with a patterned hand-kerchief. As Bald, Porter and Uribe approached, the guy abruptly stopped talking and looked towards the former Blades. So did the others.

Uribe jabbered at him in quick-fire Spanish. The latter replied in the same tongue. Which made him the CIA contact, Bald decided. An ex-SEAL might possess a smattering of local dialect for operational purposes but he wouldn't know enough to converse fluently with a guerrilla commander.

'Thanks, Andres,' the guy added in English, pausing to dab his brow again. 'We'll take it from here.'

Uribe nodded and left. To inspect his lucrative coke stash, presumably. The American watched him go and then turned to Bald and Porter. 'You guys got here fast. We weren't expecting you until later this afternoon.'

'We're ex-Regiment,' Bald said. 'We don't piss about.'

'Evidently.' The guy smiled thinly. His face was glossed with sweat, Bald noticed. 'Name's Blake Taylor. I'm from the Company.'

Bald and Porter introduced themselves and looked the man up and down. He was a typical CIA officer. White male, mid-forties with an utterly forgettable face and an accent from Nowheresville, Middle America. He was carrying a little too much timber around the midriff, probably from the years spent toiling away at his desk, analysing data and intelligence reports. His skin was so white he looked as if somebody had kept him in the cellar for the past decade.

'I'd welcome you to the camp,' Taylor said, wiping the back of his neck. 'But it's not exactly the Hilton out here. Damn hot. Ticks and spiders all over the place.'

'Won't bother us,' Bald said. 'We've spent a long time in the jungle over the years. We're used to all them creepy crawlies.'

'Rather you than me, friend. Far as I'm concerned, the sooner I'm out of here, the better. Anywhere with some fucking air con.'

Porter said, 'When did you get here?'

'Yesterday afternoon.' Taylor waved an arm at the three other guys around the table. 'Now you're here, allow me to introduce the rest of the team. This is Curtis Westwood, team leader.'

Bald trained his eyes on the guy Taylor had indicated. He was six-one and broad-shouldered, with a deep tan and a blond moustache shaped like a horseshoe. The sleeves of both arms were covered in intricate tattoos and his fingers were inked with ancient Greek symbols. He wore a black T-shirt with a Harley-Davidson print on the front and a beige baseball cap. His eyes were hidden behind a pair of Ray-Bans and he was chewing on a mouthful of tobacco. He paused to spit juice out of the corner of his mouth.

He took a step towards them. Thrust out an arm.

'Everybody calls me Hulk,' he said.

Bald shook his hand. Hulk had a grip that could snap a giraffe's neck and a grin as wide as the Rio Grande.

'Blake tells us you boys fought in Iraq, back in the day,' he went on. 'That true?'

Hulk had a gruff Midwest accent, Bald noted. Minnesota, maybe, or Montana. Somewhere with a lot of farms, where people rode horses and lived off the land and went out hunting.

'We did a few rotations. Me and Porter have kicked down a few doors in our time.'

'Always a pleasure to meet a couple of brother warriors. Bet you've got some tales to tell.'

'One or two.'

'Ain't you a little old, chief?' a ginger-bearded guy on the left of Hulk said in a Boston Irish accent. 'I didn't realise the Brits were sending us a couple of grandpas.'

Bald and Porter simultaneously arced their gazes towards the guy who had spoken. He was the youngest of the four around the table. And also the biggest. He looked like a Ken doll on steroids. His legs were the size of granite blocks. He was enormous, but without any real definition. The kind of guy, Bald guessed, who could bench-press twice his own body weight but couldn't climb a set of stairs without getting out of breath. His beard was as thick as a clenched fist. He had tattoos etched on both arms. There was an image of an IRA gunman wearing a balaclava on his left forearm, and an Irish tricolour on the other with the words 'EASTER RISING 1916' below it.

'We're not as young as we used to be,' Porter admitted. 'But we've got experience. We know how to get the job done.'

'Guess we'll see about that.'

'That's Bobby McGee,' Taylor said. 'Comms specialist and mechanic. Anything on two wheels or four, Bobby can fix.'

'Nice tats,' Bald said. 'You must be a big fan of terrorism.'

'The fuck you say?'

'Just pointing out. Your IRA tattoos. Them lot were terrorists. Thought you Yanks were against all that these days.'

'Go fuck yourself, chief.'

'Ignore his ass,' the third guy said. 'Bobby's an ignorant Mick. Can't help being an asshole.'

'Fuck you, Brendan.'

Bald turned his attention to the third guy. He was the least muscular of the four seated around the table. Which still made him bigger than the average bloke on the street. He was tall and wiry, with short clipped hair and a goatee styled like an upside-down wizard's hat. He wore a red baseball cap with a Dixie flag emblazoned across the front.

'Brendan Dudley,' Taylor said. 'Team medic and sniper specialist.'

Porter's eyebrows inched upwards. 'Good shot, are you?'

Dudley smiled, revealing a set of terrible teeth. Half of them were missing. The rest were blackened or yellowed nubs.

'Good ain't the start of it. You want someone or something dropped from a mile away, I'm your guy.'

He spoke with a strong country twang. He sounded like the lead singer in a honky tonk band, thought Bald. There was a wild look in his eyes. The kind of guy who was capable of anything, under the right circumstances.

'Dudley's something of a legend. Finished first place in the

2009 Spec Ops Sniper Competition. Which officially makes him the deadliest guy in the military.'

'From ten years ago,' Bald pointed out. 'Not today.'

Dudley stared at him, a shrewd gleam in his eyes. 'Guess we'll find out. Maybe I'll show you a trick or two. Show you how we do things down in Georgia.'

'I doubt it, mate. But you can show me how good you are at shooting in a straight line.'

'I'd tread real careful, friend. You don't want me as an enemy.'

'I'm yanking your chain, you daft prick.'

Porter glanced at Hulk. 'You're all ex-SEALs?'

'We were in the Unit,' the latter said.

'You mean Seal Team Six?' asked Bald.

Hulk nodded. 'Bobby's a little younger, but Brendan and myself fought alongside each other for the best part of ten years. Guess you could say we're blood brothers. Been through a lot together.'

'Hell, yeah.' Dudley grinned. 'Taught those Arab sumbitches a few lessons they won't never forget.'

Bald's eyes drifted towards the maps on the trestle table. He craned his neck to get a closer look. There was a detailed map of Venezuela, and a series of black-and-white photographs of the president. 'What's going on here?' he asked.

'Background report,' said Taylor. 'I'm bringing the others up to speed.'

The CIA man glanced furtively at Hulk.

'That's right.' Hulk tipped his hat at his comrades. 'See, Brendan and Bobby are late additions to the group. Had to take the place of two other guys at short notice. Wasn't no time to brief them before heading out.'

'What happened to the other blokes?'

'They had to shoot off to Europe. A business thing.'

Porter said, 'What's the plan?'

Taylor glanced at his watch. 'Get yourselves settled in while I finish briefing these fellas. I suggest you put up your shelters and grab something to eat, tend to any personal stuff. Report back here in an hour for a detailed briefing. I'll explain everything then.'

'Roger that.'

The three ex-SEALs returned to their laptops. Taylor wandered off down the camp, his smartphone pressed to his ear as he spoke to someone on the other end in a low tone. Bald and Porter wheeled away and headed back towards the accommodation area.

As they trudged down the mud-slicked track, Porter glanced back over his shoulder at the meeting house. 'What was all that stuff about their mates being tied up in Europe?'

'I'm past caring,' Bald said. 'We're here now. That's all that I give a shit about. One last mission, then I'm done with Six.'

'It's never that easy,' Porter muttered.

'This time it is. Once this is over, I'll have a nice big office, running a security company, counting my millions. Some other mug can do the grunt work for a change.' He grinned. 'Who knows? Maybe I'll give you a job, mate.'

'Fuck off, Jock.'

SIXTEEN

They left the meeting house and headed off to set up their hammocks. Uribe directed them towards a quiet area of the camp, away from the other dens and shacks. As much privacy as they could be given, in the confines of a jungle camp. They basha'd up and grabbed refreshments from the camp cookhouse. Warm bottles of Fanta, chunks of bread and fresh vegetables. Porter grazed at his food and sent a message to Strickland, confirming that they had arrived at the camp. A few minutes later, Porter got a three-word reply from Strickland. *Keep me posted.* At exactly 14.00 hours they left the cookhouse and wandered back over to the meeting house for the briefing.

Taylor was waiting for them inside. The CIA man stood in front of the noticeboard, his flabby arms folded across his chest as he watched the gang take their places around the trestle table. There were several satellite photographs and detailed maps laid out in front of them, plus half a dozen tablets and laptops connected by a series of extension leads to a whirring outdoor generator. Bald and Porter took up a bench on one side of the table. Hulk, Dudley and McGee sat down opposite. Then Taylor cleared his throat and began the briefing.

'I've just been talking with Langley,' he began. 'Colonel Gallardo has heard from his contact inside Venezuela. The lieutenant. The latest word is that Fuller will be transferred from prison to Vasquez's private estate in the next couple of days. He'll let us know as soon as she's on the move. Until then, you will wait here in a holding pattern and train for your mission. Shouldn't be more than a day or two, gentlemen.'

'That doesn't give us much time to prepare,' Porter said.

'Can't be helped, fellas. Langley's orders. You need to move out as soon as we know that the hostage is being transferred.'

'Why the rush?' asked Hulk.

'It's for her own safety. Once the hostage arrives at the mansion, Vasquez will put his personal interrogators to work. God knows what they're going to do to her.' He nodded at Bald and Porter in turn. 'I appreciate you guys are very anxious to get her out of there. The sooner we move in, the less time Vasquez and his cronies have to work on her.'

'We need more time to plan the op,' Bald said. 'Two days isn't enough.'

'Tough. This is all you're getting.'

'Thought you SAS boys were used to going in at short notice,' said Dudley. 'Flying by the seat of your pants, kicking down doors. Isn't that how you guys roll?'

'In Iraq, aye. But this is different. We're going deep into unknown territory, with no backup and attacking a heavily defended stronghold. If we don't plan this properly, it'll be a clusterfuck.'

'Sounds like we got ourselves a couple of Brit pussies, boys,' McGee cracked.

Bald stared daggers at the Bostonian. 'I didn't know the SEALs were in the habit of recruiting fucking idiots.'

Taylor stepped forward, holding up his hands in a peace-making gesture. 'Easy, guys. We're all on the same team here. No need to get anybody's back up.'

'It's all good,' said Hulk. 'Bobby here was just fooling around. Right, Bobby?'

McGee glowered at Bald, his wax-like face twitching with hatred. 'Right.'

Taylor waited for their tempers to cool and said. 'There's another problem.'

'There's a fucking surprise,' Bald muttered under his breath.

Taylor ignored him as he went on. 'According to Gallardo's contact, there's talk of a large-scale military presence being transferred to the military base. His most loyal soldiers.'

'How many?'

'Two hundred men. Possibly more. Seems Vasquez is worried

144

about the unrest spreading across the country and wants reinforcements in case his regime is toppled.'

'Any idea when they're due to arrive?' asked Hulk.

'Four days from now, we think. But that's only a calculated guess.'

Dudley said, 'Let's hope they don't get there before the hostage arrives. Otherwise we'll be blundering into a fucking suicide mission.'

'It's beginning to sound like that already,' Bald growled.

Taylor gave him a hard stare. 'We consider that highly unlikely. But the timings are very tight.'

'What's the situation, once we know Fuller is on the move?'

'As soon as our people have confirmation, you'll leave the camp for the border. Two of Commander Uribe's men will lead you to the crossing point. You'll cross the river by boat, near the town of San Vicente, eight miles from your present location.'

McGee said, 'What happens if we run into border guards?'

'Uribe has assured me that won't happen. Border security outside the major checkpoints is non-existent. You'll be taking an established route for trafficking product into Venezuela, for onward export to the West. The guerrillas control a number of such routes along the border.'

Porter sat forward, the lines above his brow forming a deep V. 'You're suggesting we rely on drug smugglers to help us across the border?'

'You have a problem with that?'

'Not us,' Bald replied, giving his mucker a look. 'It's all gravy. Go on.'

'Once you've crossed the border, you'll RV with a local contact and collect your vehicle. Then you'll head directly to the stronghold.'

Taylor reached for the map of Venezuela and tapped his finger at a point to the west of Caracas, thirty miles or so due south of the Caribbean coast.

'Vasquez's private residence is located here, north of a town called Los Altos. Seventy miles south of the capital. He's got himself a luxury spot right next to a mountain. Beautiful views, an infinity pool, underground car park. His own army of chefs and maids. We're talking seven-star facilities, in the middle of one of the poorest parts of the world.'

'Who else knows about this place?'

'Outside his inner circle, almost nobody. The residence isn't one of his official residences. It used to belong to a former general in the military. He was secretly running one of the biggest cartels in the country. Made hundreds of millions and owned this place, in addition to properties in Miami and Barbados.'

'Lucky him,' Bald remarked.

'For a while. His luck ran out when he backed the wrong side in the coup. Vasquez had the general executed and confiscated his property. Including this place.'

'How far is it from the Colombian border?' asked Hulk.

'Five hundred miles. An eleven-hour drive.'

Taylor turned his attention to one of the satellite photographs. Bald, Porter and the others crowded round for a closer look. The mansion was situated on the edge of a wide fertile valley encircled by mountains. Further to the north, immediately beyond the property, the land rose up towards a high peak. Four miles to the south, on the other side of the valley floor, was a line of low broken hills. A gravel track ran from the entrance on the southern side of the residence, past uncultivated fields, towards a junction at the main road, two miles away. The town of Los Altos was located to the east of the estate, three miles further along the main road.

The mansion was huge. There was a main residence enclosed by a security fence and a guardhouse, with towers on all four corners and several outlying buildings to the rear. Plus a luxury garden and a pair of tennis courts and a private lake looking out across the mountains. There was a gully near to the road junction, a mile and half south of the entrance, Bald noted, and a hillock a few hundred metres from the stronghold.

'What's the deal once we get there?' he asked.

'You'll make your way to a first RV at the road junction. From there, you'll debus and move forward into the gully and establish a lying-up point. Then you'll wait for the signal to move into striking distance and begin the assault. You'll go in before first light.'

Hulk scratched his beard as he studied the photograph. 'How well defended is this place?'

'Very. As you might imagine, Vasquez is a deeply paranoid individual. Especially since the failed assassination attempt. The residence is rigged up with infrared cameras, motion detectors, a sophisticated alarm system and a two-metre-high steel fence. Towers on all four corners, with security cameras overlooking the approaches.'

'What about manpower?'

'There's a permanent security detail based at the stronghold. Twelve guys. Plus six men from the Presidential Guard. Vasquez's personal bodyguard. Eighteen in total.'

'So what you're basically saying is, this place is tighter than a duck's arse.'

'If you want to put it that way.'

Bald puffed out his cheeks. 'Going to be hard to get her out of there.'

'I agree,' Hulk said. 'This is some real skin-of-our-teeth shit, Taylor. You're not leaving us with a lot of options.'

Taylor mopped his sweat-lathered face and shrugged. 'It is what it is.'

'Where's the package?' asked Porter.

'According to our source, there's a prison cell in the basement. Vasquez likes to keep his political enemies captive there. Have himself some fun with them. We believe Fuller will be held in that cell.'

'Will the president be there, when we go in?'

'We don't know. But our guess is he won't arrive until the hostage is in place and ready to interrogate.'

'One thing's for sure,' Bald said as he ran his eyes over the photos.

'What's that?' Dudley asked.

'We can't sneak into the stronghold. Not if the place is rigged up to the eyeballs. We'll have to go in noisy.'

Hulk grinned. 'My thoughts exactly, brother.'

Porter said, 'We'll need to identify possible entry points. Any armoured glass windows, any reinforced doors, strong rooms.'

'You'll find all that contained in your briefing packs. Satellite pictures, 3D renderings of the estate, architectural drawings. We've also included a report from one of the colonel's contacts. A guy who used to work on the president's bodyguard detail. He knows the layout inside out. That should cover any questions you might have.'

'Sounds like you lot have thought of everything,' said Bald.

'We're here to provide as much assistance as possible. Orders from the very top. They want you to have the platinum service on this one.'

'To help us rescue some British researcher?'

'That's what the chiefs want.'

Porter studied the satellite image for several moments. He pointed to a separate cluster of buildings situated roughly a quarter of a mile to the east of the mansion, two miles from the town.

'What's this area?' he asked, tapping a finger on the map.

'Venezuelan army barracks,' said Taylor.

Bald looked dumbfounded at the CIA officer. 'There's a barracks right next door to his residence?'

'It's no big deal.'

'I'd say it fucking is. How many soldiers?'

Taylor glanced quickly at Hulk before replying. 'Four platoons. Between thirty-two and forty guys, total. It's a small base. Cookhouse, accommodation block, armoury and an electrical substation. But also extremely well defended. Automatic doors, reinforced gates, blast-proof walls. Place is like a miniature fortress.'

'Why all the high-grade defences for a small base?'

'It's for the benefit of the president. If he finds himself under attack, he can flee to the safety of the base.'

'How are we supposed to pull this thing off with an army barracks up the road? Even if we're in and out of the stronghold in a few minutes, it'll sound the alarm at the base.'

'It's covered. We're taking care of it.'

'How?'

'That's not for you to worry about. The soldiers won't be an issue.'

'No offence, pal, but we've heard that before. We're going to need more reassurance than that.'

'Our people have got a plan. We're creating a distraction. That's all you need to know.'

'Fuck off. You're asking us to go into an area crawling with troops. We'll never make it out of there alive.'

'The barracks won't be a problem. You have my word.'

'This is a bag of bollocks,' Bald said, rising from the bench. 'I'm not getting myself dropped for the sake of some think-tank nerd.'

'You can't walk away.'

'Watch me.'

'Where are you going to go, buddy? Look around. You're in the middle of nowhere. Not as if you can just hail a cab back to your hotel.'

'I'll get one of the simpletons to take us back. One of the Mendoza kids.'

'They've left already. You've got no way out of here.'

Bald said nothing.

'Quit now, and you'll regret it,' Taylor added. 'You'll be turning down the opportunity of a lifetime.'

Bald stopped and looked round. His expression tightened. 'What the fuck are you talking about?'

Taylor smiled wickedly. 'We know about your deal with Vauxhall. The security business. Walk away, and you can forget about it. Deal's null and void. But if you stay, you'll be making a friend of the Company for life. That will lead to some business opportunities, down the line. We can open up a lot of doors.

'You have a choice,' he added. 'Work with us, and good things will happen. But you really don't want to make an enemy of the Company. We'll ruin your life.'

Bald hesitated. He wondered about the plan. He wondered how the fuck the Americans were confident of tying down a couple of hundred foreign soldiers, from thousands of miles away.

'This diversion had better be watertight,' he said.

'It is. One hundred per cent. You have my word.'

Bald gritted his teeth as he weighed up the odds. He thought about his arrangement with Vauxhall. The private security business. He figured Six might toss him a few bones, a couple of decent contracts here and there. Enough to tide him over, keep the business ticking along. But with the CIA on his side his prospects would be a hell of a lot brighter. He could make millions. After years of being a Regiment outcast, Jock Bald would finally be minted. He'd be rolling in cash.

Leave now, the voice told him, and the best you can hope for is a job working the doors of a Hereford boozer.

You'll spend the rest of your days living in shite digs and breaking up fights between pissheads outside the Nag's Head.

He sighed heavily. Sat back down on the bench. Taylor nodded at him, looked at the other faces sitting around the table.

He said, 'So. Once you're in position at the gully, you'll wait for confirmation that distraction is ready to deploy. We won't authorise the assault until then.'

Bald said, 'How long will that take?'

'Hard to say. The distraction is being handled by another team. They have their own protocols. It will be before first light. That's as much as I can tell you.'

'It had better not be any later than that. We're going to be badly exposed in that gully.'

'Shouldn't be a problem. The estate is three miles away from the nearest town, Los Altos. There's no police in that area. No military patrols.'

'I ain't interested in the military. It's the civilians that worry me.'

McGee cracked a smile and jerked a thumb in Bald's direction. 'Check this guy out, fellas. Mr SAS here is scared of a few locals.'

Porter caught sight of the vicious look on his colleague's face and stepped in before Bald lost his temper.

'He's right,' Porter said. 'Every time we've been compromised in the Regiment, on exercises or ops, it's been down to civilians. Ramblers, farmers, kids out playing, you name it. Even young couples looking for somewhere to shag. If we're in that gully for more than a few hours, someone's bound to stumble upon us.'

'It won't come to that,' Taylor replied curtly. 'Now. Let's move on to the extraction phase.'

He reached for another map and pointed to a finger of land jutting out of the north-eastern Venezuelan coast.

'Once you've rescued the hostage, you'll head directly to your extraction point. There's a fishing town here. Rio Verde. Four hundred and fifty miles from the stronghold. A reception team will meet you there.'

'Who's on the reception team?'

'Two of our guys. Ex-SEALs. They've been briefed.'

'What's the plan once we get to the extraction point?'

'You'll RV with the reception team and take a boat across to Port of Spain, on the western side of Trinidad. The traffickers use the same route to transport their product to the island, for onward flights to Europe. One of the captains will take you across.'

Porter stared at Taylor uneasily. 'We're relying on a drug dealer to get us out of the country?'

'Technically, he's a trafficker. The dealers are the guys on the streets, cutting up product with anti-malarial pills, de-worming drugs and a bunch of other crap.'

'Same difference. We're still dealing with a bloke in the supply chain. Why should we trust him?'

'Firstly, because we're paying him handsomely. Second, because we don't have a choice.' Taylor took off his safari hat and ran a hand through his hair. 'The hard truth is, we don't have anyone on the ground in Venezuela. The embassy staff moved out months ago. Orders of the president himself. All the information you have has come from second-hand sources, political exiles and electronic surveillance. The only people we can rely on are the guerrillas and their own network of contacts. Which means the traffickers. It's not ideal, I know. But it's all we've got.'

'Dude's got a point, though,' Hulk said. 'What's to stop this captain from stabbing us in the back?'

Taylor flashed a chilling smile. 'He has family in Colombia. His parents, a sister and two nephews. The mother is very ill. Cancer. We're keeping them under surveillance until the operation is over. If he tries to betray us . . . let's just say it won't end nicely for them.'

'Once we reach Trinidad? What then?'

'You'll make your way to the British High Commission. A reception team will be waiting for you there. It's all been arranged through our friends at Vauxhall. You shouldn't have any problems. Questions?'

He looked round the meeting house. Nobody said a word.

'Good.' Hulk pressed his hands together and signalled for the others to get up. 'Now, let's hit the range. Show you boys the kit you'll be taking with you.'

Taylor stepped outside the meeting house and called out to Zapata. The guerrilla came hustling over and exchanged a few words with the CIA man. Then he started abruptly down a track leading away from the main camp. Taylor followed him, with the rest of the team close behind. They made their way down a well-trodden path flanked by corridors of bamboo and rattan. Four minutes later, they reached a flat patch of land at the bottom of a gully. A wide-open space, two hundred metres long and a hundred wide. About the same size as two football pitches laid side-by-side. At either end the exposed sides of the gully rose up towards thick clumps of forest. Half a dozen shacks were arranged in an area on the right side of the gully, the walls and doors riddled with bullet holes. A dozen plywood stakes had been driven into the ground along the far edge of the gully, ninety metres away.

'FARC's old training ground,' Taylor said, sweat soaking through his linen shirt. 'Commander Uribe has given us permission to use it as we see fit.'

'Looks like they haven't used it for a while.'

'They're primarily in the drug-trafficking business these days. Less incentive to practise set-piece battles with government troops.'

'We'll need white mine tape,' Bald said. 'Timber posts, some rattan. We'll need to build a facsimile of the stronghold so we can walk through the assault.'

'Have a word with Uribe. He's placing his men at our disposal for the duration of our stay.'

Porter glanced round, frowning. 'Where's the hardware?'

Taylor didn't answer. Instead he said something quickly in Spanish to Zapata. The Colombian marched over to a patch of ground at the edge of the gully covered with loose sticks and palm fronds. He dropped to a knee and brushed the fronds aside to reveal a trapdoor hidden beneath. The door groaned as he slid it aside, revealing a deep pit containing half a dozen forty-five-gallon drums.

'Your weapon systems,' Taylor said. 'Plus equipment and armour. Everything you'll need for the mission. Delivered yesterday, courtesy of our friends at Langley.'

Bald peered inside one of the drums. He counted four weapons, each one individually sealed inside a reusable plastic bag. Small one-pound bags of silica gel helped to keep the moisture out. Taylor reached into the drum and pulled out one of the guns. He laid it down flat on the ground, untied the bag and removed a sleek rifle. It looked similar to an M16, thought Bald, except the barrel was shorter and the weapon generally looked more compact. He recognised it immediately.

'M4 carbine,' Taylor said. 'A1 variant. Five point fifty-six millimetres. Thirty-round box magazine. I assume you guys are familiar with the operating system.'

He directed the question at Bald and Porter. They both nodded. 'We know it,' Porter said. 'Spent a lot of time in the Regiment working with the M16 variant.'

Bald picked up the rifle and examined it up close. The M4 was the slimmed-down version of the M16. The same performance but housed in a more compact structure. A fine piece of hardware, in his opinion. Weapon of choice for the elite warrior. It had also been heavily modified. Like taking a Ford van and putting a Formula One engine inside. A rail system had been mounted on the upper receiver, with several attachments fitted to it. There was a red-dot sight and an additional rear iron sight and a night scope, plus a vertical fore grip fitted to the underside of the weapon. He was looking at several thousand pounds worth of weaponry.

Bald gave a grunt of approval. 'This stuff is all premium quality. Top-of-the-range components.'

'That's right, bud,' Taylor replied. 'No expense spared when it comes to helping our British friends.'

Bald stared at him but couldn't tell whether he was taking the piss.

They went through a bunch of other equipment. The other drums contained enough firepower to take over a small African country. There were four Glock 17 semi-automatic pistols to use as secondary weapons, plus lumps of plastic explosive to use as framed charges or to create a distraction charge. There was a box of L2 fragmentation grenades, three per member of the team, and four M18 Claymore anti-personnel mines. Plus black tactical plate carriers with front and rear armour inserts, with a series of pouches on the front for carrying spare ammunition clips and accessories. There were several pairs of black aviator gloves, tourniquet bandages and shell dressings, small fold-up binoculars and detachable 5.56mm sound suppressors for the M4s. Another drum was filled with ammunition for the M4s and pistols. Every item was top of the range. Taylor wasn't joking, Bald realised. The Americans really hadn't spared any expense.

'This is a lot of fucking kit,' he said.

Taylor flashed a smile so white you could build a snowman out of it. 'The Company is keen to help in any way it can.'

'Since when did your people give two shits about someone like Fuller?'

Dudley lowered the Glock he was holding and looked up at him. 'What's the problem? You don't like getting handouts from Uncle Sam?'

'I just don't understand why Langley is giving us the five-star treatment.'

McGee snorted through his flared nostrils. 'Who gives a shit? You should be grateful. At least we're not going in with whatever out-of-date crap you people use in England.'

Bald stared at him.

Porter said, 'What about comms?'

Taylor said, 'You'll be issued with Company-approved devices. They're stored at the meeting house. We'll run them through later.'

He stretched to his full height and checked his watch.

'I'll leave you boys to it. Get yourselves acquainted with your weaponry. Report back to the meeting house at eighteen hundred hours for your comms briefing.'

He trudged back down the track towards the main camp, Zapata hurrying after him. Hulk, Dudley and McGee started distributing ammunition and kit between them, while Bald and Porter took a set of yellowed paper targets from a wooden box and a pair of staplers and carried them over to the plywood stakes at the other end of the range. Bald glanced back at the three ex-SEALs, a sense of unease brewing in his guts.

'They're giving us a lot of help.'

'It's the CIA, Jock. They're not going to send us across the border with pea shooters.'

'It's not the kit that worries me,' Bald said.

'What is it, then?'

'They've sent their operations officer down here. They're controlling the intelligence, handling the briefings. They've organised everything with the guerrillas.'

'What are you saying?'

'This is more than a bit of friendly assistance. The Americans are practically running the show.'

'Thought you'd be chuffed. You were always moaning about this stuff back in the Regiment. Kit going missing. Supply fuck-ups. At least now we get access to all the high-grade hardware.'

Bald grunted. 'I can understand the Yanks throwing us a bone or two. But they're going to a lot of fucking trouble to rescue one of our own.'

'It's like Merrick said. They're involved in the operations against the cartels. They've got as much interest in rescuing Fuller as we do.'

'If you believe that.'

'Why would they lie to us?'

'Fuck knows,' Bald muttered. 'But I trust the CIA about as far as I can spit a brick. We're going to need eyes in the backs of our heads from now on. That's for bloody sure.'

SEVENTEEN

They spent two hours on the range, zeroing their weapons, sorting out their equipment and putting down rounds on the targets. It had been more than a year since Bald had discharged a weapon. The old skills were still there, but the edges had been blunted by time and a lack of practice. It didn't take him long to get back into the groove. He had spent years in the Regiment operating the M16 variant, putting down tens of thousands of rounds on the ranges in Hereford. The weapon was instantly familiar to him. Like catching up with an old friend. By the time they packed up their kit and headed back to the camp, he was feeling confident about his abilities again. He was ready to soldier.

They reported back to the meeting house at exactly six o'clock. Taylor gave them a brief lowdown on the Company-modified phones they would be taking with them. Which looked exactly like regular smartphones, but housed in protective black cases with stub-like antennae mounted on the top edge.

'The devices you're taking are military grade, battle ready and cutting edge,' said Taylor. 'Field-tested by our best people. They can operate on any network, in the most remote environment on the planet. That's important, considering the current situation in Venezuela.'

'How's that?' asked Porter.

'The crisis there has led to a number of blackouts in recent months. That could cause you big problems in terms of retaining comms with us. If the mobile towers are down, these cases allow you to turn your devices into satellite phones. Just open the relevant app, and you can start communicating with us via satellite link. There's also this . . .'

Taylor grabbed one of the phones, held it up in his sweaty paw and pointed to a weather app icon.

'This looks like a standard weather app, but it actually turns your phone into an emergency personal locator beacon. If you're compromised, tap it once and it will begin transmitting a signal back to Langley. The signal is continuous and accurate to within a couple of metres. It will keep on transmitting, even if your phone has been switched off or damaged.'

Hulk said, 'Are these things clear comms?'

Taylor nodded. 'End-to-end encryption for both voice and text. If you need to speak to us, you can do so in plain language.'

'What if we run out of juice?'

'You'll take portable charging units with you. One for each team member. These phones have been optimised for longer battery life, so they should last longer than a civilian handset.'

McGee nudged Bald. 'Don't sweat it, Grandad. We'll show you how to use these babies.'

'We're not fucking imbeciles,' Bald said angrily. 'Me and Porter have used these things before.'

Taylor clicked his fingers. 'Speaking of. You'll need to hand over any other electronic devices you've brought with you. Phones, tablets, laptops.'

Bald and Porter looked at one another.

'What the fuck for?' Bald demanded.

'Operational security. Company protocol. No foreign devices are permitted across the border.'

'The phones we've got are from Six. They're secure.'

'That's not our assessment,' said Taylor. 'Our people believe they might be vulnerable to security breaches. You can't take them.'

Porter's frown deepened. 'We should check in with Strickland. Clear this with her first.'

'This is for your own safety,' Taylor said. 'If your phones are hacked into, it could compromise your location. This is non-negotiable as far as Langley is concerned.'

'Sod it.' Bald shoved a hand into his trouser pocket and dug out the smartphone Merrick had given him. 'Makes no difference to me.'

Porter watched him slide his phone across the table. 'You're okay with this?'

'What good would them phones do us anyway? Not as if Vauxhall are going to send help if we call them, is it?'

'I'll need your phone too,' Taylor said.

Porter reluctantly took out his handset and passed it over. Taylor pocketed the devices and gave them a brief run-through of the bespoke military apps installed on the phone. Geo-spatial location software, navigation apps. Then he finished up the meeting and handed out the packs containing the blueprints and maps of the stronghold and the surrounding area. He said that he would remain at the camp to oversee their preparations until word came through from Langley to green light the operation. He would be leaving the camp the morning after the team had departed, he added. His tone suggested he was already looking forward to quitting the forest and returning to the comforts of modern civilisation. Somewhere with an AC unit.

The team spent a few hours in the meeting house, poring over the layout of the stronghold and the surrounding area. They looked at the dead ground, studied blueprints of the various floors and rooms inside the mansion and read the report from the colonel's contact about the upgrades that had been made to the building in recent years. They also looked at the layout of the nearby barracks, studying the laager points for the vehicles, the locations of the armoury and ablutions.

The Company had done a thorough job on the intelligence front. They had detailed information on the likely routes taken by the guards on patrol, the rotation of guards based at the guardhouse, the number of staff working at the residence. Everything they could possibly need.

Hulk, as team leader, took charge of the planning. He took a fresh wad of tobacco from a tin with an eagle engraved on the lid and popped it into his mouth.

'Talk us through it, Brendan.'

Dudley sucked the air between his rotten teeth. 'Way I see it, we got two main problems. One, the guardhouse. There are two guards posted out front at all times. They'll see us coming a mile away. Literally.'

'Why can't we approach from the other side?' McGee questioned. 'Sneak up on 'em.'

'Too steep, dumbass. We'd have to navigate them there hills first. We'd be exhausted by the time we hit the stronghold. Especially you. All that muscle slowing you down.'

'Those slopes are badly exposed, too,' Porter pointed out. 'Barely any cover in the five-hundred-metre gap between the trees and the fence. If the guards spotted us we'd be caught cold.'

'And we'd still have to breach the fence. Which would take time.'

'I think they're saying your idea is shite, mate.' Bald said with a smirk.

The heavyset Bostonian glowered at him with rage. Years of steroid abuse, probably, fused with a lifelong hatred of the British. They weren't going to be best friends after this, Bald decided.

Hulk said, 'Tell us about the second problem.'

Dudley said, 'The number of guards. Eighteen of them in total. We'll need to find some way of fixing them in place while we breach the stronghold and rescue the girl.'

'You're forgetting the barracks,' Bald said. 'That's another forty-odd soldiers we're potentially up against.'

Hulk spat out tobacco juice. 'Taylor says they're not an issue.'

'Do you really believe him?'

'No reason not to.'

'What fucking diversion is going to pin down those soldiers? A missile?'

'You'd be amazed at what our people are capable of. Even when they're thousands of miles away. Some of that shit, your jaw would hit the ground so hard it'd break.'

'That's why we call the shots these days, instead of your piss ant country,' McGee said.

Bald stared at him with gritted teeth. Imagined what the guy's face might look like if he gave him a knuckle sandwich.

Dudley said, 'Whatever happens, we're going to have to get in and out of there fast.'

'How long?' asked Porter.

'Ten to fifteen minutes. Once it goes noisy we're on the clock.'

'Doesn't give us a lot of time. We've got to breach the perimeter, deal with the guards at the guardhouse, engage any other targets, get inside the building, locate the hostage and bug out again before the enemy can regroup.'

'Going to be tricky as fuck,' Bald said.

Hulk inclined his head. 'You're saying it can't be done?'

'No such thing, mate. That attitude would last you about five minutes in the Regiment. Guess that's why we're still streets ahead of your gang, when it comes to doing the business.'

A smile crawled out of the corner of Hulk's mouth. 'English humour. Always had a soft spot for it.'

'I'm Scottish, mate. We're the hard people from the north. The English are the ones to the south. Bunch of pooftas.'

'All the same to me, brother. Y'all have a bunch of weird ass accents.'

Porter frowned at the map. 'There might be a way to deal with the guards.'

'How's that, friend?'

He grinned. 'We give them something else to worry about . . .'

They discussed the plan for the next two hours, thrashing out the basics, arguing the pros and cons, until they had the fundamental workings of a deliberate assault. It wasn't the most sophisticated plan in the world. But it gave them something to work with when they hit the range the following day. In an ideal scenario they would have spent a whole day working out the plan, but they were working to a shortened timeframe. They would have to refine the plan constantly, right up until the minute they set off for the Venezuelan border.

At 20.00, Hulk called an end to the briefing. They left the meeting house and stopped by Commander Uribe's tent with a list of requests for the following day. Then they made their way across the camp to the cookhouse, joining the guerrillas for plates of steaming hot rice and stewed beans. The mood around the camp was surprisingly relaxed. People were laughing and joking, watching episodes of *BoJack Horseman* on their laptops or reading books by candlelight. Understandable, thought Bald. The dissidents were in alliance with the Americans now. The Colombian army was busy fighting the cartels. The chances of anyone dropping a payload on their camp were incredibly slim.

As the evening wore on, a bunch of guerrillas headed over to another shack to watch the new *Terminator* film on a projection screen. At which point Hulk stood up and announced that he had something he wanted to show the Brits. He left the cookhouse, ducked into his shack and came back a minute later clutching a bottle of Chivas Regal.

'Fetch us some glasses, Brendan,' he ordered.

Dudley scooted over to the kitchen area and snagged five chipped enamel mugs from a shelf. Hulk unscrewed the cap on the whisky bottle and poured generous measures into four of the cups. He was about to tip some of the golden liquid into the remaining mug when Porter thrust out an arm and covered it with his hand.

'None for me,' he said.

Hulk shot him an inquisitive glance. 'You don't drink, chief?'

'Haven't touched the stuff for three years, six weeks and four days.'

'Should have seen him before then,' Bald said. 'He was a fucking mess. Saddest bloke in the Regiment.'

'For real?'

'My head wasn't in a good place,' Porter admitted. 'But that's a long time ago. I'm sober these days.'

'And a boring bastard,' Bald added.

'Sobriety. I respect that.' Hulk set the whisky bottle down, took a long swig from his cup. 'Hell of a thing to do, going clean.'

'Amen to that,' Dudley said.

'What about you?' Porter asked. 'What's your story?'

'Ain't rightfully much to tell. Georgia born and raised. Spent my teenage years raising hell. Running around, beating up wetbacks, stealing cars. Usual shit. Had a few close shaves with the law, I can tell you. Drifted around some before I figured I'd try the recruiting office. Follow the family tradition, you know.'

'You come from a military family?'

'Yessir, I do. My great-granddaddy, he served in France in World

War One. His granddaddy before him took up arms in the War of Northern Aggression.'

Bald said, 'You mean the civil war. The one where your slave-owning ancestors fought to keep black people in chains.'

'Don't give me that liberal history bullshit. We was fighting for states' rights. Slavery had nothing to do with it.'

Bald laughed. 'You've got to be thick as fuck to believe that.'

'Be careful, brother,' Hulk interrupted. 'The war's something of a sensitive issue for Brendan. His family takes a lot of pride in their part in it. Parents even gave him Lee for his middle name, after the Confederate general.'

'Been to all the big battle sites,' Dudley said proudly. 'Got myself a bunch of memorabilia too. Rifles, equipment, flags. Maybe I'll show you my collection one day.'

'Look forward to it,' Bald lied.

McGee drained his cup and refused Hulk's offer of a refill. He reached into his trouser pocket and pulled out a stainless-steel hip flask with a shamrock engraved on the front, above a map of Ireland.

'My lucky charm,' he said, noticing the look on Bald's face. 'Never go anywhere without it.'

He unscrewed the cap and swigged from his flask. Smacked his lips, set the flask down and cocked his head at the Brits.

'When did you guys join the Regiment?'

'Late eighties,' said Porter.

'Early nineties,' said Bald.

'Must have some seen action.'

'Here and there, aye.'

'Ever work in Ireland?'

'Once or twice.'

'Ever kill anybody over there?'

Bald grinned. 'We've hurt a fair few of their feelings.'

Hulk and Dudley burst into laughter. So did Porter. McGee stared at Bald with a look so cold it could stop the ice caps from melting. 'That funny to you? Killing innocent people?'

'Don't know what you're talking about, mate. The people we were fighting were terrorists.'

'They were soldiers. In a war. They wanted you bastards out of the country. Leave Ireland to the Irish. They weren't no terrorists.'

'Fuck off. You weren't there. You wouldn't know.'

'I got family. I heard stories.'

'From some old bricklayers in a flea-infested bar in South Boston? Do me a favour, pal. I bet you've never even been to the old country.'

The veins on McGee's neck bulged. His eyes threatened to pop out of their sockets. His face looked like it might explode with rage.

'Don't need no passport to know what fucking imperialism looks like.'

Bald laughed mirthlessly. 'You want to talk about imperialism, let's talk about what your people have done in the Middle East.'

'That's different.'

'Is it? What you've done over there is far worse than anything our government did in Ireland. Good fucking lads have died because of the pointless wars America started. So don't sit there and tell us about Ireland, while your own country has blood on its hands.'

'Brother's got you there, Bobby,' Hulk conceded.

McGee worked his face into a snarl. 'I don't have to listen to this shit. You ain't got the right to lecture me, chief.'

'Go fuck yourself. Stupid cunt.'

McGee shot up from the bench and stepped towards Bald, his fists trembling. 'Who the fuck do you think you're talking to? We're SEALs, man.'

'And we're the fucking SAS,' Bald said, rising to his feet.

'Fuck you.'

Bald stepped into his face. 'How about we take this outside.'

'I ain't afraid of you, British fuck.'

Bald took a step closer and dropped his shoulder, as if shaping to throw a punch. At that moment Porter lunged forward and grabbed his mucker by the shoulder, pulling him back from the Bostonian.

'Easy, mate. No need for this.'

McGee stood there, grinning from ear to ear 'That's right. Listen to your boyfriend. Pair of British pussies.'

Bald didn't respond. He just stared at McGee, entertaining all sorts of thoughts. Despite his size, it would be easy enough to beat the shit out of him. A guy as big as McGee, he wasn't built for speed. His reactions would be fractionally slower than Bald's. A quick forward jerk of his head, slamming the hard bone of his skull into the centre of McGee's face. Smash up a few bones, follow it up with a savage right hook to the jaw. Ten seconds and the guy would be flat on his back.

Satisfying?

Definitely.

But also a risky move.

You don't want to jeopardise the op, the voice warned. *Not now. Beat the shit out of this kid, and you'll be thrown off the team. You can forget about your agreement with Six. The private company. The security contracts.*

'You're lucky we've got a mission to plan for. Any other day, things would be different.'

'Keep telling yourself that, asshole.'

Hulk gave him a meaningful look. 'Take a walk, Bobby. Cool off.'

McGee held his ground for a moment longer, as if trying to make a point. Then he snatched up his hip flask, turned and trudged off in the direction of the tents.

Bald shook his head. 'We don't need this hassle. This op's going to be hard enough to pull off, without having to deal with his crap.'

'What's his fucking problem?' asked Porter.

'Steroid abuse,' Hulk said. 'Everyone knows Bobby is a pain in the ass.'

'If that's the case, why don't you tell him to sod off?'

'He wasn't our choice. He's one of the Company's guys. Taylor brought him in at the last minute. We don't have a veto.'

'I could think of a few ways of getting rid of him,' Bald muttered darkly.

'Bad idea. We need a good mechanic and comms guy. If we're on the run and we get into a fix, we're going to need his skills. Besides, five guys are better than four. With the odds we're facing, we'd be nuts to go in with less firepower.'

'We'd manage.'

'It's not happening. You're going to have to work together. Put your differences to one side. Think you can do that?'

'Just as long as that prick stays out of my way.'

'He'll stay in line. I'll make sure of it.' Hulk smoothed the corner of his horseshoe moustache. 'Not his fault, you know. What the system does to you. We've all got issues. Myself included.'

'You're an addict?' asked Porter.

'Was.'

'What was your medicine?' Bald lowered his eyes to the guy's half-full mug. 'Not alcohol, surely?'

'Painkillers,' Hulk said. 'To begin with, anyhow. Later, a whole cocktail of meds. You want to know the truth? US military is one big pharmacy these days. They pumped us full of shit in the desert. They'd inject us with stuff to keep us awake. Give us more stuff to bring us down. Then we'd get another injection before heading out again. We were taking so much stuff, everything became a blur. One minute you're on tour. The next you're standing in a bar in Houston, wondering what the fuck's going on. After a while, it got so bad that a bunch of us started self-medicating between tours. There were fellas with chemistry degrees in the service who started cooking up their own meth to help guys cope. Others were robbing pharmacies or stealing from drug dealers to fund their habits. A lot of guys were on a downward spiral, on account of all that shit the army put in their veins. I was one of 'em.'

'What happened?'

'I was back in San Diego after a tour in Afghanistan. I'd seen some shit. Did some shit. None of it good. My ninth tour in that shithole. I was done, you know? Mentally, I was already checked out of the Unit. That's when it happened. I was out in the city one night, looking to score some coke from a guy in a bar. Some stranger. My fault. Turned out, he was an undercover cop. Some sting operation they were running, looking for off-duty soldiers on product. They arrested me and threw my ass in the brig.'

'How long did you do?'

'Eight months. Followed by a dishonourable discharge and a reduction in rank and pay.'

'That's harsh.'

'The Unit knew they had a drug problem. A lot of guys were burning the candle at both ends. People were coming down with combat stress and turning to meds. They were looking to make an example of someone. Just so happened my ass was in the cross-hairs at the time.'

He took another hit of whisky and stared contemplatively at his glass.

'Had some seriously hard years after I got out. Did a lot of fucked-up shit.'

'Looks like you're doing all right now.'

'Got Dudley to thank for that. Brother was there for me when I needed him the most. Helped me go cold turkey, get my shit together. Eighteen months later, the Company tapped me up. Said they wanted to bring me in on a few operations. I kept my nose clean, did the work. Three years later, here I am.'

Bald watched him interestedly. He was seeing Hulk in a whole new light. He knew what it was like to have the military system shit on you. To be thrown onto the scrapheap. In that situation, you found out what you were really made of. Hulk could have easily crumbled. A weaker person would have ended up living under a bridge, injecting junk into their veins. Instead the guy had fought back, like a true warrior. He'd turned his life around. Bald respected that.

Hulk raised his mug in a toast. 'Here's to kicking addiction.'

He polished off the dregs of his whisky, rose from the bench and patted his cap.

'I'm calling it a night. Suggest you boys do the same. Got a long day ahead of us tomorrow. First reveille is at o-six hundred hours. We'll meet back here at o-seven hundred. Then we'll hit the range and begin training.'

EIGHTEEN

The guerrillas were already up and dressed by the time Bald and Porter rose the following morning. Two dozen of them had gathered on the training ground while Uribe read out the list of duties for the day. Others were getting campfires going, having a morning wash in the stream or lugging supplies to and from the storeroom. Bald and Porter dressed in their civvies and headed for the cookhouse. They helped themselves to plates of fried plantains and vegetables, and gulped down mugs of hot coffee poured out of a communal thermos flask. Grown locally by the farmers and brewed on-site, Hulk said. Bean-to-cup, jungle-style. It was strong and bitter. Just the way Bald liked it.

Daniela Reyes was there too. She was dressed in a tight-fitting grey T-shirt that showed off the curves of her ample breasts. She wore her hair down, long dark locks caressing suggestively against her soft cheeks. Bald was deeply impressed. She looked even more stunning than she had the previous day at the stream. He gave her a crafty wink straight out of the Jock Bald playbook and got a severe stare in return.

'Don't think she's succumbing to your charms, mate,' Porter joked.

'Matter of time.' Bald gestured to himself. 'No woman can resist this.'

'A jobless Scot without a penny to his name?'

'Fuck off. At least I still get some action. Christ, at this point you may as well go celibate. Nobody would know the difference.'

Four minutes later, Hulk and Dudley showed up. They came from the direction of the meeting house rather than their shelters,

Bald noted. He caught a glimpse of Taylor inside the house, sitting at the main table and tapping away on his laptop.

They helped themselves to coffee and food and pulled up a pew opposite Bald and Porter. 'What did Taylor want with you at this hour?' Porter asked.

'Admin,' Hulk said. 'I was briefing him on our plan. He wanted to know what we were thinking, broadly speaking.'

'What did he reckon?'

'He likes it. Says he wants to give Langley the heads-up. See if there's anything else they can add from their side. Maybe give us an extra edge.'

'He say anything more about that distraction?'

'Just what he told us yesterday. We'll check in with Langley once we reach the LUP near the stronghold. They'll notify us when the distraction is ready to deploy. Should be some time before first light. It'll tie down the barracks for fifteen minutes. Long enough for us to go in and get the girl.'

'Any word about when the hostage is being moved?'

'They're still waiting to hear. Taylor's confident they'll get the heads-up very soon, though. Says the situation in Caracas is deteriorating rapidly. Doesn't make sense for the authorities to keep her there for much longer.'

'Where's the IRA fan-boy?' asked Bald.

'McGee? Recovering, probably,' Dudley said. 'Last I saw of him last night, he was necking tequila shots with Uribe.'

'Fucking unprofessional, that. We're supposed to be training for an operation, not spending all night on the piss.'

'I'll have a word,' Hulk said.

'He needs more than that,' Bald said. 'Someone needs to give him a slap.'

'What's up with you?' Porter asked, nodding at Dudley. The redneck was scratching furiously at a spot on the nape of his neck.

'Damn ants. Fuckers were everywhere. Couldn't sleep a wink.' He grimaced. 'None of you fellas had the same problem?'

'Not us, mate.'

Bald gazed across the camp. 'Where's your basha?'

'There. That one.'

Dudley pointed to a poorly constructed hammock tied between two trees, with a waterproof poncho sheet loosely fastened a few feet above it to protect the sleeper from the rain. Bald lifted his eyes to one of the trees and indicated a dark-coloured object, roughly the size of a football, resting on one of the branches.

'There's your problem, right there. Bloody great ants' nest above your head. All you've done is give them another exit point from the tree to your hammock.'

Dudley momentarily stopped scratching himself as he squinted at the ant's nest. 'Son of a bitch.'

'Seen plenty of lads make the same mistake.'

'Anything else I should know about? Before I get bitten to shit again?'

'Watch out for any deadfall. Loose branches trapped in the trees above. One of them comes loose in the night, they'll fall right on top of you. Break an arm. And place your poncho closer to your hammock. A few inches should do it. If it's too high and there's a strong wind blowing, it won't stop the rain from coming in. You'll get drenched.'

'How do you know all that stuff?'

'Jungle phase of Selection,' said Bald. 'That's where the Regiment cut its teeth. Where we find out who's mentally strong enough to become a Blade.' He crammed another forkful of egg into his mouth. 'You lot might have the edge when it comes to the water, but in here we're the masters.'

A few minutes later, McGee trooped across from his shelter and parked his colossal frame on the edge of the bench. Hulk, setting down his coffee, gave him a searching look.

'The fuck sort of time you call this?'

'I overslept, chief. Bite me.'

McGee rubbed his eyes and yawned. The smell of whisky on his breath was so thick you could hang washing from it.

'You look like shit,' Bald said. 'How much did you put away last night?'

'Screw you. I can handle my drink.'

'Doesn't look like it from where I'm standing. Looks like the Colombians drank you under the table.'

'I ain't hungover. Even if I was, it's none of your fucking business.'

'It is if you can't perform. Maybe you want to sit this one out, mate. Let the real men do the work.'

'Eat a dick, asshole.'

Bald's muscles tautened with anger. Across the table, McGee wore a big shit-eating grin. Like he was goading Bald into a fight. Like he knew his sheer mass gave him an unassailable edge, and he could do whatever the fuck he pleased. It took every last shred of restraint for Bald to keep his fists by his side, instead of connecting with McGee's smug face.

Hulk checked his watch and stood up. 'Let's go. Time to get to work.'

A short while later, the team gathered in a circle at the edge of a wide clearing located a short distance from the gully. The low, grassy field was covered on both sides by gentle slopes and thick clumps of forest. Uribe's men had constructed a crude replica of the ground floor of the stronghold in the clearing, according to the plans given to him by Hulk the previous evening. Rooms inside the building were marked out with two-metre-tall timber posts, with strips of white mine tape around them, measured at the correct distances from one another. More posts and tape marked out the guardhouse and perimeter fence. On the ground in front of them, Hulk and Bald had sketched out a rough overhead view of the stronghold, measuring six feet by six. Scraps of paper denoted the buildings, with sticks for the fence and leaves for the mango grove in front of the mansion. Stones marked out the positions of the team members. They would run through the plan using the sandpit model, making sure everyone knew their jobs before they progressed on to the full-size facsimile.

'To get inside,' Hulk said, 'we're going to have to draw the guards away from the front gate. Along with anyone else on duty. Otherwise, we'll get cut down before we can make it to within spitting distance of the damn place.

'Our best bet, as Porter explained yesterday, is to create a diversion. If we do it right, an explosive device, placed along the perimeter fence, should divert the guards and buy us enough time to prosecute the assault.'

McGee rolled his eyes. 'We know. We've been through all this already, chief.'

Hulk shot him a look that could skin a rattlesnake. 'And we'll keep going through it, until it's automatic. That way, everyone knows what they're doing and we stand a better chance of making it out of there alive. Unless you've got something better to do, Bobby?'

Hulk stared him out. Then he picked up a stick and pointed to five stones grouped in an area outside the stronghold.

'Once we get the green light from the Company, we'll advance to the target until we reach this hillock, four hundred metres due south of the stronghold. At this point, Dudley will break to the left and establish a sniper position on top, using the bushes to conceal his position from the enemy.'

He took one of the stones and placed it to the left of the assault group. Then he took the four remaining rocks and moved them closer to the guardhouse.

'The main assault team will then advance two hundred metres to the edge of this mango grove and form up within striking distance of the gate.' He picked up one of the four stones and placed it near the corner of the fence. 'At the same time, the fifth man will carry the breaching charge and move towards the south-west corner of the perimeter fence, covered by Dudley on the high ground and the rest of the assault team at the mango grove. That guy's job is to place the explosive, crawl back fifty metres and then detonate. Bobby, that's your job.'

'You sure he can handle it?' Bald goaded. 'Maybe me or Porter should place the charge. Someone with a bit more experience.'

'Fuck you, chief. I'm good for it.'

'You look a long way from that. Christ, I can smell your breath from here.'

McGee stared at Bald. The veins on his neck bulged like lengths of tensed rope. He turned to Hulk and said, 'I'll handle the charge. You can count on me, Hulk.'

'Okay, then.' Hulk indicated the piece of paper representing the guardhouse. 'Soon as the explosive charge is triggered, that's the cue for the assault team to advance towards the gatehouse. Bobby will link up with the rest of the group before we hit the gates. We'll then engage any targets and make for the front door. We should encounter minimal resistance.'

'How can we be sure?' asked McGee.

'When the charge goes off, the enemy will naturally assume the attack is coming from that direction. They won't be expecting an attack on the gate. They might leave a couple of guys to defend that position, but no more. The assault team will then clear the main residence, locate the hostage and clear out before extracting south towards the gully, covered by the sniper.'

'Dudley's going to be exposed on that high ground,' Bald said.

'We'll be wearing olive-green clothing and using suppressed weapons. In the darkness, with no muzzle flash and firing from a concealed position, the enemy won't be able to locate him. At least for a short while. Enough time for us to carry out the mission and get the heck out of there.'

McGee said, 'What's the explosive?'

'A four-ounce lump of C4,' Bald replied. 'Should be enough to create a fucking big bang and set the corner tower on fire. We'll need to get hold of an empty container from Uribe, too. A gallon bottle should do the trick. And some washing detergent.'

A weak laugh escaped McGee's mouth. 'You planning on doing some laundry while we're there, chief?'

Bald shook his head. 'We'll pour a fifty-fifty mixture in the empty container. Detergent mixed with fuel. We'll slap the plastic explosive on the side of the container. When that charge detonates, it'll ignite the mixture inside the container and stick to anything it comes into contact with and burn it. The fence, the tower. We'll give the enemy a strong visual point of attack. They'll see the flames from the other side of the compound. It'll be like drawing moths to a light.'

Porter frowned at the model. 'How much time have we got? To mount the assault.'

'We aim to be inside and out again in less than fifteen minutes,' Hulk responded. 'That's how long Taylor says the soldiers in the barracks will be tied down.'

'Assuming the Company's plan works,' Bald added. 'If it doesn't, we're screwed from the start.'

Hulk gave him a searching look. 'You don't think we can trust them?'

'I served in the Regiment for eighteen years. You last that long, you learn not to trust the top brass about anything.'

Porter shook his head fiercely. 'I'm with Jock on this one. What can your people do from several thousand miles away, anyway? Send them a strongly worded email?'

'Drone strike, perhaps,' Bald speculated. 'Drop a couple of five-hundred-pound bombs on the base. That would sort them out.'

'I don't think that's what they're planning,' Hulk murmured.

'What do you reckon it is, then?'

The American stared at him with a blank expression. 'Your guess is as good as mine, brother.'

Bald grunted. 'Whatever it is, it needs to be fucking solid. If the CIA lets us down, we're going to be overrun as soon as that explosion rips through the fence.'

A thought struck Porter. 'We should rig a Claymore near the breach.'

'What the fuck for?' McGee wondered.

'Think about it. When that charge is triggered, all them guards will be rushing over to deal with the breach. If we put a Claymore ten metres back from the fence, we can trigger it once they're in position. We could take out ten or fifteen guys in one go. Any survivors would be tied up dealing with their wounded. Give us more time to bust the hostage loose and get out of the stronghold.'

'That's actually a bloody good idea,' Bald said, a clear note of respect creeping into his voice. 'Maybe you're not as lame as you look.'

'Piss off.'

'It'll even things up some,' said Hulk. 'That's for sure. Bobby, you'll carry the Claymore mine and the explosive device. Place 'em both at the same time and then belly-crawl back to the firing position. Dudley and the rest of us will cover you. Questions?' He glanced round at the others. 'All right, then. Let's start practising.'

* * *

173

The team spent the next two hours doing walk-throughs on the facsimile range. They looked at every possible tactical situation. What they would do if they were compromised during their approach. What would happen if the enemy showed up in force midway through the assault. They studied each other's individual arc of fire, to reduce the chances of getting accidentally plugged by their own side. They paced out the distances between the guardhouse and the entrance and the dead ground. They went through every step of the plan repeatedly, until they were thoroughly sick of it. Apart from McGee, nobody complained. Everyone understood the risks. They were going into a hostile situation, against a force that heavily outnumbered them. Their lives depended on making sure that the assault plan was tested to destruction.

Then they progressed to a real-time run-through of the assault. As close to the real thing as possible, minus the enemy targets. They wore their plate carriers and armour inserts and carried their spare clips, grenades and other accessories, along with their M4s and holstered Glock 17 pistols. Explosive charges. The whole operational load. Anything that they planned on taking with them on the night of the actual assault, right down to their choice of clothing. A pain in the arse, especially in the afternoon heat of the jungle. But better than getting to the stronghold and realising that their pacing was off because they were weighed down with too much kit.

They agreed that the use of live rounds was unnecessary. And dangerous, given the absence of any rubber-clad walls to absorb the bullets. They couldn't afford to suffer any accidents, Hulk argued. They were already facing some formidable odds. The last thing they needed was someone getting hit by a stray round. Both charges would be assembled to make sure McGee could carry them unaided, but they wouldn't be detonated during the exercise. No need. They were veteran operators, with decades of experience handling explosives. They all knew the destructive power of C4.

While the others checked their equipment, Bald assembled the breaching charge. He fetched an empty one-gallon milk container from the guerrillas' cookhouse, along with a jerry can of fuel and a two-litre bottle of laundry detergent. Then he poured the fuel and detergent mix into the plastic container, sealed the cap and fixed the slab of C4 to the side of the container using a strip of black masking tape.

As he finished setting up the charge, he caught sight of McGee assembling the Claymore anti-personnel mine. The guy was kneeling in front of a box-shaped green case with the words 'Front Toward Enemy' stamped across the side. On the ground next to the mine were two long spools of green-coated electrical wire, a satchel and a hand-held clacker firing device the size of an office stapler. Squeezing the clacker fired an electrical pulse down the length of wire, triggering the detonator. Which then triggered the plastic explosive in the Claymore. The resulting blast spewed out hundreds of ball bearings in a horizontal arc, shredding anything within a hundred-metre radius.

He watched McGee for a beat and said, 'Word of advice, mate.'

McGee looked up from the assembly and scowled. 'I've used Claymores before, asshole. May as well teach your grandmother how to suck eggs. Bet she knows how to suck a bunch of stuff, too.'

Bald stared darkly at him. 'You're carrying two explosive devices.'

'So fucking what?'

'That means you'll have two sets of electrical wire and two sets of clackers. You should mark one of them clackers with tape. So you know which one is for the charge and which one operates the Claymore. Otherwise you could trigger the wrong one. If that Claymore goes off before the breaching charge, we're all in the shit.'

McGee smirked. 'That's what you people do in the SAS? Sit around, thinking about stupid little shit like this? No wonder you couldn't defeat the IRA.'

Bald felt an irresistible urge to throttle the Bostonian. 'It's them stupid little things that lead to mistakes and get people killed. So maybe start listening to me.'

'Fuck off. I don't need advice from some antiquated haggis-eating motherfucker. I got this covered.'

Bald swallowed his anger, tamping it down deep into his guts. He looked on silently as McGee inserted the plug at one end of the wire spool to the clacker, linking the explosive to the battery. Flicked the safety bale on the clacker to the lowered position.

McGee noticed him watching with interest. Set the equipment down. 'Got something else you want to say, old man?'

Bald eyed the clacker and the green-coated wire connected to it. 'I wouldn't do that if I were you, mate.'

'Do what?'

'Linking the battery up before you plant the mine. You might trigger the thing by accident. Blow yourself up.'

'I know what I'm doing, asshole.'

He shoved the Claymore, wire and clacker inside the satchel. Slung the satchel over his shoulder, grabbed his M4 and started towards the edge of the range. Stopped abruptly in his tracks.

'Shit. Almost forgot.'

He wheeled back around, snatching up his shamrock-engraved hip flask. Across the range, Hulk called out to them. 'Assault team. Into position. Now.'

Bald hefted up his weapon and the charge and walked over to Porter and Hulk. They had formed up at their starting point, a hundred and fifty metres south of the stronghold. Dudley was already in position at their seven o'clock, lying in a prone position on top of a nearby mound, gripping his sniper variant M4. Essentially the same weapon as the carbine, but with a longer barrel to improve accuracy by increasing the stability of the round during flight. All five of them had suppressors fixed to the muzzles.

McGee waddled over to join the rest of the assault team, weighed down by his big frame and the amount of kit he was carrying. He was wearing his aviator gloves and a long-sleeved shirt over his T-shirt, the Claymore satchel hanging from his side and the pouches on his vest bursting at the seams. Porter gave him a disapproving look.

'Got enough kit there? Anything you've left behind? Kitchen sink?'

'Screw you.'

'Just saying. You're carrying a lot of gear.'

'I can handle it, old man.'

Hulk looked around to make sure everyone was ready to go. 'On my command, we'll move towards the target. Make sure you're all watching your respective arcs.'

'Roger that,' said Bald.

'Got it,' said Porter.

Hulk nodded at McGee. 'All set, Bobby?'

'Fuckin' A, chief. Let's do this!'

'Good.' Hulk glanced across his shoulder. 'Ready, Dudley?'

'I was born ready, son.'

Hulk set the timer on his watch. 'Ready . . . Go!'

As soon as the order left his mouth, McGee, Bald, Porter and Hulk broke forward across the open ground, making for the X-shaped strip of mine tape indicating the edge of the mango grove. Bald moved along at a brisk but controlled pace alongside Hulk, with Porter lagging a few paces further behind. McGee brought up the rear, breathing heavily, slowed down by the weight he was humping.

After fifty metres they reached the 'X' and then Hulk yelled, 'Assault group, going prone!'

Bald, Porter, McGee and Hulk simultaneously went down on their fronts, lying flat on the ground with a direct line of sight to the guardhouse a hundred metres away at their one o'clock and the far-left corner of the fence at their ten o'clock. The assaulters started covering their arcs and in the next second Hulk shouted another order.

'Diversion, move forward!'

Which was McGee's cue to advance. He scraped himself off the ground and hustled towards the corner fence post a hundred metres away, clutching his rifle in one hand and the explosive charge in the other, with the satchel containing the Claymore hanging at his side. After fifteen metres he dropped down and began belly-crawling the remaining distance to the post. Bald observed him through his weapon's iron sights, covering the guy while Porter and Hulk checked their respective arcs at the guard-house and the opposite corner of the fence. At their six o'clock they heard Dudley barking out, 'Sniper covering!'

Bald kept his sights focused on McGee as he inched forward. The guy was fifty-five metres from the fence post now. As he crawled down a slight dip in the land, a shiny object slipped out of the side pocket of his trousers and clattered against the rocks, catching the sunlight.

The shamrock hip flask.

'Shit,' McGee said.

Bald looked on as McGee stopped and reached around for the flask, rolling on to his left side and extending his right arm towards his knee. Like an out-of-shape guy trying to do a complicated Pilates pose.

His full weight pressing down on the satchel containing the Claymore.

A split second later, the mine detonated.

The ground beneath McGee erupted with a burst of orange flame. In the next moment there was a second, brighter orange ball as the charge triggered, and McGee vanished behind a cloud of smoke and dust as a deep whoosh rumbled across the field. Bald, Porter and Hulk flattened themselves, hugging the ground as hundreds of ball bearings whipped through the air, passing a few inches above their heads and clattering against the timber posts.

A few moments later, the noise faded.

Bald cautiously lifted his head and looked across the clearing, blinking dust out of his eyes. Tendrils of smoke drifted up from the blackened patch of earth where McGee had been crawling. The smell of charcoaled flesh hung thick in the air.

Above the hollow ringing in his ears he could hear Hulk at his side, cursing and yelling as he sprang to his feet. Bald and Porter both jumped up and followed him, rushing through the thinning haze of smoke. They stopped a metre short of McGee. Or what was left of him.

His trunk had survived the blast. The plate armour had absorbed most of the impact, the outer material burned to a crisp. The armour itself was covered in scorch marks. The rest of his body had been blown apart. His legs had been torn off at the groin, spilling his intestines across the ground. There was a ragged bloody stump where his head should have been. The area was covered with scraps of flesh and bone fragments and shreds of incinerated fabric.

Several beats passed. Nobody moved. They all just looked at McGee's body in stunned silence. Then Dudley scrambled down the side of the mound and came hurrying over. He caught sight of McGee's rag order corpse and stopped abruptly in his tracks.

'Oh shit,' he gasped. 'Oh Jesus, fuck.'

Bald glanced over at Hulk. The guy appeared to be in a state of shock. The colour had plunged from his face.

'What the fuck happened?' Dudley demanded.

'Stupid bastard must have accidentally depressed the clacker,' Bald said. 'Putting all that pressure on the satchel must have done it. Triggered the Claymore.'

Porter furrowed his brow. 'But you can't detonate one of them things by accident. Got to link the battery up first.'

'He did,' Bald said. 'Bloke had the Claymore and the battery hooked up before he put it in the satchel. Had the safety bale on the clacker lowered and all.'

Hulk looked up, the look on his face darkening. 'You watched him do that?'

'I was right next to him, aye.'

'And you didn't think to say anything to him?'

'I did. Idiot reckoned he had it under control.'

Dudley jabbed a finger at him. 'That's a crock of shit. You probably didn't say a word. Kept your mouth shut so Bobby could get himself killed. That's what happened'

'Why the fuck would I let him do that?'

'You've been wanting him off the team from the get-go. Admit it, asshole.'

'I didn't rate the guy as an operator. Got no problem admitting that. Doesn't make me a murderer.'

Dudley snorted with contempt and turned to Hulk. 'You're not buying this crap, are you?'

'He's supposed to be a Navy SEAL, for fuck's sake,' Bald said. 'He should have known how to handle a Claymore. Not my fault he blew himself up.'

Hulk was quiet for a moment. Then he said, 'Someone find Commander Uribe. Tell him we need four guys. Plus trash bags and latex gloves. Get this mess cleaned up.'

'What about Bobby?' asked Dudley.

'Pick up and bag what's left of him. We'll give the guy a proper Christian burial later. Training is suspended.'

Dudley wheeled round and headed in the direction of the camp. Hulk watched him go, then turned to the others. 'Wait here. Give Dudley a hand when he returns.'

Porter said, 'Where are you going?'

'To find Taylor. I need to tell him what just happened. He'll have to take this up the chain to his superiors.'

'What for?'

'The Company was uneasy about a five-man team. They didn't like the odds. They felt we were taking a lot of risks. Now it's just four of us, they might decide to pull the plug.'

'We're better off without him,' Bald said. 'That stupid fuck was going to screw us, mate. He could have got us all killed just now.'

'I hear your, brother,' Hulk replied quietly. 'But somehow, I don't think that's how Taylor is going to see it.'

He marched slowly off down the track leading away from the range. Porter watched him go before he turned to Bald, 'Did you do that on purpose? Tell me the truth.'

'I tried to tell him. That stupid fucker ignored me. That's how it happened.' Bald screwed up his face. 'You don't think I deliberately let that prick get himself killed, do you?'

'I know you've done some dark shit in your time. And you two were at each other's throats.'

'I'm not a psychopath. I don't go around slotting people I don't rate. Christ, if I did that, half of Hereford would be six feet under by now.'

Porter searched his friend's face for any sign of a tell. He wanted to believe Bald, but he also knew the guy was capable of anything. Given his history. Someone like that, you could never truly trust them.

He shrugged and looked away. 'Doesn't matter anyway.'

'What do you mean?'

'You heard what Hulk said. Langley will probably call the mission off now.' Porter sighed bitterly and looked him in the eye. 'You've just screwed the op, mate.'

NINETEEN

They were back in the meeting house again. Two hours had passed since the accident on the range. Bald, Porter and Dudley had led the clean-up operation while Hulk conferred with Taylor. It had taken a while to gather up what was left of McGee. The detonation of the Claymore and the explosive charge had dispersed his upper body in an impressively wide radius. There were fingers to gather up, and brain matter and eyeballs and bits of bone. They bagged the remains and buried them in an isolated spot a short distance from the camp. Taylor ordered them to retain anything that might identify his body. Rings, wallet, personal phone. Dudley insisted on burying the guy with his hip flask and led the rest of the team in a tearful prayer. He seemed cut up about McGee's death. They had evidently struck up a bond in the short time they had spent together.

Half an hour after the burial, Taylor had summoned them back to the meeting house. They had taken up their spots on the benches while the CIA officer sat at the head of the table, steepling his fingers and wearing an angry look on his sunscreen-covered face. Dudley sat directly across from Bald, giving him the stink eye.

'I've spoken with Langley,' Taylor began. 'Suffice to say, they're mightily pissed. So am I.'

'What'll happen to Bobby?' asked Dudley.

'He doesn't have any family to speak of. No partner or kids. There's a brother in San Antonio, but they're not close. The official line will be that McGee went missing while off-duty, working at an oil installation. We'll make it look like he was a low-level drug operator who got into debt.'

'Ain't right, tarring a man's name like that.'

'It's a good story. No one's going to be asking too many questions about what happened. But that's where the good news ends. This is a disaster.'

His eyes landed on Bald.

'Don't look at me,' Bald growled. 'I'm not the thick bastard who rigged up a Claymore right before a training exercise. It's not my fault that prick lost his life.'

Hulk said, 'No one's accusing you of anything, brother.'

'Speak for yourself,' Dudley said.

'The guy wasn't a professional,' Bald snapped, meeting the redneck's gaze. 'I can't be responsible for him not following standard procedures. If he'd done his job we wouldn't be having this argument.'

'Is the mission still going ahead?' Hulk asked.

'Our people are unhappy about the reduction in manpower,' Taylor said. 'Conventional military wisdom states that an attacking force should outnumber the defenders by three to one. You're drastically short of that.'

'So they're calling it off?'

'They gave it serious consideration. But given the stakes, we're willing to proceed as planned. The four of you will continue to train and carry out the mission as discussed.'

Bald wrinkled his brow. 'Any word on when the hostage is being moved?'

'We're expecting the call from Gallardo's contact at any moment. Should be within the next twenty-four hours. Could be less.'

'What about that distraction for the barracks? Can you tell us anything more?'

'Langley checked in with the team handling it. They're working round the clock. It's a big effort. We think they should be able to deploy soon after you've arrived at the LUP. Once it's ready to trigger, you'll have a thirty-minute warning to move into your final assault positions. That's all I know.'

'How soon will we move out?' asked Porter. 'Once we hear from the colonel?'

'You'll leave as soon as we get the call, confirming the hostage is en route. Any delay will simply give more time for President

Vasquez's cronies to interrogate the hostage. More time for them to torture her.'

'What about the military reinforcements?'

'They're still at least another two days away, as far as we know. But any extra delay and it'll be too late for us.'

'We need a replacement for McGee,' Hulk protested. 'Four of us makes the operation difficult.'

'I understand. But my hands are tied. There's no time for Langley to send someone else down.'

'Fuck it,' Bald said. 'We'll do better with four. No passengers.'

'Going to be a close-run thing,' Dudley said, sucking in a breath.

'It was going to be anyway. At least this way, we won't have some steroid-addicted halfwit cocking it up.'

Taylor grabbed his phone and nodded at the faces around the table. 'I'll leave you to sort out the details. Proceed with your training. You'll leave as soon as we've heard back from Colonel Gallardo.'

He ducked out of the meeting house and wandered down the main track, slapping bugs away with one hand and cursing under his breath as he dialled a number. Porter watched him go and scrunched up his face in thought.

'Why are they so keen to push on with the op?' he wondered.

'No point trying to second guess their motives,' Bald said. 'Same deal as Vauxhall. May as well read the fucking tea leaves.'

Hulk nodded. 'John's right. All we can do is keep on planning for the mission. Get everything straight. Make sure we're ready for when we get the signal.'

'You're not worried about the odds?' asked Porter.

'We've faced worse in the Regiment,' said Bald.

'But with backup.'

'Doesn't matter. It still comes down to guys like us on the ground, going in and doing the business.'

'We're heavily outnumbered, Jock.'

'That Claymore will knock out most of the defenders. That's our trump card. We detonate that fucker, we'll have the woman out of there before the remaining guards can get themselves organised.'

'And if it doesn't?'

'It will,' Bald insisted.

'Let's hope so. Because one thing's for sure.'

'What's that?'

'We're down to the bare bones now. There's four of us left and no support.' Porter swallowed hard. 'If this thing goes wrong, it's going to go badly wrong.'

They worked through the evening and returned to the range the following morning to practise the assault. There was a lot of ground to cover. They had to figure out how to work the plan with a four-man team instead of five. There was some debate over whether to abandon the sniper or slim down the assault team. In the end, they settled on a three-man assault team. The sniper's role was critical to the mission, they felt. Porter would plant the charge and the Claymore, with Dudley, Bald and Hulk covering him. He would then link up with Bald and Hulk and initiate the assault on the guardhouse, with Dudley taking down any remaining defenders from his position on the hillock.

They did a few more real-time run-throughs, rehearsing the plan to death. They wanted to get themselves well trained, refining their tactics as much as possible, so that they were ready for the mission the moment they got the signal. There was nothing else for them to do for the next few hours except train, and wait.

Taylor had told them the previous afternoon that they could expect the call from Gallardo's contact within twenty-four hours. *So we'll hear before three o'clock today*, thought Bald. *Two or three more hours on the range, fine-tuning their drills and tactics. And then we'll get the green light.*

They broke for lunch and returned in the early afternoon to practise a few basic contact drills. Nothing complicated. Just some rudimentary fire-and-move drills, getting down on the ground, then rising to their feet and breaking forward, putting down live rounds on a bunch of paper targets stapled to the plywood staves at one end of the gully. Making sure that everyone on the assault team knew how to work together, getting a feel for each other's individual strengths and weaknesses.

Hulk and Bald were equally matched, hitting their targets in close groupings. Porter ran the contact drill last, with the others looking on from the sidelines as he ran forward with his M4, breathing hard and sweating heavily as he dropped to a kneeling firing position and squeezed off two rounds at the targets, before scrambling to his feet and racing forward again. When he had finished, he stood to one side, gasping for breath while Bald, Hulk and Dudley approached the paper target.

'I'll be damned,' Hulk said, chewing hard on a wad of tobacco as he tore the paper from the stave and held it up to the sunlight. 'Look at that. Off target. Every single one of them.'

Dudley spat on the ground and peered at Porter. 'You sure you're ex-SAS?'

Hulk crumpled the target into a ball and tossed it aside. 'Try again,' he said. 'Maybe try, you know, hitting the target this time.'

The two Americans laughed and joked among themselves as they retreated to the edge of the range. Bald lingered beside his mucker, giving him the evil eye.

'Fucking abysmal. You're turning us both into a laughing stock.'

'It's a spot of rustiness,' Porter said. 'I just need a few runs to sort myself out.'

'Bollocks. Look at you. You're out of breath, for fuck's sake.'

Porter glared at him. 'It's just one bad drill. Nothing more.'

Bald stepped closer, lowering his voice. 'You've been on easy street for too long. That's your problem. All them months working jobs in London, house-sitting for billionaires. You've turned soft.'

'I know what I'm doing.'

'Them rounds you just fired say otherwise.'

Porter stared at him.

'Smarten the fuck up,' Bald went on. 'If you're having trouble moving, slow down. But make sure you get them rounds on target.'

Something snapped inside Porter. He took a step towards Bald, trembling with anger. 'Get off my back, Jock. I've got this sorted.'

'You'd bloody better,' Bald said. 'We're about to get into a scrap with a load of armed guards. If we're going to survive, we'll need to have each other's backs.'

Porter pursed his lips and stared at him.

'You might be clean as a whistle these days,' Bald added, 'but if you've lost your edge, you're going to be about as much use to us as a one-armed man in a shoe-tying contest.'

Porter stormed off and went through the drill again while Bald and the Americans watched him warily from the sidelines. Twenty minutes later, at two o'clock, they were interrupted by a shout from the edge of the gully. Bald wheeled round and saw Taylor hurrying over from the track leading to the camp.

'I just got off the phone with Langley. Colonel Gallardo has heard from his contact in Caracas. The hostage is on the move.'

'Are we sure?' asked Hulk.

'The lieutenant saw her leave the building. He made a clear visual identification. It's definitely Fuller.'

Bald said, 'When did she leave?'

'An hour ago.'

Bald thought it through. From the maps of Venezuela they had studied the previous evening, he knew that Caracas was a ninety-minute drive from the president's estate. Which meant that Fuller would arrive at the stronghold at around 15.30.

'The chiefs have given the operation the green light,' Taylor continued. 'This thing is for real, gentlemen. Finish up here and grab your stuff. Assemble in front of the parade ground in thirty minutes.'

They quit the range at once and hurried back to the main camp. Grabbed their daysacks and equipment from their bashas and carried out final checks on their weaponry, stashing spare ammo clips and accessories in the pouches of their tactical vests and taking care of any last-minute admin. Nobody wanted to leave anything vital behind. Twenty-nine minutes later, Bald, Porter, Hulk and Dudley made their way over to the parade ground near the front of the guerrillas' camp.

They were dressed in a mixture of camouflage kit, olive-green shirts and trousers and Gore-Tex boots. Some of the items had been taken from the guerrillas' stores, or from their own personal backpacks. Their OG clothing came from the supplies provided by Taylor. They were carrying their suppressed M4s with rail attachments, plus five thirty-round clips of 5.56x45mm ammo for each man, stored in the pouches on the front of their plate carriers along with their compact fold-up binoculars.

They wore their Glock 17 pistols on their belt holsters, with two seventeen-round magazines of 9x19mm Parabellum rounds. Each member of the team carried a daysack loaded up with two bottles of drinking water, fresh fruit and bread taken from the camp stores, with a poncho in case they had to lie up some-where. Also inside the daysack: three L2 fragmentation grenades, Claymore mines and shell dressings. Bald carried the empty milk container filled with detergent and fuel in his daysack. They also carried their passports, credit cards and $4,000 in carry-around cash, along with their CIA phones and portable charger units. Everything they would need for the long journey ahead of them.

Bald and Porter were leaving their Six-issued phones behind. Along with their go-bags, civilian clothing and sundry personal items. They would be taken to the US embassy in Bogotá, Taylor had assured them, once he left the camp. Arrangements could then be made through Vauxhall for their items to be returned to them.

Taylor was waiting for them beside the parade ground, dressed in his Bermuda shorts and linen shirt and a pair of Havaianas flip-flops. The guy was dripping in sweat. His shirt was soaked through. The patches under his arms were the size of lagoons. He padded at his brow and neck with a handkerchief in a futile attempt to keep his condition under control.

Zapata and Reyes stood next to the CIA officer. Reyes was bent down beside her colleague, tying the laces on her mud-caked boots. Bald allowed himself a moment to appreciate her fine arse.

'Ready?' Taylor asked. Sweat gushed down his pale face.

'As we'll ever be,' Hulk replied.

Taylor nodded. 'You'll leave at once and head for the border near San Vicente. Zapata and Reyes will accompany you.' He signalled towards the two guerrillas. 'Uribe assures me they're two of his best people.'

'As long as they get us across,' Porter said.

'We own the route,' Uribe replied confidently. 'We use it for transporting cocaine from the labs to our friends in Venezuela. It's almost a daily trip for us.'

'You must be shifting a lot of coke,' Bald said.

'What can I say?' Uribe grinned. 'Business is good.'

Porter said, 'Someone should notify Strickland. Give her the heads-up.'

Taylor nodded. 'We'll make sure she's in the loop.'

Bald said, 'What's the plan once we get to San Vicente?'

'The guerrillas have a forward staging post, on the Colombian side of the river. You'll wait there until their contact is ready to smuggle you across by boat. Shouldn't take long. You'll be using one of the main trafficking routes to cross the river.'

'Is it safe?'

Uribe nodded keenly. 'Very. My people control the land on both sides of the river. Police in that area don't fuck with us. Military don't fuck with us. Even the other gangs don't give us no shit. You won't have any trouble getting across.'

'I'd prefer it if we were going in civvies,' Dudley said. 'Something a little more discreet. We're going to stand out, dressed like this.'

Uribe chuckled. 'Lots of thieves use the same route. Traffickers. People smuggling contraband. All kinds. You won't stand out. Not on the trails. Everybody using them is breaking the law.'

'What happens once we get to the other side of the river?' asked Porter.

'One of the guerrillas' Venezuelan contacts will meet you there,' Taylor explained. 'They'll provide you with onward transportation and essential supplies.'

'Is he reliable?'

'We use him all the time,' Uribe said. 'He works for the cartels. Transports cocaine to the fishing villages. Never let us down before. He'll be there.'

'He'd fucking better be,' Bald said.

'He's being paid handsomely,' Taylor emphasised. 'The money we're paying him, he'll do his job. Once you've made it across the border, proceed directly to your objective. You'll hear from us as soon as we have confirmation that the distraction for the army base is ready.'

Bald said, 'How will we know when that distraction deploys?'

Taylor smiled and said, 'Don't worry. You'll know.'

He took a step back, nodded and winked at Hulk. Hulk laughed. Like the two of them were sharing some private dirty joke. Bald wondered about that for a moment. Then Uribe barked an order at Reyes and Zapata and the two guerrillas slung their weapons over their shoulders and motioned for Bald and the others to follow them out of the camp. Taylor said his goodbyes and shook hands with them in turn. Bald pumped his clammy hand and noticed the excitable look in his eyes. The guy looked almost elated. A considerable improvement on his mood a few hours ago. Perhaps he was just glad to be finally checking out of the camp. No more uncomfortable days in the jungle, sweating to death. Bald shoved the thought from his mind.

Two minutes later, they were setting off for the border.

TWENTY

The mid-afternoon sun poked through the gaps in the canopy as they followed a well-trodden track heading away from the camp. Daniela Reyes led the way, with Bald a short distance behind, enjoying the view. Then Porter and Hulk and Dudley, with Zapata bringing up the rear as the tail-end Charlie, his bandoliers of ammunition clinking against one another. They marched at irregular distances from one another, making themselves less noticeable to any hidden observers, with Reyes acting as lead scout, holding her weapon in a two-handed grip. Not for the first time, Bald found himself secretly admiring the professionalism of the guerrillas. They definitely weren't mugs. He almost wished they were taking part in the stronghold assault.

We could do with the extra firepower. That's for fucking sure.

Reyes set a decent pace as she led the team north through the jungle. Bald and Porter easily matched her stride, but after a couple of miles the bulkier ex-SEALs were soon breathing heavily, snatching at the clammy air as they struggled to keep up. Bald glanced over his shoulder and wrung a smile out of the corner of his mouth.

'Looks like those two are feeling the pace,' he said in a low voice.

'They're not the only ones.' Porter wiped sweat from his brow and shook his head. 'Humping kit through the trees. Last time I was doing this must have been on Selection.'

'When was that? Before or after the Stone Age?'

Porter made a screw-face. 'Know what the sad thing is, Jock? You actually think you're funny.'

'Doesn't matter,' said Bald. 'Don't need to be a comic genius when I've got you for a mate. One look at your pathetic face is enough to make anyone crack up.'

'Wanker.'

'Southern prick.'

Porter laughed and ploughed on through the forest. He would never admit it, but he was at his best when Bald was pushing him, driving him on. The Scot's merciless lashing on the training ground had fired him up, ignited some long-buried urge to prove himself. He had been a Blade once. Earned the right to wear that famous winged dagger. The pinnacle of his professional career. Had to count for something.

I might be a lot older now, he thought. *My body might be broken and battered and scarred. But I still know how to win.*

Bald looked towards Reyes and said, 'How far to the staging post?'

Reyes squinted at the track ahead. 'Another five miles or so. We'll get there before last light.' She glanced back at him, grinning. 'You're feeling tired already, gringo?'

'No chance, lass. I'm fit as fuck.'

She laughed and cocked her chin at Hulk and Dudley. 'Doing better than your friends, then.'

'They're Americans,' Bald said. 'Spend all their time in the gym, lifting weights and pretending to be fucking hard. They're not built for operating in the jungle.'

Reyes made a face. 'I thought American men were supposed to be tough.'

'You should visit Scotland. Full of rock-hard blokes.'

'Like you?'

'Exactly.' He grinned. 'You ever get out of the jungle, you should look us up. I'll show you what a real man is like.'

She gave him a look of disgust and looked ahead as she carried on. After another three miles they crossed a narrow rock-strewn stream and climbed the bank on the far side before descending a muddy slope. The canopy thinned out as they emerged from the dank, claustrophobic gloom of the jungle to the lowlands. They navigated a mass of muddy tracks and slippery undergrowth, interspersed with areas of tropical forest. Bald guessed they were getting closer to the Arauca River.

We're not far from the border now.

At seven thirty they reached the treeline at the edge of a patch of wild forest and Zapata threw up his hand and motioned for them to stop. Fifty metres away, across a bare patch of dirt, stood a single-storey wooden dwelling backing on to a wide parcel of cultivated land. A trio of tin-roofed sheds were situated a short distance from the ranch, the doors padlocked shut. There was a mud-spattered white Chevrolet Silverado pickup truck parked in a carport to the left.

A couple of guys reclined on plastic lawn chairs in front of the shack. Both were dressed in tracksuit bottoms and rubber boots. One of the guys was in his early twenties with a high forehead and heavily lidded eyes and ears like handles on a jug. He wore a bright red tank top and a gold chain around his neck as thick as a boa constrictor. The guy in the other chair looked the same, but older. As if someone had put his face through an ageing app. His skin was the texture of petrified wood. His eyelids were so low they looked like shells glued to his pupils. He had a scar on his cheek and lank black hair plastered to his scalp. Father and son, Bald guessed. The younger guy stared at his phone while the older guy sipped from a bottle of beer.

'This is the place?' asked Bald.

Reyes nodded. 'Wait here.'

Bald, Porter and the two Americans lingered in the treeline, staying out of sight while Reyes and Zapata approached.

At the sight of the two guerrillas the guys on the porch both stood up and moved towards them. Behind them, a plump woman lingered in the open doorway, peering out of the shadows.

Reyes stopped in front of the ranch. There was a brief exchange with the older man, accompanied by lots of exaggerated hand gestures and pointing in the direction of the Americans and Brits in the shadows. Bald got the gist of it.

'We've brought some people with us,' Reyes was saying. 'They're going to stay here for a short while.'

After a couple of minutes, the older guy nodded his assent and Reyes beckoned the others to join them.

The guy in the red tank top watched them as they drew nearer and nodded a cautious greeting at the party. Reyes introduced them.

'These people are the Canales family,' she said. 'Diego and his son, Junior. We'll be staying here for the next nine hours.'

Junior said something to them in gruff Spanish. Diego just stood there and smiled. Neither of them could speak a word of English, apparently. Both father and son had the worn look of people who lived a hardscrabble existence, surviving from day to day, barely making ends meet.

'Can we trust these people?' asked Bald.

'They're friends of ours. Technically, this place is a farm, but they work for us on the side.'

'Doing what?'

'Watching the trail. Supplying intelligence. Transporting supplies to the river. Many things.'

She led Bald and the others through the door and down a narrow hallway. To the left was a small kitchen. The fat woman sat at the kitchen table, peeling a bowl of potatoes while she watched some domestic soap opera on an old TV. She paid no attention to the strangers as Reyes ushered them through a door on the right and into a communal living area.

Which could have passed for a crack den, if it had been given an expensive makeover. Cockroaches scuttled across the bare floor. The walls were painted the colour of urine. There was a table in the corner with a vinyl tablecloth and a pair of worn sofas facing a TV showing a football match, and a stained mattress on the floor in the far corner. Someone had made a half-hearted attempt to brighten the place up. A handful of football shirts, scarfs and flags hung from the walls.

Hulk set his daysack down and glanced round. 'What now?'

'We wait here,' Reyes replied bluntly.

'For how long?'

'Until first light. Then we'll take the trail to the river. Four miles from this place. One of the fishermen will meet us there. He'll take you across the border at first light.'

'Who is he?'

'A Venezuelan. Freddy Vargas. He lives on the other side of the river, but makes his money taking people across illegally. He does a lot of business. Many people come across each day.'

'Refugees?'

'Some,' Reyes said. 'Others send their children to school in Colombia. Many more come to sell gasoline, or food. Anything to make some extra money.'

'Shit must be bad over there,' Dudley said.

'What happens once we get to the other side?' asked Porter.

'You'll land at Freddy's place and wait until our contact from the cartel shows up.'

Bald nodded. He knew from the charts they had consulted back at the camp that first light at this time of the year was around 04.50. An hour to walk the four miles through the lowlands to the border. Half an hour to cross the river. Which meant they would reach the Venezuelan side of the river at around 06.30. They had a long journey ahead of them once they had crossed the border, he knew. An eleven-hour ride to the stronghold. Then the assault and rescue. Then another fourteen-hour drive from the stronghold to the extraction point on the north-western coast, and a boat ride to Port of Spain, Trinidad.

If everything goes according to plan.

'We should get some kip,' he said to the others. 'Might not have another chance for a day or so.'

'We'll go on stag,' Porter suggested. 'Two-hour shifts. In case there's any trouble.'

'No need,' Reyes replied. 'We've got our people covering the approaches, looking out for movement. If there's any problems, they'll raise the alarm.'

'You lot know what you're doing.'

'We're not idiots. How do you think we survived this long?'

Bald stared admiringly at her. Impressive rack. Curves in all the right places. And she knows how to soldier.

My kind of woman.

'Get some rest,' she said. 'We leave at first light.'

They made themselves as comfortable as possible in their grim surroundings. Hulk and Dudley took the two leather sofas. Porter kipped in the armchair. Bald bedded down on the mattress on the floor. They slept through the night and rose half an hour before daylight, fumbling around for their daysacks and kit in the pre-dawn darkness.

At exactly 04.45 Reyes stepped inside the living area and told Bald and the others to follow her. They grabbed their equipment and weaponry and headed outside the ranch. The plump woman was still at the kitchen table, doing chores, the sound of canned laughter from the TV filling the air. Bald wondered if she had been sitting there all night, peeling potatoes.

The first hints of dawn were streaking the horizon as they emerged from the ranch. Zapata was sitting in one of the lawn chairs outside, his weapon resting across his lap as his dull eyes scanned the clearing and the dirt track ahead. Diego Canales and his son were kneeling down beside the sheds at the side of the dwelling. The door to the nearest shed had been unlocked and a bunch of brick-sized packets were on the floor next to the two Colombians. Bald counted more than a dozen packages in total. He looked on as the father and son stowed them inside a pair of small backpacks.

'Cocaine,' Reyes said matter-of-factly, noting the suspicious look on Porter's face.

Dudley whistled. 'Fuck of a lot of it, too. There's enough blow to keep half of New York coked up for a month.'

'Where'd this stuff come from?' Hulk asked.

'The labs. We send it to them from the camp. They process it and bring it here. Our friends look after it for us in the sheds, and then we smuggle it across the border.'

Porter glanced accusingly at her. 'Nobody said anything about smuggling a load of coke across the border with us.'

She shrugged. 'This is what we do.'

'You're using this operation to smuggle drugs. You're making us complicit, for fuck's sake.'

'Get off your high horse,' Dudley said. 'This shit's going across the border with or without us. They're just being economical.'

'This is wrong,' Porter muttered as he turned to Bald.

'What did you expect, mate? You know what these people do for a living.'

'Working with traffickers is one thing. Going across with this shit is something else. We shouldn't be doing it. They're making us a target, as well. What if the border forces find this stuff?'

'They won't. Uribe told us they control the route. Stop getting your knickers in a twist.'

'I don't like it any more than you,' Hulk said, lowering his voice. 'But we're not in any position to argue. In case you didn't notice, this is the guerrillas' rat run. We're relying on them to get us across.'

'Exactly,' said Bald. 'Now stop fucking sermonising and get a move on. We're wasting time.'

Porter stood still for a moment longer, anger pulsing in his veins. Then he took in a deep breath and the rage subsided.

Forget the cocaine, the voice told him. *Focus on the mission.*

He checked his watch: 04.54. Fourteen hours since Fuller had arrived at the president's mansion.

We've got to get across that border. Rescue her before the interrogators can do their worst.

Forty-eight hours from now, this will all be over. We'll be back on friendly soil with the hostage, celebrating the end of the mission. And this will just be a bad memory.

If we live that long.

TWENTY-ONE

They bugged out of the ranch, moving in the same formation as before. Reyes in the lead, with Bald and the rest of the team following and Zapata at the back. The two guerrillas carrying the backpacks stuffed with pure cocaine. Bald saw Reyes give Diego Canales a thick wad of dollar bills before they left. The family stayed behind at the ranch, watching the party from the doorway as they set off down the track.

The sun was glowing faintly on the horizon, lightening the star-pricked sky as they diverted off the main track and followed a narrow muddy path that corkscrewed between clumps of tall trees. The trail would take them to the river, Reyes said. After a mile or so they passed a clearing filled with a vast sprawl of flimsy-looking shacks and tents. The local slum, Reyes explained. People with less than nothing, living on one meal a day and working for a few pesos. Bald tried to feel some sympathy for these wretched souls and came up empty. He had some abstract sense of their plight. But their suffering was irrelevant to him. He wasn't interested in the misery of the masses. He was interested solely in the fortunes of John Bald. Joining the ranks of the one per cent. That was his ambition. Leave the hand-wringing to smug liberal types.

They carried on for another mile and then took a back road and continued west along the trail, on a parallel course with the Arauca River. Clusters of armed guards patrolled the side of the path, dressed in jeans and designer polo shirts, clutching their rifles and looking hard. Reyes waved at them as they passed and got a nodded greeting in return. A loose line of people plodded along the side of the road, lugging empty containers and backpacks. Early risers, heading for the river, said Reyes. They would head into Venezuela to purchase goods, then cross back into Colombia and sell their merchandise at a mark-up.

'What's left over there to sell?' Bald wondered.

'Gas, mostly. They nearly give that stuff away in Venezuela. You smuggle it across the border, make a good profit.'

'At least that stuff's harmless,' Porter said. 'Not like the load of coke we're carrying.'

An amused smile crossed Reyes's lips. She nudged Bald. 'Your friend is not a fan of our business?'

'He's a moralist, lass. Sees everything in black and white. Believes in right and wrong.'

'And you don't?'

Bald laughed. 'I've seen too much of the world to be that daft.'

'What do you believe in?'

'Rules of the jungle. There's no good or bad in this world. Just the weak and the strong. In this life, you're either the sheep in the pen, or the wolf prowling it.'

'And which one are you?'

'The wolf,' said Bald. 'Always be the wolf.'

He winked at her, hoping she would be impressed.

She smiled fondly. 'You're not like any man I met before.'

I'm in here, thought Bald. *She's up for it.*

'My boyfriend would like you,' she said. 'Maybe one day, I introduce you.'

Bald tried to mask his disappointment and surprise. 'You've got a fella?'

'In the camp.'

Bald grinned. 'We're a long way from there, lass.'

'What are you suggesting?'

'You should try a bit of Scottish while you've still got the chance. See what it's like to be with a real man.'

'Sleep with a capitalist pig.' Reyes laughed at the absurdity of it. 'Never. I rather die.'

She moved ahead of him, shaking her head. Bald watched her walk on with a hungry look in his eyes.

Half a mile later, they reached some sort of checkpoint operated by the guerrillas. A pair of guards stood beside the track, stopping each person in line and extracting wads of cash from them before allowing them to continue. Bald and the others breezed past the guards and continued along the path as it coursed north through patches of forest and swampland. At almost six o'clock the trail was busy. He saw grizzled blokes in sleeveless tops and baseball caps lugging jerry cans of petrol and sacks of freshly slaughtered meat. There were tired-looking families carrying suitcases, mothers cradling their babies. Most of the people were heading in the opposite direction, crossing over from the Venezuelan side of the river. No one paid any attention to the heavily armed foreigners. Bald remembered what Uribe had told them, back at the camp.

You won't stand out. Not on the trails.

Everybody using them is breaking the law.

Nine minutes later, as the sun rose above the trees, they reached the southern bank of the Arauca River.

Bald and the others followed Reyes across a curved patch of sand strewn with rubbish. A thin crowd of people had gathered higher up the bank, some sitting on upturned plastic crates or standing beside their bags while they waited for their turn to cross by boat.

More armed guards stood among them, scanning the water for any sign of a threat. Several brightly painted canoes with outboard motors were moored alongside the bank, their bows resting on the shingle. The boats were considerably longer than a standard kayak. Fifteen metres from bow to stern, Bald estimated. Enough space to accommodate a dozen smugglers. Or four armed ex-Special Forces operators and a couple of backpacks stuffed full of coke.

Bald squinted at the river. It was no more than a hundred and fifty metres wide. On the far side he could make out the opposite bank. Venezuelan soil. There wasn't much to see. Just a long dull belt of land dotted with palm trees and huts.

'This is the crossing point?' asked Porter.

Reyes nodded.

'Where's our boat?'

'Follow me.'

She threaded her way across the bank towards a boat with a yellow-painted hull, tied to the trunk of a tree leaning over the edge of the riverbank. A fisherman in bright pink shorts and a Taylor Swift T-shirt was kneeling beside the stern, checking the motor, while a skinny guy with an unkempt black beard folded up a tangle of fishing nets. At the sight of Reyes and the others approaching Black Beard said something to the bloke in the Taylor Swift shirt and the latter promptly stepped out of the boat and padded up the sand to greet them. Reyes said a few words to him before she turned to the team.

'This is Freddy Vargas,' she said. 'He's going to take you across the river.'

Bald looked at the guy. He was barefoot, with a lazy left eye and the worst teeth Bald had ever seen, yellowed and crooked and stubby. When he smiled, it looked like the guy was chewing on a mouthful of cigarette butts.

'You sure that thing will get us over, mate?' Bald asked, gesturing towards the boat. The paintwork on the hull was filthy. There was less than six inches of freeboard.

The fisherman's smile widened. 'I work this river for twenty years. Boat never let me down yet.'

'Freddy will take you to his place,' Reyes said. 'Miguel will meet you there.'

Bald frowned. 'Miguel?'

'Our Venezuelan contact. From the cartel. He'll deliver your vehicle.'

'You're not coming with us?'

Reyes shook her head quickly. 'Our job is done. We have people on the other side of the border who move the product on for us.'

Bald checked his watch again and made a quick calculation. If they left now, they'd reach the fisherman's home at around 06.30. From there, they were looking at an eleven-hour car ride to the mansion. Taylor had told them to be in position at their LUP by midnight.

We need to be on the road before midday, he thought. *Absolute latest. Any later, and we won't have enough time to carry out the assault.*

'Your mate had better not keep us waiting for long,' he growled. 'We're on the clock here.'

Reyes said, 'Miguel has orders from his own bosses. They'll want the cocaine to be moved on quickly. He won't mess about.'

'You're sure he's on the level?'

'We've worked with him for years.'

Vargas squinted at the river. 'We need to move now. Before the patrols.'

'Patrols?' Porter repeated.

Vargas clicked his tongue and nodded. 'Navy. They sweep the river, looking for smugglers. Got fast boats.'

'What happens if we run into them?'

'We can't outrun them. This boat not fast enough. We see them, we run for the shore. Hope for the best.'

'And if they catch us?'

Vargas made a throat-slitting gesture.

'What the fuck are you boys waiting for, then?' Hulk said. 'Enough talking. Let's get a move on.'

Reyes unhooked her backpack and handed it to Black Beard. Zapata did the same. Black Beard loaded the packs on to the boat, placing them on the floor in the stern sheets. At the same time Vargas took up his position at the tiller and motioned for Bald and the others to climb aboard. Bald went first, then Porter and Hulk and Dudley, the canoe rocking from side to side as they stepped around the fishing gear and crowded the floor beside the back-packs near the stern. Once they were seated Vargas yanked on the starter cord until the motor eventually fired up. Then Black Beard untied the line from the palm tree and Vargas operated the tiller, manoeuvring the boat away from the riverbank. Reyes and Zapata stood on the sand for a moment, watching them leave before they made their way back up the bank towards the trail. Bald looked on ruefully as the shag of a lifetime disappeared from view.

'I think your magic's fading, mate,' Porter said.

'Just a matter of time. Another hour or two, she'd have been all over me.'

Porter laughed. 'I thought you were supposed to be irresistible to women.'

'Fuck off.'

A few minutes later they were gliding across the water, heading away from San Vicente. Towards Venezuela and the stronghold. As they carried on down the river Porter looked towards the distant bank.

His stomach muscles automatically tensed as he ran his eyes over the dark line of the horizon. He forced himself to shut out the dark thoughts in his head. The ones telling him that Jock was right. That his best days were behind him. That he didn't know how to soldier anymore. He told himself to focus absolutely on the mission.

This is it, he thought. *Twenty-four hours from now, we'll either be heroes or dead.*

TWENTY-TWO

They cruised west for half an hour, the motor sounding like a chainsaw as they skimmed along the grey surface. Vargas was a steady hand on the tiller, skilfully navigating a series of sharp bends in the river. Bald and the other passengers kept an eye out for any sign of an approaching patrol, but the horizon remained blissfully clear. They passed a handful of canoes along the route, loaded down with people and contraband as they shuttled back and forth across the banks. An entire underground economy, right in front of their eyes.

The sun climbed higher into the sky, beating down on the passengers in the boat. By six thirty the heat was oppressive. They cleared another bend and then Vargas eased the throttle, slowing the motor down as he angled the canoe towards a small wooden jetty extending from a bank on the Venezuelan side of the river. Higher up the bank Bald spotted a pair of thatched-roof shacks surrounded by trees and bushes. Several fishing nets had been left out to dry, hanging from long wooden poles supported by branches driven into the ground beside the shack. A middle-aged woman in denim shorts and a loose-fitting T-shirt sat beside the poles, repairing another net. Two kids, a boy and a girl, played in the dirt beside the shack. A bare-chested guy in a pair of orange shorts was busy inspecting the drying nets.

As the boat drew closer Black Beard called out and the guy in the orange shorts scrabbled down the side of the bank and approached the jetty. The canoe bumped gently against the post and Black Beard snatched up a rope from the floor and tossed it across. The bloke in the orange shorts grabbed the end of the line and secured it around a stout post, and then Vargas switched off the motor.

'This is it,' he said. 'We're here.'

Black Beard clambered out of the boat first. Hulk followed him, and then Dudley disembarked, followed by Porter and Bald. Black Beard unloaded the two backpacks from the wet floor of the canoe and passed them to Orange Shorts, while Vargas guided the four ex-soldiers across the jetty, the worn timbers groaning under their Gore-Tex boots. They climbed the bank and passed the woman repairing the fishing nets – Vargas' wife, Bald guessed. She spared the men a quick glance before she went back to her sewing. The kids ignored them, giggling and laughing as they kicked around an old tennis ball. None of them seemed bothered about a bunch of armed guys showing up on their doorstep. Maybe it wasn't a big deal around here, Bald thought. When you lived on one of the main drug-trafficking routes, you probably saw a lot of blokes packing heat.

Vargas stopped in front of the larger of the two huts, pointed to a set of upturned crates outside. 'You wait here, okay?'

'Anyone likely to bother us?' asked Hulk.

'Not here. No one else for miles. Just us.'

Vargas swept his arm in a broad arc around him. Bald instantly saw what the guy meant. They were in an isolated area of the riverside, nestled amid screens of tangled bushes, trees and grass. To the north, beyond the huts, a rutted path ran like a lizard's tongue between slabs of dense forest. The only route to and from the Vargas property, other than the river. If anyone tried approaching, the inhabitants would hear them from a mile off.

'Miguel, the cartel guy, he'll be along soon. Bring your ride.'

'We need to be out of here in five hours,' Hulk said. 'Maximum.'

'He'll come before then. Don't worry. You'll have plenty of time.'

Vargas left them to it. Made his way back over to the jetty, chatting in Spanish with Orange Shorts and Black Beard.

The four ex-soldiers set down their weapons, sat on the crates and ate a light breakfast. Fresh fruit and stale bread from their daysacks, washed down with mouthfuls of water. Outside, the kids played tennis-football while Black Beard and Orange Shorts carted the coke-filled backpacks over to the smaller shack. Which was little more than a thatched roof supported by four poles, over a bare dirt floor. They dumped the backpacks outside the hut, next to a stack of spare car tyres and a machine that looked like a mechanical lathe turned on its side. A metal turntable rested on top of a large box-shaped unit fitted with a pair of foot pedals. A metal head shaped like a duck's bill was fixed to the end of an adjustable arm above the plate. The unit was rigged up to a small generator outside the shack. Bald had worked with vehicles long enough to know what he was looking at. A car tyre changer. Specialist equipment, usually found in commercial garages. He briefly wondered why the fishermen owned one. Maybe they had a tyre repair business on the side.

Orange Shorts and Black Beard returned to the boat and began loading up equipment. Vargas made a call on a mobile phone so old it probably needed carbon dating. The woman just sat there, mending the nets with her needles and twine.

The team checked and re-checked bits of kit. They pored over their maps and waited.

Three hours later, a few minutes before eleven o'clock, they heard a low rumble in the distance.

Bald and the others snatched up their weapons and stood up from the crates. A hundred metres away, a pair of wagons came barrelling down the rough track towards the shacks, dirt spewing behind them. At the same time Vargas, Orange Shorts and Black Beard left the jetty and climbed the bank, hurrying over to greet the new arrivals, while the woman ushered the two kids inside the larger dwelling.

'Looks like our ride's here,' Hulk said.

'Took the prick long enough,' Bald replied.

The two wagons hit the end of the track and skidded to a halt in front of the shacks. The lead vehicle was a cherry red pickup truck. A big beast of a vehicle, and nearly brand new. The car behind it was a white Toyota Land Cruiser, with a rounded body and square-shaped headlamps and rust spots on the front fenders. A late-nineties model, Bald guessed. Older than the pickup truck, for sure.

A fat guy wearing a gold crucifix got out of the pickup. A moment later, a second guy hopped down from behind the wheel of the Land Cruiser. He was medium height and build, with short black hair and gold-framed sunglasses, and a head so flat it looked like someone had dropped a piano on it. He had a pistol jammed in the waistband of his jeans. The polymer butt jutted out, digging into his slight paunch as he swaggered over to Vargas. He said a few brief words to the fisherman before turning towards the team.

'This is Miguel,' Vargas said, introducing him. 'He's the courier.'

Miguel peered at them above his shades. 'You're the friends of Commander Uribe, eh?'

'Something like that,' Hulk said.

Miguel paused as he glanced briefly at the weapons they were holding. 'That's a lot of fucking firepower.'

Hulk ignored the question. 'Where's our vehicle, friend?'

Miguel chucked a set of car keys at him and waved a hand at the Land Cruiser. 'She's all yours. Ready to go.'

'Extra gas?'

'Five jerry cans. A hundred litres. As promised. In the trunk.' Miguel's eyes narrowed. 'Got a long journey ahead of you, bro?'

'None of your goddamn business,' Dudley said.

Hulk tossed the car keys to the redneck. 'Go check the wagon, Brendan. Make sure it's all in order. Any problems, holler.'

'Roger that.'

Dudley trudged over to the Land Cruiser. Hulk reached for his CIA phone and started to walk away. 'Where are you going?' Porter asked.

'To find a signal. Check in with Taylor. Tell him we're across the border. See if he's got any updates.'

He moved off towards the dirt track while Miguel sparked up a cigarette and stood to one side of the group, shouting occasional instructions. A few metres away, Crucifix grabbed a tyre iron from inside the pickup truck, circled round to the rear and inserted one end of the iron into a hole in the bumper. Then he started rotating the handle, lowering the spare tyre stored on the underside of the truck to the ground.

As soon as the tyre was free, Black Beard lifted it up and carried it over to the changer unit in the smaller hut. He placed the tyre on the turntable, swung the arm round and positioned it over the tyre, with the duck-bill-shaped head tight against the rim.

He grabbed a metal lever and began prising the rubber beading away from the rim, working the pedals until the tyre was halfway loose. Orange Shorts tipped the packets of cocaine out of the two backpacks and passed one to Black Beard. The latter crammed the first package inside the hollow of the tyre, placing it along the deeper middle section of the rim. They shoved the rest of the coke bricks inside, and then Black Beard moved the arm back into position over the wheel and pumped the pedal, pressing down with his knuckles and spinning the plate round until the tyre popped back into place. Sealing the drugs inside.

Bald looked on as Black Beard hefted up the coke-filled tyre and hauled it over to the pickup truck. Orange Shorts grabbed a couple of toothpaste-sized tubes from a bucket beside the hut. He took a knee beside the tyre and started applying a translucent gel, smearing it across the treads.

'What's that stuff for?' Bald wondered aloud.

'Pain relief gel,' Miguel said. 'Got all kinds of stuff in it. Eucalyptus. Menthol.' He took a hit on his cigarette, exhaled. 'Fucks with the sniffer dogs, you know? They smell that shit, they back off. Can't stand it.'

'Crafty,' Bald said approvingly.

Porter gave him a reproachful look. 'I can't believe you're okay with this.'

'Even if you don't approve of their trade, you've got to respect the tactics. This is a slick operation.'

Miguel dashed his cigarette and moved off to inspect the gel-smeared tyre, giving it a kick to make sure the coke was secured inside. Then Orange Shorts slid it back under the truck and Crucifix spun the jack handle, hoisting the tyre back into place. Bald gave it a longing look as it disappeared from sight. 'We're in the wrong profession, mate. Should be doing this.'

'You're not serious.'

'Why not? Less risky than what we're doing. This lot must be raking it in.'

'Not just them,' Vargas said. 'Others get rich too.'

'How's that?' asked Bald.

Vargas pointed with his eyes at the truck. 'All of this stuff goes to the coast. Then across the sea. Some shipments get lost.' He flashed his rotten teeth. 'Then people hunt for the white lobster.'

'What the fuck is that?'

'The currents. They bring the cocaine to the beach. At a place called Suarez. People go out on fast boats and fish for the packets. Sell them back to the cartels.' He rubbed his thumb and forefinger together in a universal gesture. 'Make big money.'

'Lucky bastards,' Bald muttered.

Hulk came back over, putting his phone away. Porter nodded at the ex-SEAL. 'Anything to report?'

'No answer. I sent him a message. Told him we're across.'

Once the tyre had been secured underneath the truck, Crucifix grabbed a screwdriver and set of stick-on licence plates from the back seat. He dropped to a knee beside the front licence plate. Unscrewed it and replaced it with a clean stick-on plate secured with double-sided tape. Did the same for the back plate and dumped the old ones in the rear seat of the pickup. Then Miguel pumped Vargas's hand and gave him a wedge of dollar bills. Around the same size as the one Reyes had given to the Canales family, back at the ranch.

A few moments later, Dudley made his way back over from the Land Cruiser. Nodded at Hulk.

'Well?'

'Looks good,' Dudley said. 'Nothing wrong with her, far as I can tell. She'll get us there.'

Miguel beamed. 'See, bro. Told you.' He stepped back and spread his hands. 'Now, where's my money?'

Hulk's eyebrows climbed up his face in surprise. 'What money? You've been paid already. Our people have taken care of that.'

'Price has doubled.'

'Bullshit.'

'Think we're idiots?' Miguel waved an arm at the foreigners. 'You guys come over here, packing enough guns to start a fucking war. You're up to some shit.'

'Our business doesn't concern you.'

'Wrong, bro. Whatever you're doing, it means more risk for me and my people. We do business with you, maybe it brings some heat our way. You want the wheels, you need to pay extra.'

'How much?' asked Dudley.

Miguel narrowed his eyes in calculation. 'Twenty thousand.'

'We can't do it,' Hulk said. 'We don't have that kind of money on us.'

'Then we have a problem.'

Bald watched the Venezuelan closely. Behind him, four metres away, Crucifix leaned against the side of the truck with his arms folded across his chest. The guy also had a pistol stuffed in the waistband of his jeans, Bald saw. Vargas was standing beside Porter and Bald and Hulk in a line in front of Miguel, with Orange Shorts and Black Beard further to the right, near the smaller hut. The woman and kids were nowhere to be seen. Sheltering inside the main shack, he guessed.

Hulk said, 'You need to speak to the guerrillas. They'll pass a message to our people. They'll pay up.'

'No good,' Miguel said. 'You give me the money now. Or maybe I make a call to my friends in the police. Tell them about the four armed gringos who just came across the river.'

No one moved.

'You deaf, bro? Pay the fuck up.'

Then Bald raised his M4 and shot Miguel in the face.

The Venezuelan didn't see the round coming. His attention wasn't focused on Bald. His ferret-like eyes were fixed on Hulk, waiting for a payday that would never come.

The round spat out of the snout of the suppressed rifle and slammed into Miguel's head at close range. The shockwave liquefied his brain, spewing melted grey matter out of the back of his skull in a bright-red mush. His head snapped back and then his arms flopped and he tumbled heavily to the ground a few metres away from Hulk. As if someone had just told him he'd win a million bucks if he played dead.

In the periphery of his vision, Bald saw a sudden flicker of movement six metres away. He glanced over at the pickup truck and saw Crucifix reaching for his pistol.

Bald arced his weapon across in a flash and emptied three rounds in a quick burst at the target. Two bullets struck Crucifix in the upper chest, punching a couple of holes in his lungs. The third round chinned him as he fell away, the lower half of his face exploding in a spray of blood and bone fragments. He nose-dived to the ground and face-planted next to the truck. His chunky gold crucifix gleamed amid the puddles of blood.

A cold silence lingered over the dirt path for a half-beat. Then Bald heard the hysterical wails of the children inside the main shack, accompanied by the high-pitched shrieks of their mother. Orange Shorts and Black Beard had hit the dirt, lying face down on the ground next to the upturned crates. Freddy Vargas just stood there, rooted to the spot with fear and horror.

Porter, Hulk and Dudley had raised their weapons as soon as the first round had been fired. An instinctive reaction, drilled into them over decades of combat. Weapons trained on the two dead bodies, fingers lightly resting on the triggers. Ready to neutralise any threat.

Bald lowered his M4. So did Hulk and Dudley.

Porter dropped his gun arm to his side.

He spun round towards Bald. 'Jesus Christ. The fuck did you do that for?'

Bald pointed his gun barrel at Miguel's lifeless corpse. 'He was a problem. I decided to take care of it.'

'You didn't have to kill him, for fuck's sake,' Porter said as he fought to control his temper. 'We could have sorted this out with the Company.'

Bald shook his head forcefully. 'This guy would have shopped us either way. Doubled his money. That's what I would have done. An hour from now, we'd have every police officer and soldier in the country looking for four white guys in a Toyota Land Cruiser.'

'You killed a fucking cartel lieutenant. We just made an enemy of the cartel. They'll be out for revenge.'

'Couldn't risk him walking away. Or would you prefer to spend the rest of your days rotting in a Venezuelan jail?'

'Your buddy's right,' Hulk added. He nodded in admiration at Bald. 'That's some ruthless shit you just did. Stone cold.'

'Had to be done.'

Hulk dropped down beside Miguel's body. Rifled through his

pockets and took out the keys for the pickup truck. Tossed them to Vargas and said, 'You want to get rich?'

Vargas stood in numbed silence. He looked from the keys to Miguel to Hulk and back again. His eyes were so wide they looked like they might fall out of their sockets.

'Yes,' he said after a pause.

'Then listen carefully. Get rid of the bodies. Weigh them down with rocks and dump them in the river. A few miles downstream from here. Lose the truck, too. Anyone asks, the guys drove off and you never saw them again. Keep the coke, sit on it for a month and then sell it. You'll never have to work on a boat again. Think you can manage that?'

'Yes,' Vargas replied queasily.

'You didn't see us, right? You don't know us. Otherwise we have a problem.'

Vargas evidently saw the remorseless look in Hulk's eyes and held up his hands, shaking his head frantically. 'No problem, mister. I never see you in my life.'

Hulk pointed the tip of his rifle at the shack. 'You got food in there? Water?'

'Some, yes.'

Hulk spun round and nodded at Dudley. 'Grab whatever supplies these people have got. Make it quick. We're leaving.'

Dudley hurried over to the hut and raided their supplies. At the same time Bald, Porter and Hulk fetched their rucksacks and carried them over to the Land Cruiser, the children whimpering inside the hut as their mother desperately tried to calm them down. Hulk popped open the boot and the three operators dumped their bags inside.

Five twenty-litre jerry cans were stowed in the boot. A hundred extra litres of fuel, Bald calculated. Equivalent to twenty-two gallons, give or take a few drops. Plus the full tank. Enough fuel to cover the five-hundred-mile journey to the stronghold, and then the escape to the extraction point further to the east. All for a knockdown price, heavily subsidised by the state.

A few moments later, Dudley came jogging over with a plastic bag and two litre-containers of drinking water. 'Find anything?' Hulk asked, nodding at the bag.

'Plantains, corn cakes. Bread. Some fruit. Not much else.'

'It'll do. Dump it in the boot. Let's get the fuck out of here.'

Hulk shoved his rucksack next to the water bottles and jerry cans. Hooked round to the front passenger side door and climbed inside. Dudley was already on the other side of the wagon, taking the wheel and cranking the engine. Porter stowed his gear in the back and slammed the boot shut. Thirty seconds later they were pulling away from the Vargas property.

Arrowing down the dirt track.

Heading for the stronghold.

TWENTY-THREE

They left at exactly 11.14. Dudley took the wheel for the first leg of the journey. They agreed to drive in three-hour shifts. Make sure they were all fully rested and awake by the time they reached the road junction on the approach to the stronghold. None of them wanted to be going into the mission running on empty. They had a long twenty-four hours ahead of them. The drive to the president's estate, the assault and rescue. Then the dash across country to the extraction point once they had rescued Fuller. Hulk rode shotgun, with Porter and Bald in the back seats, their M4s flat across their laps. The two guys in the front had their rifles stored in the footwells. Barrels pointing down for easy access. If they ran into any trouble, they could raise their weapons in an instant and start putting down rounds.

The Land Cruiser was in good condition, despite its age. The previous owner had treated it well. A modern multimedia display had been retrofitted to the dash, with a bunch of brightly coloured icons and a satnav feature. Dudley punched in the address for Los Altos and followed the directions on the satnav as they roughly followed the course of the Arauca River, running west to east along the Venezuelan border. After twenty miles the road forked.

The mission can go this way, or that way, thought Bald. *Left or right. Win or lose. Live or die.*

They continued east on the metalled road. Coasting along the worn blacktop at sixty miles per hour, staying well below the national speed limit. They kept an eye open for police but getting pulled over was the least of their worries. Taylor had briefed them that law enforcement was virtually non-existent in the border-lands. Gangs and cartels competed for control of the terrain, he

213

had told them, terrorising the locals and building airstrips to ship drugs north to Miami. The police seldom ventured outside of the towns.

The route took them through the flattest landscape Bald had ever seen. Like gazing out across a giant billiard table. He saw endless stretches of farmland, fields of grazing cattle. Plains criss-crossed with estuaries and small brick-built farms, set under a cloudless blue dome. Hard to imagine they were in a country on the brink of collapse. By mid-morning the temperature had climbed into the low thirties and Hulk had cranked the air con up to full blast. Bald was just grateful Taylor wasn't with them in the wagon. The guy would be sweating his own body weight by now.

After around an hour on the road, at twelve-thirty, Hulk's phone buzzed with a message. He read it, hit Delete and put his handset away again.

'Message from Taylor. The team handling the distraction are running final tests. They're still confident that they'll trigger it before first light, but it might take longer than they anticipated.'

'How much longer?'

'He doesn't know. Just says to check in with him once we're at the LUP and await further instructions.'

Porter said, 'Any word on whether Vasquez is going to be there?'

Hulk typed a message to Taylor. Got a reply back two minutes later. 'Still no confirmation on that. But Colonel Gallardo's contact doesn't think the president has arrived yet.'

'Sounds about right,' Bald said. 'The hostage only got there yesterday afternoon. He's not going to rush over, is he? He's got to make arrangements first. Get his security sorted, all of that.'

They drove on. The road contoured around the outskirts of several small towns. Quaint-looking places with pastel-coloured buildings and whitewashed church steeples. Massive billboards overlooked the streets, the president grinning down at his people with his trademark salt-and-pepper beard and cowboy hat. In the streets below, Bald glimpsed derelict storefronts and abandoned factories and closed-down petrol stations. A whole country gone to seed. Socialism at its finest. Amid the decay he spotted a few well-kept baseball pitches and neatly trimmed gardens. Futile attempts to maintain a sense of order in a world of total economic chaos.

They switched drivers at two o'clock, and then again at five. Hulk, then Porter. Each time they went through the same routine, pulling over at a lay-by a few miles beyond the limits of the nearest town. A minute or two to stretch their legs, take a pull from their bottles of water and graze on the corn cakes, fruit and bread while they kept watch on the horizon. Then they were back on the road.

At six o'clock the road snaked around the fringes of a large town built on the southern side of a slow-moving river. Bald saw the same desperate faces as in the rural towns and villages. The same billboards. The same poverty, but on a bigger scale. They crossed the bridge over the river and carried on north along the main road. Two hundred miles to go, thought Bald. Another four hours until we get to the stronghold.

Porter kept the Land Cruiser going along at a steady clip. Hulk gazed out of the window as they coasted past another ruined town and grunted. 'Unbelievable, when you think about it.'

Bald said, 'What's that?'

'Place is sitting on the world's biggest oil reserves, and this is how people live. Like dumb animals.'

'Corruption,' said Bald. 'Way of life over here. Everyone's in it for themselves. Government included.'

'Doesn't have to be that way.'

Bald laughed. 'These people have been shat on for two hundred years, mate. They'll be shat on for another two hundred. Only difference is who does the shitting, and how much.'

'You don't believe in making the world a better place?'

'I believe in making my bank account a better place. That's my religion. Everyone else can go fuck themselves.'

Hulk glanced at him in the rear-view mirror. 'You're a mean son of a bitch, John.'

'Nah. I'm just a realist.'

'And a good soldier. I mean it. Always had respect for you boys in the SAS. Never had the chance to work up close and personal, though. Not until you showed up. Tell you the truth, it's been a privilege working with you. True fucking warrior. Your buddy too.'

'This is what we do, mate. Even Porter's not a bad operator, when he can shoot straight.'

'Hey, I'm just glad we're on the same side. Wouldn't want to be going into battle with anyone else, brother. The way you dealt with that guy back there, asking us for money? Real cold-blooded.'

'That's how we do it in the Regiment.'

Hulk nodded and went back to staring out of the window. Bald watched him for a moment, something picking at the back of his mind. He couldn't be sure, but there was something forced about Hulk's compliments. As if the guy had been repeating lines he'd rehearsed in his head.

At seven o'clock dusk began to descend across the plains, shrouding the landscape in grainy darkness. An hour later, they pulled over again. Hulk topped up the tank with two of the jerry cans from the boot, and then Bald took the wheel.

The last leg of their journey.

Two hours to their destination.

A short while later, they left the plains behind them as the road sliced through a series of valleys with mountains on either side. At nine thirty they hit a small city about two miles square, built across the valley floor. There were signs everywhere of the recent protests against President Vasquez. Bald saw shattered glass shopfronts and burnt-out cars and debris all over the place. Gangs sat on their motorbikes at the sides of the road, chatting and staring at passing traffic. Ariana Grande tracks pumped out of a stereo somewhere. For a moment Bald worried that the gang might take an interest in them, but their old Land Cruiser was inconspicuous and they rolled on past the bikers without trouble.

They steered north out of the city, and Bald knew from the maps they had studied that they were getting very close now. The satnav estimated sixty minutes until they reached their destination.

They rolled on past dark hills at their three o'clock and nine, the Land Cruiser's headlamps burning halos on the unlit road.

After ten miles the satnav prompted Bald to make a right and they bowled down another metalled road running between a range of steep-sided mountains.

The road veered this way and that along the narrow valley floor for seven miles before the landscape opened up into a wide, relatively flat plain bordered to the south by several low hills. A much higher, forbidding peak rose like a clenched fist out of the landscape to the north, black against the grey starred night.

Two miles to the east, further along the main road, Bald saw a cluster of orange lights from a mid-sized town. Which he figured must be Los Altos. To the north, near the base of the tall mountain, he spotted the weak glow from a smaller set of lights studding the surrounding blackness. A couple of miles from their current position.

The stronghold, Bald realised.

'Almost time to teach these sons of bitches a lesson,' Dudley said.

'So. Remember the plan,' Hulk said. 'We'll advance to our first lying-up position in the gully and report in to Langley, then wait for confirmation that the distraction is about to deploy. Once we have the green light, we'll move forward to our final assault positions, wait for the distraction. Then begin the attack.'

Bald's eyes wandered down to the glowing digits on the display: 22.39. Which gave them a full eighty minutes to move into their lying-up position at the gully. They were a mile due west of the road junction, according to the satnav. At this hour of the night, in this rural pocket of the country, the road was eerily quiet. They travelled along in the pitch black for another three minutes without passing another vehicle, and then Bald slowed the Cruiser down to twenty per and pointed at the satnav.

'We're three hundred metres from the junction,' he said. 'I'll drop you lot off and find somewhere to stash the wagon. Meet you at the gully.'

Dudley's face puckered. 'But that makes you the getaway driver. You'll be the only one of us who knows where she's parked up.'

'So what?'

'Getaway driver should be the fastest man on the team. Sure as shit isn't you, with that dicky knee of yours. Your buddy ain't up to the job neither, seeing as how he got out of breath on the range. I should hide the wagon.'

'No way. We need your skills on as sniper. You'll be covering us on the way out.'

'I agree,' Hulk said, giving Dudley a look. 'Your job's too important. John will stash the vehicle.'

He met Bald's eyes in the rear-view mirror. 'Wherever you hide it, make sure it's out of sight. Don't want some kid finding it and jacking our ride out of here.'

A hundred metres further on, Bald eased off the gas as they neared the junction. A single-track lane ran to the north from the main road, towards the stronghold. The gully, according to the maps they had been given, was somewhere off to their left, in an area of uncultivated fields dotted with trees.

Directly ahead of them, the main road carried on to the east, with the clustered lights from the town of Los Altos, two miles away at their eleven o'clock.

Further to the north, Bald spotted a third separate grouping of lights. Glowing white orbs, burning like beacons across the black-ened landscape. The floodlights from the army base, he realised.

They were fifty metres away from the junction when Hulk leaned forward in his seat.

'Stop here,' he said.

Bald slowed down and pulled over at the side of the road, fifteen metres west of the junction. He kept the engine running while Porter and Dudley climbed out of the Land Cruiser, clutch-ing their weapons. Hulk was the last to get out.

'Find somewhere to hide this thing, then RV with us at the gully. Pass number is anything that adds up to seven. Approach from the south and keep your weapon at your side. We don't want any blue-on-blues.'

'Roger that.'

He stepped out and joined Porter and Dudley beside the Land Cruiser. They grabbed their daysacks from the boot. Stepped off the blacktop and moved stealthily across the field parallel to the single-lane road, heading towards their designated lying-up point. A few seconds later they disappeared from view.

Bald carried on past the junction, searching for a good spot to conceal the wagon from view of passing traffic. After a mile he spotted a rough path leading off to the south between corridors of dense forest. Vaguely recalled noticing the path when they had been planning for the mission. The track was unpaved and over-grown with weeds and piles of rubbish. Which suggested it hadn't been used for a long while. He swerved off the main road and arrowed down the track for a hundred metres before he came to a footpath at the side of the road. The area looked desolate, as far as he could see. No artificial lights or sounds indicating human habitation.

Bald pulled over a few metres further along at the side of the road and parked up. Switched off the engine, snatched up his M4 from the footwell and hopped out. He opened the boot, took out the plastic container for the explosive charge. Grabbed his small daysack containing his water bottle, three extra ammunition clips and a pair of L2 fragmentation grenades. Locked the vehicle. Stuffed the keys in the side pocket on his trousers.

Hurried back down the track towards the main road.

The night was cool and dry and thick with cloud. A gentle breeze was blowing across the land, whispering through the grass as Bald approached the main road. He carried on west through the trees, paralleling the main road, using his natural night vision and the faint moonlight to guide him. Ready to dive behind the trees at the first hint of an onrushing motor.

Twelve minutes later he reached the junction he'd passed earlier. He continued west for fifty metres, counting his paces, then stopped and dropped to a crouch, checking that the road was clear in both directions.

The road was empty. Eleven o'clock at night. All the locals had their heads down, presumably.

Bald rushed across to the other side and moved through the field to the west of the minor road. After fifty metres he glimpsed the outline of an oak tree, perched on a slight rise, dimly visible beneath the light of the moon.

The oak tree marked the point next to the gully, he knew. As he drew nearer, holding his weapon sideways, a voice issued a challenge.

'Pass number?' Hulk whispered.

'Two, one, four,' Bald answered softly.

There was a pause. 'Okay, brother.'

Bald moved down the side of the gully. It was three metres deep and about twice as wide, stretching between two gently sloping mounds. To the right, four metres away, a loose tumble of rocks and dirt led up towards the oak tree. The ground either side of the gully was covered with bushes, providing some modest cover. Straight away he saw that they were badly exposed. Anyone wandering past that oak tree would easily spot the four armed men sheltered below, compromising the operation. But it was still less risky than moving closer to the stronghold and waiting potentially hours for the distraction to activate.

He scrabbled over to Hulk and Porter while Dudley kept watch over the southern approach. 'You find a spot for the wagon?' Hulk asked.

'A mile from here,' Bald replied quietly as he dumped the rucksack and container. 'No fucker will find it.'

'That's a long way from the stronghold,' Porter said.

'Not for us. Any of us can run that in a few minutes.'

'I'm not thinking of us. I'm thinking of the hostage. What if she's badly hurt? She won't be able to walk that far.'

'Then we'll revert to the backup plan,' said Hulk. 'As we discussed at the camp. Jack one of the motors inside the compound and drive that out to the Land Cruiser. Won't be a problem. President's got a whole fleet of vehicles in there.'

'What now?' asked Dudley.

'We wait. I've sent a message to Taylor. He knows we're in position. He'll call us when he's got a more precise ETA for the distraction.'

'They still reckon it'll deploy between midnight and first light?'

'That's what Taylor says.'

'They'd better not leave it too late.' Bald pointed to the oak tree. 'All it'll take is a couple of young lovers to park up and go for a shag under that tree, and we're shafted.'

'It's the middle of the night. Everybody's asleep. Road's empty.'

'Right now, maybe. But if it gets to first light and we've not heard anything, we're gonna have to move.'

'It won't come to that.'

Bald glanced at his G-Shock: 23.09. Less than six hours until first light at 04.45. Which means we might be here for another five hours or more, thought Bald, waiting for confirmation from Langley that the distraction was ready to go.

He mentally rehearsed the assault in his plan.

Get the green light from the CIA.

Advance to their final assault positions.

Wait for the distraction to trigger.

Then go in, hard.

His muscles were bunched tight with tension. *We could get the call at any moment,* he reminded himself. *All we can do now is wait.*

There was no need to organise themselves into a routine. Not when they might get the call at any moment. One guy rotated on guard duty while the others checked their weapons and kit, making sure everything was ready for the assault.

The night was still and quiet, the silence broken only by the roar of the occasional passing lorry or machine-like buzz of motorcycles coming from the main road, a hundred metres away. Above them, the moon glowed wanly behind the scattered clouds.

At 01.30, Bald looked round at Hulk and said, 'Still nothing?'

Hulk checked his phone. 'Not yet.'

'What's taking them so fucking long?'

'Patience, brother.'

The night dragged on.

Bald wondered again about the distraction the Company was planning for the army base. Not a drone strike, Hulk had suggested. Not a bomb dropped on top of the barracks. *I don't think that's what they're planning.*

So what, then?

What the fuck is it?

He checked the time again: 03.27. 'Fuck's sake,' he hissed to Hulk. 'Try them again.'

'No point. They'll be ready when they're ready.'

'Another hour and it'll nearly be first light. If they're gonna do this thing, they'd better make it quick.'

'It'll happen.'

There was a confidence to Hulk's voice that surprised Bald.

Either this bloke has a lot more faith in the CIA then I do, he thought. *Or he knows something that me and Porter don't.*

Two minutes later, Hulk's phone vibrated.

He took out the satellite-enabled device from his pocket. Swipe-answered and had a brief muted conversation with the voice on the other end of the line. Then he put the phone to sleep again. Tucked it away. Turned to the others.

'It's on,' he said quietly. 'Thirty minutes until the distraction activates.'

'About fucking time,' Dudley said, his voice laced with nervous excitement.

Hulk said, 'We'll move forward to striking distance. Dudley will take up the position on the hillock as team sniper. John, Jock, you'll come with me. We'll move into position and wait for the distraction to go off. Then Porter will lay the charge and the Claymore, return to the firing point and detonate.'

'Did they say what that distraction is?' asked Porter.

'Just that we won't be able to miss it.'

'Airstrike,' Bald decided. 'Must be.'

Hulk made no comment. Bald checked his watch: 03.30.

The distraction would kick off at exactly 04.00, he calculated.

Forty-five minutes before first light.

'Come on,' Hulk said. 'Let's go. No time to lose.'

They snatched up their weapons and equipment. Porter threw the satchel with the Claymore over his shoulder and picked up the container with the lump of C4 taped to the side of it. Then they scrabbled up the side of the gully and moved at a quick trot across the field. Making their final approach to the target.

They fast-walked north across the terrain, eyes scanning the ground ahead of them for any obstacles or signs of movement. At their three o'clock, no more than half a mile away, stood the barracks. The president's personal bolt-hole.

Bald had an unobstructed view of the base from his position. He could see the surrounding security fence and two-metre-tall gate, the main accommodation block and a separate building housing the electrical substation, enclosed within a fenced-off area at one side of the camp. The whole place was brightly lit up. Like a car showroom.

Automatic doors, reinforced gates, blast-proof walls.

Like a miniature fortress, thought Bald.

How the fuck are the CIA going to tie down those soldiers?

They crossed another barren field and reached the edge of a gravel track leading from the main road to the east, to the front of the stronghold, four hundred metres to the north. To the left of the track was a dense grove of mango trees, extending for roughly two hundred metres across the open ground. On the right, there was a mostly flat plain pockmarked with a few trees.

Beyond the mango trees, at the far end of the gravel track, stood the stronghold.

It looked more impressive in real life than the satellite imagery Bald had seen back at the camp. The estate was perhaps two hundred metres wide, enclosed within a three-metre-tall wire fence. The track led to a guardhouse at the entrance with a barrier gate.

Beyond the guardhouse, fifty metres away, stood an elegant-looking structure, two storeys tall and shaped like a shoebox, with a salmon-pink facade and tall windows and turrets at either end. At the front of the building, a long line of arches and white-washed columns overlooked a neatly trimmed lawn, decorated with bronze statues and exotic plants.

The driveway was lined with ornate lamp posts and led towards a small carriage circle at the far end, with a pair of white Ford Explorer SUVs parked around it at the six and twelve o'clock positions. A side path trailed from the driveway to a motor court and garage on the western side of the house. Through the arched gateway Bald spotted a Chevrolet Tahoe parked inside the court.

At this time, most of the lights inside the house were out. Four o'clock in the morning. The dead hours. Nobody would be awake except the on-duty guards and a few of the president's domestic staff, getting the place ready for the big man's arrival.

Our contact doesn't think the president has arrived yet.

As they drew level with the edge of the track Hulk signalled for the team to halt. He turned to Dudley and indicated a low hillock forty metres away at their nine o'clock. The slopes were grassy and covered with scrub.

'Get on the high ground,' Hulk whispered. 'Cover us. As soon as those charges go off, start putting down rounds.'

Dudley grinned. 'Count on it, son.'

He peeled off to the left and started making his way up the slope. From his position at the top of the hillock, Dudley would have an elevated firing point overlooking the grounds at the front of the stronghold on both sides of the track, covering the rest of the team as they made their final approach.

'Come on,' Hulk urged Bald and Porter.

The three of them hastened across the flat ground in front of the stronghold, racing towards the clump of mango trees on the left side of the gravel track. They hit the grove and jogged forward for two hundred metres until they neared the edge of the trees. Then they dropped flat and moved into a prone position a hundred metres from the mansion, concealed from view by the line of mango trees. At this distance, with the light coming from the grounds, Bald could see the two guards posted at the guardhouse, patrolling up and down behind the barrier gate.

The pair of them looked like an old time double-act. One of the guards was maybe five-six or five-seven and thickset, with a round head and dark buzz-cut hair. The other guy was tall and skinny, all sinewy muscle. Both were dressed in dark suits.

Both wielded rifles.

Bald checked his watch.

03.58.

Two minutes until the distraction triggered.

He glanced past his shoulder at the barracks, half a mile to the east, straining his eyes as he looked for any sign of movement. He saw nothing except the harsh glare from the floodlights above the security fence, the distant glow from the town.

Time scraped past.

Bald felt his muscles tautening. Adrenaline coursed through his bloodstream. Any second now.

04.00.

Silence.

He stole another glance at the base.

Nothing happened.

'What's taking them so bloody long?' he muttered, turning to Hulk.

The American said nothing.

Then Bald saw the fire.

TWENTY-FOUR

The fire came from the fenced-off building on one side of the barracks. The electrical substation, providing power to the base and surrounding towns and villages. Bald saw it erupt almost without warning. A furious zapping noise ripped across the air, the sound of circuitry shorting. Like the sparks from a million live wires. There was a searing flash of light, and then a gout of orange flames and smoke spewed out of the structure and drifted into the air. The fire spread rapidly across the substation, engulfing it. The lights briefly went out across the base before they switched back on again as the backup generator kicked in. A few moments later several more lights flicked on inside the accommodation block. Bald could hear shouts and cries. At the same time, an alert sounded over the loudspeaker in Spanish.

At his side, Porter said, 'What the fuck is going on?'

'Power surge,' Bald replied. 'Substation must have been over-loaded. Caused one of them transformers to blow.'

'Told you the boys at Langley would come good,' Hulk said.

Bald swung round and looked towards the American. He looked strangely composed. As if he had expected this. As if the surge wasn't a surprise to him at all.

Bald said, 'This is the distraction?'

Hulk nodded. 'Specialist hackers have taken control of the security systems at the base. They've sealed the automatic doors shut. The front gate too. The soldiers are trapped inside their barracks. Right now, the base is in lockdown. We've turned their fortress into a prison.'

'How long for?'

'Until they can break open the doors manually and crash

through the gate. That'll take some time. Fifteen minutes, Langley reckons.'

Bald snapped his gaze to the east, straining his eyes. Beyond the columns of smoke and flames he saw that lights at Los Altos had been extinguished. The whole town was in darkness. The lights were still on at the president's place.

'Emergency generator,' Hulk explained. 'Mansion runs off its own backup supply in case of power failure. Same deal as the barracks.'

'What if the soldiers call for help?'

'Won't work. The hackers have knocked out the power in the surrounding area. Communications towers, mobile masts. Whole area is off the grid. They can ask for help but their messages won't get through.'

'You should have told us,' Porter fumed.

'There's no time for this. You need to get those charges planted at the fence, right now. Clock's ticking.'

Bald grunted. 'He's right, mate. Get moving.'

Porter stared at the barracks for a fleeting moment. The flames quickly spread, churning noxious grey smoke into the sky. Alarms were piercing the air. Emergency announcements were being made over the loudspeaker in Spanish. Porter could imagine the chaos inside the base, the soldiers frantically trying to break out of their barracks blocks as the fiery inferno raged a short distance away.

Fuck it.

Time to move.

He picked himself up off the ground and grabbed the container with the explosive charge.

'Remember,' Hulk said in an undertone. 'As soon as you reach the firing point, detonate the diversionary charge. That'll draw the guards over like flies to shit. Once they're in range, hit them with the Claymore.'

'Don't link them batteries up until you've set the charges,' Bald added. 'Don't want to get blown to shit like Plastic Paddy.'

'Got it,' Porter said. 'Cover me.'

Then he advanced beyond the grove, the container in his right hand and the Claymore satchel hanging from his side. His M4 was attached to a sling connected to his plate carrier vest, allowing Porter to anchor the weapon across his back. A necessary adjustment they had made back on the training ground. The guy planting the charges needed both hands to rig up the devices and link them to their respective batteries. No way he could do that and keep hold of his weapon at the same time.

Porter ran on for twenty metres, then dropped to his front and started crawling on all fours towards the south-west corner of the fence, a hundred metres away. At his six o'clock, Bald and Hulk were checking their arcs, peering through the night scopes attached to their weapons. Dudley would be covering Porter from his position atop the hillock, three hundred metres to the rear, Bald knew. Ready to drop any guards who spotted Porter.

Bald arced his sights across the ground near the guardhouse. Mr Tall and Buzzcut were chatting to one another and pointing in the direction of the fire coming from the army base. The blaze was glowing brightly, lighting up the night sky.

Not a missile.

Not an airstrike.

A cyber-attack.

The plan was solid, Bald thought. With the soldiers trapped inside their base, they would be unable to rush over once the charges kicked off at the president's estate. They would eventually smash their way out of their barracks, of course. But by then it would be too late. The assault team planned on spending no more than a few minutes inside the stronghold. A real in-and-out job. Get in, get the hostage. Get the fuck out again.

He refocused on Porter, watching him through the green glow of his night scope as the guy reached the fence and planted the charge near the base of the tower. Then he backtracked ten metres and set up the Claymore, placing it so that the front was facing the same section of the fence where the explosive charge had been planted.

Porter inserted the blasting caps into the fuse wells, slinked away from the fence and began unspooling the electrical wires connected to the mine and the diversion charge.

He slithered back to a point fifty metres from the Claymore and sixty metres from the fence. As far as the wires would extend.

They had rigged two thirty-metre lengths of wire together for each device, allowing Porter to put as much distance between himself and the breach as possible.

Now he lay down in a sparse patch of scrub, detached his M4 from the leash buckle and laid it flat beside him on the ground for easy access. Gripped the clacker for the charge in his right hand. Clacker for the Claymore next to the rifle. Bald looked on as his mucker did a mental three-count.

Then Porter squeezed the firing lever.

The boom was deafening. Like a million carburettors backfiring. A deep rumble shook the ground as a huge orange fireball gushed upwards from the fence, belching flames and smoke into the pre-dawn sky. The explosion tore through the wire mesh, creating a breach big enough to drive a truck through. Flames coated the detergent-and-fuel-soaked tower, and from somewhere inside the grounds Bald heard the machine-like wail of an alarm. Above the shrilling and the hiss and roar of the flames, there was a chorus of panicked shouts.

He swung his M4 back to the main gate. Through his night-sight, he could see several figures streaming out of the front entrance of the main building, a hundred and fifty metres away. Counted eleven of them in total. Well-built guys dressed in plain long shirts and trousers and boots, armed with M16 assault rifles. Some of them were fiddling with bits of clothing and kit. The off-duty guards. Woken up by the surge at the barracks, probably. Now in full-blown panic mode.

The guards had clearly fallen for the trap the team had set. Bald watched them racing towards the breaching point, believing that they were under attack from that corner of the stronghold. At the guardhouse, Mr Tall and Buzzcut had turned away from the barrier as they watched their eleven comrades sprinting across the compound. Buzzcut shouted out to one of the passing figures. The guy paused briefly and yelled something back. Bald couldn't understand him, but it sounded distinctly like an order.

Don't move. Stay here. Watch the gate.

The guy ran on. Mr Tall and Buzzcut stayed put.

'Guards heading for the breach,' Bald reported. 'Eleven of them.'

'Claymore, ready!' Hulk called out to Porter. 'Coming your way!'

Bald tightened his fingers around the grip on his weapon and scanned the breach, searching for any sign of the enemy.

At first he couldn't see a thing. The smoke was too dense. The flames were still eating away at the base of the tower and the surrounding wire.

Then he glimpsed a figure surging through the large hole in the fence. A copper-skinned guard in a long-sleeved white shirt and a pair of sandy-brown trousers. He had his rifle aimed in front of him, shouting at the top of his voice as he headed for the killing zone directly in front of the Claymore.

A couple of metres behind him, six more guards were spilling out of the breach in a rough chevron formation. They looked like infantry at the Somme, charging across no man's land.

Then Porter detonated the mine.

TWENTY-FIVE

Bald felt the shudder in his bones as the Claymore kicked off. There was a whoosh as the explosion fanned outward across the front of the stronghold, shredding the area around the fence. Then the clattering of steel, and in the background the agonised screams of men as hundreds of metal fragments tore into the onrushing guards, smashing bones and lacerating vitals.

The smoke cleared, revealing a scene of carnage. There were body parts everywhere. The ground was a bloody tangle of limbs and intestines and torsos. Bits of flesh dangled from the torn ends of the wire-mesh fence. The Claymore had wiped or killed or maimed most of the guards. Bald saw one man sprawled beside the fence hole, screaming hysterically as his bowels slopped out of a wide gash in his stomach. Another guy had been severed at the torso. Bald saw his upper body lying next to the breach. Couldn't see the guy's legs anywhere. The Moon, maybe.

'Move!' Hulk roared. 'Make for the guardhouse!'

Bald scrambled to his feet alongside the ex-SEAL. They surged clear of the mango grove and broke across the strip of ground between the trees and the perimeter fence, rushing through the flame-illuminated scrub. The guardhouse was a hundred metres away. The smell of burning metal and the putrid stink of burnt flesh thick in the air. Bald could hear the cries of dying men and the shriek of the sirens inside the mansion, the distant hiss and rumble from the electrical fire raging further to the east.

Fifty metres away, Porter shot to his feet as well. He ran over to the rest of the assault team and reached Bald and Hulk in another few strides. Then the three of them dashed towards the guard-house, forty metres away at their one o'clock.

Behind the front barrier, Mr Tall and Buzzcut had turned away from the entrance, transfixed by the massacre at the breach. They were in a state of shock, probably. They hadn't expected to see their mates get blown to shreds. They would be wondering what to do. Go over and help or stay put and defend the entrance?

Then Buzzcut evidently heard the pounding of boots and spun round in surprise. His eyes flicked from the barrier gate to the gravel path. To the three armed men running towards them.

The guy had just enough time to register a look of dumb surprise. He opened his mouth as if to shout a warning to his comrade. Then he spasmed as Dudley plugged him from four hundred metres away. Two unseen bullets slapped into his neck and shoulder. The guy did a drunken pirouette before he fell away, dead flesh slapping wetly against concrete.

Mr Tall saw his mate dying and lost his nerve. He turned and bolted towards the guardhouse. Diving for the nearest available cover.

A smart move. But taken way too late. Hulk opened fire, giving him the good news with three rounds from the M4. The first bullet smacked into Mr Tall's kneecap, shattering bone. The second and third shots struck him higher up, punching holes in the side of his torso. He landed a metre or so away from the guardhouse, writhing in pain before Dudley finished him off from long-range with a couple of well-aimed shots to the face. Blood gushed out of the holes in his head in bright-red jets.

Bald added the guy's death to the clicker-counter in his head.

Two dead at the guardhouse, he thought.

Eleven guards cut down by the Claymore.

Thirteen targets dealt with.

That leaves five fuckers to put down.

They charged through the barrier gate, sidestepped the slotted guards and moved quickly down the driveway towards the front of the main building, fifty metres away. Bald could hear the blood rushing in his ears, his heart beating furiously inside his chest. Hulk was moving alongside him at his three o'clock, with Porter lagging a couple of paces behind, breathing heavily.

'Fuck's sake, keep up!' Bald shouted back.

They scudded forward, passing the carriage circle and the two white Ford Explorer SUVs Bald had spotted earlier. From across the stronghold he heard an anguished cry of pain. He looked over his shoulder in the direction of the breach and saw three rounds thwacking into a wounded guard crawling away from the flames, smacking into his arms and legs. Dudley's handiwork. At first Bald thought the redneck's aim had been piss-poor. Then he saw another injured guard jerking wildly as he stumbled away from the breach, two rounds nailing him in the back of the leg.

Dudley isn't shooting to kill, he realised.

The guy was deliberately clipping the wounded guards. Making sure they couldn't walk or use a weapon. As a bonus, their hideous screams would draw over any remaining guards, luring them to their deaths.

Effective.

But also fucking cruel.

Then Bald heard a crash.

He swung round just in time to see two burly guards bursting out of the mansion. The guy in front was a bald-headed man mountain. His shirt and trousers looked like they had been shrink-wrapped around his enormous muscles. The second guy looked like the Man Mountain's long-lost twin. Only paler and thicker around the midriff. He was round chested and chubby faced, with cropped black hair that sat like a leather skullcap on top of his head.

They broke forward across the covered porch, gripping their M16s. Rushing head-on to meet the three attackers.

Twenty metres away from the assault team.

Bald registered all of this in a microsecond. There was no way that Dudley could put the drop on them, he knew. The redneck was too busy shooting up the wounded men at the breach.

It's down to us now.

Bald already had his weapon raised. His right hand was clasped around the trigger grip, his left hand securely holding on to the fore grip for stability. Fire selector switched to semi-automatic.

He angled his sights up slightly, aiming for Man Mountain's trunk. It was a nice big target to aim for.

The guy was fifteen metres away when Bald fired twice.

The bullets scythed through the air and smacked into the guard as he raced forward, striking him in the jaw. The lower half of his face disintegrated in a spray of blood and teeth. The guard jerked backwards as if he'd run into a clothesline. He fell away and landed so heavily Bald half-expected the ground to shake.

Two metres to the right, Skullcap was dropping to a kneeling firing stance beside a marble statue of a naked Hercules. Porter came up alongside Bald, breathing raggedly as he fired twice at the Venezuelan. The first round was all over the fucking place. It smashed into the statue several inches to the right of the target, taking off a chunk of Hercules' penis. His second effort was marginally better, slapping into Skullcap's right ankle. The guy howled in pain and reached down to clutch his shattered leg.

At which point Hulk opened fire. He swept forward, loosing off a couple of quick rounds at the target. Skullcap spasmed as the bullets thumped into his shoulder blade and chest, knocking him backwards. As if someone had just struck him across the face with a sledgehammer. Hulk fired again, drilling him in the guts. The deal-closer.

The guard slumped down beside his comrade, his weapon falling from his grip and clattering to the ground. He was dead before he kissed the paving slabs.

Bald stole a glance at Porter. Wondered again if his old mate had lost his edge. No time to berate the guy. Keep the momentum going. Don't stop.

He broke into a run, moved swiftly past the two slotted guards. Another quick look over his shoulder at the south-west corner. Both the wounded guards had stopped moving. Bald couldn't see any more movement coming from that direction. The defenders had been annihilated. If anyone else was still alive, Dudley would neutralise them.

Fifteen men down, he calculated.

Three targets left. Including the two guards in the basement.

'Keep moving!' he barked.

They raced on. Away from the sounds of the dying men at the breach and the smell of charred flesh and metal.

In another dozen paces they reached the porch, pushed through the front door and swept into the hallway. Moving in a rough formation, with Bald on the left, Porter in the middle and Hulk to the right. Weapons up, telescopic stocks resting against their shoulders, index fingers feathering the triggers. Ready to double-tap any lurking targets. Dudley would remain in position outside the compound, covering the approaches to the mansion, keeping an eye on the barracks and putting down any wounded guards at the breach.

The siren was even louder inside the stronghold. They crossed the hallway and hit the marble-floored foyer. Which looked like something out of a drug kingpin's wet dream. The walls were covered in gold and marble detail. A diamond chandelier the size of a spaceship hung from the ceiling. There were gold statues of naked women mounted on columns, expensive-looking oriental rugs, huge paintings of the president and his mistresses.

On the left side of the foyer a blood-red-carpeted stairwell led up to a central balcony overlooking the entrance, with a portrait of the president in his military garb hanging from the wall. A door off to the left opened into a dining room. To the right, another door led to a private library. Both doors were open. At the opposite end of the foyer, ten metres away, an arched entrance led to a great room facing out towards a terraced patio and swimming pool, with corridors veering off to the left and right. The corridor to the left, Bald knew, led towards the kitchen and pantry. There was a door midway down that corridor that provided access to the basement.

That's where we'll find Fuller.

They knew all this because they had spent countless hours at the camp, poring over floor plans and mapping out the distances from one room to the next. They knew the layout better than their own mothers.

They advanced with controlled aggression through the foyer, Hulk and Porter clearing the library area on the right. Bald moved on and caught a glimmer of movement at his left.

Coming from the dining room.

He swivelled round. Arced his sights across the space.

Finger tensing on the trigger.

Then he saw her.

A middle-aged woman in a housemaid's uniform, cowering beside the long dining-room table. Bunch of polishing and cleaning kit on the floor beside her. She screamed at the sight of Bald and threw herself to the floor, babbling in Spanish.

In the same beat, Bald saw the blur of motion at his three o'clock.

He spun round. Saw a guard appearing around the corner from the great room. A solidly built guy in a denim shirt, with oily black hair and stubble that looked like it had been scrawled on his face with a sharpie.

Rifle pointed directly at Bald.

There was no time to react, Bald knew. The guy with the oily hair was midway across the foyer. The business end of his rifle was lined up with Bald's centre mass. A distance of five metres. Almost impossible to miss at that range. No time for Bald to bring his weapon across, aim and unleash a couple of rounds of his own.

I'm fucked.

In the next half-second he heard two rapid light cracks.

Not from the guard's rifle.

From across the foyer.

Porter, giving the target the double-tap special.

The guard gave out a howl as the first round thumped into his groin, hot lead tearing into his balls. The second bullet struck several inches higher, slapping into his chest. Keyhole surgery, Regiment-style. The guard dropped his weapon and fell backwards, arms flailing. He knocked over a china vase before he flopped to the ground. Blood pooling around him, mixing with the broken shards.

Bald spun round. Saw Porter standing in the middle of the foyer, weapon still trained on the slotted guard. There was no time for Bald to say anything to him. He just nodded his gratitude. Bloke just saved my fucking life, he realised.

Maybe I was wrong.

Maybe he's not over the hill just yet.

Hulk moved towards the dining-room doors and barked at the terrified woman in Spanish. She didn't move. He stormed inside, grabbed her by the arm and pulled her to her feet, repeating the same words as he pointed at the porticoed entrance. Bald understood what the American was telling her. *Get the hell out of here.*

The maid understood. She stumbled out of the dining room, hands shaking and eyes wide with fear as she hurried towards the front door. Hulk watched her go before turning to the others.

'Move on,' he growled.

They pressed on through the foyer, crossed a great room lined with more nude bronze statues and headed for the corridor to the left. Bald guessed that five or six minutes had elapsed since the cyber-attack on the barracks. Hulk reckoned it would take the soldiers fifteen minutes to smash their way out of the base. Minimum.

We need to be out of here by 04.15, Bald reminded himself. *We've got ten minutes left to find Fuller and bug out. Otherwise we'll get overrun by forty fucking soldiers.*

The voice inside his head told him to hurry the fuck up.

He looked ahead as they hit the corridor. The kitchen was located through a bland grey door at the far end, eight metres away.

Four metres away, on the left side of the corridor, he spotted the unmarked door that led directly down to the basement.

He was two metres from the door when Porter suddenly halted, glanced back down the corridor in the direction of the grand room, wearing a look of puzzlement.

'Where the fuck is Hulk going?'

Bald followed his mucker's line of sight. He saw Hulk marching off in the opposite direction from the rest of the team. Making for the corridor that veered off to the right of the great room, leading towards the master suite and family bedrooms.

'This fucking way!' Bald shouted out. 'Over here!'

Hulk didn't appear to hear him. He carried on down the other corridor, turned the corner and disappeared from view.

'Stupid bastard,' Bald muttered.

'Should we go after him?' asked Porter.

'No time. Fuck him. We'll get him on the way out. Come on.'

He wheeled round and quickened his stride as he hurried over to the unmarked basement door. The alarm was still sounding as Bald wrenched the door open and trotted down a metal staircase, boots pounding on the treads, Porter breathing heavily at his six o'clock.

They hit the bottom of the stairs, crossed another foyer and emerged into a long fluorescent-lit corridor.

The basement was dusty and dank. Not at all like the luxurious quarters on the ground floor. Bald saw three metal doors on the right side of the corridor. There was another door on the left side of the room, seven metres away from the assaulters. At the far end a separate corridor led off to the right, towards the president's private wine collection, but Bald wasn't interested in expensive French plonk. Not today.

The first door on the right housed the boiler, Bald knew. The second door led to some sort of interrogation room.

The prison cell was behind the third door.

He saw movement from the door on the left side of the corridor. The guardroom.

Two guards were rushing out of the room, guns ready to go. The first guy out of the door was a lanky streak of piss in a brown polo T-shirt and jeans. The guy behind him was a greasy fucker, with slicked-back hair and a black chevron moustache. Like an eighties porn actor. Bald guessed they had heard the muffled reports of the explosions and gunfire outside and had decided to hurry upstairs to find out what was going on.

The lanky guy was three paces outside the guardroom when he caught sight of the two Brits bearing down on them. He saw Bald levelling his M4 at his face, at a distance of four metres. Close enough for Bald to make out the individual beads of sweat on the fucker's brow.

The lanky guy looked at Bald with bug eyes, face registering horror. He raised his weapon. Then Bald drilled him through the head. The two rounds bored holes through his skull, his brains painting the wall behind him a bright mushy red. Bits of gooey matter slicked down the wall as Porter emptied two rounds into the greasy fucker, nailing him in the chest before he could return fire. He jolted like someone had just rigged him up to the national grid. He dropped to the floor next to his comrade in a tangle of contorted limbs, blood disgorging out of the exit wounds in his upper back.

Bald took a moment to admire his work. Like a painter stepping back from the canvas to take in his masterpiece. Then he made for the cell door. Tested the handle. Locked. He stooped down beside the lanky guy. Snatched a set of keys from his belt, moved back over to the door. He struck gold with the third key, unlocked the deadbolt and yanked the door open, iron hinges groaning in protest.

He pushed through the gap and stepped inside. Porter stayed back in the corridor, covering the approaches.

The cell was small and dirty. Three metres by three. There was a stained mattress on the floor, a bucket in the corner. A single light bulb dangled from an exposed wire. Thick scent of piss and sweat hung in the air.

A red-haired woman sat on the edge of the mattress. She hastily backed away from the figure standing in the doorway and pressed herself against the wall. Her hands were visibly shaking as she raised them above her head. Eyes as wide as saucers.

'Please, no,' she said in a frail tone of voice. 'Please, don't kill me. Don't.'

It took Bald a few moments to recognise the woman. Her white blouse was blood-stained and torn in several places. Her jaw was swollen. She had a deep cut on her lower lip and purpled bruises on her arms. Her long hair was matted and filthy.

Caroline Fuller looked bad. But not as bad as he had feared. Vasquez and his interrogators hadn't yet done their worst.

They had reached her in time.

'Please. Don't do this,' she begged. 'I don't know anything.'

Tears stained her cheeks. She said a few more words in Spanish. The same desperate pleas, but in the local tongue.

'Caroline will panic,' he remembered Cantwell telling them in

London. 'You're going to have to calm her down before you do anything else.'

'It's okay, love,' Bald told her in as soft a voice as possible. 'We're from London. We're here to bring you home.'

Fuller stopped trembling. She lowered her hands and looked up at Bald with a mixture of hope and disbelief.

'London?' she repeated. A flicker of recognition in her eyes. 'You mean—'

'We're the good guys,' Bald replied. 'We've been sent here to rescue you. We're getting you out of here. You need to come with us.'

Fuller studied his face for a moment, as if wondering whether to trust him.

'Where?'

'We'll explain later. Right now, we need to fucking move. Can you walk?'

She nodded and struggled to her feet, wincing with pain. He wrapped an arm around her waist and helped her along. They shuffled out of the cell and started back down the corridor, with Porter. Fuller paused as she spared a brief look at Lanky and Pornstar.

'The guards . . . they're dead?'

'Aye,' Bald said.

'All of them?'

'Aye.'

'Good.'

Bald hurried alongside the academic, with Porter moving a step ahead of them. It had been a surgical operation so far, thought Bald. They had decimated the guards. Rescued the prisoner. Even Porter had rediscovered his old magic.

We're going to win.

All we've got to do now is find Hulk and bug out.

'Hurry,' he urged Fuller. 'Fucking move.'

They hustled back down the corridor and climbed the staircase leading to the first floor. Fuller grimaced with every step, slowing the two ex-SAS men down. Bald willed her to move faster. He reckoned seven minutes had passed since the cyber-attack on the base.

Eight minutes left to get out of here.

He followed Porter out of the basement door and looked down the corridor. No sign of Hulk. The American was nowhere to be seen. He had fucked-up big time. Which was strange. And definitely out of character. The guy was a solid professional. Hulk didn't strike him as the kind of guy who fluffed his lines on the big night.

So why the fuck did he head off in the wrong direction?

They paced back down the corridor and cut across the great room. Fuller tilted her head quizzically at Bald. 'We're going the wrong way. Exit is down there.'

'One of our lads got himself lost,' said Bald. 'We've got to fetch him first.'

'There's three of you?'

'Four,' Bald explained. 'Two other lads. Americans.'

An uneasy look flashed across her face. 'They're here?'

'One of them. The other bloke's outside. Sniper, covering the approaches. Anyone tries coming through the front door, they'll get dropped.'

Fuller said nothing.

They swerved round the corner and pushed on down another corridor, moving as quickly as Fuller could manage. They passed an office on the right, and a games room and a guest bedroom. Beelined towards the door leading to the master bedroom at the opposite end of the passage, twelve metres away.

The door to the suite was ajar. Porter picked up the pace and barrelled shoulder first into the room. Bald piled in after him, left arm still supporting Fuller.

They stepped into a room the approximate size of a London penthouse. There was a four-poster bed with golden posts and a diamond-encrusted crucifix hanging from the wall. A separate door led through to a gold-tapped en-suite bathroom. There was a walk-in closet to the left, with the president's usual array of cowboy hats on a long wooden shelf above a rack of white linen jackets and trousers, and framed pictures on the walls. The president, hanging out with different celebrities. In one snap he was giving it the thumbs-up with Charles Bronson. In another he was bumping fists with a retired heavyweight boxer.

To the right of the bedroom there was a private sitting area with a pair of leather armchairs arranged around a glass coffee table. An antique fireplace with a cavalry sword mounted above it. Mustard-coloured velvet curtains pulled across a tall window.

Hulk was standing in front of the fireplace.

The American had his M4 hanging from his sling, barrel down by his right side. He had drawn his Glock 17. Gripped it in his right hand. His close-quarters weapon. Chambered for the 9x19mm Parabellum round. A better tool for shooting in a confined environment.

In his left hand Hulk held his satellite-enabled phone. The guy was pointing the antenna in different directions as he searched for a signal. Like a scientist with a Geiger counter, checking for radiation.

Bald was about to ask him what the fuck he was doing when something caught his attention in the corner of his vision. He shifted his gaze back across to the fireplace. There was a polished wooden cabinet next to it, the shelves filled with baseball trophies and memorabilia. Autographed baseballs and gloves. Pennants. Photographs of the president shaking hands with players. The president was a big baseball guy, apparently. But that wasn't what caught his eye.

Next to the cabinet, he saw a strong-room door. A big steel thing, roughly the dimensions of a Smeg fridge.

The light on the panel next to the door glowed red.

Locked.

The voice whispered to him.

Something is badly wrong, John Boy.

'What the fuck is going on?' he growled.

The American lowered the phone. Looked from Bald to Porter to Fuller and back again. A sly look in his eyes that Bald hadn't seen before.

'Following orders,' he said.

'What are you fucking talking about?' Porter snapped. 'We're here for the hostage. Those are our bloody orders.'

Hulk stared blankly at him. 'We have another mission to carry out.'

Bald felt something like acid leaching into his guts. He glanced again at the strong-room door.

'What mission?' he asked.

But he already knew the answer.

'We're not here for the hostage,' Hulk said. 'We're here to kill the president.'

TWENTY-SIX

Nobody said anything for a long beat. Hulk watched the two Brits and the hostage carefully, his weapon at his side. The siren continued to wail in the background, overlapping the faintly audible cries of the wounded men pleading for help. The savage pounding between Bald's temples grew louder.

Porter said, 'You've got orders to slot Vasquez?'

Hulk nodded.

'From who?'

'Who d'you think?'

'The CIA?'

Hulk nodded again. Fuller was listening intently, Bald noticed.

'Why?'

'Regime change. There's a plan in place. The people running this thing have got their own man waiting in the wings. Pro-American guy. We scrub Vasquez out of existence, put him in charge.'

Bald felt a bayonet twisting inside his guts as he listened. Several thoughts clicked together inside his head. Questions that had been nicking away at the back of his mind.

The CIA's keenness to help to coordinate the mission. The directive from headquarters to push on after the fatal accident on the range.

The intelligence they had provided. The manpower and resources.

The Company is keen to help in any way it can.

A lot of effort to rescue a British citizen, Bald had thought at the time.

But not if you were planning to murder the Head of State.

'You fucking lied to us,' Porter said.

Hulk said, 'Not our call. Langley told us to keep you out of the loop. Didn't know if you could be trusted.'

'Where's Vasquez now?'

'In there.' Hulk pointed at the strong-room door. 'Son of a bitch crawled inside before I could drop him.'

'You told us he wasn't supposed to have arrived yet.'

'We lied. Had to. If you knew Vasquez was already at the mansion, you might have got suspicious.'

Bald turned his attention to the door. It looked solid as fuck. He had seen similar rooms before. The walls and ceiling would be bullet-resistant and blast-proof and soundproof. Steel sheeting, probably, placed over concrete blocks reinforced with rebar. The room would have its own ventilation system, comms and emergency supplies. The president could stay holed up in there for days if necessary.

'No way of busting that thing open,' Bald said. 'Not with a few M4s and grenades.'

'We have a way.'

'How?'

The American indicated his phone. 'Soon as I've got a signal, I'll speak with Langley. The strong room is rigged up to the Internet. Satellite modem, for continuous comms in the event of a power cut. We've got people who can hack into the hardware remotely. Same deal as the army barracks. They can unlock the door for us in sixty seconds.'

'From two thousand miles away?'

'They're good at what they do.'

Porter said, 'This is fucking madness.'

'You're looking at it the wrong way, brother. We put a hole in Vasquez, we're going to be rich.'

'We?' Bald repeated.

Hulk said, 'Me and Dudley. Once the new guy is installed as president, we'll handle security for the oil installations. Worth a lot of money. Langley says that you're to join us, taking control of the contracts. Help us out now, you'll have millions of dollars coming your way.'

'How much?'

'Ten per cent of the profits. We'll hire a couple of hundred guys to do the work, split the company profits between us four ways. You'll be richer than you ever dreamed.'

Bald glanced at the clock on the far wall: 04.09.

Nine minutes since the hackers had locked down the barracks.

Six minutes to get out of the mansion.

We're running out of time.

Porter shook his head, shaking with anger. 'We're not getting involved.'

'Too late,' said Hulk. 'This thing is already in train. The new guy has got his own people on the ground. They're rounding up the generals as we speak. Making them an offer they can't refuse. Twenty-four hours from now, he'll declare himself the new president.'

'Does Six know about this?' Porter demanded.

'Company business. Doesn't concern them.'

'This is bullshit. We didn't sign up for this shit.'

'You want to get rich or not?'

'Sod the money.'

Hulk said, 'We're killing a corrupt dictator. Nobody's going to be shedding tears over this fat—'

He stopped mid-sentence. Eyes narrowed, head canted to one side. As if he'd heard something. Then Porter heard it too. A soft whimpering.

Coming from behind the mustard-yellow curtains.

Hulk back-pocketed his phone and spun round. Keeping his Glock raised, he grabbed hold of the velvet drapes with his left hand and yanked them back.

Standing in front of the window was a young maid.

She was dressed in the same domestic uniform as the woman they had seen fleeing out of the dining room. But she was ten or fifteen years younger. Mid-twenties or thereabouts. *Around the same age as Sandy*, thought Porter. She was dark-eyed and slender, with heart-shaped lips and long flowing hair the colour of ground coffee.

She saw the Glock pointed at a spot between her eyes and began trembling. Lips quivering, a look of terror in her eyes as she begged and pleaded with Hulk in tearful Spanish.

Hulk kept the pistol raised.

'Sorry, sweetheart,' he said. 'No witnesses.'

The American's index finger tensed on the trigger.

'No!' Porter shouted.

In the corner of his eye, Bald saw his friend bringing up his rifle.

Aiming it at Hulk.

The American was fast. He reacted in a lightning flash, wheeling towards Porter and firing once before the latter could discharge a round. The Glock barked maybe six or seven feet away from Porter. A loud crack boomeranged around the master suite as a nine-milli bullet jetted out of the snout and thumped into Porter's face. The round struck him like an uppercut and sent him sprawling into the wooden cabinet, body clattering against the shelves of baseball souvenirs. He sagged to the floor, blood gushing down his face from the hole in his head. Instant death.

Fuller screamed.

The maid darted past Hulk and scampered out of the room, screaming wildly. She ducked out of the door, disappearing from view before the American could get a bead on her, Hulk cursing under his breath.

'Fucking bitch . . .'

He started after her, then shook his head. Bald stood frozen to the spot and stared at his dead mucker. Fragments of Porter's brain matter slicked down the wood panelling. The guy's mouth was open in an 'O' of mild surprise. His eyes gazed lifelessly at a spot on the far wall.

'Oh God,' Fuller sobbed. 'Oh, Jesus Christ.'

Hulk slid his gaze across to the Scot, Glock hanging by his side.

'Let's not get emotional, here,' he said coolly. 'Your buddy didn't want to get on board. He was going to fuck this thing up for all of us. You can see that, right?'

Bald tore his gaze away from Porter. At his side, Fuller was weeping pathetically.

'Fuck him,' Bald replied tonelessly. 'Cunt was soft anyway.'

Hulk's phone trilled. He took it out, read a message. Looked up.

'Do you still want to get rich, brother?'

'Always,' said Bald.

Hulk waved the Glock at Fuller. 'Take her outside. One of the wagons out front. Stick her in the back. I'll speak to Langley and deal with the president.'

'What about the Land Cruiser?'

'Change of plan. We've lost too much time. Dudley just messaged. He's seen figures spilling out of one of the barrack blocks. Must have smashed open the door somehow. Any minute now, the soldiers will be ramming through that front gate. We need to get out of here, right the fuck now.'

Bald glanced again at the clock: 04.11.

'Get moving,' Hulk went on, his voice urgent and tense. 'I'll be out in two minutes. Then we'll get the fuck out of here and crack open the beers.'

He turned away and dialled a number on his phone. Bald grabbed hold of Fuller and made for the doorway, arm wrapped around her waist. Her body shaking with fear and horror. The first time she had seen somebody die, probably.

They left the master suite and traced their steps back down the corridor, heading towards the great room. In the background, Bald could hear Hulk's voice as he spoke to the person on the other end of the phone. Giving them instructions. Fuller staggered alongside him, moving slowly, tears glistening on her dirt-smeared cheeks.

'You can't do this,' she croaked.

'Shut up,' Bald said. 'Walk faster.'

'Please. You're making a mistake.'

'Not from where I'm standing.'

'They just killed your friend. Don't you care?'

'He was a lame bastard. Now fucking move.'

She kept begging with him as they moved across the great room and hooked a left, beating a path back down the foyer towards the front porch, ten metres ahead of them. Through the open doorway, Bald could see the nearest of the two Ford Explorers resting at the side of the carriage circle, four metres beyond the porticoed entryway.

Our ticket out of here.

He was banking on the key fob being left inside the vehicle. A reasonable assumption. Standard procedure for close-protection teams. You didn't want guys having to search their pockets for the keys if the principal needed to make a hasty exit. Easier to leave them in the wagon.

Then he noticed something else.

A slender figure writhing on the ground to the right of the SUV.

Dressed in a black-and-white uniform.

The older maid had been shot. The woman Bald had seen in the dining room. She had taken a bullet to the guts. Both hands pawed at her stomach as a dark and glistening liquid pumped out of the hole, staining her apron and slicking the driveway. Bald wondered who had shot her. Stray round, maybe. But unlikely. Or perhaps Dudley had mistaken her for a target fleeing the building. The injured woman's agonised sobs carried across the driveway, mingling with the fainter moans of the wounded men at the breach.

No sign of the younger maid. Bald hoped she had found somewhere safe to hide.

'Listen to me,' Fuller said, gasping for breath. 'I'm trying to help you.'

Bald ignored her pleas and roughly marched her towards the entrance. They passed by the bullet-riddled guard Porter had dropped several minutes earlier. Felt like hours ago now. They were four metres from the front door when Fuller abruptly pulled away from Bald. He tried yanking her towards him but she stood her ground.

'For God's sake, listen, you bloody fool. We can't go outside.'

There was a sudden transformation in Fuller's voice and posture. Like an actor breaking character in the middle of a show. Like a mask had dropped from her face. The weak, tearful figure he had rescued from the cell had been replaced by a much more confident woman. A hard look in her green eyes as she spoke.

'It's a trap. Don't you see? As soon we step out of that door, they're going to kill both of us.'

'Who?'

'The Americans, you idiot.'

Bald's expression tightened. 'Why the fuck would they do that?'

'Because they're not here to do a deal with you. They're here to frame you both. You and your dead friend.'

Bald felt something cold and wet trickle down the base of his spine. The pounding between his temples was deafening now. He shook his head.

'Bollocks.'

'It's the truth,' Fuller insisted. 'They're setting you up. They're going to murder President Vasquez, kill you and pin the blame on you two. That's their plan.'

A question prodded at him. 'How the fuck would you know that?'

'I'm not a researcher,' Fuller said calmly. 'I'm with Six.'

TWENTY-SEVEN

The words hit Bald like a fist. For a moment he couldn't speak.
Couldn't move. He simply stared at Fuller, a hollow feeling
spreading though his chest. Outside, the maid with the gut-shot
continued to scream. Begging for help that would never come.

'Bullshit,' he said. 'You're lying.'

Fuller's lips upturned. 'Don't believe me? Phone Madeleine.
She'll tell you the truth.'

Bald peered at her. 'How do you know Strickland?'

'She's my boss. I report directly to her.'

Bald hesitated. He looked back in the direction of the great
room. Hulk had said he would need two minutes to get on the
blower to the agency, unlock the strong-room door and dispatch
Vasquez. Maybe fifty seconds had passed since then.

We're almost out of time.

His cold grey eyes skated back to Fuller.

'Why would the Yanks want to frame us for slotting the
president?'

'There's no time to explain now. You're going to have to trust
me.'

Seconds ticked by. Bald remembered the questions they had asked
themselves back in London. What Porter had said. 'We're going to a
lot of effort for some unknown academic.'

'Don't believe me? Who do you think shot her?'

Fuller thrust an arm in the direction of the housemaid on the
driveway.

Then he understood.

Dudley.

The sniper hadn't shot her by accident, Bald realised. He was
too good a shot for that. Which meant that he had deliberately

251

plugged the maid as she had bolted out of the front door. From Dudley's vantage point on the hillock, four hundred metres away, he would have been able to line her up as soon as she had emerged from the mansion.

'Why?' Bald asked.

Fuller said, 'They shot her for the same reason they wanted to kill that maid behind the curtain. They're covering their tracks. They don't want anyone else to know they were here. Believe me, they're not going to let you or me walk out of here alive.'

No witnesses.

Bald looked from the wounded housemaid to the great room.

Left or right. Win or lose.

Live or die.

Less than a minute until Hulk finishes up.

'We've got to go,' Fuller said, panic rising in her voice. 'You need to decide. Right now.'

Bald thought about the money. The millions he'd make. He thought about Porter lying on the bedroom floor. The lights out in his eyes, a hole in his head the size of a poker chip.

Who do you trust, John Boy? Hulk and Dudley?

Or the woman?

He looked back towards the front door. They weren't in the sniper's line of sight now, but Dudley would spot them as soon as they set foot outside the door, Bald knew. They would have to go through the kill zone to reach the Explorers.

We'd never make it.

He reached a decision.

Nodded at Fuller.

'Is there another way out of here?'

She thought quickly. 'Kitchen. They brought me in through the garage when I first arrived. There's a door that connects from the motor court to the utility room. We can escape through there.'

Bald cast his mind back several thousand years. He remembered sweeping through the barrier gate, making for the entrance. The motor court and garages on the western side of the stronghold. The Tahoe SUV he'd spied through the gateway.

'Come on,' he said.

He started down the foyer.

'Wait,' Fuller said. 'Do you have a phone?'

'Just the one the Americans gave us.'

'Lose it. The CIA will be able to track it remotely.'

She scuttled over to the dead guard. The guy with the shredded ball sack and the oily hair. The guy who had been a split second away from slotting Bald. Fuller knelt down beside him and rooted through his clothing. Dug out his phone and stashed it in her jeans pocket. She grabbed the guard's pistol from his belt holster too. A Browning Hi-Power semi-automatic. Tugged back the slider to see if there was a round in the chamber. Pressed the mag release button on the side and checked the clip. Full magazine. At the same time, Bald took out the handset Taylor had given him and tossed it aside.

Fuller nodded at him.

'Okay,' she said. 'Let's go.'

They set off down the foyer. Away from the squealing maid. Away from the front doors, and certain death. Towards the great room.

Fuller was moving freely now, chopping her stride as they hurried towards the corridor off to the left, adrenaline juicing her veins. As they turned the corner, he heard two muffled cracks in the distance. Coming from the other side of the great room.

Hulk.

He's just executed the fucking president, Bald thought.

Any second now, he's going to be leaving that room.

'Hurry,' Bald rasped.

They pushed on, putting more distance between themselves and Hulk. Barrelled past the door to the basement and crashed through the grey door at the far end. Fuller led the way, Bald hurrying along a metre or so behind as she dashed through the kitchen and levered open a door next to the pantry. They hurried across a bare tile-floored space with a sink and several bins and washing machines. Swept through another and emerged at the side of the building, facing out across the motor court.

Fourteen minutes since the attack on the barracks.

The Tahoe was parked in the middle of the blacktop. A boxy beast of a wagon with paintwork the colour of graphite and a golden bow-tie logo fixed to the chrome grille. Run-flat tyres fitted as standard.

'Get in,' Bald ordered. 'Quick.'

His heart was beating faster now as he circled round to the rear passenger door and dumped his rucksack inside. There was a neglected bulletproof vest on the back seat. Left inside the vehicle in case the principal forgot to wear his own armour, presumably. Bald snatched the vest, swerved round to the driver's side door and hopped up the step while Fuller climbed into the front passenger seat. He shoved his rifle barrel-down at his side and looked round for the keys.

He didn't have to look far. The previous occupant had left the key fob on the plastic tray in the middle of the console. For convenience, Bald imagined. The bodyguards would have had a system going on. Park the car, leave it unlocked with the key in the tray, ready for the next guy.

The Tahoe was an automatic. He foot-tapped the brake and depressed the start button. The engine fired up. A whole galaxy of lights lit up on the dash. The needle on the fuel gauge showed a full tank. Enough for a journey of least four hundred miles.

He thrust the spare vest at Fuller. 'Here. Shove this down your side of the door.'

'What for?'

'We're in a soft-shell vehicle. We're gonna be driving right past that sniper, on your side. It'll stop any rounds ripping through the door.'

She nodded quickly. Pressed the vest against the side panel on her door.

'Stay low,' he ordered. 'And for fuck's sake keep your head in the footwell.'

He switched the lights off. The beams would simply make the vehicle a more obvious target. He down-shifted the lever on the side of the steering wheel to the Drive position. Released the parking brake.

Then he stamped on the accelerator.

The Tahoe roared as it surged forward. Bald gripped the wheel tightly, speedometer needle rapidly arcing upwards as he steered the wagon out of the motor court and through the arched gateway. Towards the carriage circle and the driveway and the front gate, fifty metres away. He slalomed around the two Explorers parked around the carriage circle, swerving to avoid the gut-shot maid. Hit the driveway and arrowed south, picking up speed. To his right Fuller was staying low in her seat, her chest tight against her thighs and her hands laced over the back of her head. Like an aeroplane passenger adopting the brace position.

In the rear-view mirror, he caught a glimpse of Hulk. The ex-SEAL was rushing out of the mansion and bringing up his M4 rifle. Aiming at the fleeing Tahoe.

'Stay the fuck down!' Bald thundered.

In the next fraction of a second, the rear windscreen shattered as three rounds punched through the glass and thumped into the rear headrests, rocking them back and forth with explosive force. Shattered glass fragments and torn bits of stuffing flew through the air as two more 5.56mm bullets sliced through the air and struck the upholstery. Bald dropped as low as he possibly could, steering almost blind. Foot to the pedal, aiming for the gate. Another round zipped past him, inches above his head. Buried itself in the front windshield.

Keep fucking going.

If we don't make it out of here, we're dead.

Hulk was emptying a ferocious amount of lead at the wagon. Bullets clanged off the rear fenders and ripped through the body-work in a deafening metallic clang. Bald kept the Tahoe pointed at the gate, mashing the pedal and gripping the wheel with white-knuckled hands. Thirty metres to the barrier gate now. Bald willed the wagon to go faster. Rounds hammered off the boot, clattering like hailstones against the bodywork. Twenty metres.

Ten.

There was a loud thump and clatter as the Tahoe rammed through the barrier. They hit the gravel track with a jolt and bombed south towards the main road, four hundred metres away. Mango grove on their right, the hillock somewhere further to the south. Engine snarling, the speedometer needle creeping past the fifty miles per hour mark. Fuller keeping her head down, the spare vest pressed against the side of the door.

Bald floored it.

We're not out of the woods yet.

We've got to get past Dudley first.

The track would take them directly past the hillock on their right. They would have to endure Dudley's fire before they could get away, he knew. He guessed there would be a delay of a few seconds while Hulk raised the redneck on the phone.

The Brit and the woman are fleeing in the Tahoe. Stop them at all costs.

They raced past the trees. Two hundred metres to the main road now. Two hundred metres to freedom. Beyond the treetops, he could make out the dark hump of high ground overlooking the stronghold.

Dudley's sniper nest.

They were a hundred metres from the road when the first two rounds cracked against the windscreen, spider-webbing the glass. The bullets thumped into the headrests above Bald and Fuller, showering flakes of foam over their heads. Another pair of shots cracked against the front of the wagon, ricocheting off the grille. He heard an urgent hiss as Dudley brassed up the run-flat tyres, peppering them with rounds. A moment later they were sliding directly past the hillock and the side window above Fuller exploded. Glass cascaded over Bald and Fuller, sprinkling the footwells and grazing their hands and faces. Rounds hammered against the panelling on the door on Fuller's side, thumping into the spare bulletproof vest. Bald drove on. Twenty metres to the main road. He dropped his speed and flicked the wheel sharply to the left. The wagon lurched heavily as it drifted into the turn. Tyres screaming in protest, loose gravel clattering against the panelling. Bald fought to maintain control of the wheel. There was time for Dudley to fire two more rounds, bullets glancing off the shattered frame of the rear windscreen.

Then they were pulling away and surging east.

The shooting ceased.

Bald raced east and then south. After two miles he hit the road junction and made a sharp left, tearing along for a mile until he took the turn for the rough path he'd spotted earlier. He steered down the track for a hundred metres, the Tahoe shuddering over the potholes as he peered through the cracked glass. Found the spot where he'd ditched the Land Cruiser a few hours ago and slammed on the brakes, pulling up a metre behind it. Hit the engine stop button and sprang open his door. Fuller had sat up in her seat. Turned round to look at him, slivers of broken glass glinting like ice in her hair.

'What are you doing? We can't stop now. We need to be on the road.'

'This ride's no good,' Bald said. 'Tyres are shot to bits. Run-flats are only good for fifty miles. We'll need to switch vehicles. Besides, we can't drive this thing across the country. Bullet holes all over the fucking shop. We'll stand out like a dog-lover in China. Come on.'

He jumped down from the Tahoe, gripping his M4, and moved round to the rear door. Grabbed his rucksack containing the water bottles, L2 grenades and spare clips from the back seat. Hastened over to the Land Cruiser and dived behind the wheel while Fuller clambered into the passenger seat.

Bald fired up the engine and K-turned in the path. Then he sped back towards the main road, slung a hard right and rocketed east. Past the blacked-out town of Los Altos, towards the distant mountains.

Every so often he glanced at the rear-view, watching for headlights, but he saw nothing. Just a dense empty blackness. Understandable. The soldiers might have broken out of the barracks by now. The Americans were most likely too busy making their own escape from the stronghold. They wouldn't have time to focus on hunting down Bald and Fuller. Not at the moment. *Besides*, Bald reminded himself, *We ditched that phone the CIA gave us. Those fuckers won't have any way of tracking us.*

We're safe.

For now.

They raced on for four miles and then Bald eased off the gas and kept the Land Cruiser ticking along at ten miles below the speed limit. He wasn't worried about drawing attention from the local cops. They would have their hands full for a while, dealing with the effects of the blackout. There would be panic in the streets. Looters plundering shops and offices. Criminals roaming free.

He glanced over at Fuller. She sat in tense silence, staring at the phone she had snatched from the dead guard. She looked a little shaken up, but otherwise seemed to be okay. He got the distinct impression this wasn't the first firefight she had been involved in.

'Where are we going?' she asked.

Bald said, 'We're thirty miles from the coast. We'll head in that direction, lie up in one of the fishing villages and bribe someone to take us out to sea. Get to one of them islands. Aruba or Curacao. Then we'll find a way to contact Vauxhall. Tell them what's happened.'

She looked up from the screen with wide eyes. 'That's your big plan?'

'Better than nothing. Their president has just been capped. We need to get out of this country, before we have every soldier and police officer in the land looking for us.'

'We can't go to the villages. It's high risk. They might shop us to the authorities.'

'It's Venezuela,' Bald said. 'Inflation's running at a million per cent. People haven't got two pennies to rub together. They'll take the fucking money, if it's on offer.'

Fuller shook her head. 'It's too dangerous.'

'You have a better idea?'

'We need to speak to Six. They'll find a way of getting us out of here.'

'Power's out.' Bald nodded at the pitch-black landscape. 'Most of the immediate area is in the dark ages. We've got no way of contacting your bosses.'

'The grid won't be down for long,' Fuller said confidently. 'Another half hour or so. The people behind the hack are under orders not to cause unnecessary damage to the infrastructure.'

Bald glanced at her again. 'How the fuck do you know that?'

'It's part of their plan. That's all I can tell you.'

'Bollocks. Those pricks just tried to kill me. I deserve answers.'

'This is an intelligence matter. Need-to-know only. You're not security cleared. I'm not authorised to discuss this with you.'

'I don't give a fuck. I just saw my oldest mate get blown away.'

Fuller gave him a funny look. 'You didn't seem too cut up about his death, as I recall.'

'Had to make it look like I didn't give a shit,' Bald replied dismissively. 'Play along with Hulk.'

Fuller stared at him, as if trying to decide whether he was telling the truth.

'I'm taking a big risk here,' Bald went on. 'If it wasn't for me, we'd both be dead. Now tell me what the fuck is going on.'

She fell silent for a beat. Bald glanced over at the digital clock on the Land Cruiser's multimedia display: 04.43. Almost first light. The faintest bluish glow was visible on the horizon, beyond the rugged dark slopes. The road flowed river-like through the valley floor, twisting past blacked-out villages and small towns. To the north, several miles away, Bald could see a far steeper row of mountains. Somewhere beyond those peaks, he knew, was the Caribbean coast.

'Six sent me out here to establish contact with a colleague,' Fuller said at last.

'Another spy?'

Fuller shook her head. 'An American. From the CIA. Chris Keeble. He said he had information he wanted to share with me and he couldn't risk discussing it via electronic communications. He insisted on a face-to-face meeting.'

'Why would this bloke reach out to you, rather than his own people?'

'He'd gone rogue. The Company was looking for him. He didn't know where else to go.'

'So he turned to you?'

'I'd worked with him in the past. We had a good rapport. I guess he felt I was someone who wouldn't sell him out. Six decided to send me over here to meet with him. Find out what he had uncovered. That's what I was doing when the security forces showed up at my hotel and arrested me.'

'All that stuff about you being an academic . . . that was a load of crap?'

'Not exactly. It's a cover identity I was using. A legend. It's becoming standard practice now at Six. The days when SIS officers could operate clandestinely abroad are over. Facial recognition software means you're picked up and identified as soon as you step off the plane these days. So they train up people like me instead.'

'Like you?'

'Deep-cover officers, with legitimate careers and carefully constructed backstories who can travel around and operate with a degree of freedom. We're spies, but we have professional careers with the appropriate qualifications and backgrounds. Six populates our online profiles and make sure nothing slips through the net that might give us away. Tagged photographs on someone else's social media feed, that sort of thing. Some of us work in the sciences, others in business or at universities. Typically, jobs that require international travel and meeting a lot of new people. I've got a legitimate paid position, I pay rent on a flat in Bethnal Green and have a circle of friends that don't know anything about my career with Six. I've even had academic papers published. As far as my parents and family are concerned, I was going to Venezuela to do research. No one was supposed to suspect a thing. Then it all went wrong.'

Bald said, 'What happened?'

'Someone at the CIA must have realised Keeble was going to spill his guts. They lifted him, but not before our meeting.'

'What did he tell you?'

'He said he'd been working closely with his colleagues in Bogotá. A top-secret operation. He'd been briefed about it and wasn't happy about what they were planning to do. Said the Company was plotting to murder Vasquez and put a new guy in charge. Someone more amenable to American interests. Someone who wouldn't be so welcoming to the Iranians and Russians. He said they were going to make sure it was done cleanly, with nothing to link the killing to Langley.'

'Who else is involved?'

'Keeble's bosses. And people above them, he said. He didn't have names. But his gut feeling was that it went right to the very top.'

'The US President?'

'He didn't have proof, but he thinks so. It's hard to imagine anyone at Langley signing off on this without presidential approval.'

'Jesus Christ.'

'At first, I wasn't sure whether to believe Keeble,' Fuller said. 'I mean, it sounded outlandish. But two days later, he disappeared. That's when I knew he must be on to something.'

'Why did he go to you, though? Why not go to the press? They'd have a fucking field day with this stuff.'

'He didn't have concrete proof. And he was afraid that his superiors would try to silence him if he went public. He wanted to cut a deal with us instead. Information about the conspiracy, in exchange for a new identity. He figured we could sit down with our friends at Langley and tell them what we knew. Threaten to leak everything unless they backed down. That was the plan we discussed, anyway. I was preparing to notify Vauxhall when the security forces broke into my room.'

'How did they find you?' asked Bald.

'The Venezuelans had been watching Keeble. Must have followed him to our meeting. So they knew I was involved. I tried to flee the country but they caught up with me before I could escape. Before the CIA could get to me.'

Bald looked at her. 'All this time, the Company knew you were working for Six?'

'Yes. My guess is that's why they hijacked the rescue op. They could kill Vasquez and get rid of me at the same time. Two birds, one stone.'

'Does Six know about any of this?'

Fuller shook her head. 'I don't think so, no. It was a CIA-led operation, under directive from the White House. Vauxhall didn't know anything about a plan to assassinate Vasquez.'

'Or maybe they just didn't want to admit it.'

Fuller considered this, then shook her head. 'No. That's not Strickland's style.'

'You people are capable of some evil shit. I've done my fair share of dirty work for you lot down the years.'

'Point taken. But generally speaking, we don't go around murdering heads of state. Not even as favours to Washington.'

Bald said, 'Why would the Yanks bother trying to frame me and Porter for the hit? Why not just kill the president themselves?'

'Plausible deniability. The Americans didn't want to look like they were involved in an assassination attempt. That would be a bad look for them, obviously. There would be an international outcry. And it would completely undermine the new man's credibility if it looked as if he was a US-sponsored puppet. They needed a scapegoat. Someone to carry the can, so it didn't look like an inside job.'

'So they decided to pin the blame on us?'

'That wasn't the original plan. According to Keeble, they were going to carry out the attack using four disgraced ex-SEALs. Real mavericks. They'd go in, execute the president and melt away again.'

'What happened?'

'The plan changed. My guess is that they heard about the team being prepared to rescue me and decided to hijack the operation. They could kill Vasquez, murder you and your friend and claim that a pair of British mercenaries were behind the attack.'

'And they'd have the security footage to back it up.'

'Exactly.'

She fell silent again and stared out of the windscreen, lost in her thoughts. Then she swallowed and said, 'Keeble told me something else, too. Before he went missing.'

Bald glanced at her. 'What's that?'

'He said the Americans weren't the only ones involved in the plot to kill Vasquez. He believed they had outside help. The cyber-attacks were being handled by a third party.'

'Who?'

'Someone who's worked with Six before. No one you've ever heard of.'

'Try me, lass.'

Fuller stared out the window at the dense blackness beyond. 'A political fixer,' she said. 'From London. A former friend of mine, actually. Julian Cantwell.'

TWENTY-EIGHT

Bald tightened his grip on the wheel. His muscles tensed with rage. The pounding between his temples flared up again. Like knuckles rapping against wood. Fuller evidently saw the dark look flash across his face and crinkled her brow.

'What is it?' she asked.

'I know that name,' Bald replied through gritted teeth.

The lines on her brow deepened. 'How?'

Bald told her about the briefing in London. The introduction to Julian Cantwell, the portly, red-haired dandy in the three-piece suit. The discussion about Fuller. Her panic attacks, their time at university together.

'That sounds like Julian,' Fuller said. 'He always dressed like it was the 1920s, even when we were at Oxford together.'

'He doesn't strike me as a mastermind hacker. Thought all them lot were sad bastards, like. Sitting in basements in their Y-fronts, wanking off to weird porn.'

Fuller smirked. 'Julian doesn't do the hacking himself. He's not computer literate. Barely knows how to operate a mobile phone. His employees have to show him how to do everything. But he's emotionally manipulative. Very good at getting other people to do what he wants. They're the ones who do the actual grunt work. He just sits there and takes all the credit.'

'He reckoned you two were good pals.'

Fuller smiled feebly. 'We were, once. For a short while. But we're not in touch anymore. I can't even remember the last time we spoke. Ten, fifteen years ago? Something like that.'

'Why would he bullshit about your relationship?'

Fuller thought for a moment while she checked her phone for a signal. 'Someone must have sent him on a fact-finding mission.

His masters would have wanted to know what Madeleine and the others knew about the conspiracy. He certainly didn't go there out of any concern for my well-being.'

'He reckoned you suffered from panic attacks.'

'I used to. Six toughened me up, though. You can't be weak-minded and survive for long at Vauxhall.'

Bald wrestled with a puzzling thought. 'Why would the Yanks outsource the cyber-warfare stuff to Cantwell? They've got their own hackers, surely.'

'Same reason they wanted to frame you. Using domestic hackers was too risky. Even if they were very careful, they'd leave digital fingerprints all over the place. It had to be someone from the outside. And Cantwell was a known entity within Washington circles. He was someone they could trust.'

'Fuckers thought of everything.'

'Almost,' Fuller corrected. 'They didn't count on me escaping. If we make it out of the country, we can still expose what the Company has been doing.'

'They'll deny it,' Bald said. 'They always do.'

'Probably. But we can still go after Cantwell. The Americans couldn't have done this without his help. We can twist his arm. Get him to give up what he knows. Names, dates. Information we can corroborate. He could be a goldmine of intelligence on who else is involved.'

'We've got to get out of this shithole first,' Bald pointed out.

Fuller nodded nervously.

'What's the plan now?' he asked.

She glanced at the time on the display: 04.54. 'The grid should be back on in a few minutes. Keep driving north. I'll reach out to Vauxhall as soon as I have a signal. We need to tell them what's going on.'

They rolled on through the valley. Bald stuck to the main road snaking north from Los Altos, zigzagging between dark brooding hills and the outlines of coal-black towns. Heading in the direction of the mountain range fringing the coast. He didn't have a specific destination in mind. His primary concern was to put as much distance between themselves and the Americans as possible. Every couple of minutes Fuller woke the phone up from sleep mode and checked for a signal. Frowned when she didn't find one and put the handset back into its digital coma.

After two miles Bald spotted a few lights twinkling in the distance from a township in the foothills. A sure sign that the power was back up and running. At which point Fuller woke up the dead guard's phone again and manually tapped in a long number. He glanced over her shoulder and caught the first three digits: *212*. The area code for Caracas.

'Who are you calling?' he asked.

'British embassy,' Fuller said. 'I'll speak to the resident Six officer there. Get him to put me through to Vauxhall.'

'Why can't we just head straight for the embassy? Stay there for a while?'

'Absolutely not,' Fuller replied bluntly. 'For a start, neither of us is supposed to be here. We're off the books. If we show up at the embassy, it's going to directly implicate the British government. Besides, they can't help us. A few hours from now, we're going to be the most wanted people in the country. We can't risk leaving through the air or seaports. The authorities will be looking for us everywhere. Anywhere densely populated is a no-go.'

'They could sort us out with clean passports.'

'The Venezuelan intelligence services already know my face. They'll know yours, too, once they take a look at the security footage. It's a non-starter.'

'How the fuck are your mates going to get us out of here, then?'

'Madeleine will have a plan. She won't let us down.'

Fuller tapped the Dial icon and clamped the handset to her ear. Bald drove on as she spent several minutes jumping through hoops on the phone. The switchboard transferred her to an emergency out-of-hours number. The duty officer who took the call seemed reluctant to disclose the private number for the cultural attaché. There was some displeasure at the thought of disturbing him at such an early hour. But Fuller was persistent. And very persuasive.

The call with the attaché, a guy called Anthony Herd, was much shorter and to the point. There was a quick back-and-forth with a groggy-sounding man. She obviously knew the guy. There was an easy familiarity in her voice as they spoke. She didn't introduce herself, didn't bother with any preamble. She just launched straight into it. Explained that she was in trouble, without going into too many specifics, and needed to be patched through to Vauxhall. The voice on the other end mumbled something and hung up.

Bald said, 'What's the situation?'

'Anthony, the local resident, is calling Vauxhall now. They have my number. Madeleine is going to call back on a secure line.'

'Whatever plan they're gonna cook up,' Bald growled, 'it had better be fucking good.'

'They'll get us out of here.'

Fourteen minutes later, her phone buzzed again. Bald saw the blue-green glow of the display light up with an incoming call. He thought: five o'clock in the morning in Venezuela. Ten o'clock in the morning in London. Strickland would be at her desk, hacking through her in-tray.

Fuller went to swipe-answer.

Bald said, 'Put her on loudspeaker.'

Fuller looked at him.

'Strickland knows me,' he added. 'She'll want me to listen in. I'm going to need to know the details of the exfiltration plan.'

She paused, then swiped and tapped at the touchscreen again. A moment later, Bald heard a familiar Glaswegian-accented voice on the other end of the line.

Strickland said, 'Caroline? Are you there?'

'Here,' Fuller said. 'I'm okay.'

A light sigh of relief sibilated down the line. 'Where are you?'

'Fifteen miles from the stronghold,' Bald cut in. 'Heading north towards the coast.'

There was another long pause. 'John? Is that you?'

'Aye.'

'What the hell is going on?'

'The op turned into a clusterfuck,' Bald said. 'Porter's dead. Vasquez too. The Americans almost slotted us as well. They fucking set us up.'

He drove on while Fuller briefed Strickland on the situation.

She gave a concise summary of events. Everything from the time of her capture by the Venezuelans to the escape from the mansion. Strickland said very little. She listened in silence as Fuller told her about the CIA-led plot to assassinate Vasquez. The cyber-attacks. Cantwell's involvement. Hulk putting a hole in Porter's head. Their attempt to frame Bald and Porter for Vasquez's death. Bald interrupted occasionally, adding details here and there.

'Where are the Americans now?' she asked.

'We left them at the stronghold,' Bald said. 'They'll be on the road. If they've got any smarts about them, they'll be heading back down to the Colombian border. Getting the fuck out of Dodge.'

'And President Vasquez?'

'Dead, as far as we know,' Fuller said.

'Jesus,' she muttered. 'This is a disaster.'

'Did you know about any of this?' Bald demanded.

'Of course not. Why would you think that, for God's sake?'

'Wouldn't be the first lie you told us. You fed us that bag of bollocks about Fuller. Told us that she had nothing to do with your people.'

'That was necessary to keep her cover story intact. We didn't want to share that information with the Americans in case it leaked. We were trying to protect her. Nothing more.'

Bald grunted. 'It's getting fucking hard to know who to trust these days.'

'We're on the same side. We didn't have anything to do with the Vasquez hit. You have my word, John. From one Scot to another.'

'I'm not interested in your bullshit. Just get us the fuck out of here. We need an emergency extraction, right bloody now.'

Strickland said, 'We're working on it as we speak. But it's going to take some time to arrange a rescue team. This is a complicated operation, as you might imagine.'

'I don't give a monkey's,' Bald snapped. 'Tell your people to hurry up and pull their fingers out, before we have the whole fucking country searching for us.'

'We understand the urgency. We've got our best people on the

267

case. As soon as our assets are ready to move in, we'll let you know. In the meantime, head for the emergency rendezvous location. I'll send you the coordinates once this call is over. Once you get there, you'll await the rescue team and prepare for immediate extraction.'

'What's the RV?'

'An old airstrip, to the east of your position. One of the air bridges used by the cartels to export cocaine to Europe. The traffickers abandoned it a while ago but the strip is still intact. You'll make your way there and wait for the team to arrive.'

'Do the Americans know about it?'

'We don't share every operational detail with Langley, John.'

'Your team had better not keep us waiting long. We're going to be exposed, sitting around waiting for an aircraft to come in.'

'We're doing the best we can. Keep this phone switched on. I'll be in touch as soon as we have more information.'

She clicked off. The phone screen darkened. Then brightened again, trilling to announce a new text. Fuller glanced at it before showing the screen to Bald. The message contained two strings of numbers. Latitude and longitude. Fuller finger-punched the icon for the satnav on the multimedia display and selected the option for lat and long. She typed in the coordinates and tapped Drive.

The map zoomed out. A bright-blue line showed the route from their present location to their destination to the east. An isolated spot, thirty miles due south of the coastline and at least fifteen miles from the nearest town. A 250-mile journey, according to the satnav. Roughly six hours away. Estimated arrival time at around 11.00.

Fuller said, 'Is there enough fuel in this thing to get us there?'

Bald did a quick mental calculation. The jerry cans in the back, plus the two-thirds in the tank. 'Yeah. Plenty.'

She was silent for a while as she stared out of the window at the slowly rising sun. Bald followed the route on the satnav and said, 'I thought you lot didn't have any assets on the ground over here.'

'We don't.'

'What assets was Strickland talking about just now, then? For the rescue team.'

Fuller thought about it for a few seconds, shook her head. 'I don't know. Let's just hope they get it sorted soon.'

'You're worried about them Venezuelans?'

'Not just them. The Americans. They'll be mobilising any reinforcements and allies they have. The Company will do whatever it takes to stop us from getting away.'

'They can't track us, lass. We ditched the electronics. They're out of the picture.'

They both stared quietly ahead. After a while she turned to him and said, 'I'm sorry. About your friend.'

Bald shrugged. 'He was a Blade. You wear that beret, you know the deal. When you step through that door, one of two things happens. You're either the hero who saves the day, or the fucker who gets one between the eyes.' He was silent for a moment. 'It's not him I feel angry about.'

Fuller angled her head. 'Who, then?'

'That maid. The one Dudley nailed.'

'Why her?'

'Killing her is one thing. But with the skills he's got, that Yank sniper could have put one in her head. Could have ended her life painlessly. Instead he plugged her in the guts. That was deliberate. The sick cunt wanted her to suffer.'

They carried on towards the emergency RV, the sun glowing behind shreds of cloud as they headed east. They stuck to the main roads, avoiding the quieter secondary roads. A conscious decision. They were using the traffic to hide in plain sight, making the Land Cruiser less conspicuous. And hence less likely to attract the attention of any passing cops. Bald kept an eye on the horizon, looking out for military checkpoints. If they spotted one, he would detour on to the next dirt path or trail and box around the checkpoint before re-joining the main road several miles further along.

They cantered through rolling green valleys, the peaks wreathed in early morning mist. Small villages scattered like dice along the slopes. Bald was running on fumes now. After a few hours the landscape flat-lined and they catapulted along the coast, the Caribbean at their left, denim-blue against the morning sky. They passed squalid villages and strips of empty white beach and hotels fallen into disrepair. Bald vaguely recalled something Freddy Vargas had said to him. Something about white lobsters and go-fast boats. He shook off a wave of tiredness and glanced over at the satnav: 09.00.

Two hours to their destination.

Not much further now.

A few more hours and we'll be out of this place.

Forty-nine minutes later, Fuller's phone buzzed again.

Another incoming call from Strickland. She swipe-answered and tapped to put it on loudspeaker, Bald listening in as he kept the Land Cruiser coasting along the nearly empty road.

'We've made some calls,' Strickland said. 'A rescue team is being assembled to come in and extract you. They're being briefed right now.'

Bald said, 'Who are they?'

'A detachment of soldiers from 22 SAS. D Squadron.'

'They're coming over from Hereford?'

'Colombia. They're out there on a team training job. Along with a bunch of guys from the Special Boat Service. Training up local security forces to help fight the emergent cartels. They'll going to fly across in a Hercules C-130 and pick you up.'

A question stabbed at Bald. 'Your fucking errand boy Merrick didn't mention anything about a load of Regiment lads being right next door to us.'

'The D Squadron guys aren't supposed to be out there. We couldn't risk telling you in case you were captured by the Venezuelans and compromised their operations. You understand, John.'

More fucking lies, Bald thought. Rage pounded in his veins. 'How many lads are we talking about?'

'One section. Air Troop. That's all we can spare.'

Bald nodded to himself. Technically there were supposed to be sixteen guys to an SAS troop, but in his experience they were always short. We're looking at anywhere from eight to a dozen operators.

Plenty of firepower.

Enough to take on anyone who tries to ambush us.

'What's their ETA?' he asked.

'Twelve o'clock. They'll be in the air in the next thirty minutes.'

Bald looked over at the satnav again and make a quick calculation. They were around eighty minutes from the RV. Which meant that they would be waiting for the Hercules for approximately an hour.

'What happens once we're out of the country?'

'A reception party from Six will be waiting for you on the ground in Colombia. One of our guys from the embassy in Bogotá will meet you there. He'll provide you with clean papers and drive you to another airfield. You'll then be flown back to London for a full debriefing.'

'Those reinforcements had better be on the button. We can't be hanging around there for long.'

'They'll be on time. Just get to the RV. We'll get you safely back home. Then we'll take care of Cantwell and his chums.'

TWENTY-NINE

They left the main road at ten o'clock and cut inland, swathing past sparsely forested fields and the occasional smallholding or village. A few minutes later a helicopter roared overhead, alarming Fuller, but it soon raced off towards the coast. Bald stayed calm. He wasn't worried about the chopper. He very much doubted the Venezuelans knew what car they were driving. Not unless the Americans had tipped them off about the Land Cruiser. And they weren't about to do that. They'd want to catch Bald and Fuller themselves. Kill them before they could spill their guts.

After thirty minutes the road degraded as they took another turn and the Land Cruiser juddered and rocked over muddied tracks as they headed south through a wide plain punctuated with clumps of forest. They were miles from the nearest town now. Twenty miles from the northern coast. The middle of nowhere. The Venezuelan backwoods. The only signs of habitation were the rough trails criss-crossing the landscape and the power lines trailing through the plains. They rolled on for another two miles, between corridors of trees, and then the satnav cheerfully pinged to announce that they had arrived at their destination.

Bald eased off the gas and crept along for two hundred metres until they hit the eastern edge of a long narrow airstrip surrounded on all sides by walls of tall-canopied forest. The strip looked to be at least a kilometre long and more than fifty metres wide. To his right, a few hundred metres further along, he saw a pair of aluminium-roofed huts on a grassy patch on the side of the strip. The strip itself was little more than a stretch of rough ground, dotted with weeds and puddles.

An isolated area, Bald thought. *No one will be looking for us here.*

He checked the time: 10.04.

Fifty-six minutes until the Herc was due to land.

Fuller said, 'What now?'

Bald nodded at her phone. 'You got reception on that thing?'

She tapped the screen awake and squinted at it. 'Two bars. Why?'

'We'll need to check the condition of the airstrip. Make sure there's no obstacles. Feed that information back to Vauxhall, so they can pass it on to the pilot.'

She looked doubtfully at the strip. 'Can the Hercules really land there?'

'It'll be tasty for the lads on board. But the Herc can handle it. You can bring them things down on really rough ground. As long as the strip is long enough, she'll be fine.'

He steered the Land Cruiser left and trundled south, towards the southern end of the strip. When he was level with the threshold Bald slewed the wagon round and stopped in the middle of the airstrip, facing north towards the other end of the makeshift runway. He reset the trip meter on the odometer, then turned in his seat to face Fuller.

'We'll drive up the length of the strip,' he said. 'Measure its length and look for obstructions. You'll check your side, I'll do mine.'

'What are we looking for?'

'Potholes, ditches, large rocks. Any shit like that. Make sure this thing is fit for purpose.'

Bald pumped the gas and started down the middle of the airstrip, keeping the Land Cruiser to a fixed speed of twenty miles per hour. Fuller ran her eyes over the right side of the strip while Bald checked the ground to the left, paying attention to the foliage and looking for any overhanging branches that might snag against the Herc's wingtips. The strip was in decent condition, despite its age and neglected surroundings. He noted a few clumps of weed and divots, but nothing to cause the crew serious difficulties. Fuller reported that everything was clear on her side, and then they reached the northern threshold and Bald tapped the brakes again. He looked round, checking the radius of the turning circle. The Herc was a big beast of an aircraft, with a forty-metre wingspan. If the circle wasn't wide enough there was no way the crew would be able to swing her round for take-off.

He made a note of the distance on the trip odometer, told Fuller to wait in the Land Cruiser and then climbed out. Wandered over to a patch of grass, took a clump of it and let the blades tumble to the ground, gauging the direction and strength of the wind. Stood up and strained his eyes at the horizon, looking out for any obstacles. Telephone lines, electricity pylons, tall trees. He hurried back across to the Land Cruiser and hopped up into the driver's seat.

'Send a message to Strickland,' he said. 'Tell her that the airstrip is running north to south and we have a north-by-northwest wind blowing. The pilot should approach from the south. The airstrip is fifteen hundred metres long and is serviceable. They need to watch for high trees when they come in.'

Fuller rapidly typed out a message on the phone, nodding along as she repeated to herself. 'North-by-northwest wind. One-point-five kilometres long. Approach from the south. High trees. Got it.'

She zapped off the text and said, 'What now?'

Bald pointed to a shaded area at the edge of the canopy, fifteen metres due west of the turning circle to the north. 'Head for that spot and wait in the shade. When that Herc lands, it's going to approach that circle, swing round and drop its tailgate. As soon as it does, we'll leg it from the canopy to the aircraft and get on board.'

'Where are you going?'

'To hide this wagon.' Bald waved a hand in the general direction of the shacks at the side of the strip, five hundred metres to the south.

'Shouldn't we leave the car here? In case we need to make a quick getaway?'

Bald shook his head. 'Some randoms might stroll up the track and spot it. Run off and sound the alarm. Better to hide it. The motor's hot now, anyway. Americans will be looking for it.'

Fuller reached down into the storage compartment on the passenger-side door and snatched up the Browning Hi-Power pistol. Sprang the door lever and jumped down to the ground, shoving the Browning down the back of her jean. Set off towards the shaded area at the edge of the turning circle.

Bald watched her move away, then drove back south for six hundred metres until he had almost drawn level with the two shacks. To the left of the nearest shack was the overgrown path he had spotted when driving down the middle of the airstrip. The path led through to a small clearing in the forest, about the size of a tennis court, containing the rusted hulk of a Cessna light aircraft and several forty-gallon drums. He parked the Land Cruiser beyond the Cessna, concealing it from view behind a thin scattering of trees. Then he dismounted, grabbed his daysack from the back seat and his M4 rifle from the footwell, and jogged back towards the airstrip. A few minutes later he reached the shaded patch of ground near the forest. Fuller was checking something on the phone as he approached.

'What's the news?' he asked.

'Madeleine says they've passed the information on to the pilot. He's being updated.'

'Any word on their ETA?'

'They're on schedule. Left their camp ninety minutes ago.'

Bald checked his G-Shock: 10.22.

Thirty-eight minutes until the Herc was due to land.

They took up their positions on the verge beside the turning circle. The palm trees provided some much-needed cover from the scorching mid-morning sun. Fuller checked her phone and took pulls of water from the bottle in Bald's daysack. Bald alternated between staring at the horizon and glancing at his watch. Counting down the minutes until the Herc was due to come in. His heart started to beat faster.

Any minute now, thought Bald.

Once the aircraft had safely touched down it would make for the turning circle at the other end of the runway. The tailgate would lower and the lads from Air Troop would set up a defensive perimeter while Bald and Fuller hurried up the ramp. Then the Herc would rev its engines and catapult off again. If everything went smoothly they would be back across the border in a couple of hours.

Twenty-four hours from now, I'll be back in London and on the beers. And I'll never have to deal with those twats at Vauxhall again.

Bald watched and waited.

Fuller's phone buzzed. She read the message and said, 'Rescue team is five minutes out. Making its final approach.'

Freedom, thought Bald.

Fuller smiled.

He looked south beyond the airstrip, straining his eyes at the horizon. For a while he saw nothing except the occasional smudge of cloud in the sky and the belt of jungle below.

Then he saw it.

The distinctive shape of a Hercules C-130 transport plane, faintly visible against the sky.

The Herc was a few miles to the south of the airstrip, coming in low and fast above the treetops. The landing gear lowered, the orange lights glowing on the wingtips. Mechanical drone of the four turboprop engines blasting across the clearing. Bald felt a flood of relief sweeping through his veins at the sight of the aircraft.

Finally. We're getting the fuck out of here. It's almost over.

As he looked on, the Herc started to bank sharply to the right.

For a terrifying moment the aircraft seemed to hang in mid-air, as if suspended.

Then it plunged to the ground.

THIRTY

The C-130 fell suddenly out of the sky. Bald saw it lurch away to the right before it dropped on its belly and pancaked into the foliage a mile or so away from the strip, disappearing from view behind the canopy. There was a dreadful beat of silence before the thunderclap of thirty thousand kilograms of aircraft exploding with a deafening boom. Flames and black smoke mushroom-clouded into the air above the crash-site, the fumes from the burning jet fuel blackening the sky.

'Dear God,' Fuller gasped.

Bald watched the fire for several long seconds, in a kind of trance. He saw Fuller to his right, staring at the scene in horror, the colour draining from her face.

His first thought was, *No one's surviving that crash*. Anyone who hadn't been killed on impact would have been consumed by the blaze. His second thought was for the Regiment lads who had been on board. A dozen or more outstanding soldiers, no doubt.

Then a realisation socked him in the guts.

Our ticket out of here just went up in flames.

We're shafted.

'What . . . what the fuck happened?' said Fuller.

Bald didn't respond. He wasn't an aviation expert. But he knew that the Herc had a reputation as a reliable old bird. Workhorse of the RAF.

'We need to call Strickland,' he said at last, trying to piece together a plan. 'Someone needs to tell her what the fuck just went down.'

Fuller nodded vaguely but kept on staring at the flames fountaining up from the jungle. Her face white as uncut cocaine. Then her training seemed to kick in and she shook herself out of her stupor and reached for her phone. Not an easy thing to do, Bald knew. Focusing on the job at hand when you had just watched several comrades plummet to their deaths. Fuller was clearly made of strong stuff. A toughened operator. Tougher than the likes of Hugo Merrick, for sure.

She was about to hit Dial when Bald saw something else.

A cloud of dust, pluming into the sky towards the southern end of the strip. A kilometre away.

The plume was getting bigger.

Fuller saw it too and froze. Thumb poised on the screen.

'Vehicles?' she asked.

Bald nodded.

'Civilians?'

'Maybe.'

Or maybe not.

He dropped low amid the undergrowth and told Fuller to do the same. Staying in the gloom at the very edge of the jungle canopy, Bald tore the pocket binoculars out of the pouch on his front vest and quickly unfolded them. Peered through the lenses at the approaching dirt cloud. Saw the magnified image of a pair of bulked-up SUVs trundling north along the airstrip from the direction of the track a kilometre away. A black Ford Expedition. And a white Ford Explorer.

The same colour and model as the wagons he'd seen parked outside the stronghold.

Bald looked on as the two SUVs skidded to a halt in the middle of the airstrip, opposite the shacks. Six hundred metres away from Bald and Fuller.

Two figures debussed from the Expedition.

One of the guys was stocky and barrel-chested and wore a pair of wraparound shades. The bloke next to him was physically gargantuan. He looked like he belonged in a freak show. He made the guy with the shades look like a dwarf in comparison. His hands were like wrecking balls. His legs were so wide you'd need a dozen hippies to hug them. Both figures were dressed in the unofficial uniform of mercenaries. Dark trousers, Gore-Tex boots and bulletproof vests over their short-sleeved shirts. Aviator gloves. They were both armed with M4 rifles attached to slings. The rifle looked tiny in Freak Show's grip. Bald didn't recognise either guy but from their builds and stances, he was willing to bet that they were ex-Special Forces.

Then he saw the other two figures getting out of the Explorer.

A sinewy redneck in a red baseball cap.

A tanned guy with a blond horeshoe moustache and heavily tattooed arms.

Both gripping their rifles. Hulk with his short M4, Dudley with the sniper variant.

He recalled what Taylor had told them at the briefing. The extraction plan.

There's a fishing town. Rio Verde.

Four hundred and fifty miles from the stronghold.

A reception team will meet you there.

Two of our guys. Ex-SEALs.

Hulk and Dudley must have alerted the reception team, he realised. They would have raised the alarm with their mates as soon as they had bugged out from the president's mansion. Those guys would have rushed over more or less immediately, aiming to intercept Bald and Fuller from the east, before linking up with their mates.

'Shit,' he growled as he watched the enemy through the binos.

'What?' Fuller whispered. 'What can you see?'

'The Americans. They've got backup. Two of the bastards.'

'How did they find us? This RV is a secret.'

'Maybe one of your mates at Six tipped them off,' said Bald.

'No. Can't be. Madeleine runs a tight ship.'

'Bastards must have had some way of following us here.'

A thought scraped fingernail-like at the base of Bald's skull. He shoved it aside and looked on through the binos. Six hundred metres to the south, across the dirt runway, the four figures formed up next to the shacks and had some sort of conference. They were looking around, scanning the ground either side of the airstrip. There was a lot of gesturing and pointing going on. Bald considered retreating into the jungle, but quickly dismissed the idea. There was still a chance that the Americans might take a quick look around, find nothing and head off again. In which case Bald and Fuller could race over to the Land Cruiser, check it for tracking devices and move out. It would be a bad move to flee into the jungle, thought Bald. They had no supplies. Fuller was physically shattered after their escape from the mansion and the long drive across the country. They would have to cover miles to get to the nearest town, with no certainty that they would be able to steal a car or get help. Better to stay put and see how it played out.

Hulk took out his satellite-cum-smartphone and made a call while Freak Show and Dudley cleared the shacks. Then Hulk beckoned to Shades and the latter carried over a map, placing it flat on the dirt ground. The others crowded around Hulk as he took a knee beside it and tore off a blade of grass, tracing it across the map while he listened to the person on the other end of the line. He paused. Looked up. Looked down again, as if trying to reconcile the landscape in front of him with the details on the map. Then he pulled out a pair of compact binos from one of his vest pouches, unfolded them and looked through the glasses at the forested area beyond the northern edge of the airstrip.

There was another pause.

Then Hulk thrust out an arm.

Pointing directly at Bald and Fuller.

Hulk knows exactly where we are. He's pinpointed us.

We're fucking blown.

In the next breath, the American grabbed the map and shot up, yelling orders at the others as they leapt to their feet and scrambled towards the Expedition.

'Fuck.'

'What is it?' Fuller asked, fear creeping into her voice.

'They're on to us.'

Bald made an instant calculation. He was cornered with Fuller at the threshold of the airstrip, with dense primary forest to their six o'clock and to the east and west. There was no chance of legging it to the Land Cruiser now. The wagon was hidden in the secluded area next to the airstrip, six hundred metres away. The ex-SEALs would cut them down long before they could reach it.

He reached a decision. Lowered his binos and arced up his M4. Squeezed off two three-round bursts at the tiny figures clustering around the SUV, peppering the shapes with hot metal.

At six hundred metres, Bald was firing at targets beyond the M4's maximum effective range. But he wasn't shooting to kill. He was stalling for time, forcing the enemy to get their heads down. Stopping them momentarily in their tracks. Giving himself and Fuller time to make a run for the jungle.

He put down a third burst and spun round, yelling at Fuller madly.

'Head for the trees! Move yourself!'

Fuller got the message. She spun away and hurried falteringly towards the treeline. Bald loosed off a fourth burst, turned and ran after her before the ex-SEALs put down fire on them. Bullets cracked and slapped into the undergrowth and the tree trunks either side of Bald in a hail of splinters and dirt, missing him by inches. He was moving on pure adrenaline, going as fast as his legs could carry him as he raced towards the denser patch of forest. Ahead of him the terrain was a green curtain of tall trees, prickly bushes, shrubs and ferns, reducing visibility to less than fifteen metres. In there, if anywhere, they stood their best chance of giving the Americans the slip.

Then he heard a crack and a sharp cry at his six. He glanced over his shoulder. Saw Fuller dropping to the ground two metres behind him, hissing through clenched teeth. A bullet had grazed her left hand, slicing through her skin. Another round thumped into the undergrowth, three or four inches to her right.

Bald raced over, ducking low as he grabbed her by the wrist and dragged her to her feet. 'We've got to fucking move! Come on!'

Fuller stumbled forward, almost tripping up as they raced further away from the turning circle. The canopy overhead thickened, the light faded to a grey gloom as they plunged deeper into the jungle.

Bald could see no more than a dozen metres in front of him now. They were surrounded by a screen of vegetation in every direction. He pushed on, moving effortlessly through the terrain. Fuller struggled to keep up, taking in ragged gulps of breath. The ground underfoot was a sea of dead leaves and fallen branches and mosses and gnarled roots, slowing her down.

They ploughed on for another twenty-five metres and then she let out a torrent of curses. Bald wheeled round and saw her thrashing wildly as she tried to tear herself free from a prickly bush, ripping off the sleeve of her blouse. He rushed back, unhooked the barbs from her clothing, grabbed the torn material and shoved it in his pocket. He didn't want to leave any obvious signs for the enemy to pick up. No point making their job any easier for them. Fuller was gasping for breath, hands planted on her legs, like a runner at the end of a race.

'I've got to stop,' she said hoarsely. 'Please. Just for a minute.'

'We can't,' Bald replied firmly. 'Bastards are on to us. Come on.'

Fuller rose unsteadily to her feet. The fighter in her. She wasn't ready to give up yet. Bald glanced back in the direction of the treeline. They had covered about a quarter of a mile since rushing into the trees. He figured they had a six-minute head start over the enemy. Maximum. But with the state Fuller was in, the enemy would soon catch up with them.

We'll never give them the slip. Not at the rate we're going.

'I don't understand,' she said. 'How are they following us?'

'Tracking device. Only explanation. One of us is bugged.'

'But we got rid of phones.'

Bald looked hard at her. 'You sure you're not wearing anything?'

'Of course not.' She narrowed her eyes at him. 'What about your equipment? Where's all that stuff from?'

'The CIA gave it to us. At the camp.'

'Have you checked it?'

'I'm not that bloody stupid. You can't bug grenades and shit like that. There's nowhere to hide a tracker in any—'

He stopped. Lowered his gaze to the rifle he was holding.

The thought, scraping across his skull again. Something to do with the buttstock.

We've looked everywhere.

Except we haven't.

He hastily dropped to his knees beside Fuller and took a closer look at the retractable stock. It appeared newer than the rest of the M4, Bald thought. Almost brand new. No scuff marks, no signs of wear and tear.

He lifted up the lever on the underside of the stock, gripping the rear plate with his other hand. Pulled on the stock, detaching it from the rifle. Set the stock down and inspected the hollow metal tube jutting out of the end of the receiver.

Secreted inside the tube was a small black unit, no bigger than a thumbnail.

A red signal blinked on the front of the device.

Fuller looked over his shoulder. 'What is it?'

Bald angled the receiver upwards, tipping the transponder out of the buffer tube. Showed it to her. 'Those pricks bugged our fucking weapons.' Anger pulsed inside his chest. 'They've been tracking us since the moment we bugged out of the stronghold.'

He stared at the transponder unit for a beat. The kernel of a plan formed inside his head.

'What are you waiting for?' Fuller snapped. 'Get rid of it.'

'It's too late. They'll be on us soon enough, with or without this thing. We've got no chance of outrunning them.'

'You're not suggesting we take them on?'

Bald shook his head. 'I've got a better idea.'

'What?'

'No time to explain.' He dropped the transponder, and crushed it beneath his boot. Picked up the broken device and stuffed it in his pocket. Slid the stock back onto the tube and straightened up. 'Get your arse in gear. Follow me.'

They set off again through the forest. Fuller was moving with obvious difficulty now, limping heavily. Bald carried on, eyes shifting left to right as he scanned the ground. He was making no effort to cover their tracks now. The opposite, in fact. He grabbed branches and snapped them in half, kicking over dead leaves on the ground to expose their paler underside and brushing past plants and bushes. Deliberately luring the enemy towards them. With all the signs Bald was leaving behind Hulk and the three others would have no problem following their trail through the forest.

Which is exactly what he wanted.

They moved on for another eighty metres, and then he found exactly what he was looking for. A slightly elevated piece of ground on his left flank, partially obscured by a thin line of trees, with a mostly flat area of trees and bushes to the right and a rough trail running between them. The perfect position in order to make his plan work, thought Bald. He drew up twenty metres from the high ground and pointed it out to Fuller as she caught her breath.

'This is what we're going to do. We're going to move up fifty metres past that position, then put in a dogleg and come back on ourselves but to five metres to the left, on that high ground. That's going to be the baseline for our attack.'

Fuller looked at him with alarm. 'What are you planning?'

'We're going to put in a linear ambush,' said Bald. 'We'll set a trap and let them walk right into it. Then we'll launch a follow-up attack. Wipe out any survivors.'

'Will that work?'

'It's our best chance of getting out of here alive.'

'What if they don't fall for it?'

'Then we're fucked,' Bald said. 'But it's either this, or we let them hunt us down like dogs.'

She nodded.

He turned and moved on, quickening his stride as he broke past the area of high ground to his left. Bald paced out fifty metres beyond that point, counting it off in ten-metre increments in his head, just like he had once done in the Regiment. Then they broke left and put a loop in, doubling up on themselves as they manoeuvred south on a parallel bearing to the path they had just taken. Bald moved along for fifty metres until he reached the slightly elevated point he had indicated to Fuller. He found a hollow next to the trees, facing out across the lower spread of forest opposite, five metres away. Fuller had taken the Browning Hi-Power out of her jeans waistband and gripped it in her good right hand.

'You know how to use that thing?' asked Bald.

'I've fired them once or twice,' she replied, in a way that suggested she had used them a lot more often than that. She wouldn't be much use in a firefight, he decided, not in her present condition, but if their backs were to the wall he was confident that she could at least loose off a few rounds at the enemy.

'Wait here,' he said. 'Stay low and keep your head down. I'll be back in a few minutes. If those fuckers show up on our flank, start putting down rounds.'

'What about you?'

Bald grinned. 'I'm going to leave them a nasty surprise.'

He grabbed the daysack, slung it over his back and rushed forward from the hollow. Moved down from the slope and broke through the trees until he hit the edge of the rack, five metres from the hollow.

Bald guessed he had no more than four or five minutes until the Americans caught up with them. They would be slogging through the forest, navigating the near-impenetrable maze of thorny bushes and trees and slippery undergrowth. Moving as fast as they possibly could. He assumed they were no more than three or four hundred metres away.

Just enough time to set the trap.

This is going to be a hard fight, John Boy, the voice warned him. *Hardest of your life. You're taking on four ex-SEALs.*

Not good odds.

Maybe not, thought Bald. *But I'm not ready to die like Porter. Not fucking yet.*

He darted off the track in the opposite direction from the high ground, listening out for the arrival of the enemy. With the curtain of forest all around them the Americans weren't going to be visible until they were no more than fifteen or twenty metres from the ambush point.

But I'll hear them a lot further away than that.

He took a couple of paces into the trees and broke off three thin branches, snapping them down into peg-sized lengths, each one roughly six inches long. He carried the pegs back over to the track and paced five metres south, heading away from the hollow. Stopped again and dropped down beside a sturdy tree at the side of the path. Shook his daysack from his shoulder and pushed four of the pegs into the ground at the base of the tree, forming a small box. Retrieved one of the fragmentation grenades from the sack and placed it inside the box, securing the grenade in place between the pegs.

Then he reached into a pouch on his vest and pulled out a bundle of paracord: a four-mil diameter length of interwoven nylon strands. He pinched the end of one of the dark individual braids and pulled on it, unwinding it from the rest of the cord.

Bald threaded the thin material through the splayed pin on the grenade, squashed the ends together and eased the pin out slightly, so that it was only held in place by a hair's breadth.

A moment later he heard voices in the distance. Men shouting at one another in urgent voices. At least two of them.

The enemy.

Bald couldn't make out what they were saying. Just the general timbre of their voices. Urgent, aggressive. Like a hunting party closing in on its prey.

They were around two hundred metres away from the ambush point, Bald estimated.

Hurry up, John Boy.

He snatched up the daysack and the pegs and counted five metres forward, kneeling down again beside a smaller tree. He went through the same process. Planted the second grenade in another peg-box. Looped the braid through the pin. Teased out the splayed pin fractionally.

He took the other end of the nylon string and trailed it across the track at a right angle for two metres. He wedged another peg into the ground and wrapped the cord around it three times. Then he took the rest of the string and anchored it to another branch at a ninety-degree angle, making sure it was taut. As soon as anyone set foot on the tripwire lying across the track, the peg would come out, pulling on the wire and yanking the pins out of the two grenades at almost the same time. The trees would shield Bald and Fuller from the blast, directing it outwards in a lethal killing arc. Clobbering anyone who was caught within the killing zone.

He snatched up a fistful of leaves and sprinkled them over the length of the wire across the track, making sure it was hidden. He scattered more rotting vegetation over the grenades to obscure them as well. In the distance, beyond the claustrophobic green curtain, Bald could hear the voices. They were more distinct now.

There was a wild holler, and then he heard Dudley yelling out to the others that he had found something. The signs Bald had left behind for them, presumably. They were no more than a hundred metres away now.

They'll be here in a couple of minutes.

Bald paced further along the track and took out the water bottle from his daysack. He wasn't worried about being seen by the enemy. *They're still not close enough to see me yet.*

He emptied the remaining liquid, placed the bottle on the ground a couple of metres due north of the hidden tripwire, nestling it at the side of the track. Then he pulled out the strip of torn-off material from Fuller's blouse and hung it at eye-level from a nearby bush, making sure it was visible to anyone coming up the track.

He stepped back and surveyed his work. The water bottle and the shred of clothing would instantly catch the eye of the lead scout. The enemy would follow the signs he had left, spot the discarded water bottle and the material hanging from the bush. Assume that their quarry had been drinking some water before rushing off moments earlier.

They would be hurrying forward, concentrating on the signs in front of them.

Not looking at the ground at their feet.

They wouldn't see the tripwire until it was too late.

That was the plan.

Not the greatest trap ever set. Not foolproof.

But it's the best I can do.

He scuffed the ground, kicked a few leaves over and snapped a few branches, adding to the signs near the path. The enemy was dangerously close now. Bald could hear twigs snapping beneath boots, the guys crashing through the bushes, making a ton of fucking noise.

They're almost right on top of us, he realised. Sixty or seventy metres away.

He sprinted up the track for ten metres. Doglegged back around to the high ground on the other side of the path and hit the hollow next to Fuller. Turned to her and pointed out a spot five metres further along the hollow, facing out across the approach to the tripwire.

'Get over there,' he said. 'Watch the track. As soon as you see the lead scout approaching, give us the thumbs-up.'

'Then what?' she asked, voice fraught with tension.

'Once they trigger the tripwire, the grenades will go off and cut down everyone on the team. I'll mop up. Make sure you keep your head down and don't fucking move. If it goes sideways and they start overrunning us, take as many of the fuckers down as you can but make sure you save the last bullet for yourself,' he added. 'Trust me. You don't want Dudley getting his slimy hands on you.'

She nodded with a look of grim determination in her eyes. Clasped her right hand around the Browning Hi-Power and crawled across the hollow, lying flat on her stomach with the trees four metres away, along the side of the track. Bald shifted two metres across to the right and went static, putting himself in a prone firing position between the two grenades, with a line of sight over-looking the trail. He extracted a spare thirty-round clip from his pouch and placed it beside him for easy access in case it went noisy.

Then he waited.

He heard Dudley again. The redneck's voice was full of aggression as he urged the others on. Any moment now. To the right, Fuller focused on the approach to the track. Waiting for the first sign of the enemy.

Bald felt his muscles tense. His mouth was dry at the prospect of a firefight. He felt that there was a fifty-fifty chance the ambush would succeed. He was banking on a lot of things happening. The lead scout charging forward, not paying too much attention to the overall scene. The rest of the guys bunching up tightly behind him.

If the ex-SEALs were thinly spread out, with multiple metres between them, the grenades might only take out half the team. Or the enemy might approach the trail in a linear formation, strung out like a clothesline across the ground.

If that happens, thought Bald, *we'll find ourselves in a heavy fire-fight. We'd start taking rounds from all sides. No way we'd survive that.*

Five seconds later, Fuller looked round and gave him the thumbs-up.

Enemy in sight.

Bald flicked his gaze back to the tripwire. The track ran from left to right in front of him, six metres away, with the approach to his right and the water bottle and scrap of torn fabric at his eleven o'clock. Fuller was a few metres away to his right, observing the enemy.

A beat later, the four Americans slid into view.

They were fifteen metres away from the ambush point, cutting their way along the track in a tight patrol formation. Dudley was in the lead scout position, with Hulk three paces further behind. Shades was third in line, with Freak Show several paces further back, lagging slightly behind the others. Weighed down by his monstrous mass. They were moving in quick, aggressive steps, scanning the area ahead of them.

Stalking prey.

Five metres from the tripwire, Dudley momentarily halted. Bald saw the redneck squinting with mean eyes at the trail and felt the knot in his guts tighten.

Shit, he thought. *We've been rumbled.*

Then Dudley pointed out the water bottle and torn clothing to Hulk. 'Looks like we're on these bitches. Ain't gonna be far from here, Hulk.'

He started down the trail, increasing his pace. Like a dog with its nose to the ground, picking up a powerful scent. 'I've got you now, you son of a bitch.'

Hulk and the other two guys abruptly picked up the pace as well. Dudley was surging a few paces ahead of the team leader, full of aggressive intent. Eyes pinned to the water bottle and the fabric hanging from the bush a few metres ahead of him.

Two metres from the tripwire now.

Behind him, Hulk was looking closely around him. Taking in the bigger picture. He looked down at the ground. Looked at the trees at his twelve o'clock and the flat area of jungle to his right. Then he glanced up at the high ground to his left.

Stopped.

There was a flash of panic in his eyes as he caught sight of Bald lying flat on the ground six metres away.

'Wait!' he cried to Dudley. 'Stop right there!'

In the next instant, the redneck's boot came down on the tripwire.

There was a light metallic ping as the wire tugged on the two grenade pins. Like a cord being plucked. A sound that every soldier instantly recognised. Dudley froze. He had time to realise that he was fucked.

Then the grenades detonated.

The blasts ripped across the trail, two booms thundering in rapid succession as the first grenade went off a microsecond before the second one, five metres to the rear. Dudley was two feet ahead of the grenade nearest to the water bottle. The blast punched him in the back and knocked him to the ground, fragments shredding his legs and back. Hulk was six or seven feet behind the redneck. He took the brunt of the explosive force, caught between the grenade to his front and the one to his rear. He disappeared in a flurry of smoke and hot dirt and metal shards. The second grenade fragged the two guys behind Hulk, putting Shades and Freak Show on their arses as shrapnel tore through the surrounding vegetation, smashing into tree trunks and slicing through branches.

Dudley rolled onto his back, screaming in pain at his injuries.

In the next moment, Bald levelled his sights with the redneck and opened fire. Two aimed shots thumped into Dudley's chest. Bald gave him another double-tap to the head just for good measure, finishing him off. At the same time he spied Shades lying on the ground, five metres away to the right, his rifle slanted upwards as he aimed at the high ground in a futile attempt to return fire on the shooter. Bald eased out a breath as he calmly lined up the muzzle with the ex-SEAL and put two quick rounds into the target. One round winged Shades on the jaw, shattering his teeth and jawbone. The second bullet punched a hole through his sunglasses and bored through into his skull, mashing his brains. He joined Dudley in whatever afterlife he believed in.

Half a second later, Bald spied a swift motion to his right. Four metres away. He caught sight of Freak Show staggering away from the trail. The rearmost guy in the formation, several paces behind the others. Therefore the one who had been furthest from the grenades when they had blown up. His legs were smeared with blood but otherwise he had got off lightly. A combination of the thick vegetation and the guys in front of him absorbing most of the fragmentation. He had taken a beating, but he was still in the fight.

Now he was limping up the slope towards the hollow. Bringing up his rifle as he charged at the ambushers. Following the standard drill for anyone caught in a linear ambush.

Don't run.

Don't try to escape the kill zone.

Head directly for the attackers and engage.

The guy was halfway up the slope when Bald heard two sharp cracks at his right.

He saw Freak Show tumbling away, an avalanche of flesh and muscle mass back-sliding down the slope. Blood arcing out of a hole in his head. He came to a rest at the side of the trail, a ragged lifeless heap.

Bald glanced over at his right. Saw Fuller standing there with the Browning Hi-Power raised. Gave her a nod. *Good work.*

Four seconds after Dudley had tripped the wire, Bald sprang forward and scrambled down the slope, weapon raised. Ready to nail anyone still drawing breath.

Through the acrid wisps of smoke he could see that the trail was slicked with blood and viscera and splintered bits of wood and tiny metal fragments. Carnage.

These guys might have been hardened ex-SEALs.

But I'm the fucking SAS.

Freak Show and Shades were both utterly still. No signs of life. Dudley was slumped on his back, riddled with fragments and bullets, his mouth agape. Bald gave him a solid kick, partly to check he was dead and partly just because it felt fucking good. Then he moved down the trail towards Hulk.

The guy was all kinds of messed up. His hands, face and neck were stippled with bits of metal. The blast had slashed open his groin. His guts were hanging out in a glistening coil, slopping onto the dirt beside him. A mortal wound. Bald wasn't a doctor, but he could tell from looking at the guy that he didn't have very long to live. A few minutes, maybe. He kicked away Hulk's rifle and knelt down beside him. The American looked up at him with dimming eyes.

'Jesus,' Hulk croaked. 'Jesus . . .'

He groaned in pain. His lank hair was plastered to his scalp. His breathing was shallow and erratic.

'A trap . . . should have known.' He attempted a blood-stained smile. 'Almost had you there. Brother.'

'I know.'

He coughed up blood. 'I'm sorry. About your buddy. Ain't nothing personal.'

'You had your orders. I'd have done the same thing. How it is.'

'He had family?'

'A daughter.'

Hulk nodded, as if this meant something. Bald looked at the dying American. 'It didn't have to come to this.'

'No.' He groaned again. 'Glad . . . it was you. Losing to a warrior. No shame in that.'

Hulk convulsed as a wave of pain racked his body. 'Shit . . . so cold.'

He offered up a trembling hand.

Bald held it for a couple of seconds. One soldier respecting the spirited efforts of his vanquished opponent. A ritual that stretched back into the mists of time.

Hulk's breathing became shallower and more erratic. His body shook again, and he said something that Bald couldn't understand. Then his grip relaxed. The light faded from his eyes.

Bald closed his eyes. Rose to his feet. Took one last look at the dead former SEAL. Then signalled that it was safe for Fuller to move forward. She scaled down the slope, glancing around at the bodies littering the trail. A dazed look on her face. She gazed at the bodies as Bald moved up and down the track, grabbing various bits of kit. He took Freak Show's Glock as a backup weapon, along with a pair of spare clips of 9x19 Parabellum from his vest pouches. Stashed the pistol in his holster, then set off with Fuller back down the trail. Retracing the earlier route they had taken through the forest.

Seven minutes later, they were back at the threshold of the airstrip.

They paused again at the fringes of the jungle while Bald crouched in the gloom and observed the vehicles from a distance through his binoculars. Making sure that ex-SEALs hadn't left someone behind to guard them. Once he was sure that the coast was clear, he gave the order to Fuller and they broke across the open ground to the wagons. In their rush to pursue their targets the Americans had left both the Explorer and the Expedition unlocked, with the keys in the console trays. Bald checked the boots and found an emergency medical pack in the back of the Expedition, along with fresh bottles of water and a pair of jerry cans. He unscrewed the cap on one of the cans and gave it a sniff to check whether it was diesel or fuel. Then he hurried over to the secluded area off the airstrip, climbed behind the wheel of the Land Cruiser and drove it down the track and north, pulling up next to the two Fords. He transferred the medical kit and the jerry cans to the Land Cruiser, snagged a pair of sunglasses left on the dash of the Expedition and a baseball cap from the back seat of the Explorer. He also lifted a laptop he found in the rear of the Expedition. Six might want it, Fuller had said. There might be something useful on the hard drive.

He shoved the laptop into a leather holdall he found in the back of the Expedition and dumped it in the rear of the Land Cruiser. Fired up the engine while Fuller climbed into the front passenger seat.

'What now?' she asked.

'RV is burned,' Bald said. 'We can't stay here. The Yanks know about it, and the place will be crawling with locals and helpers soon enough, once they see that the Herc has gone down. Not as if they can send us another plane, either. Have to find another way out.'

Fuller thought for a beat. 'We'll have to find somewhere to lie low. It'll take Madeleine a while to sort out an escape plan.'

'We can't wait that long. Security forces will be out looking for the assassins by now.'

'What else can we do? Not as if we can risk going to any of the big fishing towns or ports. They'll be looking for us.'

'I've got an idea.'

Bald tapped the satnav icon on the tablet-sized display and typed in the name of a small town two hundred miles to the east.

He remembered the name of the place Freddy Vargas had told him about.

Suarez.

Fuller frowned at the screen. 'Where are we going?'

'The coast,' Bald said. 'A place where they hunt the white lobster.'

He explained his plan. They would head to the town, recce the beach and steal one of the fishing boats. The place was on the north-eastern tip of the country, on the Gulf of Paria, ten miles from the coast of Trinidad. A small settlement far removed from any of the big towns or cities, in an area of the country dominated by the cartels and hence a no-go area for the police. But with a lot of fishermen who made extra money from selling the cocaine they captured. Who would therefore have reliable fishing boats with two-hundred-horsepower motors, capable of ferrying them across the Gulf. They could make the crossing to Port of Spain in a couple of hours, Bald said. Then hand themselves in to the British High Commission. There were regular flights to the other islands in the Caribbean: Barbados, Saint Lucia, Antigua. From there, they could catch a plane back to London.

They left the airstrip and drove east. Fuller updated Strickland on the way, letting her know about their escape plan so she could contact the High Commission in advance and prepare for their arrival. When they were twenty miles clear of the strip, Bald pulled over at a lay-by, tore off his bulletproof vest and belt holster and broke down his rifle into its component parts. He shoved the weapons, the vest and the clips into the holdall with the laptop. Then he picked up the medical kit and cleaned and dressed Fuller's wound while he went through their cover story. If anyone stopped them, they would claim to be British tourists, a man and wife, on an edgy adventure off the beaten track. They would claim that they had been held up at gunpoint and robbed. A gunshot had been fired during the scuffle, hence the bullet graze on Fuller's left hand. The sunglasses and baseball caps would help disguise their appearances.

They reached Suarez at six o'clock in the evening. Almost an hour before last light. The town was situated on a small plain between low hills, with a curved strip of sand facing out towards the sea. Bald did a quick mobile recce, driving slowly through the streets. He saw a lot of deteriorating homes and rusted vehicles and bins overflowing with rubbish. A big pastel-coloured church in the middle of the town. He didn't see any police. But there were a few too many locals in the streets for his liking. Kids playing football, people going to and from work.

He steered back out of Suarez and pulled up in a lay-by a couple of miles away. Then they waited for last light.

At 18.50, as the last band of light glowed on the horizon, Bald gunned the engine and motored back into the town. The streets were darker and quieter now. Easier to move around unseen. He arrowed down the gridded streets, parked the Land Cruiser outside the church, grabbed the holdall and dismounted. Locked the wagon and quick-walked with Fuller across the main road, heading for the beach.

Bald had a rough plan sketched out in his head. They would wander down to the beach, holding hands, like a couple going out for a romantic evening stroll, and take a look at the set-up. Looking for anything suspicious. Then they would hang back and wait for an opportune target. They were looking for a go-fast motorboat with a small crew, two or three guys at most. Small enough for Bald and Fuller to overpower. He ruled out stealing an empty boat. They would need a skipper, he said. Someone who knew the waters and was confident of getting them across to Trinidad.

They would have to make their move when the beach was empty, Bald knew, in case any passers-by sounded the alarm. But he felt they wouldn't have to wait long for an opportunity. Some of the local fishermen were bound to go out at night, when there was less traffic at sea. They would head out late in the evening, returning at dawn the following day to sell their catch.

In the fading light, they walked up and down the sand, from one end of the beach to the other. Several colourful fishing boats were moored bow to stern in the shallows. Nobody in sight. They carried on past the boats for fifty metres and found a spot to lay up among the palm trees running alongside the beach. Anyone watching them would have assumed they were a couple of lovers disappearing for a shag in the bushes. Bald set down his holdall and watched and waited, eyes fixed on the boats.

Ninety minutes later, beneath the wan moonlight, he spied three skinny guys making their way down to the beach. They were carrying a bunch of fishing gear, Bald saw. Fishing nets, bait, crates. He watched as they waded into the shallows and made for a small fishing vessel with an outboard motor. Bald scanned the ground further up the beach, making sure they were alone. Then he slid his Glock 17 out his holster, grabbed the holdall and broke forward from the shadows, Fuller hurrying along at his side, clutching her pistol.

The fishermen didn't see him coming. Not until he was in their faces. The nearest guy was standing in the shallows, passing up supplies to the two blokes in the boat. He wore a hoodie and shorts and had silver stud earrings in both ears. He heard Bald at the last instant, spun round. Alarm flashed across his face as his eyes locked on the pistol. Bald trained the Glock on Stud's centre mass while the two other fishermen stood up on the boat and froze. Even in the semi-darkness, he could see the fear stencilled across their faces.

Stud jabbered Spanish at him. Bald kept his eyes on the guy but addressed Fuller. 'Tell this prick no one gets hurt if he does exactly as I say. If he tries to run or call for help, I'll cap him and his mates. Tell him.'

Fuller translated.

Stud's face whitened with fear.

'Tell him he's got a couple of passengers tonight. He's going to take us across to Trinidad. Port of Spain. If he tries anything, he dies. If he tries to shop us to the authorities, he dies. Understood?'

Fuller translated again. Stud nodded quickly. He understood. Bald cocked his head at Fuller. 'Get in the boat. We're leaving now.'

Several minutes later, they were pulling away from the beach. Speeding out towards the Gulf. Towards safety.

Bald kept a watchful eye over Stud and his mates, but from the terrified looks in their eyes he doubted they would do anything stupid. Ninety minutes later, they were closing in on the Trinidadian coast. Lights from the port twinkled on the horizon.

For the first time in a week, Bald felt the tension easing out of his muscles.

'It's nearly over,' he said to Fuller. 'Thank fuck for that.'

She wore a pensive look on her face. 'I'm not so sure.'

'What's the problem? We got rid of the Yanks. We're out of the country. We'll be home and dry in a few hours. We won, lass.'

'Not yet.' She paused. 'We've still got to deal with Cantwell. He's going to pay for what he's done. Mark my words . . .'

THIRTY-ONE

Three days later, at precisely seven o'clock in the evening, Julian Cantwell stepped out of the King's Arms pub and began the short walk back to his secret base of operations. A fine rain was falling, settling like mist across the village of Swanton, nestled in the Oxfordshire countryside. He crossed the main road, turned left at the quaint village green and strolled confidently towards a building on the other side of the square, overlooking a small pond.

The old post office had cost a pittance to acquire. The building had lain vacant for more than a year before Cantwell had purchased it, through a series of shell companies arranged by his business partners. It was a classic village post office, with stone walls and a red-painted letter box, next to a wooden door ringed with roses. The original sign still hung from the wall, and the only hint at the change in ownership was the name of the new company fixed above the entrance: 'WhiteSpear IT Solutions, Ltd'. The name had been a necessary addition, to ward off any curious locals who might wonder what was going on inside. Anyone who googled the company would be directed towards an anonymous website, written in stolid corporate-management speak, with lots of talk about values and diversity and mission statements, without giving away any actual information on what the company did. There was no phone number on the website, and any messages sent to the email address were answered by one of the individuals who worked inside the building.

The post office building, with its superfast broadband connection, twenty-four-hour access and innocuous location, was the perfect cover for Cantwell's secret project.

Teams of hackers, recruited personally by Cantwell and vetted by his American friends at Langley, worked in eight-hour shifts inside the building, with four-hour breaks between one team departing and the next arriving. To avoid drawing too much attention to themselves, the hackers lived in digs in Oxford, nine miles away. They were bussed into work at the start of their shifts, entering the building through the same back entrance used by delivery vans. The blinds were drawn at all hours and the hackers were not permitted to leave the building during the day under any circumstances. Most of them had no problem sticking to the rules. They were talented but emotionally fragile individuals, laughably easy to manipulate. The few who had questioned Cantwell's methods, or their purpose, had been swiftly dealt with. Suicides, drug overdoses, car crashes. Cantwell couldn't afford any weak links. They were playing for high stakes. The risks were enormous. Discretion was critical.

No one in the village knew anything about the operation. As far as they understood, Cantwell was an eccentrically dressed overweight Londoner who ran a small start-up out of the old post office. Something to do with computers and spreadsheets. The sort of boring subject that discouraged further questions.

What really went on inside, of course, was much more sinister.

He took in a draw of breath and fought off a wave of tiredness. He had been holed up at the post office for the past three days, working round the clock with his hackers on their next planned operation. Had argued that they should lie low after the Venezuela job, but the Americans had insisted on pressing on. Their boss wasn't famous for his patience. The next mission had been green-lit to take place two days from now. His people had been working flat out to get everything ready in time. If they pulled it off, it would be a major victory. A hot thrill ran through Cantwell just thinking about it. But he also had a certain feeling of trepidation. They were moving too fast, he feared. Mistakes had been made in Venezuela.

On the face of it, the mission had been successful – Vasquez was dead – but the attempt to pin the blame on two rogue Brits had gone badly wrong. Five ex-SEALs were dead. In the absence of an easy scapegoat the new president was in damage-limitation mode, blaming nameless 'foreign elements' for the assassination.

Worse yet, the hostage had apparently escaped. No one had seen or heard from her since, which was disconcerting. Cantwell had shared his concerns with his fellow conspirators, but they had assured him that it was being dealt with.

Nothing to worry about, they had said.

Cantwell wasn't so sure.

He turned right past the square, swinging past a row of parking spaces as he made for the entrance to the post office building. He spotted a delivery van parked on the other side of the pond, next to a row of terraced houses. Cantwell vaguely remembered seeing the same van parked nearby earlier that afternoon. Or the same model and colour, at least. He wondered for a moment if he was being watched. But then again, there were so many delivery drivers these days. Streets were clogged with them.

Calm down. Probably just another driver doing his rounds.

No one knows you're here.

He reached the entrance, rooted through his pockets for his keys. Twisted the key in the door lock and stepped inside. The ground floor of the post office had been extensively remodelled, with laminate flooring and white-painted walls and desks, but Cantwell had retained the original oak ceiling beams. A nice touch, he felt. A nod to the building's rich history.

At five minutes past seven, the workspace was empty. The previous shift had clocked off at six o'clock, with the second team not due to arrive until ten. Cantwell had left soon after the earlier shift, popping over to the King's Arms for a pint of Guinness and a steak pie and chips. His usual routine. He would spend the few hours in his private office, catching up on the news, checking over the details for the next operation. Sleep for an hour or two on the sofa, before the next shift arrived.

He fumbled around in the darkness, looking for the light switch.

Found it.

Flicked it on.

Then he froze.

Two figures were sitting on a pair of office chairs at the nearest workstation. A man and a woman.

Cantwell recognised them both.

'Hello, Julian,' Madeleine Strickland said.

The man — Cantwell couldn't remember the chap's name — said nothing but stared at him with a look that suggested he would very much like to rip his throat out.

He automatically looked back towards the door.

'I wouldn't try to run,' Strickland continued. 'You wouldn't get very far. Our friends at Five have got a surveillance team outside.'

Cantwell swallowed. 'The delivery van.'

'Yes.' Strickland waved at the silver-haired man with the black look in his eyes. 'You remember John Bald, don't you?'

'Of course,' he lied quickly. 'From the briefing.' He shifted his gaze back to Strickland. 'What are you doing here?'

'We'd like to have a chat with you.'

'You should have called. Put something in the diary.'

Strickland shot him a smile so thin you could hack through bamboo with it. 'Actually, we'd prefer to speak to you alone.'

Cantwell frowned. 'How the hell did you get in?'

'We have technicians who are very good at that sort of thing.' She gestured to an empty chair. 'Have a seat, Julian.'

'Think I'll stand.'

'Suit yourself.'

Cantwell glanced at Bald. The guy's right hand was stuffed inside the pocket of his leather jacket and gripping something bulky. A gun, perhaps. He couldn't tell.

'I assume you know why we're here,' Strickland said.

Cantwell thought quickly. Six knew about his business in the old post office, obviously. MI5 had been running surveillance on him, possibly for days. Which meant someone had tipped off the security services about his secret project. But on the other hand, they might not know very much. This could just be a fishing expedition, he thought. They might be setting a trap for him. He must tease out what they knew.

'Is this to do with Caroline?' he asked.

'In a way.'

'Where is she?'

'We're keeping her in a safe location. Somewhere your American friends won't be able to find her. She works for us, of course, but I assume you know that already.'

Cantwell stayed quiet.

'She told us everything,' Strickland said.

'I'm not sure I follow, Madeleine.'

'Caroline met with a CIA officer in Caracas. He told her chapter and verse. We know about the CIA's involvement in the plot to assassinate Vasquez. We know your role in the operation.'

'That's your evidence? Some second-rate gossip one of your spies picked up? You don't seriously believe that, do you? I'm just a political fixer, for God's sake.'

Strickland smiled again and folded her hands. 'We know more than that. A lot more. You see, John managed to retrieve a laptop from Venezuela. There's a treasure trove of information on there. Messages, emails. Phone logs. Transcripts. And we found something else, too. Details of another assassination plot.'

There was a triumphant gleam in her eyes as she went on.

'We've been watching you. We know what you've been up to in this place for the past few days. You've been colluding with the Americans to kill the Turkish president.'

'You can't prove that.'

'Oh, but we can. Right now, our people are questioning a dozen hackers taken from a number of addresses in central Oxford. They'll soon agree to cooperate, once they understand the charges they're facing. It's over, Julian. You're done.'

Cantwell sneered at her. 'You don't know the half of it.'

'What the fuck do you mean?' Bald growled.

'It's not just Turkey and Venezuela. It's much bigger than that.'

Strickland stared at him in surprise. 'There are others?'

'There's a list,' Cantwell said. 'Heads of state who have been targeted by President Drummond.'

'How many?'

'More than you'd imagine. Ukraine, Iran, Mexico. Several more. All those countries who are hostile to American interests. Specifically, to those of President Drummond.'

'That's got to be a fucking long list,' said Bald.

Cantwell shrugged.

Strickland said, 'This comes direct from the president?'

'Of course. It's his new foreign policy. He's very proud of it.'

'Why?'

302

'Drummond wants a new approach to dealing with the West's enemies. Soft power is dead. The old tools of propaganda, financial manipulation and sanctions no longer work. Something more muscular is needed.'

'So he planned to have their leaders killed instead?'

'It's the simplest, most cost-effective way of getting rid of those regimes. We can then replace them with ones that are more sympathetic to our interests. It's regime change, without having to go to the fuss of invading a country and spending trillions of dollars.'

'But also highly illegal. You're talking about a systematic programme of extrajudicial murder.'

Cantwell swatted away her words. 'Spare me the lecture. We've been assassinating people every day in the Middle East. What's the difference between taking out some minor terrorist and a despotic leader who is opposed to our interests? I'd argue that there's more justification for taking out the ruler.'

'And you simply decided to go along with the plan?'

'They reached out to me. Wanted to sound me out. It was all very hush-hush, of course. They couldn't be seen to be officially sanctioning the killings. That would trigger a public backlash. People are still weirdly averse to knocking off our worst enemies. It had to be done covertly, with the help of people like me.'

'Like you?'

'People who believe in what we're trying to accomplish,' Cantwell said.

'And what is that, exactly? Wiping out anyone who gets on the wrong side of the president?'

'We're trying to restore the West to its former glory. We've lost our nerve. The West is terrified of intervening in other countries' affairs these days. We draw red lines and issue strongly worded condemnations and expel a few diplomats, and nothing more. The merest hint of military action sends our politicians running for the hills. All that has done is embolden our enemies into believing that we're fundamentally weak. It's time we were more proactive. Show our enemies that we are capable of something harder edged.' He tipped his head at Bald. 'You of all people should understand the value of that.'

Strickland shook her head. 'That doesn't justify murder.'

'It's a small price to pay, for helping to reassert the West's strength on the world stage. You should be thanking me, in fact.'

'Load of bollocks,' Bald said with a snarl. 'You were doing it for the cash. The Americans were getting a share of the oil profits. Don't tell me you weren't getting the same.'

'We were going to be handsomely rewarded for our efforts. I won't deny that. But it was never just about the money.'

'What was the plan for the other leaders?' asked Strickland. 'More blackouts?'

'Not always. In some instances, we'd shut down the grid. In other cases, we'd cause dams to flood. We would crash trains, cause explosions. Whatever the mission required.'

He was bragging now. Demonstrating his genius.

Bald said, 'You can do all that, from this old building?'

'You'd be amazed what you can do with a few talented young hackers and an Internet connection.' Cantwell paused. He winked at Bald. 'You can even bring down planes.'

Bald looked at him. His hard, lean face was burning with indescribable hatred. 'The downed Herc. That was you?'

'Let's just say that I'd be very careful the next time you get on a plane.'

'There were twelve Regiment lads on that plane. You fucking killed them, you sick bastard.'

'I'll remember to wear a poppy.'

Bald's neck muscles tensed. He looked as if he might spring out of his chair and strangle Cantwell. 'You'll pay for this.'

'I doubt it. Not with the friends I've got.'

'They're not your friends anymore,' Strickland said. 'Not after today. Once the Company realises the operation is blown, they'll go into damage-limitation mode. They'll be covering their tracks.'

'I don't need them. I have people higher up.'

'Drummond?' Strickland laughed bitterly. 'I wouldn't count on his loyalty, Julian. What do you think he'll do once we threaten to leak this stuff? He'll sell you out in a heartbeat.'

She was right, Cantwell knew. But he was thinking something else, too. He was thinking about the president, and what he was prepared to do to his enemies. If he was willing to sanction the killing of foreign leaders, he wouldn't hesitate to silence Cantwell.

Time to take a chance.

'What do you want?' he asked. 'Cooperation?'

'We're not here to a cut a deal with you,' Strickland said.

'What, then?'

'Obviously, we'd prefer to stop this conspiracy from becoming public knowledge. Six is tainted by association. Although we had no inkling about your devious scheme, the operation involved British assets working illegally on Venezuelan soil and resulted in the rescue of a British spy. If this became public, it would cause deep embarrassment. So we're going to give you a choice. Disappear – go quietly, leave the country and live under a new identity, and we'll promise to leave you alone.'

'And if I refuse?'

'Then John will put a bullet in your head.'

'You can't be serious.'

Bald pointed to his face. 'Do we look like we're joking, mate?'

Cantwell shook his head in protest. 'I can't just leave. My whole life is here. I've got my company. My wife ...'

'We'll arrange for her to join you, once you've settled in to your new life.'

'But where would I go?'

'Somewhere far away, well off the grid, where the Americans won't think to look for you. Laos, perhaps. Or Paraguay. We'll help you with the details, supply you with clean documents.'

'You're asking me to give up my life, for Christ's sake.'

'Should have thought about that when you were sending those fucking SAS lads to their deaths,' Bald growled.

Strickland said, 'It won't be that bad. We know you've got money stashed away in various places. Wherever you go, it will be more than enough to live in relative comfort. But you need to decide now.'

Cantwell took in a deep breath. He was being offered a life sentence in exile. Living on reduced means, in some impover-ished backwater, far away from the political connections and spheres of influence that he thrived on. An anonymous, sad little existence. He couldn't think of anything worse.

Except he could: death.

He saw Bald glowering at him with a look of pure hatred in his eyes. No question that he would put a bullet in Cantwell's head, if Strickland gave him the order.

'Well?' Strickland asked.

'Okay,' he said after a long pause. 'I'll do it.'

'Good man.'

'What happens now?'

'There's a car waiting outside. You'll leave the country immediately. But first, we'll have to make your disappearance look like a suicide.'

'What for?'

'To make sure none of your old friends decide to come looking for you, of course.'

Strickland reached into her coat pocket and pulled out a small white card with a few handwritten lines on it.

'This is a suicide note. You'll write this out on a piece of paper, in your own handwriting, and sign it. It will be left next to the body.'

'What body?'

'Five will send a team to the morgue. Get a John Doe to take your place.'

'But they'll know it's not me, surely?'

'There's a level crossing three miles up the road. The body is going to be found there. Or what's left of it, after a high-speed train has smashed through it. He'll be carrying your wallet and keys, wearing your watch and ring and clothes. We'll cut off the fingertips before dumping it there, to prevent fingerprint identification.'

Cantwell eyed the card she was holding. 'What does the note say?'

'Just a generic suicide letter. You're very sorry, you can't go on, that sort of thing. Nothing to implicate you in this affair.' Strickland glanced impatiently at her watch. 'We really do need to hurry up, Julian. Write the note.'

Cantwell dithered for a few moments longer, but he could understand the logic of her position. A body would make his death far more plausible than simply vanishing into thin air. And the death certificate would provide his wife with a generous insurance payout, he reasoned.

He sat down at the desk next to Strickland and copied out the card on a blank sheet of paper, hand trembling as he wrote. Signed his name at the bottom in his characteristically flamboyant flourish, handed the note and pen and card back to Strickland. She pocketed them and stood up.

'Excellent. Now, let's go. Your car is waiting.'

He started towards the door.

Which is when he saw Bald pull his hand out of his jacket pocket and move towards him.

Armed with an electric cattle prod.

Bald lunged at Cantwell before he could react, bumping him in the arm.

He let out a scream as a sharp stabbing pain spread through his arms and legs. His legs folded, and he dropped to the floor. Bald gave him another whack with the prod, shocking his torso. The pain was unbearable. Worse than anything Cantwell had ever known. He couldn't breathe.

He was dimly aware of someone dragging his enormous mass across the floor, towards the small kitchen at the rear of the building. A chair in the middle of the room. Noose hanging from the ceiling beam above it.

He tried to resist. Bald bumped him again. Shockwaves of pain ripped through his skull. His world went black, briefly.

When he came to a few moments later, he realised he was standing upright on the chair. Meaty hands grabbed the rope tied to the beam.

Secured it around Cantwell's neck.

Cantwell saw the look in the Scot's eyes. Through the pain fogging inside his head, he grasped what was happening.

'Don't,' he mumbled. Snot streamed out of his nostrils. A warm, moist patch spread across his groin as he pissed himself. 'Don't do this.'

Bald ignored him. Turned to Strickland and said, 'Get the clean-up team ready. Tell them to start dusting everything down.'

Strickland left the room.

Cantwell froze.

Bald looked round at him.

'Time to take your last flight, mate.'

'No,' Cantwell cried. 'No!'

'This is for all the lads you killed,' said Bald.

Then he kicked the chair away.